Venture and Venus

a Jack Muldoon Story

by

Michael McDonough

ISBN: 978-0-9546655-1-7
A CIP Catalogue record for this book is available from
the British Library

First Published in 2010 by Michael McDonough

Front Cover Illustration courtesy of Syra Larkin
Editing and Proof-reading by Mary McElroy
Typesetting and Cover Design by Oscar Duggan.

Printed in Ireland by Gemini International Ltd

Published with the assistance of The Author's Friend.
For more information about assisted publishing, including
catalogue and titles, visit www.TheAuthorsFriend.com

Venture and Venus
a Jack Muldoon Story

Dedication

I dedicate this book to my skiing and army friends and acquaintances.

Acknowledgements

I acknowledge the support of my wife Greta. Our children Stephen, Martin, Alan, Michael and Clare helped me reach the finish line, as did our super grandchildren, Leah and Cathy.

Jock Kelly and Denis Leahy contributed story lines. Local neighbours helped format the French'/German and Latin and kept the computer on track.

Anne Duff Griffin helped edit the manuscript.

Syra Larkin kindly provided the illustration used on the front cover. It is from the third part of the triptych *Elemental Connections* by Syra Larkin - www.syralarkin.com.

Wrapped in a Donegal-tweed overcoat and a peak cap pulled well down as protection against the cold, Lieutenant Jack Muldoon looked out of place among the more traditionally-dressed ski resort pedestrians. He passed the '*zimmer frei*' - 'rooms to let' signs in the windows of St Anton am Arlberg. Jack knew that the 3-star 'Schwarzer Adler', 'Hotel Post' and the many other small hotels at this end of the fashionable Austrian ski resort would be outside his budget bracket. He humped his unwieldy soft case, stuffed with all his projected needs for his four weeks' stay in St Anton, but without an immediate plan for accommodation. Like Dickens's 'Micawber' he believed that something would "turn up". His brown leather shoes, made by Tuttys of Naas for the Kildare squire, were no protection against the frozen snow as he slithered and slipped his way down the dimly-lit street.

Jack had skied in a much smaller ski village the previous year and, while on a one-day visit to St Anton with a Donegal-priest friend Louis McCormac, had fallen in love with this home of the Kandahar race. This ski race was established in 1924 in Murren by Sir Arnold Lunn, President of the Ski Club of Great Britain, in honour of Lord Roberts of Kandahar. The historic start to the sport of downhill ski racing was transferred the following year to St Anton on the invitation of Hannes Schneider of the Arlberg Ski School and renamed the Arlberg-Kandahar ski race.

Jack and Louis were captivated by the complete package that was St Anton and vowed there and then to book a four-week holiday for the following year. They were also fascinated by its history as the beginning of skiing as a sport. The Arlberg technique of skiing, devised by Hannes Schneider of the Arlberg Ski Club, helped to popularise skiing. It was founded in 1901 in St Christoph.

A typical village of the Arlberg region of Austria, St Anton's population was about two thousand people, the villagers surviving on farming, but more so ski tourism since the end of the Second World War. The street down which Jack walked reflected both facets of the village's life, comprising small hotels and farmhouses, some incorporating ground-floor accommodation for cattle. Cows in the Tyrol, and in the Alps in general, were stall-fed in the villages in winter with hay saved in the upper meadows in summer. The hay was stored in a myriad of picture postcard huts, to be transported down on sledges later in the year as required.

The flower boxes on the balconies, bedecked with hanging geraniums in summer, now sported regular mounds of glistening snow set in sagittal order. Jack's eager eyes soaked in the winter village scene that had so captivated him the previous year. He tingled with excitement, and not a little trepidation, at the prospect of skiing on the surrounding snow-covered mountains.

"Looking for a bed?"

The young spectacled man spoke as he made his way down an exterior stairway from the upper level of an old roadside building. Jack had just turned off the main street at the church and was about twenty yards beyond the municipal cattle trough. He squinted into flecks of snow in the badly-lit side street. The stranger was smiling broadly as he spoke, despite his obvious difficulty negotiating the narrow stairway, hampered as he was by a large gear bag and a pair of skis. About thirty years of age, Jack figured, and an American he thought, mostly because of the accent.

Jack didn't immediately answer the open-ended question about the bed. Dumping his own gear he moved quickly up to the first landing and took charge of the long skis, which were defying control by their owner and had formed an awkward 'x' on his back, previous, Jack figured, to taking flight. He stood them upright against the timber stairs.

"My name's Jack Muldoon. I'm certainly looking for a place to stay. Are you American?"

"Chris Davenport." The young man thrust out his hand and fixed Jack with a business-like, steely blue-eyed gaze. "American, okay, but not the US of A, although my parents are from the States. We live in the Argentine where my father mines. I'm on a European trip, been here for the past three weeks and need to move on - are you interested in taking this place?" He nodded his head upwards in the direction of the top of the stairs.

"This is a farmhouse, but Frau Gasper lets a room over the cowshed at a really good price."

He looked back at the building as he spoke and explained that the adjacent large double door and the shed behind were directly under his bedroom, and housed the cows.

With no plans and a cold winter's evening making its presence felt, Jack was pushed towards finding a room as soon as possible. He agreed to look at the accommodation and followed Chris up the stairs, three at a time. 'So Micawber was right, something did "turn up",' he thought.

"You Irish are a rare breed out here." The words were thrown in a haze of frozen breath over the shoulder of the Argentinean as he fumbled with the door key.

Jack surprised himself as he venomously spat out a response.

"You're the only Argentinean I've ever met, anywhere!"

He hadn't an inferiority complex about his nationality; however he'd met a number of English colonial-types on the train, males, who showed surprise at the infiltration of the Irish to ski resorts in the Alps. The Ski Club of Great Britain was a select group in St Anton and Jack had spoken to a few who questioned if the Irish 'had' an Army and this in particular may have been what stuck in his craw.

Chris turned quickly and Jack's reflexes went into on-guard mode until he saw and heard Chris's laugh.

"I've heard about the Irish temper and now I've met it full frontal."

The young Argentinean threw his arms around a startled Jack, beating him on the back in the mode of *bonhomie*. Not a space invader himself, Jack nevertheless felt obliged to respond in kind.

Chris threw open the door to reveal an attic-type room furnished as a bedroom - a single bed under a sloping roof and a washbasin near a window overlooking the roadway. It was clean and smelt of the timber framework.

"Is there a lavatory?"

"Down the stairs at the back of the cowshed," Chris threw in this snippet excitedly and looked relieved that the room had been well received.

"You're joking!" For no particular reason the word cowshed linked with human lavatory facilities jarred with Jack Muldoon.

Without responding Chris sped down the stairs, moved to the right of the main barn doors, opened a small door, and there it was. Jack, who had followed Chris closely, saw an adequate lavatory facility illuminated by a single light bulb.

Jack figured that Chris's overly enthusiastic approach stemmed from the fact that he had contracted for a longer stay and now for some reason needed to go. He followed him back up the stairs and around the building to the front of the living accommodation. A portly, smiling lady with wrap-around apron and slippers opened the door and greeted Chris in welcoming tones.

"Ah, Chris, you've found a friend."

"This is Jack Muldoon, Frau Gasper. He's just arrived from the Emerald Isle and would like to rent the room."

Jack ignored the Emerald Isle stuff, shook hands and they all shuffled into the hall, where immediately his saliva started to flow, stimulated by strong cooking smells from the kitchen.

"I guessed you were leaving soon Chris, but so soon?" solicited the landlady.

Chris's only response was to look towards Jack and seek assurance that he was indeed ready to move in that very evening. The price was agreed and Frau Gasper fussed her way up to the room, carrying a change of bedclothes, towels, and a cover for the eiderdown. Jack discovered later that Chris had booked for a further week at least and now for some reason or other he was getting out.

'What a stroke of luck for me,' Jack thought, as he unpacked his belongings and took stock, 'and the price is right!'

"Hello." He looked up and was surprised to see Chris Davenport's head push around the door. Jack's immediate response was to hope that the room really was his and that there was no last minute hitch.

"I was wondering if you'd be interested in a pair of skis? I won't need them and they're one hell of a drag." Chris poked the tips of the skis into the room at chin level, by way of introduction.

Jack had neither boots nor skis and they were of course next on his agenda of required skiing items. He had used hired skis in Galtür the previous year but longed to have a pair of his own, although the idea was more in fond hope than reality.

"They're very good, the best of Kandahar bindings. Look!" Jack sat open-mouthed on the bed. As Chris and his skis made a full entry into the bedroom he stood up and, head bent forward, moved from the sloped roof over the bed area to view the skis. Because of the slope encroachment, the skis couldn't be stood upright, but Jack could see that they were long, about two metres.

Chris noticed Jack sizing up the length of the skis; a fact which he realised could be an issue in their sale. He quickly tried to diminish Jack's concern.

"That's very good for skiing in this area," said the vendor, "the longer the better." Chris spoke with confidence as he stood with a ski in each hand, looking in admiration from one to the other; 'too much in admiration,' Jack thought, 'like a soldier on inspection with something to hide.'

Jack carefully studied the all-important steel edges and noticed that one section was loose. His critical attention to the loose edge nearly reduced the confident smile of the vendor. Although the Argentinean's smile faded a little, he muttered something about extra screws and switched his lip-wrenching grimace full on again. The skis were Attenhoffers, made of laminated strips of hickory with sections of edges held in place by screws, two in each section. The Kandahar binding, designed to hold the boots in place on the skis, had a spring that allowed only a forward release in case of a fall.

"How much?" Jack had a very limited amount to spend but needed skis. He felt apprehensive, not only about the suitability of the skis but also about his ability to say no. Here he was in the epicentre of the ski world making a big decision about skis. The idea that he might seek advice, even from his friend Louis, did cross his mind.

Chris threw 'knots on himself' at this show of interest and presented more information on the giant timber skis.

"They've only been in use for two seasons. They're very good, Attenhoffer Molitors, 215 centimetres long." As he smelt success Chris's eyes narrowed behind his Chaplin-style glasses.

"How much?" Jack repeated his direct question.

"About ten pounds?" He hoped to lesson the impact of cost by giving the price in Jack's currency.

"What's that in real money?" Jack asked questions, but in reality he was fully immersed in the spider's web.

"About eight hundred Austrian schilling."

"That's a lot of money - how about two hundred schilling?" said Jack.

The salesman smile faded as Chris scrambled to save the deal. "These are pure laminated hickory, they'd cost you treble in the shops."

Jack could see that the stranger had little choice, the alternative being to lug them around Europe for the next few months.

"Okay, it's a deal!" The skis changed hands for two hundred schilling and Chris left.

Jack spent the next half hour opening and closing the bindings like a child playing with new toys on Christmas morning. He even tested them for walking skills in the narrow confines of the bedroom floor.

At this stage of the evening he was hungry, but it was late and he was vague on how best to get food. The deal with Frau Gasper was for bed only, so he would need to make other arrangements for eating. He eventually fell asleep wondering how a Japanese soldier could live on a handful of rice a day.

The Irish State's maximum monetary travel allowances of twenty pounds, plus Jack's army pay, but mostly his weakness in the budget department, were the reasons why seeking suitable accommodation had a high priority. Lieutenant Jack Muldoon hoped to get some sort of a job in the village and join a number of others in the ski bum category. He would in fact be one of a number of young people from Europe, America,

Australia, and New Zealand, living from hand to mouth and with a firm focus on skiing. He had met some of them at the Bahnhof, the station restaurant, on his arrival from Ireland via 'The Golden Arrow', Victoria Station, London. The Bahnhof restaurant at St Anton's railway station was a popular eating and drinking centre as well as the hub of coming and going; beer and food there were reasonably priced. White-aproned waiters picked their way through well-established footmarks in the snow from the kitchens of the Hotel Post, carrying loaded trays at shoulder level. The surprise was that food from this up-market hotel was sold in the railway station at much lower prices.

Next morning Jack awoke to the sound of cattle being fed and an odd contented 'moo'. He pulled on his ski bottoms (converted golf pull-ups), and donned a new blue sweater, knitted by a female friend, under his ski jacket.

It was half eight according to the clock on the church tower. The tower had a traditional onion-shaped dome, with icicles dropping from the eaves and a thick coating of snow on the roof. The morning was crisp and the covered cattle drinking trough by the roadside was iced over, the water from the tap a silver frozen snot. The nearby bread shop was open and people were arriving and leaving, carrying batches of bread of different sorts. The aroma from the bakery dragged him by the nose into the crowded shop.

"*Ein Brotchen, bitte.*" Although almost illiterate in German he managed to order and pay for his bread roll. With a cheery "*Danke*" he stepped on to the ice-covered road and nibbled the bread from inside the paper wrapper as he made his way through the village towards the railway station. Just beyond the station complex, a level crossing led to a number of houses, one of which was the Strauss family's 'Hotel Trittkopf'. It was here that he was to meet his friend Father Louis.

He walked slowly, taking in the atmosphere. The sun was just beginning to glint on the snow-covered roofs and people were walking around, going to work perhaps, wearing warm coats and hats as protection against the cold. He checked the thermometer at the end of the railway station and saw the marker at eight below.

'And that's at the station,' he said to himself. 'Imagine the cold at the top!'

Everything in this strange environment was a cause of wonder for this Irishman from a small isolated island home, situated in a temperate climate off the European mainland.

Just beyond the railway level crossing was the entrance to the Vallugabahn cable car. This was the largest lift in the village and was capable of carrying thirty people to the top of the Galzig Mountain - 2,185 metres, and linked to the 2,650-metre Valluga by a smaller car. Further to the right was the Gampen chair lift, which staged at the top of Gampen Mountain and continued to the top of Kapall - 2,330 metres. It appeared to be working, but he didn't see anyone on the chairs and the seats were folded up.

"Come on in, Jack." Louis was sitting in the hotel breakfast room reading an out-of-date English newspaper.

"How are things? Where did you stay last night?"

Louis was a thirty-five-year-old priest based in a north of England parish. He stayed in this nice family hotel while Jack scraped the barrel. A tall, confident man with a pair of dancing brown eyes and a personality to match, he was a magnet to whomever he encountered and never lost a friend.

Priests were held in very high regard in the Tyrol and the family members of the Trittkopf, led by Mama Strauss, were typical of the strong Catholic ethic in St Anton. The physical centre of their faith, and one of the main cultural influences, was the village church, both from the outside and inside, with its beautiful Baroque trappings on the altar and around the pillars. A group of skulls laid out on the window-ledge at the entrance were a traditional reminder of the transience of life. When Jack first visited, his eyes were drawn to the skulls and as he dipped his finger into the holy water, it skidded on the ice in the font. It seemed a long way from the soft entrance to mass in the west of Ireland where he was from, or even from the Curragh of Kildare.

Johan, the second-youngest boy in the Strauss family, confidently assisted the priest by leading the small congregation every morning and on Sundays in the prayers of the mass. His voice had a deep and round vowel sound, in keeping with the Austrian-Tyrolean speaking resonance that echoed so naturally around the walls and altars of the church.

"All is well, Louis. Would you believe it, I have a room not far from here and for three hundred schilling a day."

"Well done," said Louis, beaming at Jack and dramatically dumping the large morning paper on the breakfast table.

Jack, over a cup of tea and crispy bread rolls, described his purchase of the Attenhoffer skis.

"Wait 'til you see them Louis, they're fantastic."

"How about the boots?"

"I'll hire them I suppose." Jack was still recovering from the purchase of the skis.

"Well, I'm going to Pangratz's shop after breakfast; we could both get our gear there." Louis moved things along.

Over breakfast Louis questioned Jack on how he managed to get four weeks' holiday from the army. He knew that leave of that length was not automatic and he had listened to Jack's descriptions of his trials and tribulations while they were planning the trip.

Lieutenant Muldoon's account about getting funded and being allocated four weeks' leave, despite what he considered to be a good relationship with his own Commanding Officer, had been fraught with difficulties. He filled out his application for leave about three weeks in advance, but ostrich-like had kept his head in the sand until shortly before departure time.

"I was told that my chances of getting four weeks' leave were nil," admitted Jack. "I was mess caterer, and that, combined with my work in the gym, was an insurmountable obstacle it seemed. The Adjutant informed me that nobody was allowed to 'skive off' in February."

Louis could see that Jack had been through the mill and that celebrations were due.

"But you made it, *a cara*."

"I suppose four weeks was a bit much, but then that's the length that we had planned - didn't make much sense as an excuse - but it takes three days to get here by road, rail, and boat - it's hard to change when your mind's made up - sometimes the weather is bad and you could lose a week's good skiing - it's a bit much really, considering I was turned down for an appointment with the FCA in Bailieborough - I don't think I'd have gone at all if not granted the four weeks - I know that bollix O'Connor was against me going, he might have to do more work while I am away." Jack puked out a whole diatribe of thoughts about escaping from the Curragh.

Louis had the picture and wanted to move on, but Jack had the bit in his teeth and needed to tell the whole story.

"Shit and double shit - I made that application in plenty of time but nobody bothered. If I didn't get the four weeks, I wouldn't have come at all." Jack could feel his heart deaden and his mouth go very dry at the prospect of missing out on this return trip to the Arlberg.

"You're not going to tell me you deserted." Louis missed his saucer with the teacup and almost spilled the lot.

"I nearly spit my heart out when the word came through. I sat on the bus to Dublin sweating with effort and relief." Louis could see the child-like determination in the face of his ski friend.

L ouis and a light-headed Jack left the hotel in the direction of 'Pangratz Ski Hire Shop'. The man of the house ran the business, supported by Mama and a teenage son. Like the Strauss family, Mama was a devout Austrian Catholic and on receiving a phone call from the Hotel Trittkopf, was delighted to host Father Louis. Mama Pangratz appeared in the shop as soon as Jack and Louis announced their names and, before they could get down to the serious business of selecting ski equipment, they were ushered into the parlour and presented with a meal of ham, bread, and tea. This was to be a Thursday evening occasion for the four weeks of their visit at the express wishes of Mama Pangratz. Although intended as a purely social visit, Jack availed, ski bum-style, of the opportunity to have a free meal and eat his fill, while Father Louis picked at the food and tried to have a conversation, although he and Mama Pangratz didn't have a common language!

Jack presented his newly acquired skis (which he had collected en-route to the shop) to Mr Pangratz, who viewed them with quizzical interest. However, they had the regulation binding of the time and in a few minutes were fitted with a pair of second-hand leather ski boots. The boots had an outer and an inner cover, the outer being capable of being laced in the loop-style of mountain boots, following the tying of a inner boot in normal lacing form. The safety strap held the boot to the ski in case of release. Jack stepped outside on to the snow-covered road and tested the new equipment by sidestepping up a small bank and snow-ploughing down to the door of the shop. Mr Pangratz sold Jack the boots for next to nothing because of their age and condition, and not a little because of the visit of Fr Louis.

"Hey, you look the part," said Louis. "There'll be no stopping you now!"

"Watch out the Austrian ski team – here comes the Irish terror!" Jack knew in his heart, however, that before long he'd be sorely tested on the ski slopes.

Equipped and fed, they walked back towards the church where Louis needed to make arrangements with the parish priest about saying mass each morning. The housekeeper answered and, using a prepared sentence in German, Louis asked to speak to Father Stremitzer. He handed the housekeeper an introductory letter for the parish priest from a friend who had been in St Anton previously; this had been his conduit to the Strauss family and their Hotel Trittkopf. The introduction worked and they were led into a musty front room. A sorrowful Christ on the cross over the fireplace dominated the room, which also consisted of a well-used fire grate, an ornate mantelpiece, a dining table, chairs, and a heavily carved sideboard set on the polished timber floor. It reminded Jack of the front rooms he had seen in Irish convents and monasteries.

Before he could lead Louis down that observation trail, the door opened, ushering in the venerable parish priest. He addressed them in German. Neither of the two Irishmen could reply in kind, but on cue Louis introduced himself in Latin and explained his business.

"*Salve, Pater Stremitzer, Veni ex Parochia in Anglia septentrionali. Hae litterae testemontales explicabunt omnia, spero.*"

Father Stremitzer replied in Latin also and gave Louis the support he needed for the four weeks of morning mass, and welcomed him to St Anton am Arlberg.

"*Acceptus est ad nostram Parochiam Sancti Antonii. Contentus sum quod celebrare sanctam missam hic pro quattuoc septimanas. Qualis hora erit idonea?*"

"*Mane ad horam septiman et dimidium.*"

In fact, Father was very happy to help and explained that an American priest, Father Bush, would also be saying mass every morning.

Asked about his ski experience Louis admitted his novice status.

"*Incepi solum annus ultimups. Spero continuare, Deo volente.*"

Having settled their business, the two priests continued to chat to one another in Latin, whereupon they all shook hands and parted. Stamping their way back to the Trittkopf, Jack congratulated Louis on his conversational use of Latin.

"The Romans would be proud of you - the Pope would be proud of you!"

All this preparatory work had given our two heroes a bit of a thirst and so they decided to call into the Bahnhof for *ein kleines* beer. A fair number of people were sitting around, some eating and others just chatting and drinking. They got into conversation with tourists from New Zealand; sheep farmers from the North Island who had taken a six-month European break. They were evidently good skiers, describing some of the runs that morning and talking excitedly about the Osthang, a very steep route under the cable car and covered in bumps. As he listened to their stories, Jack knew he'd a lot to learn. They spoke of slalom runs down through the bumps at speed. Although invited to join them, Jack and Louis viewed discretion as the better part of valour.

One drink led to another. The level of excitement was regularly raised by the arrival of new groups on the train and the departure of others. In what appeared like minutes, hours passed and they decided to have something to eat.

"You're in the first class section, they have tablecloths here, but you can eat the same Hotel Post food in the lower section for much less."

Good advice from a New Zealand sheep farmer!

They ordered two *Wienerschnitzel* and another *grosses* beer. They had progressed to the large beer at this stage. A group of local people sat at the next table. At least they sounded local, using local accents and local phrases.

"Grüss Gott, wie geht's?"

"Servus Johann, sehr gut."

"Danke, Pfüatdi."

The conversation was about work on the Gampen-Kapall ski lift. Apart from the maintenance of the lift machinery and the seats, the slopes had to be worked on, levelled and smoothed every morning for the skiers later in the day. An army of part-time workers, some locals but mostly other nationalities, did this job. Called *Pistenhelfers* they worked from seven until ten in the morning, were given an *Arbeiter* (workers) breakfast and lunch, and had free use of the chair lift for the rest of the day as payment. Georg Werner, the Austrian manager of the Gampen lift, was setting things up for the next weeks; the previous group of foreign *Pistenhelfers* who had worked on the last shift had just left by train for their homes.

"What do you think, Louis, should I have a go, would I be able for it?" Jack was excited and asked the question to involve his friend.

"All you have to do is ski with a shovel and be able to dig. Yes, I saw some of them '*schaufeln und treten*' this morning."

"What's this *schaufeln* business?"

"It's just shovelling snow out of the way and firming it down with the skis to make a *piste* for the ski tourist. If it snows during the night, you work with the others to step down the mountain and tread the snow flat; otherwise you ski down to bad patches, fill them in and tread down, or dig bumps up and fill in between them to make the *piste* level."

"Sounds like a lot of work, but I came here to ski and this is skiing at the rough edges." Jack could hardly contain his excitement and as he finished his meal, he listened intently to a young Italian signing up with the manager. They spoke in English but he recognised the Italian accent. He heard the manager do the deal and present him with his *Pistenhelfer* identity card.

"I suppose you're not interested, Louis?"

"Got it in one, Jack. Anyway, I'll be saying mass at that time of the morning."

Jack spoke to the young Italian. His name was Ricardo; he was from near Rome, a village called Frascati in the foothills, and was on a visit to a married sister in Vienna. She was only recently married to an Austrian doctor and, in typical Italian style, was lonely for her family. So, during a mid-term break from Università di Verona, he had been dispatched to re-attach the family cord and bring back news. As it turned out, his sister was invited to spend time with a distant relation in the Tyrol, and so Ricardo finished up in St Anton for a week's skiing. He heard about the *Pistenhelfer* job and, never having worked with his hands before, thought that a week working would be exciting and he would have a tale to tell in Rome when he returned.

"You've signed up as a galley slave?"

Ricardo laughed at Jack's attempt to inject humour into the situation. "Yes! I start tomorrow morning at *halb sieben*."

"Is it easy to be taken on?" Jack was excited about the prospect but still expected difficulties to emerge.

"No trouble, he's looking for people because a large group of American students left this morning."

Jack Muldoon could barely believe his luck. He had always intended doing something to make a few bob and saw this job as a gift from heaven. He wasn't going to make any money, but a free meal and free lift tickets were exactly what he needed. He approached the Austrian manager of the Gampen-Kapall lift system and introduced himself.

"You're the first Irishman to look for a job, can you ski?" Georg was serious about the skiing question: this requirement was of course essential!

Jack decided not to be insulted, gave his details, and showed his passport. A quick trip to the office for a passport photo and his identity card was completed and signed by the manager and himself.

"Tomorrow at *halb sieben.*"

"*Danke.*"

"Well Louis, I'm one of the employed, from now on please address me as *Herr Pistenhelfer*!"

With a job in his pocket, he rowed back a bit on the beer, apart from celebratory Schnapps, and hit the scratcher at about midnight. He spoke to the son of the family, who was making an unsteady entrance to his home at the same time. Jack needed to be up and away at about seven, thus leaving thirty minutes to make it to the lift.

"*Jawohl, mein Freund. Ich arbeite zu der Zeit im Hotel Post. Ich kann dich wecken.*"

Jack picked up that he would get a call in time, but wasn't sure if Bruno would remember. He decided to set an alarm in his mind as a back up; he had tried that before and it usually meant that he wouldn't sleep at all, or at best fitfully.

'I should have brought the orderly with me', were his thoughts as he lay in this strange room on the eve of a very exciting experience in his life.

Apart from his trip to Galtür the year before, Jack had had an introduction to a primitive form of skiing in the Curragh Camp while a lieutenant in the Army School of Physical Culture (ASPC). On one famous day in March, the commandant in charge returned from a holiday abroad, alight with enthusiasm about skiing and in possession of a pair of boots and skis. By a stroke of luck the snow arrived and on Monday morning Commandant Donal McBennett arrived at the gym on skis.

"Come over here to the window, quick!"

"Jesus, Mary, and Joseph, what's that?"

The two corporals were talking about a snow-splattered figure, pipe clenched in mouth and wearing a Cavalry glengarrie at a jaunty angle. The Commanding Officer of the ASPC released the binding levers, stepped out of the skis and slapped them together to remove excess snow. Probably for the first time ever, the civilians at Farrell's bus stop were treated to the sight of a lone skier flashing past the post office, heading down the hill towards the Master Baker's house to turn *en route* to the gymnasium. For the rest of that period of snow, everyone in the gym had a go. Jack really enjoyed the exercise, despite his inability to control either of the skis to form any sort of coordinated unit and having to use the same boots. Most of the skiing was done on the butts of the rifle ranges, or from the ladies' tee on the first hole of the golf club. Memories of a *sortie* to the nearest forest to ski down a firebreak flooded his dreams.

His next ski progression involved taking a recruit platoon to the Glen of Imaal on the instructions of his CO. The memories of recruits collecting snow in buckets so that the officers could practise skiing on the fast-melting snow clarified. In fairness, everyone - recruits, Non Commissioned Officers (NCOs) and men, had a go using the same size ten ski boots. Before all snow faded from Kildare and Wicklow that year, Jack and Donal McBennett spent many hours testing their skills on skis, on some occasions after dark by moonlight when Jack Frost firmed up the mushy snow. This was Muldoon's initiation, leading to the trip to Galtür and now St Anton am Arlberg.

"Jack, Jack, *mein Freund*, get up, it is time." He got the call after all and he had slept. He jumped up and hit his head off the sloped ceiling.

"*Danke*, Bruno. Shit! Oh, my head!"

This was his prayer replacement as he struggled into the gear. Bottoms, polo neck, socks, jacket, and the new (well, new to him) boots. He clambered down the stairs carrying his skis, poles, gloves, and cap. When he reached the street it was still dark, apart from the lights of one or two shops, and the time was five to seven. He parked his skis outside a bread shop and bought a bread roll.

Munching the roll on his way up the street he met some people and responded to their '*Grüss Gott*' or '*Servus*' with a warm feeling in his heart. Here he was in the Tyrol, on his way to work as part of the ski community!

'This is what life is about and they nearly didn't let me go!'

"Hi, Jack." It was Louis, breviary in hand, on his way to say mass.

"Hello Louis, this is some trick, me meeting you on my way to work in an Austrian ski resort. In the blink of an eye we're out of sight as far as Ireland is concerned, England in your case, of course."

"Wonderful, isn't it? What time do you start? I'm due in church at seven twenty."

"Half past for me. See you."

They passed on, caps pulled well down to protect their ears against the below-zero temperatures.

When Jack got to the office he saw a stationary lift and was surprised that nobody was around. He knew there were about twenty others on the *Pistenhelfer* team and it was ten past seven.

'Maybe they're late starters, or they meet somewhere else and arrive at the lift at the exact time,' he thought.

He passed the time by trying on the skis and moving about a bit. At half past there was still no action.

"*Grüss Gott!*" Jack was startled by the voice from the gloom. The skier had arrived from the direction of the mountain and immediately set about opening the office and starting the machinery. It took Jack a while to get his message across. Eventually, he discovered that the workers were at the top of the mountain and had started making their way down. He wondered how and why? The arrangement was for *halb sieben.*

"Ja, that was the time." The skier had some English. Eventually the penny dropped; *halb sieben uhr*, half to seven! He felt such a fool and was very disappointed at not having made it on the first morning. Bad enough in normal circumstances missing your group and feeling lost, but on the mountains the feeling was magnified.

'Half to - what a dog's dinner! I suppose I'll have to wait 'til tomorrow.' The mistake about time ate into his feel-good factor. As he stood there musing and swearing, the machine started up and the mechanic began moving the chairs slowly around. Slowly, because as each chair passed his position the mechanic checked to see that the seat could move up and down and at the same time cleaned the seat. Jack watched for a while and saw that this job was going to take a long time to complete.

"Can I help?"

The Austrian eyed him up and down and when he discovered that he was a registered *Pistenhelfer* he grunted agreement and gave him the job of cleaning each seat. This was the worst part of the operation, but Jack was delighted to get started and would have agreed to anything. Certainly he would be on time the next morning, for what he perceived as a much more exciting, even romantic job on skis.

At about half nine he saw the rising sun sweep the *Pistenhelfer* team over the skyline. He watched the *Schauflers* work their way down the ski slope; they timed their work to keep just behind the shadow. By then also, practically all the seats had been cleaned and he had moved to another job. There was a pile of cloaks to one side ready for distribution to the skiers in case the weather was cold and it was snowing. The task was to fold them in piles of ten for easy distribution. He was still folding the *mantels*, as they were called, when the *Pistenhelfers* landed. The *Gauleiter* boss of that group, Wolfgang Gruber, was a six-foot burly local, with a voice like a growl. He started talking to the mechanic through the haze of their cigarette smoke. Jack knew that he was a part subject of the conversation, because they looked in his direction with intent.

'I hope this doesn't mean that I'm stuck with this job from now on,' Jack thought. 'It was okay to be a dogsbody and do this bottom-of-the-pile job in order to stay with the team, but not every morning.'

As it turned out, one of the new workers, a young American, couldn't ski very well, at least not well enough to descend with a large shovel and keep stable enough to dig and flatten out the bumps on the snow. Jack, on the other hand, expected that his work preparing the runs in the Glen of Imaal and on the Wicklow firebreaks and his session in Galtür the year before had provided him with the right skills.

"Will you be able to ski with this shovel and dig?" Wolfgang spoke Humphrey Bogart-style through his cigarette.

Jack on skis was led out to the side of the lift offices and supervised as he dug a bump of snow and filled in the space beside.

"*Jawohl, halb sieben heure morgen früh,*" said the ganger of the work group, as he handed out meal tickets to everyone. The ticket entitled the bearer to get an *Arbeiter* breakfast and a lunch on that particular day. Jack made a mental note of the start time. No mistakes in the *morgen*.

"Where were you this morning?" the young Italian questioned him.

"It's a long story - you can be sure that I'll be here well on time tomorrow. How did you get on?" Jack thought Ricardo looked a bit bruised in spirit.

"It was very difficult, that fellow Wolfgang is a real brute. He's the type that probably looks forward to taking down the Christmas decorations." Ricardo watched Jack for a reaction and perhaps sympathy for his account of Wolfgang's attitude to his efforts. "I was always having trouble, but he kept shouting at me to keep up. I'm not sure if I'll be able to survive. It sounded exciting last night but…" His voice trailed off, as he looked up at the route the team had taken from seven to ten that morning.

"Well, you must have been better than the American, he got the chop."

"Chop?"

"Yes, he's been downgraded to the job I was doing this morning," said Jack with relief in his voice.

They had to go up to the restaurant at Gampen to avail of the *Arbeiter* breakfast, so they jumped on one of the chairs and started their journey to the top. As they glided slowly upwards, Jack admired the scenery and pointed out the animal marks between the trees. He thought they might be foxes or rabbits, but then he didn't know what wildlife survived during the very harsh Tyrol winters. Ricardo was just as uninformed as he about nature, so he used the time on the way up to Gampen to talk about his sisters and mother. Jack could see that he was the family pet and was having trouble surviving in this big bad world.

"Tips up," said Jack as they arrived. For beginners, getting off the chair lift was a big challenge and the attendant at the top had to be ready to stop the lift if somebody caught their ski in the snow, or just fell in a heap when deposited by the chair. Beginners on the way down, brought up to better snow by the ski instructor and returning by lift, were a real problem and required a lot of organising on both phases of their journey. However, they were the paying customers and were the important focus of all the work, including the *piste* preparation by Jack and his fellow *Pistenhelfers*.

The type or amount of breakfast was optional, so Jack and his newfound friend had Spaghetti Bolognese and a beer. It was a strange experience for Jack at ten o'clock in the morning, but he realised that this job was the key to keeping body and soul together for four weeks. Breakfast and lunch were the payment for working, which included free skiing on the Gampen-Kapall route. Dinner would have to come out of his own funds, as would paying for other routes in the resort and whatever gear and gear maintenance was required.

And so Jack and Ricardo spent the rest of the morning skiing up and down the mountain. At Galtür, Jack had developed a racing snow-plough, but during his one-day trip to St Anton the previous year, he had seen how the better skiers managed, with skis parallel and feet together as far as possible, so he started working on this technique. He had learned to stem turn, which was a good transition skill. At least in the stem, the skis can be parallel after the turn.

Lunchtime in the Gampen restaurant was an experience for the new arrivals. The room was full of skiers of all descriptions - locals, foreign visitors, some young and, like Jack, looking for support to live and ski. Other more sophisticated tourists, mostly English from higher social levels on a ski experience, lived out a way of life aimed at building a character platform for a future in the public services anywhere in the 'Empire'.

Jack and Ricardo made their way down that evening from Gampen to St Anton. The lifts stopped at five o'clock and by that time most skiers were heading home to change and prepare for the pre-dinner celebrations. Afternoon tea dances were a part of the social scene and it was *de rigueur* that all should change from skiwear into dancing clothes. Despite his overall lack of funds, Jack, who had identified the level of social sophistication in a ski resort the year previously, decided to prepare for this epic trip and had invested in a number of items of clothing to make ski life more enjoyable and fruitful. He sought advice from some of the more 'with it' officers. In particular, those in the camp who had show jumping experience with the Army Equitation Team. Kevin Berry and Brendan Cullitan both recommended Agars of Trinity Street and Jack went there one afternoon with a blazer in mind.

"Yes, of course", said Mr Agar, "we'll have no difficulty in fitting you out, sir."

Jack was used to being measured for uniforms and this was a similar exercise. Old Mr Agar produced a tape and went about the business of measuring his client with an efficiency born of experience in the trade as master tailor.

Jack had only a vague notion of what he wanted, but knew that something along the lines of the English blazers he had seen in Loughborough on his athletic courses would suit.

Each visit brought him closer to the finished article. At first, pieces were held together with pins and Mr Agar made the necessary adjustments. On the fourth occasion, however, there was little adjusting to do. Jack had written to an English company for a badge, a *Discopoles,* to be placed on the breast pocket, and as this had arrived he anticipated having the finished article on his next visit.

"Yes, very good, that's great." Jack was happy with the result.

"Look at the back, sir, what do you think?"

Jack felt good as he stood in front of the long mirror. The man himself, Mr Agar, supervised the final fitting, supported by an assistant who spent most of his time on his knees, measuring tape around his neck and pins clenched in the corner of his mouth. Although in the back of Jack's mind lurked the amount to be paid, nineteen pounds, the craftsmen never mentioned filthy lucre and when he stepped out of the shop carrying the brown parcel, an envelope containing the bill was tucked discreetly into his inside pocket, placed there without comment by the assistant tailor. As he walked down Trinity Street, high spirits led him across the street towards Jury's bar. He sat on the bar stool drinking a pint of the black stuff and couldn't resist the urge to open the package and finger the smooth English barathea inside.

'My God, what stuff! Watch out any women in my line of sight!'

In truth the purchase wasn't only for the purpose of being attractive to women, but the result instead of a slightly inflated ego, brought on perhaps by having to look good in military uniform and the psychological ingestion of respectful salutations by NCOs and men in the five years since his commission.

Jack and Ricardo parted and headed for their separate dwelling places. It felt good being a part of the ski fraternity, walking in the strong mode determined by the large ski boots and with a pair of skis over one's shoulder. Because of the icy condition of the snow-covered roads, care was necessary, and progress was often only possible by using the poles as a third point of balance. When Jack Muldoon reached his abode, he mounted the stairs, planted his skis and poles outside the door, threw himself on the bed, and reviewed the situation. In next to jig time he was asleep, although he had intended heading up to the Bahnhof for a bite and a few. When next he awoke it was ten o'clock, so he stripped and dived under the large duvet cover - certainly a step up from the Curragh version of bedclothes which, in winter, required the support of an army greatcoat.

Jack wound and set an alarm clock he had borrowed from the Strauss family; a repetition of the previous day would not occur. True to plan, the clock went mad at six o'clock. Jack reduced it to quiet with a long swing of the right arm and went through his plan of action. Up, wash, shave, clothes; push-ups - reduced to ten because of the physical nature of the holiday; boots on, glance around, out the door, skis picked up at speed, and clatter down the stairs. The cold hit him like an incision across the McBurney's point, immediate and clean. His boots crunched in the frozen snow in unison with the few other worker-types who were up and away at this early hour. The heady aroma of freshly baked cakes of bread hit his nostrils.

"*Grüss Gott, ein Brötchen bitte.*"

He resisted the urge to buy a number of cakes, but stuck to his limit and bought the regulation simple piece of bread. 'After all,' he thought, 'I'll get fed for free after work, so why waste money?' This frugality had started in the Curragh as part of preparation for the four weeks in the Alps. On he trudged over the railway line, and across to the chair lift. He could see the cigarettes of a number of people glowing in the dark and knew that today he had the right time. About five locals were engaged in animated conversation. He recognised some of the words, although what they were talking about was a mystery, which made the situation all the more surreal.

"Are you one of the workers?" A tall blonde girl with an American accent asked.

"Yes, I was supposed to start yesterday, but got the start time wrong. Were you here?"

It was also Amy's first time as a *Pistenhelfer* on Gampen and she was looking forward to the experience. From a skiing area in the States, working on the slopes held little or no fears for this much-travelled Amazon. In Europe for the season, she had already been in St Anton for at least three weeks working as a chambermaid. This, plus a couple of seasons in the snowfields of the Rockies under her belt, made her an experienced ski bum.

"The hotel work is okay, but I only get to ski two days a week. I make a few - enough of that shit, I'm on skis from now on, money or no."

Others shuffled in penguin-like from the gloom. Gradually a group of about twenty-five gathered around the leader Wolfgang, as he began his brief for the morning.

"Get up to the top, we'll collect the shovels there and work our way down. I'll give you instructions when we get up. Any questions?"

Jack recognised the format; this guy Wolfgang must have been in the army during the war. He was about forty-five years of age. 'That fits,' he thought. The rest of the group, including locals, were so covered up that not even their sex was distinguishable in the dark of the winter morning. He stuck with the American, selected a *mantel*, and waited for the chair lift to start, which it did in about five minutes. He was eager to get up and going, but the locals appeared more interested in chatting than getting to work and set the rate of progress. On this occasion they talked about the Austrian ski team and in particular about a local representation, and the threat imposed by the French or Swiss teams. He managed to pick out enough key words to unlock the conversation.

"Away we go." The American girl took charge.

Their chair came around and they pulled down the seat and settled in for the journey up to Gampen and on to Kapall. As they slowly progressed up the slope their eyes became accustomed to the dark, aided by whatever light was reflected from the snow below. Jack hadn't noticed any new snow in the village, but as they made their way upwards it became obvious that there had been a fall during the night, not much, but enough to coat the pine trees and cover the ground with a thin covering of new snow.

"We'll have to do a bit of *treten* as well as *schaufeln*," said Amy.

"Sounds like hard work," said Jack. "Is all this done on skis?" Jack had already identified the functions of the job but welcomed the experienced knowledge of the American girl.

"That's for sure, you have to be ready to move from place to place at speed and that can only be done on boards."

They both snuggled in and pulled their hoods up as protection from the biting wind. Their bodies shook as the pulleys rattled over the pylon at the top of the first rock outcrop. When they reached Gampen some of the crew got off and headed over to the restaurant with supplies of provisions.

The lift jerked off again and from this point the slopes were clear of trees and the wind even colder. Above the timber line each pylon loomed into view at about twenty yards distance and the seat, attached to a steel rope, rattled over the sprung pulley wheels on the pylon, and sank down to form an arch to the next one. The machinery and the hypnotic movement seemed out of place in this natural environment, but the rhythm was fascinating, set as it was in the midst of such stunning mountain beauty. It was still not daylight when they arrived at the top, but in the background there was a slight brightening of the sky behind the mountains. The lights in the village below sparkled in the frosty air. A row of lights crept into view and stopped at the station before moving off again - the Arlberg Express heading for the tunnel!

On arrival at Kapall, the 'hards' from Austria headed to a small shed close to the arrival point. Smoke belched from the chimney and a rake of shovels rested innocently near the door.

'The instruments of torture,' Jack thought.

Jack had lost his lift partner in the gloom and just as he was about to join the crew in the hut, he was touched on the shoulder.

"Hello, Jack." It was the young Italian.

"*Buon giorno*, Ricardo, how's she cutting?" Jack had already explained some 'Irishisms' to Ricardo.

"Apart from the early getting up, things are cutting very well." Although Ricardo was putting a good face on things, in Jack's opinion he looked stuffed with trepidation. Not that his own eyes weren't out on *cippins* as he absorbed the black and white scene.

They took off their skis, placed them against the paling outside the hut and entered the crowded space. In pride of place stood a red-hot pot-bellied stove, around which sat a gaggle of local workers. They had by now taken off their boots and were warming their feet from a variety of angles and distances. One of them occasionally touched the red-hot metal and added the pungent smell of burning cloth to the already high level of odour - a mixture of outdoor toilet, burnt toast, and the smell when a red-hot horse's shoe is placed on the hoof by the smith; add to this the smoke of rough tobacco and a tinge of unwashed bodies.

The high-octane smell had an immediate effect on the more genteel of the *Pistenhelfers*. Jack fought against the worst effects of the odour and allowed the heat to ease the accumulated stress of the cold on the slow chair lift from St Anton. He noticed however, the gradual whitening of the face of his Italian friend.

In about fifteen minutes the locals began to lace up their boots and Wolfgang gave them some instructions in German. "This is it, we're on our way," Jack was eager to start and he trooped out to the door with the rest. Just at this point, however, Ricardo turned from white to all the colours of the rainbow and looked like he was going to be sick. He muttered something to Jack, who tried to make a space for his friend near the door. Wolfgang at once showed his other side and began to care for the stricken Italian.

"Bring him outside into the fresh air."

Once away from the heat and smell of the hut, Ricardo recovered his normal colour, but not before he had unloaded his stomach, followed by some time heaving and spitting and eventually producing nothing but air and phlegm. 'Not a pretty sight,' thought Jack, as he held the shoulders of the unfortunate Roman, uttering the usual platitudes for such occasions.

"You'll be all right once you get rid of what's in your stomach," and "if your mother could see you now!"

Jack knew they were getting there when the young Italian laughed between spits and stomach heaves at one of his hard-man quips. In the middle of this tattera, the main event of the morning was being established. The sun, although not yet visible, was beginning to push back the darkness, and shapes at the top of the mountain became buildings or groups of people. The *Pistenhelfers*, both local and imported, began to unwind. Skis were slapped down on the soft snow to be matched to leather ski boots, tied on, and fixed firmly in place with a final push of the Kandahar lever. The main support of the exercise was of course the shovel, and each worker grabbed one and made movements suited to the role of *Pistenhelfer* in preparation for the morning's work. Skiing with a shovel is a special exercise, apart, that is, from digging or flattening the snow. The shovel, about four feet high, consisted of a stout wooden handle and a broad metal plate. Working with this implement on skis was one thing, but to ski using the shovel instead of poles was a special skill. The locals were very adept and, like all youngsters, did the work well, but also engaged in horseplay and *craic*. Jack and the stricken Ricardo got themselves ready like the rest.

"I don't think it's a good idea for you to work today. Can you make it down to the village on your own?" asked Wolfgang.

"I don't feel too bad now."

"Nevertheless, you should either go down on a chair, or, if you're able for it, ski down. You go down with him, in case he gets into any trouble."

Wolfgang's last remark was to Jack who, having missed the day before, really wanted to be a part of the team on this morning. He hadn't much choice however; this request from the *Gauleiter* had a military ring to it.

"Okay, will I come up and join you when I leave him down?" Jack tried to salvage something.

"No, stay with him for a while and join the team tomorrow." Another direction from Wolfgang!

"Shit and double shit!" Jack wondered if he'd ever get going as a *Pistenhelfer*.

"What did you say, Jack?"

"Nothing. Let's get started. Take this shovel, we could ski with free hands, but there are a few narrow catwalks on the way down and we'll probably need something to act as a brake."

Jack had seen the Italian's skills the day before and, not unlike himself but even more so, he had difficulty in getting the snow-plough to hold on one or two of the connecting paths on the way between Kapall and Gampen. He had also seen the local workers slow their way down the same catwalks by turning the shovel upside down and leaning back, putting weight on the blade as it scraped along. As they started down Jack could barely make out the path, as the light was poor and somehow the route seemed different. The *Pistenhelfers* took a more direct track, but he figured that the easier route he had been directed to take with the sick man was indeed the best choice. He waited until the sun began to appear at the top of the mountain and when it was about two hundred yards behind, he led off with Ricardo. They hadn't made much progress when the sun caught up and bathed them in warm sunlight. Almost at once they felt better and, best of all, the way down became clear.

The route to Gampen looked easy enough, right down to the group of trees just before the catwalk which connected both *pistes*. They zigzagged their way down to the trees, but not without a fall or two, brought about by the heavy frozen ruts under the thin layer of overnight snow. Ricardo had a problem with his left safety binding and every time he fell, the left ski shot down the slope until it was stopped by a fortunate twist into a bank of snow or by hitting some obstacle like a tree or rise in the terrain. One of the accepted 'boy meets girl' ploys was associated with the regular release of skis when the binding opened accidentally. Many a beautiful peaches-and-cream lass met their knight in armour in this way, he having swooped in to collect an errant ski and trudged up to the thankful female.

Stepping up with the ski over his shoulder to Ricardo was Jack's 'not romantic' task on this occasion. Without a pole to help he was under severe pressure and he had to leave his shovel where it was and ski down to collect it when the Italian was reorganised.

'I don't need this fucking hassle,' thought Jack

On the other hand, he figured that the exercise might prepare him for the work with the group for the rest of the time.

'Ricardo probably thinks I'm a nice guy.'

As this malfunction happened more and more frequently, Jack

accumulated frustration. Catching the ski was the first part of the exercise, but putting it on again was a real pressure.

"Kick your foot, there's snow on the boot - more, it's still there - here - hold it, there's ice. I'll take it off with the shovel."

Then the young Roman falls down and the process has to start again.

Whereas their efforts at the start were made more difficult by the cold and Jack's inadequate gloves, the blazing sun and the heat reduced him to a sweating subaltern and Ricardo's face became a rosy red, a combination of heat and frustration.

"Maybe I should take my skis off and walk," Ricardo searched for a solution to the many embarrassing stops and starts.

"Have you ever tried walking in deep snow?" asked Jack. "It's impossible! That's why they invented skis!" 'How the hell did the Romans conquer the world?' he thought. 'This guy is indeed the soft underbelly of the Roman Army.'

After about twenty falls of different causes and seriousness, Ricardo was beginning to lose all control, both physical and mental. He even broke the hard-man golden rule and sought his mother's assistance. "*Mama mia*," he whispered in Italian to his mother. However, mostly by dint of the force of gravity, they reached the clump of pine trees through which the catwalk ran to join the slopes, leading to Gampen and home. This was the point at which the shovel's reversed action was supposed to play its part as a snow brake.

"I think you'd better go first. I can watch and shout instructions if need be, okay?"

Ricardo nodded and managed to look even more terrified, if that were possible. Jack faced him down the path and instructed him to lean well back on the upturned shovel. He let him slip a bit just to get the feel of it.

Ricardo's eyes were fixed like a rabbit's in torchlight as he reluctantly edged on to the steep icy path - wide snow-plough, tips together and heels pushed out to a v-shape.

"Oh never mind, just do as I've told you and when you get to the bottom of the path, turn uphill. Don't continue down to the left or you'll break the speed limit and perhaps your neck."

"Break what?" More white of eyeball, and a slight pivot upwards towards the hill - 'the wrong thing to do!' thought Jack.

Without waiting to reply, Jack gave the Italian a little push and down the 200-yard narrow path he went. The shovel seemed to be doing its thing for the first few yards and he set off at a 'Canterbury Gallop', but gradually poor Ricardo lost the ability to exert power on the brake, mostly, Jack suspected, because of his increasing lean uphill. As he began to pick up speed his right arm started to pain. Amazingly he collected enough gravitas to take immediate action, and decided to change the shovel to the other side. Jack watched this mid-flight adjustment with horror. Ricardo without brakes on a steep, narrow, icy slope - his snow-plough, because of his exaggerated backward and upwards lean and resultant lack of edging, became ineffectual. In those two seconds without brakes, he increased speed dramatically.

"Jeezzzus!" Jack's expulsion of feeling was not meant as a prayer. By this time the runaway skier was totally out of control and unfortunately did not fall at once. Instead he struggled to stay upright, jettisoned the shovel, and reached a high level of speed. The runaway Italian then hit a three-foot bump and took to the air.

'He's fucked if he hits those trees.' He did and he was!

As Ricardo disappeared in a flurry of snow and coloured jacket, Jack scraped his way slowly and with great trepidation down to his exit point.

'Take it easy, this is serious, supposing the poor "*hoor*" is killed?'

With his heart in his mouth, Jack made his way carefully to the suspected point of the demise of Ricardo.

'After all, he was a poor auld skin.' Jack had already begun to think in the past tense.

The sight that met his eyes was part expected, and yet he was not prepared for the total integration of human and natural environment that was Ricardo, the snow, and a particular pine tree. The unfortunate Italian had become impaled with both legs astride its girth. That impact on its own was enough, but the minor branches on the lower level of the tree had eagerly found soft tissue into which they were embedded in celebration of this man-tree thing. The young man had been projected upwards and was held, crucifix-like, in the tree, at about four feet above the ground.

'Could be Christ getting his own back on the Romans,' was one irreverent thought and despite his military training Jack was not immediately thrust into action. Instead, he surveyed the horror of what was his erstwhile ski companion. The figure showed no life, made no sound, and the sight of blood dripping from the projected branches was in itself a silent indication of ebbing life. At last Jack moved into action, well, stumbled into action would more appropriately describe his movements. He pushed forward his Kandahar binding lever and unwound his leather safety straps. On stepping out of the Attenhoffers, he sank into about three feet of soft snow and laboriously ploughed his way up to where Ricardo hung. His first feelings around the body gave him some hope; he felt rather than saw that the branches had pierced the flesh on the sides of the body, not the central parts nor the head; the face appeared okay. However, the young Italian was held in a fierce embrace.

"Ricardo, Ricardo, can you hear me?"

Jack peered around to see if there was any reaction and was pleased to hear a low moan. He kept looking at the face for more signs of life and eventually the eyes opened.

"Ricardo, I'm here, how do you feel?" He realised that it was a stupid question, but wanted to begin a process of extraction from the arms of the tree with some degree of cooperation. However, Ricardo appeared to fall into unconsciousness again and, as he slumped, he partly slipped backwards into Jack's arms and made it possible for him to continue the slide towards the snow with a little extra force. There were one or two checks as timber wrestled with flesh and sinew, but eventually the Italian was landed on the ground. His eyes didn't open, he didn't speak, nor did he move or groan. Jack remembered his first aid training.

'Keep cool and act promptly.'

'Keep the patient warm.' There wasn't much he could do about keeping him warm except to keep his clothes around him and he did that.

'Send for a doctor if the case is serious. That's a good idea, but the skiers haven't started yet and if I leave him he could come to and…'

'Make sure that breathing is easy, loosen clothing around head and neck, and keep onlookers well away.' He loosened the clothing but onlookers weren't a problem.

'Treat bleeding first. Now here's where I can help, perhaps,' he thought. He looked for blood and saw that there was serious bleeding from one of his arms just above the elbow, and there was also heavy bleeding on his right thigh. He had a handkerchief which he tore in two, then tied it around the arm above the wound, broke a bit of stick from one of the branches that had come away from the tree and twisted it around to form a tourniquet. Almost at once the rush of blood slowed, so again he performed the same task on Ricardo's thigh with the same result. He took off his own jacket and wrapped it around the upper body of Ricardo and took stock.

'What to do? Obviously I must get help and that means leaving him here.'

Without delay he followed his own footprints back to his skis, seized his shovel and snow-ploughed down towards St Anton as fast as he could. Mostly the Attenhoffers did their job, but unfortunately there were a number of falls, which of course slowed his progress. At last he reached the bottom of the ski lift. The work group had not arrived down as yet, but the secretary was in the office setting up for the day.

"*Fräulein bitte, bitte. Ich habe grosses problem.*" She looked at the distracted coatless creature at the window and looked scared. Eventually she opened a window and asked in perfect English if he had a problem.

"Thanks be to God!" He explained that one of the working group was badly injured and in need of help.

"He's lying at the entrance to the final slope, just at the end of the catwalk on the right."

Events moved very fast from that point. Just like a lifeboat launch, two locals came running up the road, collected the rescue kit and the four-handled sledge, loaded it on the chairs, and headed up the mountain. At this time skiers were beginning to gather at the bottom of the slope and the rescue move caused a great deal of excitement. Jack went with the rescue sledge, but had difficulty keeping up with the team when they dismounted from the lift. They took off in the direction of the accident like 'shit through a goose', one in front, the other at the rear, both holding the arm extensions of the sledge. They threw a few words to one another in German, but from the moment they got the sledge fixed up at the top of Gampen they wasted no time in zooming down to the stricken Italian.

When Jack arrived at the scene, Ricardo was already strapped into the 'blood wagon' as recreational skiers irreverently called the rescue sledge. The tourniquets had been eased and tightened, and the rescue team were nosing out on to the slopes from the base of the tree. Gunter, the leader, set the pace and chose the route, while the rescuer at the back slewed right and left in an effort to keep the sledge on line. They made straight for the doctor's house just beside the lift. A searchlight had been switched on, illuminating the forecourt of the house, thus facilitating immediate entrance to the doctor's front door. Doctor Victor Flunger stepped out just as Jack arrived, by which time the two rescuers had loosened the security straps from the patient, opened his jacket, and were administering to him in readiness for the doctor. In a short time Ricardo was being treated in a mini hospital room in the house.

Jack waited in the hall, shocked at the serious nature of the accident, but relieved that the patient was in good hands.

"Was there an accident?" The questions from the group of onlookers varied. It was obvious that there was an accident, but the detail was missing. It was disclosed that a young person had been injured and that he was being transported from St Anton to a hospital somewhere. Jack, who had been at the epicentre of the accident early on, now gained information about the accident from others.

"How is he? Is there any information about the accident?" Jack spoke to a young skier.

"I think he's dead".

A local lady rejected this response. "No he's not. The doctor says he was saved by the first aid."

Gradually it emerged that, although he'd lost a lot of blood and had a break or two, Ricardo was going to survive.

Dr Flunger appeared and spoke quietly to Jack.

"He's a lucky man. Another ten minutes and he was dead. He's stabilised as of now and will be brought by ambulance to the Regional hospital in Innsbruck. You did a great job; the tourniquets were excellent and saved his life. Have you medical experience?" Dr Flunger placed a hand on Jack's forearm.

"I did a course in the army as part of my training." Jack liked the phrase 'medical experience', coming as it did from the medic in charge.

"Well done, he's a bit distressed; would you like to go with him in the ambulance? It would help if you would," Dr Flunger looked at Jack seriously.

Having agreed to help, Jack rushed to his accommodation, changed out of his ski wear, quickly packed a case, told his landlady Frau Gasper about his mission and joined the ambulance. Ricardo was awake at this stage, trussed up in splints and with untold bandages and tubes. They talked about the accident. Ricardo's account of the kamikaze run down the catwalk opened Jack's mind to what inexperience and terror can produce. Inexperience, in that anyone with a whit of sense could see that a skier of Ricardo's practise, taking account of his very weak snow-plough, was not in a position to adjust to a backward facing shovel as a brake. In other words, Jack made a bum decision in the first place.

"How do you feel? Is your arm very sore?"

"I feel great, but only because we're on our way to hospital. You saved my life, Jack."

Jack was flattered, but knew that he was partly responsible for the debacle. When they arrived at Innsbruck General Hospital he was given the opportunity to stay the night. The nurses were very friendly and Jack was calm enough to notice that they were mostly young and very attractive. One in particular was very pretty and even a mite sexier than the rest, supported by nice slim legs on well-rounded hips.

"Would you like to join me for a meal tonight?"

With smiling eyes and dancing flaxen hair, she enthusiastically accepted Jack's invitation. Jack's conscience, however, was drip-feeding negative information about the idea of going on a date in such tragic circumstances. He managed to push all the negative influences to the back of his mind and looked forward to his date.

He spent some time with Ricardo's sister. She had just arrived at the hospital and carried the responsibility of reporting back to the family in Rome. Although married in Austria, this accident to her brother carried a lot of weight, even more than her duties to her new husband. He spoke to them both and learned that Ricardo had no intention of rejoining the St Anton *Pistenhelfer* team this ski year, or for that matter, ever! With this information secured, he felt relieved of any responsibility for getting Ricardo back in action and could therefore concentrate on the business to hand: attending to the needs of Heidi, the beautiful young Austrian nurse. He had been provided with an apartment close to the Innsbruck hospital by the St Anton rescue services, so he retired there to prepare for the night out.

"Hear my song Violetta; hear my song beneath the moon."

A mixture of shower water, soap and singing helped to set the scene. This called for the Trinity Street blazer. The medical team, whose invitation was responsible for his visit, had made meal arrangements in a local hotel and so financing the evening out was partly met. A meal, including a few drinks, wine etc., and then a quiet romantic walk in the town was the plan.

Now that Ricardo was in no real danger, Jack could relax and then get back to St Anton. When he arrived in the 'Hotel Alpenrose', he sat back in a comfortable lobby chair and waited for his date to arrive. The foyer of a hotel is a place where the world meets and parts. A couple came to the desk and looked for a room; he looked ill at ease, while she appeared confident and calm. She encouraged her young man to enquire after their booking.

"*Haben Sie ein Zimmer auf den Namen Schwarzkopf?*"

The clerk played his part, but couldn't resist putting the youngster under pressure.

"Will you and your wife require a call in the morning?"

"Well, we may, but on the other hand…"

"Yes, we will require a call and breakfast of English fry with all the trimmings."

The 'wife' eyeballed the clerk. Checking into a room without being married was not usual and especially so in Ireland. Maybe it was the same in Austria, but one way or another, Jack applied Irish norms to his assessment of this situation. Jack couldn't resist seeing all. This was one of his weaknesses, seeing what went on around him and incorporating the detail into his consciousness and, as a result perhaps, not giving enough attention to his own problems and possible solutions.

"*Grüss Gott.*"

There, in a shimmering green dress and lovely high-heeled shoes, stood his date. She was more beautiful than he remembered. Shining hair, blue eyes and a smile to kill for.

"*Wie geht's* - you look lovely."

Heidi blushed slightly and thanked Jack for his complimentary remarks. Side by side they walked into the dining room. She was small, but her elegant posture and gait matched her to Jack's greater height. They looked good together. Gunter pounced. He had trained in the 'Grand Hotel', Bad Gastein, and loved his role as headwaiter. He brought them to a table near the centre of the room, drew back one of the chairs with razor-sharp precision and just the slightest shriek from the chair's contact with the highly-polished wooden floor.

"We would prefer a table by the window please."

Jack's statement was without compromise and left little choice to Gunter, who wheeled away swiftly to a table nearer the windows. The view from their new table was breathtaking. It presented a panorama of the town and the mountain background, lit by the Alpen glow of a dying winter's evening. Although upstaged by the young couple, Gunter held no rancour and serviced the table with professional aplomb. A golden lighter flicked a red candle lit, glasses slid into position, some forks taken away, and almost everything on the elegant table rearranged in celebration of the arrival of Jack and Heidi. Gunter took charge again, held Heidi's chair and slid it expertly under her young frame. It wasn't possible for him to get around and assist Jack into his seat - but he did! He then snapped his fingers and a waitress appeared, as if by magic, with the biggest menu cards Jack had ever seen.

Jack's experience in the officers' mess stood to him and he felt at ease. Gunter spoke German with Heidi and a lot of what they said about the menu was lost on Jack, so he studied the wine available and let them get on with menu issues. He realised quickly, however, that the wine selection would depend on the food, more or less, and so he tried to get in on the discussion between his date and the headwaiter. Only then did he understand that their conversation wasn't about food at all.

"I am from the same village as Heidi and I know lots of her friends, one in particular."

Heidi blushed.

This wasn't the sort of information that fed into Jack's plans for the evening. Here the headwaiter was having a *tete a tete* with his partner; this was the antithesis of an early boy-girl relationship between Jack and Heidi.

"We'll both have '*Wienerschnitzel und pommes frites*' and a bottle of Riesling '52."

His tone of voice jolted Gunter back into his role as headwaiter. Picking up the menus at speed he backed towards the kitchens, pivoting at about ten paces, as on the drill square, to a front movement. Heidi's eyes opened a little wider and returning Jack's felicitations they touched glasses. The Austrian-type champagne, which had been provided by Gunter as an aperitif, tasted crisp and fresh and gradually the atmosphere eased.

"I know that you work in the hospital and presumably stay in that locality, but where are you from Heidi? Is it true what the headwaiter said?" He sipped from his glass but kept his eyes on his date.

Jack learned with some surprise that she was from St Anton. Her father had a small farm just above the village under the route of the Vallugabahn. He loved farming and particularly working with his cattle, high up on the Alpine pastures during the summer. As the tourist trade strengthened after the war, he and his wife kept farming, but developed their house for accommodation and as a restaurant.

He had started as an Alpine Storm trooper specialising as a MGD8 medium machine gunner. After the *Anschluss* in 1938 he, like all the others, was assimilated into the *Wehrmacht* and later he was transferred to a *Luftwaffe* unit in Vienna. Shot down over London in 1941 he spent about four years in a prison camp in Manchester. He got on well with some of his guards and on release at the end of the war, spent some time with a family there. His wife and Heidi were forced to leave their home to work in a factory in Munich and it wasn't until '47 that they were allowed to return to St Anton and received his letters. As a result of her father's experience in England, Heidi, on reaching the appropriate age, went to train as a nurse in Manchester; hence her good English.

"I enjoyed Manchester and I completed my initial training there, but I really loved Hove in Sussex, where I studied midwifery."

"Is there a midwifery unit here as well?"

"Yes indeed, but I was in emergency today to help with the avalanche victims."

"Avalanche?"

"Yes, didn't you hear, a whole village was nearly wiped away? They were building a lift station above Lermoos and a rock explosion started a bad lawine - I mean avalanche - about six people were killed and dozens injured." She put down her cutlery and used her hands to emphasise the gravity of the event.

"God, our little escapade didn't deserve the attention we got." Jack was beginning to feel that he had overdone his role as supporter for Ricardo's arrival in Innsbruck.

Heidi kept her eyes on her plate as she responded.

"Everyone gets the same treatment here," she said, with pride in her voice.

The evening cruised ahead. Gunter behaved, the meal was good and the drink facilitated Jack's ability to converse at ease. Over coffee and dessert, he suggested that they take a stroll around the town.

"Maybe we could visit the *Bierkeller* area and hear a zither play." Jack had recently seen 'The Third Man', and the zither music and rhythms had a romantic niche in his thoughts.

That agreed they set off. Heidi pulled up her jacket hood and her face, framed in a fur surround, made a pretty picture. They walked side by side through the winter fairyland, across the bridge over the frozen river and into an area comprising narrow streets, restaurants, and *Bier-kellers*. Halfway down one of the streets, they heard the sound of a band playing German folk songs. Heidi took his hand in hers and, like children, they skipped on quickly to the corner of the street which led to a little square surrounded by three-storied buildings with ornate, wood-carved balconies. There, on a covered bandstand, sat the brass band being conducted by a tall man with a wide moustache and sporting a hat with the required feathers and badges.

"Umpa umpa, stick it up your jumpa!"

"What did you say?"

"Oh, I was just singing." Jack realised that the childish musical games of the mess might not be appropriate or understood.

They excitedly joined the crowd around the band. Heidi sang the chorus and he joined in as best he could.

"In München steht ein Hofbräuhaus - eins, zwei, g'suffa!
Da lauft so manches Fassl aus - eins, zwei, g'suffa!
Da lauft so manches Fassl aus - eins, zwei, g'suffa!
Da hat so mancher brave Mann - eins, zwei, g'suffa!"

In fairness, Jack was in a 'la la'-mode until the 'eins, zwei g'suffa', but he gave that part 'lackery'. Some of the songs involved holding hands, linking elbows and chain movement, right hand left hand, around the crowd. It was just like dancing at a ceilidhe. He watched for Heidi's return; he loved seeing her smiling face weaving its way around the chain to arrive once more by his side.

"*Ein Proooosit, ein Proooosit*
Der Gemütlichkeit
Ein Proooosit, ein Proooosit
Der Gemütlichkeit."

By the time they left the music and moved into one of the *Biergarten*, any formality that existed between them was gone. On one occasion during the dance their cheeks brushed and their eyes met, searching for a response. No words were spoken but, from then, any chance to embrace was eagerly taken, on a fifty-fifty basis so to speak! Jack felt happy, just occasionally he thought of life in the mess - not being there made him even happier. They had a few beers, discussed his work in Ireland, her work in the hospital, music, sport and life in their respective countries.

Placing her lips close to Jack's ear Heidi whispered, "I think it's time we went back, I have an early start tomorrow." He tingled to the touch of her lips.

They walked back to the hospital, stopping at a picturesque stone bridge to admire the frozen river. When they arrived at the gates of the nurses' quarters they paused and, without speaking, Jack held her close and buried his face in her sweet smelling neck. He felt her body respond and she pressed her hips strongly against his - he was taken by surprise and could only utter her name.

"Heidi…"

Before he could respond further, she held him firmly, looked into his eyes and softly said, "I must go now Jack, but I'll see you in St Anton at the weekend. I'll be up there with some friends for a few days' skiing."

… and she was gone, leaving just a faint trace of her perfume hanging on the cold evening air.

Next morning early, Jack made his way to the hospital. He experienced the usual hospital ward activity and when he reached the bedside, Ricardo was sitting up perky as you like, and he had visitors. Mr and Mrs Biglia had made the trip from Rome and were ensconced on each side of the bed, gazing in rapt attention at their beloved only son and listening to his account of the accident and of Jack's part in his rescue.

"*Mille mille grazie ifinitte.*"

"She says that our family are indebted to you, Jack, and that you must visit us in Rome so they can show their appreciation." Ricardo explained.

Jack looked sheepish and muttered something like "it was nothing". He felt more guilt than before because he knew in his heart that he was partly responsible for the accident. 'If he hadn't been so much in a hurry to get back to the *Pistenhelfers* - if he'd more tolerance and understanding of the young Italian - if he'd waited for the lift to start and gone down with him.'

'I'm a bad man,' he thought, 'and this praise only makes it worse - nevertheless, I might take up the invitation to Rome! Never cut off your nose to spite your face!'

The trip back from Innsbruck was uneventful. Jack took in the beauty of the winter landscape and marvelled at the road route up the mountainside but his mind was elsewhere and Heidi had pride of place.

It was late afternoon when they reached St Anton - the driver and his crew had indulged in a long meal stop at a roadside restaurant. Jack went straight away up to the Trittkopf to relay his adventures to Louis.

"Would you like the real or the edited version?"

"You look like the cat that got the cream. I thought you were on a mission of mercy."

Louis had been informed of Jack's role in bringing Ricardo to hospital by Dr Flunger.

"Yes, the main mission was to look after Ricardo. I'm glad to report that my first aid worked and he's on the mend, although still ensconced in the hospital in Innsbruck. His mother and father are sitting by his bedside."

"Good, you're a credit to the old sod - I suspect that you played more than one game of cards - out with it!" Louis enjoyed hearing about the adventures of his young friend.

Jack told Louis about his time with the young nurse and the plan to meet the following weekend. He eagerly sought information from Louis about how his skiing went and his plans for the morrow. In his own case he was excited about his first real *Pistenhelfer* outing. The temperature stood at minus 2 and it had started snowing heavily. That meant *treten* would be the order of the day from top to bottom, without much work for the shovels.

Louis described his day. He'd said mass, no problems, had a late breakfast and, feeling in need of a ski lesson, hired an instructor called Peter. He did some snow-plough and stem turns with him on the learner slopes, and spent the rest of the time skiing up and down on the Gampen-Kapall run. He was excited about his progress and looked forward to demonstrating his new skills to Jack.

"Okay, Louis, great, I'm off; see you tomorrow."

Out through the double doors of the Trittkopf into the swirling snow went Jack; over the railway line past the Schwarzer Adler and Hotel Post, and down the main street to his room over the cowshed. The night was still buzzing. He could hear zither music from the cellar restaurant and further down a snowball fight between exuberant skiers, happy that the slopes would be deep in snow in the morning. Up the stairs and into the room he went; before lapsing into slumber land he pondered with awe on his setting and the difference between the plains and the Alps, Heidi, Heidi, Hei…snzzzz.

Up like a lark, he checked the clock and planned his arrival for work - a bread roll, possibly touch base with Louis, on to the chair lift to be there at half six. On with the gear - 'Bloody hell, these boots take some putting on - poles, gloves and skis, what else? Do I need to hide my passport and wallet? That's the first place anyone would look.' He hid them anyway, glanced around and scuttled down the stairs. The excitement and freedom of his new life more than compensated for the lack of security and it was a happy young Irishman that set out on what he hoped would be his first real experience as a *Pistenhelfer*. He felt as free as a bird and couldn't resist jumping from the third last step on to the snow-covered road.

'Yahoo, happy is the dealer in the big ace pot.' He felt the impact of his landing on his ski quads and thanked God he was himself.

The gates were down at the level crossing. As the train rumbled by, it gave the impression of a Weimar supply transport unit going to the front. The rear carriages were loaded with motorcars, to be reoccupied by their owners when the train had passed through the Arlberg tunnel. It was difficult, and sometimes impossible, to keep the pass open during the winter and it was normal practise to travel via the tunnel in this manner. The Arlberg tunnel, over six miles long, was opened to rail traffic in 1884 and electrified in 1923, just before the war.

Jack waited for the line of clanking goods carriages to pass. A few empty spaces gave him an opportunity to see to the other side of the track. He spotted Louis waiting, on his way, no doubt, to the church to say mass, albeit a bit early. When the barrier lifted they made arrangements to meet.

"Why not call up to the Trittkopf when you get down. I'll be at breakfast 'til about ten o'clock and you're welcome to a cuppa."

Passing the Vallugabahn cable lift Jack saw no lights or movement, and wondered how they prepared their runs. 'A much bigger job, and then, maybe they don't *piste* the upper runs at all - probably not.' Certainly the Osthang, which is directly under the cable car, was not worked on, and the giant bumps were the terror of the resort. This was a run that Louis and Jack intended doing when they 'came of age'.

"*Grüss Gott, wie geht's?*"

"*Gut, danke.*"

Jack was greeted enthusiastically in the Austrian dialect by Wolfgang the leader and by the local and foreign workers. His escapades with Ricardo had evidently upped his status.

The number of workers had increased. As well as the Americans, there was a contingent from New Zealand. He recognised one of the group from the first night in the Bahnhof and knew they were good skiers. It was still dark when the lift started up; they all grabbed a *mantel* and sat on the chair lift. He was alone and had time to sit and take in the Alpine winter environment.

The great pines groaned aghast as their tops were crowned with fantastic white plumes. Occasionally snow fell from an over-laden branch, formed a snowball as it hit the ground and rolled out of sight, adding to the giant jigsaw-pattern marks in the fresh snow. In the distance the mountains were outlined against a sky gradually being brightened by the rising sun. He was so excited by it all that he couldn't resist shouting to the pair just ahead.

"Isn't this really something?"

They couldn't hear him clearly over the rattle of the cable on the pulleys, so they just waved back. To communicate in any way was enough and he was engulfed in a wave of contentment. Above the tree line, things were much more austere; long ridges of snow had been formed by the wind and he could see that there was work to do before beginners could ski with safety. The top of the lift was covered with snow and someone had cleared just enough to let the chairs arrive and leave.

A galvanised shed covered the arrival area and as he swung in he could see the glow of a single electric light bulb swinging from the roof, plus the red spot of Herman's fag. Herman was the man in charge of this terminal section of the lift operation. He was responsible for the safe arrival of the skiers, their dismounting and exit to the slopes. The steep slope from the dismount was a cause of much anxiety to beginners. The slope was bad enough, but a sharp turn at the bottom complicated matters even more. Often a beginner would fall at the bottom having frantically and inelegantly exited the chair, thus creating a pile-up of bodies and skis. Under the best of scenarios this traffic 'marmalade' would be a cause of hysterical laughter, but sometimes the Kandahar bindings would not release and either a ski would break or there could be damage to limbs. Under these circumstances Herman and his assistant had an important function to perform. Herman had been an NCO in the *Wehrmacht* and was very reliable.

"Whoops! That's not easy."

Jack ploughed down the slope and around. He blamed the *mantel*, which he still wore, for his inelegant exit from the chair lift. He joined the shadowy figures of *Pistenhelfers* as they made their way over to the hut and the fire. His previous experience on Kapall had not been a rewarding one, but he tried to block all that from his mind, including the descent with Ricardo. The fire was welcoming, but the overpowering smell of stale socks and cheap cigarettes was the same. Again the young locals hogged the fire and the conversation. Jack was asked a question about his trip to Innsbruck. It appeared that the ambulance crew had carried back stories about his meeting with the nurse, and the locals in the crew, as well as tease him about the boy-girl thing, decided to christen him Romeo.

'Shit, I don't need this.' In reality he wasn't sure if he should be pleased or not.

The name offended his hard-man image to some degree, so he decided not to respond so that the tease might die for lack of reaction. The move to work was initiated by Wolfgang who tied up his boots, stubbed his fag, and set out into the gloom of the morning and rattled his poles on the outside of the corrugated hut as a signal to get moving. Jack was keen and wasted no time donning his skis and getting the shovel at the ready. Gradually, all the *Pistenhelfers* assembled, the last being the local Austrians, who were still engaged in conversation about a ski competition in St Anton involving some of their erstwhile school friends.

Once Wolfgang began his brief for the day there was total attention to his directions. The object of the day was to tread the mountain from top to bottom and provide a suitable ski route. Wolfgang was skilled in picking a route, following the ridges and hollows of the terrain, thus facilitating natural weighting and unweighting in an even flow from top to bottom. Three teams were organised; each led by a local worker. Jack was allocated to the team on the left of the decent, led by a local called Heinrich.

"Okay, here we start. Romeo, follow me."

So much for Jack's attempt to remain anonymous, or at least avoid being saddled with the romantic label. They got into line and started treading downwards. The snow was deep and each step required the lifting of the knees and skis with a deal of effort. By this stage the sun had risen and Heinrich followed the accepted 'keep with the sun' rule. The work was tough physical exertion by any standard and in about ten minutes the Irishman was sweating heavily but happy to be involved.

'This is the life, they'll never believe me.' Jack could still hardly believe that he'd achieved such a heroic life-style.

"No, not like that - watch me."

Heinrich was most enthusiastic about his newly acquired role as leader of the group and, as well as setting out the path, he pounced on anyone not treading to his satisfaction. His demonstrations were perfection and resulted in a smooth *piste* without ridge of any sort.

"Watch me - lift your knees."

Jack and an American girl got the brunt of his attention that morning, but were allowed praise where their efforts were an improvement. It's not easy to tread new snow, particularly when it's fairly high and in some instances they almost had to lift their knees to their chins to clear the surface. Not alone that but one step wasn't always enough, and a smooth finish often required several attempts by the Piestenhelfer. Heinrich had eyes in the back of his head and seemed able to spot the slightest weakness in the work. It didn't bother him that his team were sweating like pigs and ready to drop.

Heinrich propelled himself up the slope at great speed to any inadequate worker, pointing out the weakness and making corrections with applied enthusiasm.

"He has double-jointed legs."

Jack agreed with the American girl, but noted that Heinrich's legs were like tree trunks. Great strength, he figured, probably a 474 in somatotyping and the result of generations of physical work and honest, good food. Keeping pace with the sun's rays was, no doubt, an accepted policy for physical and psychological reasons - to be warm and to feel good. Jack was feeling the pressure and was always glad of the opportunity to rest when they passed beyond the sunlight. The Attenhoffer skis were working well, but because of their length, the tips needed to be lifted vigorously every step in order to clear the excess snow. This movement was an added pressure and the muscles on the front of his tibia complained of the strain.

Jack sweated his way down the mountain, goaded on by the local leaders and by his own enthusiasm for the project. His dropping sweat made little blue holes in the snow and on one occasion when the group waited for the sun to catch up, he gashed a vigorous hole in the snow in relief of a need to clear his bladder. Once, as they were *treten* down the slope, the American, Jennie, exited a patch of pine scrub like a woodcock fleeing a copse of hazel wood, trousers down and white bum exposed she left a yellow trail in her wake. She blamed her inability to set her skis in the squatting position in a mixture of snow and twigs, although she seemed nonplussed and enjoyed her moment of fame then, and the recounting of the event. Of such tough stuff were female *Pistenhelfers* made!

"Not hard enough, and keep in time with Don Carlos." Don Carlos, who was on Jack's other side, was Spanish-Mexican, originally from Spain. "It's no good if you don't work together - you should know that, Romeo."

Jack accepted Heinrich's advice and ignored the reference to his trip to Innsbruck.

"How are you getting on, Carlos? A bit like working in the Legion I suppose?" Jack spoke, keeping time with his *treten* efforts.

"I've never been to Morocco, but I know that they used to call the members of the Legion '*les novios de la muerte*' - the bridegrooms of death." Jack didn't expect such a historically-informed response from the Spaniard.

"That's a bit over the top for this crowd, but the mixture of members of the *Pistenhelfers* are a bit like the flotsam and jetsam that joined the French or Spanish Legions, without the criminal background that is - at least, as far as we know."

"Less talking and more work." Heinrich interrupted the history lecture.

"*Legionarios a luchar; Legionarios a morir.*"

"What's that?" said Jack, as Heinrich moved out of earshot.

"Oh, just the motto of the Legionnaires - onward to fight, onward to die!"

"That's us all right - keep going or Heinrich will have our heads!"

Their work on skis was an enjoyable but tough exercise, which developed comradeship among the workers and carried a badge of status in the village. The experience was often a subject of conversation in the

Bahnhof restaurant. The deeds of these self-styled desperados invited admiring glances and questions from young Inghamss's' girls, for example, thus opening an avenue for further and deeper connections between couples. Inghams, the London-based travel agent, employed young 'well-bred' English girls as representatives; most of who had been to Swiss finishing schools and as such could ski and speak German. They were ideal for the job and graced the slopes and attended all social activities, as well as doing whatever ski reps do. In St Anton they stayed in a hotel at the lower end of the village, which was, for the likes of Jack, to become a natural evening retreat.

The day's work done, albeit early at ten o'clock, Jack felt self-satisfied - his first day as a fully-fledged *Pistenhelfer*. The work was hard, but the feeling of satisfaction prevailed and it was a happy young subaltern that stomped his way up the hill to the Hotel Trittkopf to his friend Louis. He opened the inner front door to be met by the smell of breakfast and the sound of rustling papers and conversation. Jack absorbed the contrast between the slog of the *Pistenhelfer* and that of the tourist skier preparing to move to the slopes from the warmth of the family hotel. Louis crumpled his newspaper onto the breakfast table displaying a wide smile under dancing brown eyes.

"And how's the *Pistenhelfer* on his first morning?"

Jack's explanation of his morning was principally a focus on the fundamentals of *Pistenhelfer* work, and of the skills and strengths required on that first morning. He described the pressures of time and precision involved to an open-mouthed Louis.

"All the way down? How many people? How did the skis stand up? Have you free lifts for the rest of the day? Did you enjoy it?"

Louis listened and understood that Jack needed an opportunity for reaction and relaxation. Louis was enthralled by the idea of being a *Pistenhelfer*. In particular he admired the chance way in which Jack had not alone secured a room for very little, but also had achieved a work position almost by accident.

Most of the hotel patrons were leaving to prepare for a day's skiing and Heinie, the daughter of the Strauss family, had not as yet cleared the tables.

Jack, with support from Louis, took advantage of the situation and ate everything in sight - bread rolls, cheese, and fruit from the ten or so tables in the breakfast room.

"How'd the church session go?"

"All according to plan, and surprisingly enough there were quite a few in attendance." Louis looked pleased.

"Locals?" Jack had heard that the local young ski-instructors were following the path of Manna rather than God.

"Yes, some of those surely, but also quite a few visitors, Americans mostly."

They made their way down to the Trittkopf ski cellar, collected Louis's skis and boots, and headed over to the chair lift, weaving their way through the *skischule* classes to get to the entrance. The red-jacketed instructors, wearing distinctive Tyrolean Ski School badges, chatted to one another and stamped skis on the snow like thoroughbreds waiting for the off. There were always a few problems before classes started, such as the upgrading or the downgrading of some pupils. The head of the ski school tested and graded everyone on the first morning. For the student, the problem mostly was that they were separated from a friend or relation for a substantial period of the holiday by virtue of being placed in a higher or lower class. In very difficult cases, which sometimes resulted in tears, the stronger student was allowed to transfer downwards. Ski instruction was taken seriously and military discipline transferred naturally through the ex-army ski instructors. Quite a few of the older instructors had been members of wartime Alpine units.

"I can't go on - Cecil is a better skier than me and yet he's allocated to a lower class."

Sometimes the young skiers were so besotted with one another that competence on skis rated much lower than relationships, and their ability to appreciate the grading programme was diminished. The instructors know this of course and often enhanced what might have been an unexciting morning by dividing lovers. The wails only added to the pleasure of the moment.

Jack was of the age of the young majority, but was removed from any sympathy for the divided by dint of his professional role as a *Pistenhelfer*.

Louis and he were ensconced on the now familiar chair lift and surveyed what was becoming quite a busy ski slope. The chair gave them the opportunity to easily view over the slopes for about half a mile in each direction. Although it was early, there were a fair number of skiers 'shaping' their way down to St Anton from Gampen, and to Gampen from

Kapall. The competence of each skier was easily seen and Jack and Louis became involved in an exercise to 'shoot down' the weaker skier. If a targeted skier looked a bit tenuous and not firm on the skis, they would use their poles as rifles and try to shoot down the unfortunate target. This meant identifying the weakness of the skier and importantly, their advancement towards a particularly difficult part of the *piste*. Bang! If the skier fell, it was a score for the rifleman and the more dramatic the fall the better the pleasure.

"There's one, he's a certainty. When he gets to the ridge - ready, fire - yes!"

Down he went, much to the amusement of the two marksmen involved in this *Schadenfreude* exercise, even though they themselves were heading for at least two falls on the next run. Louis was a bit of a fall expert and was up to his usual form on this visit to St Anton.

Off they went. One thing about skiing; most people hate being on their own and take great care to arrange their rendezvous. It's one thing playing a round of golf in a nice green familiar environment, but the Alps are a different story. Alone on the mountaintop, late afternoon, light failing, rising wind and pellets of snow into the face, and the gremlins of fear and isolation take charge. Although Jack always felt excited by the adventure, the sight of the village lights and a bit of company on the final slopes was reassuring.

When they reached the restaurant at Gampen, Jack met a few of his fellow workers. They were mostly having a feed of *Wienerschnitzel* and fried potatoes or pasta and a beer. Working from early morning eats up the calories and for most ski bums this was the main meal of the day. Jack and Louis enjoyed their lunch, and an *Apfelstrudel* and coffee finished off Jack's mid-day treat. He pushed back the chair to make room for his Gussie Goose type stomach.

"You look like the cat," said Louis, black ski outfit and white smile. "I was thinking of a trip up to Valluga. Are you on?"

"Is it a bit late?"

"Don't be such a wimp."

"Okay, you're on. I'll show you who's a wimp."

And so Jack and Louis skied down to the Vallugabahn, bought their tickets and got on the thirty-person cable car. This was Jack's second time to travel on this cable car or, for that matter, on any cable car lift. They held their breath as the gears clicked into place and the car swung out over the ski slopes below. Up and up to the first pylon which was perched on a crag about 300 yards from the station. Somebody squealed as the car rattled over the pylon rollers and drooped down to continue its inverted arch to the next pylon and so on to the top of Galzig mountain, 2,185 metres! A slow tentative docking and the man in charge opened the door and lowered the platform linking the car and the station.

Klaus Glos assisted his wife Monika in the restaurant '*Die Schuss*', situated at the top of the final slope into St Anton. A group of Swedes had livened the place up a bit and the rounds of Schnapps had developed into a singsong, before they eventually geared up and headed down to the village.

"I need to get some hay to the cows before dark," said Klaus to his wife.

The cows were housed in the village and stall-fed during the winter months. In summer Klaus and family members spent time on the lush Alpine pastures further up the mountain, herding the cattle and cutting and saving hay. The hay was stored in mountain huts and a sledge provided the ideal transport system to get the hay down to the village. Klaus had limited space to store hay in the village itself, so sledge by sledge in winter suited.

"It's very late; will you have time to get up and down before dark?"

Monika was worried, mostly because of the injuries Klaus had sustained during the war. He made light of his leg injury, so she didn't mention it often.

"I'll be okay, I can use the path when the skiers are finished - the sledge is already loaded at the back of the upper meadow hut, so I should have plenty of time."

She didn't mention that she thought he was getting a bit past this heavy type of work. He had a fierce pride in his role as a farmer and with such long links to the past in St Anton. She bit her tongue and said a prayer to St Christoph for his safety.

"*Pfüatdi*," and he was off.

As she wiped the pots she watched him limp up the hill and out of view. He picked a route close to the rocks where the snow was less deep and left a zigzag trail in the snow. Skiers shot past at speed and tucked down to meet the final *schuss* to St Anton. One or two stopped at the door to drink a warm *glühwein* before finishing their journey. Monika was kept busy that afternoon, and what with the passing trade and preparations for a fondue party that evening, her trudging farmer husband soon left her mind.

"*In München steht ein Hofbräuhaus - eins zwei g'suffa,*" he sang the *Bierkeller* song as he walked along and his thoughts went back to his training with the local Tirolerer Corp before the war. He remembered the excitement and the loyalties among friends in the Corp. Most of these friends and about twenty other young men from the area were now gone, dead that is. What was worse, the survivors were unable to celebrate any special time associated with service to the *Wehrmacht*, and although they did meet and talk, it was quietly in their houses and with a select few.

He strayed from the normal path of skiers and mentally noted fallen trees and the marks of the animals of the forest. A pair of Alpine grouse stuttered from a clump of trees and winged their way to another stand of pine. He knew they were there. In the old days he might have joined a group of locals on a Sunday after mass to go hunting. The grouse were prime targets for eating and for their feathers, used to adorn the Tyrolean hats worn on Sundays and festivals. Nowadays, however, the birds were becoming scarce and he protected the pairs in his area. There was talk at local government level that he was creating a game preserve on his land, an area off-limits to skiers and local hunters. True, he had offered some of his farm for this purpose, but being on the sunny side of the valley he reckoned that skiing and business must come first. The other side of the valley, including Rendel, was much steeper, had no lift, was prone to avalanche, and therefore was the obvious choice as a nature reserve. He stuck the ski poles he was using to assist his ascent aggressively into the snow as an act of frustration at the conflict of interests!

He made steady progress and reached the hut in about two hours - three o'clock on his army-issue watch. His expert eye noted the light conditions and with a quick puff of his carved meerschaum pipe, he pulled the sledge out from behind the hut and started his downward route. The pressure of the sledge and hay felt just right and he braced back, digging his heels well in.

'Monika thinks I'm past it, well past it in some senses, but when I get into my mountains anything goes.'

Grunt, ease, slip, swivel, lift, right, left, right, left, and jump, hold. Gradually sledge, hay and man made their way down the mountain. At last he reached the catwalk around the Steisbachtal at the tree line.

'From now on it's easy.' His heels were tipped with steel half moons and, even in the frozen snow, man and sledge eased their way down as one.

Jack and Louis looked down at the sloping ground from Galzig, over the shoulder leading to the catwalk from where the Steisbachtal and the Schindler Kar met. A tightening of the stomach muscles and a sharp intake of breath; vertigo and the diminishing evening light played their part - this nervousness was born of the relationship between their ski abilities and the snow challenge. It was with great care, and partly in an effort to delay the trial, that they slapped their skis on the frozen ground, and took time as they married the boots to the Kandahar bindings.

'That won't come off,' thought Jack as he wrapped the safety strap tightly around the leather boots. Safety straps are supposed to be used to hold on to the skis if they leave the foot, but Jack felt safer using the long leather strap as an additional way of securing the boots to the bindings.

"I suppose a prayer is out of the question, Louis?"

"Even God isn't much help in this situation. It's true that *Pistenhelfers* don't work on the slopes up here. Apart from the ski marks, I don't see any marked route." Louis was beginning to feel the pressure and wondered if they had bitten of more than they could chew.

"There are a few poles here and there, can you see what colour they are?" Colour coding of routes and levels of difficulty are indicated by poles with the appropriate colouring as markers, black being the highest grade.

They eventually saw a possible route and set off. It was difficult going as the snow was thick and had crusted slightly on top. Jack found that a long traverse and a dynamic stem turn was best practice and with Louis following closely they made good progress. After about an hour the mountain shoulder with a catwalk along the side became visible.

"What time do you make it?"

"It's just four."

"I don't see anyone around and the light is fading." Louis was definitely anxious.

The sun had dipped behind the mountains, leaving a bright afterglow, but not enough to light the valley. The catwalk or path around the shoulder of the mountain was their target, so they set off, with difficulty at first, through the fairly deep rutted snow. Someone had followed the same path earlier, so they felt reassured, and as they got closer to the beginning of the path Jack began to sing and call to Louis, who responded in kind.

Jack yelped like a beagle on the scent as he left the rutted snow and leaped over a ridge onto the path. Louis followed and they increased speed significantly. Jack's goggles were useless out of the sunlight so he pulled them down to hang around his neck. The breeze blowing up the valley was cold and penetrating, and it was more by feel than sight that he wound his way around the narrow winding path on the mountain. Occasionally he edged to a halt, taking care not to spill over the steep slope down to the valley floor.

"Sorry, shit!" Louis marked one of these stops by crashing into Jack - skis, legs, and poles all over the place! At least they stayed on the track, but the delays ate into whatever daylight remained and soon they saw glimmers of light appearing from houses far below, indicating that night had arrived.

"Onward ever onward!" Away they went, Jack still in front and setting a faster pace. His heart in his mouth, but things went well and he narrowed the plough and sped down the path. Glancing back on a bend, he thought, 'Louis's not there, I hope he's okay.'

He felt confident and even increased the speed. The path provided a pitched bank on the corners and he enjoyed the feeling of increased momentum as, in his own mind, he flashed around each bend. It was fairly dark when it happened. Just around one acute turn, he saw through squinting eyes what he thought was a tunnel. No tunnel on the route, but elation was in control and without any reduction in speed he ploughed into a tightly compacted bale of hay on a sledge!

Louis saw what happened. He had arrived in a much more careful manner and saw the impact and the outcome of the suddenly increased mass on the velocity of the bale of hay.

K laus eased his way down the path, as he and his father before him had done many times before - from the front, leaning back and digging his heels in on this particularly steep and icy part. He was thinking of goulash soup and bread when he heard and felt the impact behind him. Despite his best efforts the hay took off! Leaning in towards the mountain on his right, he let the sledge proceed on the outside edge and before it left his view he saw the red and blue figure impaled on the back. This was his first experience of this kind, but his cool immediate actions mirrored many of his reactions to experiences in the army and as a machine gunner on the *Heinkel* bomber.

Jack was stunned as his chest slammed into the timber of the sledge. With his skis securely held, face and head in the sweet smelling hay, he was but a compliant passenger on that runaway hay-sledge.

Louis and the farmer watched the show with differing interests. Miraculously the sledge followed the path and even negotiated a few minor curves, but about 100 yards down it disappeared over the edge.

No time for introductions! Off they went, one in search of his hay and the other seeking a lost friend. Because he was on skis, Louis got to the bend first and to his amazement - zilch! The sledge must have negotiated that sharp bend and headed down the path. Away he went and still no sign of anything. 'What the hell, it couldn't have gotten this far!' One more bend and still no Jack or the sledge and more importantly no runner marks on the snow. 'It's icy and maybe they wouldn't leave a mark.' He looked back up the path and realised that he had come about 200 yards and would have great difficulty getting back up to the farmer. He looked over the edge and sweated at the sight of the steep tree-lined slope down to the floor of the valley far below. He tried to sidestep up the catwalk, but the path was too narrow and the rear of his skis kept catching in the bank of snow. He took them off, but kept slipping on the ice and made no progress. He finished in a heap even farther down.

'This is bad, Jack could be dead!'

To wait, or go down and raise the alarm; he thought of the options and tried not to panic as he peered anxiously up the path - and there they were!

The sledge, released from its restraint, had taken off down the path at an increasing speed. The momentum registered with Jack, who had recovered from the impact of the timber on his sternum. He rolled his eyes right and saw the bank of snow flash by and on the left nothing – well the tops of trees, but he couldn't take that in as a possibility. He closed his eyes and held on to the sledge.

'You and I are in this together,' he thought, and they were! His skis held firm in the hay; man and sledge were as one.

Klaus looked on in horror as events developed. He remembered that he'd been encouraged by his wife not to go; but then the hay had to be brought down to his lovely herd of Simmental cows.

'What the hell were they doing on this route at this time of the evening?'

Despite the fact that they were making good money from skiers, he felt resentment at the desecration of his mountains by lowlanders. He trudged down after the sledge and was more than pleased and a little horrified when he saw the load had keeled over and stopped against a broken pine tree about four feet over the edge. Avalanches often piled into this valley breaking the tops of strong pine trees as if they were matchsticks. The sledge could have plummeted out of control down the sides into the deep valley, but instead it held firm against the tree. He breathed a sigh of relief. '*Mein Gott! Danke.*'

Before he had time to extricate himself, Jack heard the farmer's efforts at making a route back to the path for the sledge and its passenger. Their conversation was limited, but the farmer had good English and encouraged him to stay still until the boots were released from the skis. Jack wasn't injured and once pulled out of the hay was able to re-establish contact with the Attenhoffers and follow the sledge down the next narrow section to a level platform, about 200 yards further on - in fact to where the worried Louis waited. They had a few words with the farmer and even offered to help him down to the village. He seemed keen to have them ski down before dark and convinced them that he was well able to complete the trip with the hay.

"He knows what he's at, he looked happy to be rid of us."

They made their way down in the near dark and finished with an exciting *schuss* down the final hill to the platform of icy snow in front of the Vallugabahn cable car. Sportsmanlike, they shook hands: "That was some run, we got more than we expected!"

Unhitched, they made their way to the Bahnhof, stacked their skis against the paling and pushed open the door. They were met by a cacophony of sound and the smell of cigarette smoke and bodies, the usual when skiing finished.

"Wait 'til I tell you about Jack here. This is one for the books."

Louis left out nothing and even added somewhat, which was the norm for tales told between skiers. And so Jack and his love affair with a bale of hay, was sent on its way around the world via the range of multi-countried skiers present.

"Philip was heading home to South Africa so we gave him a real St Anton send-off."

Philip was one of the *Pistenhelfers*. Jack had spoken to him once or twice and learned that he lived with his father and family on a farm in Kenya close to the forests of Mount Kenya. He had skied on the snow near the peak often. Their usual way of getting to the top of the ski run was unusual: donkeys. Yes! Trained donkeys crossed with zebra, walked down to the bottom of the run as soon as they had delivered their skier to the top and begin the process again.

"A carrot's a wonderful motivator."

Jack and Louis joined in the festivities even though they had missed the send-off. Beer and a Schnapps chaser was the order and they were in the mood to join in.

L ouis was a strong character. Ordained as a priest in Ireland and posted to a parish in England, he quickly became a highly appreciated member of the parish team. He never stepped away from opportunities to innovate in religious matters or social exercises. For example, there was a young aspiring actor in the parish boys' club, which was linked to the local school. Joe was an enthusiastic actor in the club's drama society and played a range of leading parts. His recent role as Willie Wee, in 'Under Milkwood', was considered by many to be exceptional. Louis saw the potential in Joe and, as Joe had indicated his intention to leave school feeling frustrated with the education system, felt that he should at least receive further exposure in the English language. Louis wasn't prepared to let this young man fail to develop his obvious talent and sought to motivate him by offering him the opportunity to stay in the drama society and to use the library in the Rectory.

"Read Thackeray, Shakespeare, and Dickens over the next year and report to me every Friday night." He did and from then on Joe was hitched to a star and he and Louis remained friends.

Louis became parish priest and so his opportunities for innovation increased. He learned to fly in the local aerodrome and when it was proposed by the parish council that a new church be built (the old one was costing a lot, year after year in repairs), Louis's counter-proposal, which was typical Louis and which excited the committee members, was accepted.

"I propose that we put our money into servicing a struggling parish in northern Canada."

The idea was that four members of the parish expert group would go to Canada for a year and provide medical, social, and religious support for the Eskimos and others, in an area of Tundra about the size of Ireland. Louis, of course, was to play the important roles of priest and pilot. The venture was a great success.

Meanwhile, Joe had made progress in the world of acting and film. He made a breakthrough in films and although forced to accept very strict contract conditions to get his first big job, the film made him. The success was like a flood and he was invited to venues to publicise the film all over the world. One such invitation was to New York, where Ed Sullivan interviewed him on his television show. At this time Joe was in touch with Louis in Canada, and in the Green Room after the show he convinced Ed Sullivan that he should interview Louis. The Irish connection added to the issue and Louis was invited to the show to talk about his life and the Canadian project.

Due to the isolated nature of the area in northern Canada, Louis lived close to the working group from England and got to know the individuals very well. In particular he related to a young married couple, both doctors, and was very impressed with their closeness, both as a couple and as a working team. This experience made a lasting impression on him and as a result he remained a staunch admirer of the married state.

There's more, but it suffices to say that Louis was no lightweight and could box his weight on the slopes, in the church, or in the Bahnhof restaurant. His parishioners loved him, were excited by his ski trips to Austria and if anyone returned from holidays or business, a selection of foreign coins, including Austrian schilling, would appear on the Sunday plate!

Our heroes drank a few, but eventually the pangs of hunger had their effect. Louis didn't eat in the Trittkopf as evening meals were not served, so in order not to spoil the party, food was ordered in the Bahnhof. *Wienerschnitzel* and double portion of chips was Jack's favourite and today was no exception. They both had *Apfelstrudel* for sweet - what else?

The restaurant filled up as skiers called in before going on to eat elsewhere, or to dance in one of the *Bier-kellers*. Next to Jack and Louis's table in the Bahnhof sat a group of English-speaking men and women. The conversations spilled over and Jack began to talk to a beautiful young English girl whom he thought he recognised. She was with an older German man, older than twenty-four that is, whose English was adequate but not fluent. Their light conversation was interrupted by pauses, geared to bring the German man into the circle.

"I have it! I know where I saw you last! I saw you in my brother's bedroom." The penny had dropped for Jack.

"What's his name?" the English girl responded to Jack with a grin and the mischievous arch of a beautiful eyebrow.

Jack had a brother Jim. On one occasion, while on a trip to a dance to Dublin, Jim had secured a signed picture of a J. Arthur Rank film starlet, who was visiting Dublin as part of a film promotion. On his return home Jim had crept up the stairs very late and grinned as he placed the large autographed picture on the mantelpiece of his and Jack's bedroom.

Hopping on one leg as he struggled to pull on his trousers next morning the picture of the pretty girl caught Jack's eye.

"Who's that?"

"That's the girl I was at the dance with."

"Gimme a break - who is she?"

"I told you, I was with her last night."

Jack was impressed but doubtful, for no reason other than jealousy. Now here in St Anton he was to learn the real connection. Her name was Jane Thornly, in St Anton on her holidays alone and staying in the Hotel Post. She had met the German man the day before, skied with him for a day and had plans for the next day also. Before arranging to 'give her a shout' the next evening, Jack learned that she was at that dance in the 'Gresham Hotel', but not with his brother! She had signed photographs for many as part of the film promotion.

Monika worried about Klaus on that trip up to the pastures. She was uneasy and watched the descent route anxiously. He had said that he needed the hay as they were running low down in the village; otherwise she would have sent somebody to meet him and have him park the sledge until the morning. He had a lamp, so she watched for its flicker in the dark. She loved their life up on the slopes, but felt he was getting a bit beyond this hard work. It was dark and she was about to organise a search party with the assistance of neighbours when she saw the torchlight flicker in the distance. Gradually the light grew and at the crest of the final *schuss* she saw the form of the hay and her husband. She blessed herself and thanked St Christoph.

"I had a bit of an accident, a skier ran into the sledge and nearly pushed it over the ridge down to the valley."

"Was anybody hurt, are you all right?"

"The skier hit the sledge fairly hard, but he only hit the middle truss and the rest of him was cushioned by the hay."

"He was lucky, you were lucky. Have they gone on?"

"I should have asked them to call in, but they seemed to be anxious to get away. Anyway, I must get down to the cows; I'll take this down in the morning."

When Jack hit the 'scratcher' that night, the smell of the hay and the lowing of the cows had a special significance, but next morning he had problems getting out to meet his *Pistenhelfer* deadline. A bruised chest, which had been immunised by alcohol the night before, came home to roost. The legs were okay but he had pains emanating from his sternum, which made getting the clothes on a bit of an ordeal. He dreaded to think about the boots and skis.

'Feck it, I'll manage. After all, I'm a commando!'

It was a struggle but eventually and slightly sweated up, he stepped down to *terra firma* from the steps to his room. He got a bit of a shock when he noticed a sledge, very similar to the one he had run into the night before, parked outside the hay-shed. Looking at the sledge caused him to lose concentration and when he shouldered the skis his centre of gravity shifted, his feet rose in front, and he landed on his arse.

'The curse of the dreaded sledge - get me out of here!'

He stopped at the shop to get a bread roll, and strode up the main street. He looked into the Post, smelt the breakfast smells and thought of his appointment that evening with the lovely Jane. When he reached the chair lift the workers had already started up, so he pulled on a *mantel*, wiped the seat and joined the *Pistenhelfer* migration to Kapall.

"It'll snow before noon and we'll have plenty of snow stepping tomorrow morning."

As they sat around the pot-bellied stove Wolfgang issued this prognosis and emphasised the importance of being there, and on time, the following morning. As well as stepping down to the village, there would be clearing to do around the lift so that the chairs could pass over the ground and people could easily mount.

"I want four of you to stay at the top today and clear a way for the first skiers at nine o'clock."

Jack kept his head down until those appointments were made. Anyway, the locals grabbed these jobs. Jack figured that they liked to be away from the influence of Wolfgang, who was a bit of a slave driver and needed to harass the foreign *Pistenhelfers*.

"*Fertig! Schaufeln und treten, meine Kinder.*"

And off they went, each with his or her shovel.

"This isn't mine," said a slim, sweet-smelling American girl.

"They're all the frigin' same," said a nasty young man from New Zealand.

Some shovels were lighter and had a smoother handle, but there was one lethal ton-weight job that everyone avoided. Anyway, it was usually those who wouldn't leave the fire who got the worst shovels. This American girl always waited until it was just time to go before she went to the shed they called a toilet. Sometimes she selected a shovel early, brought it to the toilet and left it outside. Big mistake, the shovel was in danger of being changed while she peed or whatever. Then the moans would erupt. She managed later however, to acquire a boyfriend who gladly took the responsibility of watching 'her' shovel; as such were alliances made.

Off they went, a straight ski down to a piece of ground covered with large bumps. The technique worked well; firstly, make sure that your skis are well planted across the slope. Then strike with the shovel just where the bump flattens out, and keep going until the blade is well in. Secondly, press down on the handle until the side of the bump is dislodged and repeat until the bump is gone and the hard shell with soft inner remains. Then stamp those pieces into the ground between what was the dislodged bump and the next one. And so a fairly level patch of ski run replaces the platera of bumps, not appreciated by beginners. Heinrich supervised this process with an eagle eye.

"It's too hard, I can't break it." It was the shovel-sensitive American girl again. Not all the girls had this problem and some were expert, so she got no sympathy from Wolfgang or Heinrich, nor was her boyfriend allowed to help. She didn't last the week. Jack saw her working in the Hotel Post later, where room maids were paid, unlike the *Pistenhelfers*, and could leave to ski as soon as they had finished their quota of rooms. Most were free to ski at about two o'clock in the afternoon and some made it sooner.

The group of twenty-five descended on a bumpy patch, flattened it out and swooped like a flock of starlings to the next area of operation. Normally the sun and its progress down the hill determined their rate of descent, but this morning there was no sun and the clouds covered the high mountains almost to the bottom of the tree line. Occasionally the rising wind blew the clouds away, allowing a view of rolling bands of snow swirling down the valley. Some of the trees on the high ground were already coated and the work team felt the effects of cold drops of rain and hail. Wolfgang had been right in his forecast and it looked like tomorrow would indeed be a high stepping day. Following a stop to pull up hoods or put on caps and gloves, the *Pistenhelfers* worked on through the Gampen station and down to the village. Looking back didn't afford much satisfaction on this occasion, as the work of the group wasn't visible. It looked as if a giant hand of freezing snow had grasped the mountains, making Jack and the rest of them in this wild environment feel very small and vulnerable.

With a gruff, "*Bis morgen früh*", Wolfgang eventually released the group and they jumped on the chair lift, snuggled into the *mantels* and headed up. There were a few skiers already starting up, but the workers didn't have to queue - just duck under the chain at the other side of the lift station and take a seat. This was a great advantage during the day when the queues could sometimes be very long.

The smell of cooking, the coffee, and the heat hit the working group when they came through the double doors. For Jack the feeling was a major experience. Living in a hostile and strange environment, far away from the security of the Curragh, the mess, and the army rules, and yet he was a part of an operational team with all the respect and security that went with it. Among working friends, he stamped to the food queue and pushed a tray towards the glorious range of food. He felt very happy at that moment, no problems, no worries, and among friends.

"*Ein spaghetti Bolonaise bitte, mit Kaffee.*"

He handed in his breakfast ticket. The lady took it and automatically placed Schnapps on the tray. He looked surprised.

"*Einen Schnapps fur die Pistenhelfer,*" she explained.

It seemed that this was traditional and could be availed of three times a day. 'A bit like the workers in Guinness,' he thought. As he carried his loaded tray down to join a few of his co-workers he felt ten feet tall! All the talk at the table was about skiing and a young New Zealander expounded on the merits of the Osthang, the giant run under the cable car to Galzig.

"It's easy if you keep to the fall line and use the bumps to ease the back of the skis around."

It didn't sound so easy to Jack, who had only recently picked up the stem turn as a progression from the racing snow-plough. Feeling the effects of the Schnapps, he skied down and made his way to the Trittkopf.

Louis had finished breakfast and was sitting reading his breviary.

"Hello there, how'd it go?" asked Louis.

"Do you mean last night or this morning?"

Louis had left the Bahnhof early the night before, in line with his policy of returning to his room in the Trittkopf before midnight, and keeping his priesthood a secret.

"Well, start with last night; here, have a cup of tea."

"Thanks, well last night was a real surprise. The girl I spoke to, Jane Thornly is her name, and she's a film-star."

"I've seen her in a film, how do you know her?"

Jack told the story about the signed picture, his brother and how he had recognised her.

"And what's more, I hope to meet her again before the end of my holiday." Jack fed on Louis's congratulatory remarks.

They talked for a while over tea and decided how to approach the skiing. It had started snowing heavily but nevertheless they planned to ski and, because of his conversation in Gampen with the New Zealanders, Jack was keen to go up the Ferrenherrenhugle and ski the Osthang for the first time.

"I'll go along, but this is a big one."

"In for a penny, in for a pound, to hell with poverty, we'll kill a chicken." Jack knew that he was pushing the boat out a bit far, but realised also that a verbal commitment was necessary if they were to progress to serious challenges - and this was one!

"We're the chickens, and I hope our necks are not at risk. I presume all farmers with hay sledges have been confined to quarters?" Louis looked at Jack with serious intent but with a twinkle in his eye.

They got the cable car to Galzig and looked down on the scene of the sledge accident the evening before. A bird's-eye view of the path around the side of the mountain, which had been their route the evening before, provided them with a clear picture of how close they were to a real accident.

"If the sledge had gone over the side, with you as an appendix, it would have been requiem time," said Louis quietly. Jack gulped and in an effort to lift the spirits quipped:

"Look to the here, the now, through which all the morrows rush to the past; and the here, the now, is the Osthang in a snowstorm."

"That's very poetic."

"Yes and with a little help from James Joyce."

They cleaned their goggles and waxed their skis before setting off from Galzig. Ski wax came in lumps, about the size of a bar of soap, red for soft snow, blue for ice, and silver was supposed to be the solution for all conditions. As Jack rubbed on the red wax, he noticed that one of the edges had come adrift, so he tightened the screw and checked the remainder. They slid their skis back and forth like a racer at the start, and set off. The visibility was cat! Neither could see very well and, as they sweated up, their breath fogged up the goggles on the inside. This meant stopping, prising the goggles clear of the face and allowing them to clear.

Jack felt okay. He thought he was skiing all right, but then they hit the Osthang. As he looked down the slope, he saw that all of it was covered in enormous bumps and the gradient was steeper than he had ever experienced. He tried to remember what had been said at breakfast about the way to ski this type of terrain, but what seemed easy with Schnapps and an arse on a chair was turning into something of a nightmare.

'I'm sitting back; try to get over the tips as you turn.' Talking to himself didn't seem to make any difference and, as he progressed, he got worse and fell on almost every turn. He was both disgusted and embarrassed. About halfway down, a skier, doing exactly what he thought he should be doing, passed him. He tucked in behind and had a go at imitating his every move and position. The effort of making a turn on almost every bump and of keeping the tips of the skis downward worked at first, but eventually had its physical effect and after about ten yards he was out of control. This was the voluptuous panic he had heard about and he knew he needed to pull the communication cord. At that point he steered the skis hard left and had almost completed the turn when suddenly he was pitched arse over tip, literally. He heard a breaking sound as he fell over the tips, which had firmly embedded in a steep bump. There was a dragging sensation on his legs, particularly his right one, as he toppled over the skis. He held on to the poles as he skidded down the steep slope and tried to stick the tip of one into the snow to bring his head up and slow his decent. Eventually he stopped in a haze of sweat, snow and confusion. He looked into the snow from very close quarters, about an inch, and wondered what the hell he was doing in this God-forsaken hole. However, given a minute or two to recover, he sorted himself out. He had both poles, both skis, but his goggles were gone.

'Good riddance, I couldn't see with the feckin' things anyway.'

He readjusted his cap, stood up, and without saying a word to Louis, who was having his own problems, started skiing down. Something was different; it felt easier on the right turn for some reason. Then he saw it! The tip of the right ski was broken across about a foot from the top. It hadn't severed completely, but he could see the timber gape and flap like a broken branch on a tree. He bent over, pulled the offending piece clear and threw it into the bushes at the side of the piste. Funnily enough, things were much easier from then on. On the right turn particularly, he was able to plant and turn with greater ease. Success breeding success, he enjoyed the trip despite the bad visibility and his lack of eye protection.

'Should've broken a bit off these bloody Attenhoffer skis before now.'

"Heidi, stop dreaming and give me a hand with this bed."

It was bed-making time in Innsbruck General Hospital. Matron was due any minute in ward 43 and she was not to be trifled with. The two nurses on the ward were on top of the job however, and Heidi had allowed herself a brief minute of contemplation of events the week before.

She was concerned about how her parents in St Anton would react to her association with the young Irishman, Jack. She realised that she had been a bit foolish in agreeing to meet him at the weekend, but he had opened a new world to her where responsibilities were taken lightly and living seen as an opportunity for adventure. Her parents liked Josef, her tailor boyfriend in St Anton, and more importantly, they liked his family, and both families had been friends for many years. In fact Heidi's father and Herr Kerber had served in the Alpine Unit, before her father went to the *Luftwaffe* in Vienna.

'Anyway, Jack and I are only friends,' she thought, 'but why then the conflicting sentiments of happiness and guilt?'

She shook her head and decided to look on the bright side. Two of her nursing friends were coming with her to her parents' home in St Anton for the weekend. They were all delighted that the first heavy fall of snow was predicted and they each spent time gazing out the hospital windows at the gathering storm. It had already started - a thin filigree of snowflakes was floating silently down between the hospital buildings.

Mostly all country girls, they had learned to ski almost before they could walk. Heidi had skied to school in St Anton every day and had won quite a few of the school slalom competitions. Her strong legs were testament to her ski and farming background. Josef was a very good skier also, but he spent most of his time in his shop nowadays. He had trained under his father as a tailor and if he was not in the shop selling ski and walking gear, he'd be involved in making clothes including ski pants. Their shop was on a very good business site, right on the main street.

K laus Glos was up and about as usual next morning. He came down the timber stairs; a carved climbing scene, including ropes and belays, was set below the banisters from top to bottom. His wife, blown in the kitchen door by a flurry of snow, had her arms full of neatly cut logs which he had prepared and stacked against the outside wall during the summer. He remembered the fallen tree that he had seen on his way up to the meadow the day before, and made a mental note to collect it before it was covered with snow. He liked cutting and splitting wood and was on top of the job of having 'one-year-old' dry blocks stacked and ready for the fire.

"Here, let me do that."

He took the logs from Monika, stacked some and put the rest into the large central tile-covered stove. As he opened the shutter the heat hit his face; he pushed in about five logs and closed it quickly. Sitting down with his back to the warm tiles he began his breakfast.

"What nationality were the two skiers you met yesterday?"

"Irish, at least that's what the one who was impaled on the sledge said."

When he had finished the breakfast, he headed down with the sledge to where the cows were housed. It was snowing quite heavily by the time he reached the railway crossing and he waited patiently as a train passed north to the Arlberg tunnel, loaded as usual with a variety of cars and containers. One other figure, tall and dressed in black, waited also. He had come from the Hotel Trittkopf and carried a book of some sort. As he studied the frame and head he thought there was something familiar about him.

'Very like the man on the slopes yesterday - yes, it's him!'

When the train passed and the gates lifted, he was sure. It definitely was one of the skiers of yesterday, but the coincidence of seeing him again so soon was surpassed by the next discovery. As they got closer to the church the man in front let down his hood and began to unzip his anorak. He turned sideways to open the door and Klaus saw the Roman collar. "He's a priest," he whispered to himself.

Klaus passed the church and turned right down to the water trough and pulled the sledge down to the byre beside the house of Frau Gasper. He cleaned out the cow stall, spread some straw, and filled their hay boxes. As the cows munched contentedly he pitched the hay from the sledge up to the loft.

'There will be more hay needed before the end of the week by the look of things,' Klaus thought.

He rolled up his sleeves, washed his hands and began to milk. The music of the milk hitting the bucket brought a big she-cat out of her lair. Tail perpendicular, she rubbed her head against his trousers and mewed pleadingly. He was thinking about the priest skier and didn't notice the cat but when he did, he turned his right hand and sent a stream of steaming milk sideways, but nowhere in particular. Pussy knew her stuff; in a flash she stood up, opened her mouth, and swallowed the warm liquid without spilling a drop. He milked the six cows in about two hours, strained the milk and stored it in large delph bowls in the dairy at the back of the cowshed. These Simmental / *Fleckvich* Alpine cows were docile and yielded a high butterfat level of milk. Their meat was highly valued also, a not unimportant factor in a land where the *Wienerschnitzel* was universally popular.

'Herself will be down later to skim the cream from yesterday.' His journey back wasn't rushed and he had time to make a few social calls. Firstly he visited the church to find that the mass was over and the priest had left. The sacristan, Hans Kerber, a long-time servant of the parish, was getting things ready for the next mass.

"*Grüss Gott Hans, wie geht's?*"
"*Alles gut, Ach Klaus, sehr gut.*"

Hans didn't have to look around to recognise the visitor to the church. They also had been in the Alpine Corps together and had seen active service against a group of dissidents from the next valley. In fact Hans had saved his life on one occasion. They were on patrol from the valley between Valluga and the village of Zurs during the winter of 1940 and Klaus had fallen from an observation position on the Trittkopf mountain, and lay badly injured on a ledge about 1,000 metres up. He was alone, wasn't roped and could have lain there until he died if Hans and his mountain dog hadn't found him the same day. Both his legs were broken, but due to the first aid skills of Hans, his strength and courage and his minute knowledge of the area, Klaus was saved. Hans carried him for two days before they both could be rescued.

He spoke about the visitor priest and his experience the evening before. Hans explained that Louis would be saying mass every morning for four weeks, and that he was Irish but working in the north of England.

Klaus was a close friend and had hopes for a developing relationship between his daughter Heidi and Hans' son. Josef was a good lad and worked hard. He had been walking Heidi out for about a year, but they had been friends even when they were in kindergarten. His wife, he knew, was looking forward to the day when they would be married and both families could spend time together. Frau Kerber and Monika were members of the church decoration society and they enjoyed their long conversations at the meetings on Wednesday nights. As well as the tailor's shop, the Kerbers had a small hotel at the end of the village and a considerable amount of farmland stretching down the valley.

"I saw you pulling the sledge down to the barn this morning. Are you able for all that - we're not getting any younger you know."

"Are you sure you weren't listening to your Greta, interpreting what Monika said to her?" 'It's bad enough having this network working now, imagine what it'll be like when the young 'uns tie the knot,' he thought.

"Seriously though, take it easy with that sledge."

Klaus thought it was time to change the conversation. He liked doing the physical things and especially things he could do alone. He enjoyed nothing better than heading up the mountain to the Alpine meadows and had fond memories as a child tending cattle for weeks at a time, in the summertime of course. It was these visits to the high mountains, above and below the tree line, that gave him such regard for the natural environment. He understood the lifestyle of the wildlife living in the meadows, the trees, and high up on and above the glacier. The many lakes dotted around attracted a special wildlife both indigenous and migratory.

Since the development of ski tourism, much of the natural environment had become threatened however, and now chamois and ibex were rare in his part of the Alps. Tourists arrived to study nature and, on the last occasion when a group had stayed in his house, the peregrine falcons and the rare golden eagle were high on their list of attractions. These mountains were formed millions of years ago, when the seabed was forced up to form the high-ridged mountains of the Alps. Visiting geologists delighted in picking their way along the limestone-exposed relics of the seabed, now three or four thousand metres up.

The money from the Marshall Plan (The European Recovery Programme), which in his village facilitated the building of the Vallugabahn in 1948, should have been a boon to the area and it was, as far as economics was concerned. But Klaus could see the effects of the let-loose skiers on the environment and he feared for the future. Soon there will be a restaurant on the top of every Alp, he joked to himself - more in sorrow than amusement.

"I saw a pair of Alpine grouse in the trees about four hundred metres from my house," he announced as a contribution to the change of subject. "I figure that there are no more than about twenty pairs in the whole valley from St Christoph to here. God be with the days when we could bag at least ten brace of cocks every Sunday without affecting the stock."

Hans, who was much more laid-back about environmental issues, argued that tourists bring in the money. "You can't make omelettes without breaking eggs," he quipped.

"Who said anything about breaking eggs?" snapped Klaus. "If the basic nature of the area breaks down we are nothing but an amusement centre and we might as well put up plastic mats on the slopes and ski all year around."

"That's a good idea, can you ski on plastic? We could have skiers here in the summer!"

Klaus could see that there was no point in talking about the environment with Hans. His views were strongly coloured by the needs of his hotel, the productive valley farm and the tailor's shop. His wife Greta was a potent force in this mix.

A green pressure group had been established in the village to keep pressure on the village council and on the regional government about environmental issues and how Marshall Fund money might be spent. Most of the council's time so far had been taken up with increasing the scope for skiers.

Another big issue was the avalanche protection measure on the northern side of the valley. Ramps were being built above the tree line in order to divert the beginnings of avalanche snow, thus protecting the houses and hotels built on the north side of the river and making it possible to build more accommodation. Skiing, firstly on the Rendel slopes and eventually all the way down the valley, was part of this plan. Avalanches were the natural terror of the Alpine community, but big business was creating a new ethic supported by local businessmen like Hans. Apart from an agreement to create a wildlife park somewhere, business developments were mostly the top priority.

These two men were connected in a social and historical way, but were poles apart on nature and the protection of the wonderful natural environment that was under threat.

Klaus pulled the empty sledge up the street as part of the excited movement of skiers all heading to the lifts or to the *skischule*. The experienced skiers strode purposefully, skis held confidently - tips down, ends up, poles hanging from the hand draped over the ski ends, sometimes one pole in the other hand. The whole picture was of a man or woman at ease with the exercise. Beginners on the other hand gave a completely different impression. They were ill at ease on their feet and the fact of raising their centre of gravity by having skis on their shoulder; usually wrong way around, added to their instability on the slippery surface. Occasionally they were upended; skis and poles tossed and splayed like matchsticks to the accompaniment of wild shrieks and peals of laughter.

This exercise of walking and looking cool was practised easily by the experienced skiers, but the ski instructors, in their distinctive red Austrian Ski School jackets, were the epitome of confidence and set the example of what everyone wanted to be. Somehow, they were always accompanied by at least one gorgeous, leggy female obsessed by the magnetism of these 'cock of the walk' creatures. It could be argued that this village impression was not important to one's efficiency on the slopes, and maybe that was so, but there was a bird of paradise game being played in the village between people and especially the young. Prowess on the slopes was a part of this game and the effect of a fluid flash of expertise impressed, but was mostly lost in the blink of an eye before identity could be established, like the blue and gold flash of a kingfisher from bank to bank in a stream.

This growing tourist environment was having its effect on the young locals; their heads were being turned, so to speak. Most young men were sucked into the festive life. In the past, festive occasions were confined to special religious occasions - Sunday afternoons, holy days, marriages, and even funerals. Now, every evening was a time for drink, dance, and whatever else was on offer from the modern misses on holiday and enjoying the company of the brown, strong, ski-efficient Karls, Rudolphs or Heinrichs. Some local men had gone so far as to quit the village and go away with well-off, sometimes once-married Americans, to the States.

Attendance at mass was low among this group, much to the chagrin of the parish priest and the village elders. Louis had gotten an earful of this state of affairs from Fr Stremitzer, who spoke each Sunday from the ornate pulpit in the church. Unfortunately those for whom the words were intended were usually absent!

All of this human flow in detail was lost on Klaus Glos; he was intent on getting home and busying himself with a few household chores before lunch. He allowed himself a break to visit the church; he blessed himself with holy water, knelt in the quiet church and said a prayer. The new timber seats still had a beautiful pine smell and he allowed himself an extra flush of pleasure.

He thought about the work he and the other villagers had devoted to the selection of tall straight pine trees from the timber line above the village. They were planked and stored in the timber yard under cover for three years, before being sent to Innsbruck to be made into the finished seats that graced the church today. The ends were carved in the traditional manner of the Tyrol and the two-inch thick seats were smooth and straight still, despite the variations of heat over the seven years of use.

He looked around before he left and admired what he and his villagers considered to be one of the most ornate and well-balanced churches in the country. The many little golden cherubs gazed in awe and admiration at Christ standing on a golden globe in ornate flowing garments, displaying his Sacred Heart and surrounded by clouds and the singing seraphim. As he pulled on his cap outside the church he met one of the members of the local environmental sub committee. Their discussion was about the last meeting and the plans to develop Rendel and link with Lech, Uber Lech, and Zurs. Because of the post war money from the Marshall plan and investments from local entrepreneurs such as Hans and others, short and long-term plans poured off the desks of planners in Innsbruck and Lendel.

Jack awoke with the dearth of skis clearly in mind. He had the opportunity the evening before to replace them, but drinking in the Bahnhof had intervened and one thing had led to another. It wasn't that he hadn't considered the implications of being ski-less, but youthful folly played its part and you can guess the rest. The fun of breaking the ski had opened a whole basket of communication with skiers of various sorts in the Bahnhof. The Osthang descent had its effect and they were ready to be a part of any ski-related experience of the day. They didn't launch straightaway into a description of their adventure, but waited for the slightest chance.

Firstly, they got involved in a bizarre card game. The players all knew one another by name and were as close in social terms as a group of third-year university students. Perhaps more close, in that the cement that held them together was based on working as a team under the direction of the military-type control of the local leader of the *schaufeln* and *treten* regime. Louis was fully accepted in the Bahnhof and acted as a kind of patron, although in truth he would have liked to be 'one of the lads'.

"Right let's start. Three of clubs, jack of hearts, two of diamonds, ace of spades; right Louis, take a sip."

The game involved about eight people sitting around a table. First up, everyone contributed a pint of beer, which was placed in the centre. The dealer then shuffled a pack of cards and began by placing a card in front of each participant. The cards were turned up as they were dealt and the deal was continued without interruption until the first ace arrived.

"Only a sip, Louis, put the pint back with the others."

"Why only a sip?"

"The next ace drinks 'til he can see the bottom of the glass, the next finishes the glass."

"But there's another ace."

"Yes, my friend, and whoever gets that has to pay for the pint!"

Usually in this game of chance, one or two get to drink a lot and some a little.

This was the milieu into which Jack and Louis landed. When the game disintegrated, Louis headed for the hotel, while Jack, despite the fact that he was detailed for work in the morning, continued to drink and socialise. On the social side, events took a turn for the better and, without much planning or realisation, he found himself with a group of newfound friends stepping down into the heat of a dance Bier-keller. He wasn't dressed for the part, but neither were the others and, ski boots and all, they clumped their way down the narrow stairs past the zither-playing local at the entrance. The inside of the hall was like a Monaghan wedding; the floor was a mass of sweating men and women of all ages, shapes, and sizes. Before he could make any decisions he was approached and asked to dance by a young English girl. He straightened himself up and tried to look in control, but realised that he had reached a point of no return and that evacuation would be the better option.

"Would you like to dance, Jack?"

He recognised her as one of the Inghams's' girls and knew that she skied like an angel.

"I'm a bit under the weather. Why would a beautiful creature like you want to dance with me?"

He slipped his arm around her waist. An old-time waltz in leather ski boots is a difficult exercise but nevertheless he managed. He didn't try anything adventurous, and the floor was so crowded that a gentle sway was a maximum achievement. Barely halfway down the hall it started. His face flushed, and the room began to spin. He knew the symptoms and realised that he had about one minute to get out into the cool air. Just like Cinderella, he hit the ground running and in four giant steps he climbed the stairs and launched himself past the startled zither player into the night. He didn't get sick at once so he kept running, unaware of direction. On and on he ran until his rhythm steadied and he began to enjoy the movement.

Eventually he arrived in the Nasserein, another built-up area in St Anton, and decided to go into a large hotel complex and wash up. On the way out he encountered a *Pistenhelfer* member from Australia. He looked like he had had a few as well and invited Jack to join him at the bar. He had recovered from the sick feeling, brought on, he figured, by the heat in the dance area - 'never blame the drink'! They started off drinking small beers but the conversation and the drink tempo soon progressed until they qualified to join a drink-and-sing group of mad Swedes. It appeared that everyone sang a diddley-di song, drank a beer, placed a hand under the table, lifted the table, and used the other hand to lift a glass of Schnapps and let it down in one fell swoop.

It was great fun but, perhaps typical of many of young Swedish males, the drink level was major. After about four of these table exercises, Jack slipped out to the jacks and thence out into the cold night air. He was comatose and felt no pain. He wasn't steady as he headed up the village, and on one occasion he overcorrected and fell into a bank of snow which had been cleared from around the doors of an adjacent building. He didn't fight the fall but lay back in the soft snow and studied the brilliant show of stars above his head.

"Joxer, what is the stars?"

"Joxer, what is the moon?"

He considered these imponderables from a comfortable supine position. The stars were beginning to respond when he heard giggly-type voices above him. He revolved his eyes in their sockets until they focused on an open window in the building beside him and identified that the girls' voices were from rooms on the fourth floor.

"I can see him in the snow. Is he all right, he isn't moving?"

He figured they were worried about his well-being and curiosity urged investigation. He turned face into the snow to allow a horse-type elevation - knees first and then total erection. This adventure on his part prompted a quick slam of the two windows and quiet. In spite of the on-off nature of the evening, he felt calm and relaxed. Somehow, he had reached the eye of the storm and the calm lent him a maturity of connection with his environment and his ability to control events. The physical self behaved; he stood upright and walked in a designated direction, although he felt somewhat divorced from his extremities. It amused him that he succeeded in walking through the narrow parameters of the door and through the selection of 'opes' and corridors in the building. With the possibility of getting to the sacred source of the voices from the windows, he climbed and walked and turned and climbed and walked, all without thought about direction. Eventually he stopped at a door, as if directed by a magic hand. The writing on the wall said, 'This is the holy grail'. Drawing breath he knocked quietly, and then a little louder.

"What do you want - some of us are trying to get a little sleep here."

"Sorry."

The sleepy-faced woman in neck-to-toes nightgown and hair curlers spoke from the door directly behind him.

Rather than continue knocking he tried another alternative. It never occurred to him that this might not be the room of the talking windows. He pushed the door gently and wasn't surprised when it gave way with just the slightest squeak. A further push; the room was dark and smelt of bodies, bedclothes, toothpaste, perfume, and socks. As he entered, his orientation was restored and as if by magic he was able to relate the windows with the outside where he had been. No sound, which was strange, and as he tiptoed into the room his eyes became accustomed to the semi-gloom.

"Titter, titter, he-he."

He was reassured by the sound of mini laughs from within the bundles on the various levels of the two-story bunks. Rather than risk a confrontation, he lay down in the centre of the floor, just as he had with his younger brothers and sisters as part of a going to bed play time. He knew that from the prone position he would be more difficult to identify and so it was. Even the breathing stopped and then, "Jane, do you see anything? Is he gone?"

"I don't know; the door is still not fully closed."

Jack was forced to make a sound, a kind of snuffle, and this led to more twittering but importantly, one of the girls sat up in bed and switched on a wall light above her head on the top bunk close to the windows. The light revealed, apart from the young girl sitting up in bed, two other double bunks with a body in each.

"Hello, my name is Jack. I had a few I'm afraid and I'm here on instinct. I thought that you were talking about me from the window."

Jack took the initiative and in jig time was engaged in conversation with the five girls from Inghams's' Travel Agency. One of them, Susan, was a ski instructor; at least she was qualified as such, although she didn't teach. She it was who had switched on the light and she and Jack conducted a conversation before the others joined in.

"I'm Susan. I think I saw you on the slopes today. You approached the chair from the worker's side. Are you a *Pistenhelfer* by any chance?"

Jack was happy to claim a part in the work of the *Pistenhelfers* and as he and Susan started to converse, the others joined in.

"We were split between this and the next room, but one of our group invited a male friend to share with her and we arranged the bunks in here." This line of conversation revealed that the 'friend' sharing the next room was Chris Davenport of Attenhoffer fame! This was the reason for his quick evacuation of Jack's bedroom!

"I must scarper, girls, sorry for bursting in. I'm glad to have met you all."

He and Susan made an appointment to meet at Gampen some lunchtime.

Louis was a poor second to Jack in the drink stakes. He was amused by the antics of the young in all respects and especially young males like Jack. The drink game in the Bahnhof was to him an opportunity to be a part of 'lads' life and he loved being on the fringes of activity; having the opportunity to view from close up without being involved in the work of the pack. Being a priest, he had of course a number of restrictions in relation to all aspects of social behaviour. Everybody was living life to the full and the white heat of involvement on the slopes relayed in intensity and detail to all aspects of social behaviour. His usual routine, however, was to stay the course until about twelve o'clock and then head for bed in order to be fresh for early morning mass.

He saw Jack leave the Bahnhof and intended to retire to the Trittkopf shortly afterwards. A range of individuals attended the table and he engaged in conversation left and right. Nothing of note, that is until an American lady from his far right estimated his distance, focused on him and created a channel of conversation. He noticed her perfect teeth and their role in framing her words. This observation came about partly because of his difficulty in hearing over the high-pitched babble, but also because he had noticed her before and thought she looked sad. Anybody looking sad attracted Louis like bees and flowers and so he moved in tow with the thirty-something blond American to a quieter corner of the railway restaurant cum waiting room.

"I'm Louis. Are you here alone?" She raised her eyes in a welcoming rather than a surprised look. Avis explained that she was American and had come to St Anton as part of a rehabilitation programme.

"A rehabilitation programme?" An obvious starting point for Louis, but he was surprised at her elimination of the normal small talk, usual on a first encounter. And more - she grasped the nettle and launched straight into the essence of her private life, as it related to her trip to the snow slopes of the Arlberg.

"Well, it's a long story. I was married in Boston to a college friend and on graduation we both started up a printing business. He, Joe, was the financial side and I ran the business from the point of view of customer relations, general management, and promotion of our product."

Louis was happy to have a conversation with this beautiful woman and although nervous of the serious portent of her story, and despite a 'where angels fear to tread' feeling in his heart, he encouraged her to tell him about her problems. It was like opening a sluice gate - the story just poured out. Louis wondered what he had let himself in for, but figured that allowing her to unload would in itself be a relief, whether or not he was able to offer any solutions. He reckoned that there must be a down side to the story despite the idyllic start. Funnily, apart from his name, she hadn't sought any information vis-à-vis his background, not even about his nationality.

As if reading his mind, she raised her hand to her mouth and lifted her eyebrows in surprise.

"Oh I'm sorry; here I am rattling on *ad nauseam* without asking your permission."

"Don't worry, I did think that we were just having a chat, but if I can be of any help I'm very glad to be of service. Actually, I'm in the business of advising people and although on holiday, I'll do my best."

"Oh, you're a doctor, but I can't be just throwing my problems on you on your holidays." She made to stand up but Louis gently placed his hand on her sleeve.

"Well, I'm not a doctor as such, but I can at least listen, if that would help."

Avis didn't ask any more about his profession and figured he must be involved in the paramedical world in some form or another, and continued with her story, but did a fast-forward to what she considered to be the crux. The business went okay at first and then she became pregnant. It wasn't that her pregnancy influenced events overmuch, but as she advanced in pregnancy she had difficulty in handling all the management items and Joe, her husband, arranged that a member of staff, a woman, would step in and take over some of her responsibilities. When she went into hospital to be treated for an illness that was affecting her and the unborn child, the support female took over the functions in the office under the supervision of her husband.

Louis was a little ahead of her at this stage but tried to concentrate on what she said rather than what he thought might happen. Anyway, he was right in some respects, but couldn't have foreseen the level of tragedy that evolved. Yes, Joe did strike up a relationship and her replacement became a replacement in every respect. That was bad enough, but her illness became a set of serious medical complications, the child died in the womb and Avis lost her child and her womb in one fell swoop. Instead of being supported by a dutiful loving husband she rested alone in hospital and was informed of goings-on in the office by her friends. She went through tough times afterwards and at the finish of the saga, Joe left with his new love and she went home to her parents. Her mother and father were very supportive in every respect and her solicitor father sought to get her share of the business. Some of the money, supposedly lodged in shares, failed to surface, and although he kept a focus they had no success. Her father and mother were not very wealthy, and despite being an only child she benefited only minimally.

Avis was devastated by the fact that she had lost a child, a husband and her ability to have children. It played, it appears, on her mind to such an extent that she became ill and needed psychiatric help. Her psychiatrist recommended a trip to Europe - the classical treatment for affairs of the mind among a certain level of social life in the USA, but also an opportunity to start again - a kind of post war 'bachelor' girl.

Certain strands of her story were familiar to Louis, who had of course often advised in the confessional, but the international setting added a film-like aura to Avis' account of her life. She looked like a film star and Louis had a number of human emotions on his plate - what a pity such a beautiful woman should be so damaged and how could her husband be such a rotter! He realised that her getting better probably depended on the emergence of a normal life and the support of friends. Her obvious attachment to her errant husband was a problem; she kept referring to the good life they had before the break-up and feelings about how difficult it must have been for him when she was in hospital.

About an hour later Louis excused himself and headed for the Hotel Trittkopf and his beautiful single room. He'd made an appointment for the following evening in her hotel, but he wasn't naïve and didn't need advice about how to handle relationships with this American lady. This wasn't a casual meeting; they'd seen one another over a crowded room so to speak, but then she'd dealt a hand to Louis that required careful study. When he reached his room he thought about her a bit. He looked in the mirror after he'd washed his teeth, raised his arms in the Charles Atlas' style and decided that he still had a fair musculature. He went to bed and read his breviary for about a half hour.

Jack made it back to his room at about half three and felt at ease as he slipped into bed. The next morning, however, was not so serene, and having dressed, shaved, and gathered his gear, he was shocked to realise that he had no skis. The broken top of the Attenhoffer was a sharp reminder of his mishap on the Osthang and of course the chances of getting re-equipped quickly were slim. What to do? He remembered he'd been offered a set of skis by the *Pistenhelfer* organisers when first he started and he decided to take up this offer, if he could. Anyway, he set off, piece of bread in hand, up to the lift, and as usual met Louis on his way to mass.

"How did it go last night? There was a lot of beer being knocked back."

"To tell the truth, Louis, I'm afraid I over-stepped the mark, but all's well so far. I'll need to borrow a set of skis from the lift people - if I can."

"There's a spare pair in the cellar in the Trittkopf. Why don't you nip up and borrow them? I know somebody left them behind after a holiday last year and they've been there since." Louis was happy to be able to step into a simple *Pistenhelfer* support role, particularly following his complicated conversation of the night before.

This was great news and Jack had only to go into the Trittkopf, down the stairs and take the skis in the corner of the ski cellar. Louis had described where they were and the make, so he'd no difficulty in making his selection and scampering down the hill from the hotel to the lift station.

Equipped with a new set of skis, but bereft of his beloved Attenhoffers, he set off up the lift to where the *Pistenhelfers* were gathering at Kapall. Even in one week the light had increased, and he could easily see the cabin where the team gathered as he swung around the descent route from the chair. Although the boots were not a perfect fit he did manage to tie them to his skis. The more modern skis were very different, shorter and wider than what he had been using. Most ski bums were equipped with the most up-to-date ski and boot. They didn't bother much with dress, but the skis and boots had to be right. This message was getting home and he intended spending some time looking into ski shop windows after work. Futile if you haven't the money, but now that he had a job he was considering an upgrade.

He sat in a corner of the cabin listening to the chat of the locals and taking in the ambience that at its most basic made young Romans sick, but like a drug became addictive and called participants back to become involved again and create the stuff of memories. Jack knew that these moments in the corrugated iron shed around the venerable pot-bellied stove were special.

"Arbeiten meine damen und herren."

The *Pistenhelfers* call to arms was, as usual, received with a variety of reactions. The locals ignored the warning, the hardened *Pistenhelfers* were slow to stir, and the newcomers, which at this stage included Jack, were prompt and sought reassurance from Wolfgang and Heinrich with their eyes and body language. It had snowed heavily for about three hours during the early morning and this was definitely *treten* time and the lines were drawn on the snow. The aim was to create a smooth *piste* about 100 yards wide from top to bottom of the slope. Jack delivered on his work contract well, despite unfamiliarity with the skis. During the few opportunities he had to ski however, he didn't manage to his satisfaction.

"These skis are shit." And so the seeds of discontent about the skis he had borrowed in the Trittkopf were sown, and after work, when he met Louis, he was charged up with the idea of getting a new pair. At lunchtime they walked down the village to have a look in the sports shops. There were many skis on offer, but it was a pair of Kneissl Combi with Marker bindings that grabbed Jack's attention. They were blue, bang up to date, and perhaps a little pricey. There were others, but he kept coming back to the beautiful Kneissls. The price would be a problem.

Heidi and her friends were without doubt free for the weekend. Hospital leave had a funny habit of coming unstuck, but not on this occasion. After work she, Andreas and Frieda would catch the 5.30 train from Innsbruck and be in St Anton at 9.25, where Heidi's father would be there to meet them and bring them by horse and sledge to her home. She knew she had an appointment on Saturday evening with Jack and, although excited by the prospect of meeting him again, knew that her mother and Josef were also very much in the equation. The excitement of meeting Jack in Innsbruck would need to be tempered with a dose of stark reality. She wanted excitement in her life, but the lines of family and locality left her with little scope for change. True, the work in Innsbruck was a break from life in St Anton, but she knew in her heart of hearts that there was no escape. She liked Josef, he was sensible and one day would be a strong business influence in the village, but deep in her heart she felt that this was not enough.

She and her friends engaged in animated conversation from the moment they left the hospital. Frieda and Andreas were from Vienna and although they had skied in Innsbruck, this was their first visit to St Anton, considered to be the real heart of the Tyrol; at least that's what Heidi had told them over and over.

"Will Jack be there to meet you?"

This innocent question pressurised Heidi even more and she went to some lengths to explain that the meeting with Jack was fine, as far as it went, but from now on it would be platonic in nature. Naturally they were both disappointed and didn't fully believe her, but in deference to Heidi's obvious anxiety, refrained from mentioning the liaison again. The trip in itself was enough to satisfy their sense of enjoyment but, like all young people, romance had a high priority.

As the train steamed into St Anton the three girls gathered their things and stepped down the four steep steps from the carriage to the station platform. The two worlds, the pragmatic travel world and the leisure ski environment, met in a swirl of steam from the mighty engine of the Arlberg Express. Heidi had hardly touched the ground when her father lifted her in his traditional bear hug.

"Mein kleines grosses Fräulein, Herzlich Willkommen."

She warmed to his welcome but realised that her friends were standing open-mouthed on the platform clutching their overnight bags. They knew who he was and absorbed, still open-mouthed, the picture of the tall, moustached, breeches and stocking-clad man, performing a happy large dog-like welcoming dance with Heidi.

"Papa, das sind meine Freunde, Frieda, und Andreas."

Almost at once he became a military man and bowed to the two girls, seized their hands and planted a kiss. He was a simple farmer, but the Austro-Hungarian culture still provided a strong ethical influence and it was with great care and concern that he herded them out of the station to the waiting carriage. The family horse, hitched to an ancient sledge, waited quietly with one rear leg in the rest position. Klaus loaded the bags on the back while the girls giggled excitedly together. That done, he helped each girl up to her position on the sledge.

"Das hält euch warm meine Damen."

The rug arranged around their knees, Klaus climbed on to the driver's seat and, with a pleased glance at his excited daughter, he shook the reins and muttered an Austrian giddy-up sound to the horse. Off they went, down the path from the station and across the railway lines, to the comforting clip-clop of the horse's ice shoes on the frozen snow. This hoof music, the hiss of the sledge rails, the sound of the harness bells, and the excited chatter and laughs of the young nurses presented a joyous Pickwickian scene to skiers heading back to their hotels and *zimmers*, to rest and prepare for an evening of social leisure.

The horse Betsie had an easy time since the arrival of the snow and was now full of wind and piss, like an officer's charger. She grunted on the steep patches and let off an odd fart or two when she could relax. Young girls may not notice bodily functions for social reasons, but nurses are a different breed, and whenever Betsie blew wind, they roared with laughter. They were clever enough, however, to link these peals of laughter with elements of conversation, in deference to the sensitivities of the father-figure driver. On they jangled up the slope towards the house. Heidi's mother had no clients for meals at that time, so she lit the surrounds of the house and waited apron-clad at the door. When Betsie arrived in the courtyard, Monika opened the door fully which added considerably to the light in the yard. She joined the barking dog in welcoming her daughter and her friends from Innsbruck.

"Grüss Gott mein Fräulein." The meeting was rapturous. Heidi introduced the girls, and Klaus unhitched the horse, walked her to the stable and pushed the sledge to its corner in the yard. A wall of heat and

animated conversation hit him when he opened the kitchen door. The table was set and they had already started eating. Josef came up in conversation.

"He's been waiting for you, I know. He never lets a day pass that he doesn't mention your name - so his mother told me." The woman of the house warmed to her favourite Heidi-connected subject and watched carefully for her only daughter's reaction.

Heidi had mixed emotions. She felt a certain excitement at the possibility of meeting Jack again. Their close encounter in Innsbruck was still a fond memory but sometimes a thorn in her heart. She bravely met her mother's eyes, however, and waxed somewhat enthusiastically about meeting Josef during the weekend, but without detail; her mother noted this subdued reaction.

Heidi and her friends had fun settling into the piled high duvet-covered beds, so carefully arranged for them by Heidi's mother. The northwestern wind rose during the night and Heidi peeped out to see the snow silently falling, covering all their arrival marks at the kitchen door.

Next morning Klaus was up early. He did the usual chores - brought in some timber, cleared the snow away from the doors with a large hand-held snow-plough and moved mountains of snow easily to a designated area of the yard. He unlocked the dog's door; the dog opened one eye, viewed the white curtain of snow and settled deeper into his pile of hay. Klaus studied the sky for a moment, and came to a decision about the weather and what would occupy him for the rest of the day.

'Thanks be to God, I don't have to clear a way up to the meadows.'

As he opened the door into the warm kitchen, the smell of freshly-baked bread and the gentle laughter of the girls welcomed him. They were seated at the table, attended by the aproned form of his wife Monika. Irene the village girl, who helped with the house chores, was getting on with the business of preparing the dining room for lunchtime patrons. She managed nevertheless to keep an ear cocked for the news from the hospital in Innsbruck.

"We had an accident case from St. Anton last week. A young Italian, he was working as a *Pistenhelfer* it seems, was treated by Dr Flunger and brought to us by ambulance," said Frieda.

Heidi lifted her head from the cereal bowl and glanced sharply at her friend who was geared to continue, so she thought it time to give her version of the story.

"He'd been bleeding pretty badly, lost a lot of blood, but by the time he came to us he'd been stabilised. Some of his wounds were serious and he was in the hospital for about a week."

"Did he come back here?"

"No, his parents collected him and brought him home to Rome."

"I don't think it's a good idea to have those youngsters from non-skiing backgrounds working in the mornings as *Pistenhelfers*. What if he'd been killed?"

Heidi's father's opinion was discussed for a while. The question of insurance came up, but nobody was able to clarify the situation in that regard one way or another, and one or two questioned on how the *piste* could be prepared without the volunteer army. Klaus got the opportunity to climb on his hobby-horse about the threat that skiers were to the natural environment, but before he could get into full flight Monika cut the conversation short by swooping on the table and beginning the task of clearing up after breakfast. The clatter was too much so he moved outside to continue his work.

'It's all right for him and his environmental committee, but many people in this area depend on skiers for their livelihood. Josef for example, he makes a good living out of ski-pants and skis and his parents depend on tourists to fill the hotel. Live and let live I say!'

Slotting logs into the fire and closing the shutter sharply added a final punctuation to Monika's thoughts on environmental issues.

Heidi and her friends began to organise themselves for a morning's skiing. They intended playing on the slopes from Gampen down, using the chair and the slalom hank - a t-bar about 300 meters long. Frieda was only a learner and, although the others were expert, they decided to ski the easy runs with her. The sun had come out by eleven o'clock, so they were in great form as they left the house and skied down to the *skischule*. Heidi kept an eye on Frieda but there was no need to worry; her colleague had a mean racing snow-plough.

'Enough to get her safely anywhere,' she thought.

When they arrived at the area below the *skischule*, Heidi took charge and led the others to the start of the slalom hank. There's not much room for nearness in skiing, every movement should be exactly right. Like many from the village, Heidi had skied to school and had competed at the age of six. She was an example of the importance of teaching sports' skills at an early age, a practice that in turn made Austria a leader in world competitive skiing.

Klaus completed a few jobs at home, put on his good clothes and headed down to a meeting room in the Hotel Post to plan development and the environment in St Anton. Today they were to discuss a report based on a survey carried out by students from the University of Innsbruck. The professor in the Department of Environmental Engineering, Dr Gerd Hissler, was to present the report and explain its significance for Austria and in particular St Anton.

As Klaus arrived at the hotel foyer, his friend Hans stepped out of the toilet.

"*Grüss Gott*, how are things Klaus, is Heidi home?"

"She arrived last night with a couple of friends - they're out on the slopes as I speak."

"Josef will be happy to get the news; he's looking forward to meeting her."

Klaus wondered why the couple had not connected before this. 'After all, she arrived on the last train and had plenty of time to drop down to the hotel. Maybe not, it took time to settle in. On the other hand one would have expected them to make arrangements by post or phone?' These thoughts were reflective of the table conversation the evening before.

They checked at the desk. One of the Alber family was on duty and was able to inform them that the professor from Innsbruck had arrived the evening before, had his breakfast and was in the lounge reading the morning paper. As they walked into the room a traditionally-dressed man with leatherhosen, knee-length socks, and a jacket complete with horn buttons folded his newspaper, stood up and walked towards them. Hans addressed him as Herr Professor and introduced him to Klaus who clicked his heels, bowed, and took the hand of the professor.

Klaus gaped and gasped as the professor turned and continued a conversation with Hans. He suddenly realized that the expert from Innsbruck was in fact Captain Gerd Hissler who had served with him in the *Luftflotte* - a branch of the *Luftwaffe* established by General Kesserling in 1941 in northern France, in preparation for the proposed invasion of Britain. They had flown together in Junkers 88 on recognisance sorties over the south of England, he as a gunner and Captain Hissler as pilot. Klaus had changed in appearance somewhat since then and wasn't surprised at not being recognised. As he walked behind the dapper ex-pilot, he saw in his mind's eye mornings when the same physique eagerly walked across the tarmac towards the parked rows of Junkers. The crew, as well as gunners like him, consisted of a photographic team whose aim was to capture the defences on film, both air and ground. They were all involved in a risky exercise; on some occasions the flight level could be as low as a hundred feet in order to expose costal and inland defences or troop build-up.

The Colonel had a reputation as a daredevil and using the excuse of seeking a closer look at defences, had flown under Tower Bridge, London! All his crew, including Klaus, didn't gain the same enjoyment from what they considered an unnecessary escapade. However, news of his exploits reached the ears of Goebbels, the Propaganda Minister, and through him Field Marshall Goering, head of the *Luftwaffe*, and he was summoned to Berlin and presented by the *Fuehrer* with the Iron Cross, First Class. He fulfilled his potential and when the invasion plans were put on hold, as a result mostly of the opening of the eastern front, he went on to fly the Junkers 87 dive-bombers, in which he had gained experience in Spain with Franco.

As they settled around the table in the meeting room, Klaus noted that Colonel Hissler was wearing his military civilian dress badges, including the Iron Cross. Although most of the environmental committee meetings were held without formality, this special meeting was significantly taking place in a room with a large window overlooking the valley and facing south. The table was set with note pads, information leaflets, pens, water glasses, and Dr Hissler's seat placed at the top, facing the picture window. He had already visited the room, walked unhesitatingly to the top chair, placed his brief case on the table, looked down the valley and, hands deep in the pockets of the leatherhosen, rocked back and forward on his toes and heels.

"What a wonderful country we have! We must work hard to ensure that it's preserved from the destruction that has already begun in countries under communist domination." He had a habit of mixing politics and environmental studies.

By this time five other local members had arrived and were gathered in groups in the room; they used Dr Hissler's statement as a signal to take their places. Their chairman, who happened for this term to be Klaus's friend Hans, accepted his role and started proceedings.

"*Jawohl! Mein Herr Doctor.* You're very welcome to our part of Austria. We look forward to your words of wisdom at this crucial stage of the development of our land. May I introduce you to our committee?"

Klaus sat about four places from where Hans had started his introductions. He had an opportunity to recognise that the Colonel, starting with a 'recce' of the room, had followed with a strong political statement and more or less nailed his flag to the mast.

The resistance to the German army after the *Anschluss* had been from a group of local communists on the Lech side of the valley. He, Klaus, had been involved in that exercise, which had finished in a bloody battle in the tunnel. It was probably this nerve that Dr Hissler had attempted to touch when he made his opening remark and perhaps also, he thought, to salvage something from the disaster for the Germans that was the end of the war and the communist domination of Eastern Europe.

"Next, I have the pleasure of introducing a local landowner who has both a practical and environmental reason for being a member of this committee. Herr Klaus Glos."

When Klaus stood up in recognition of his introduction, the penny dropped for his erstwhile colleague from the *Luftwaffe*.

"*Mein Gott, Herr Gauleiter* it's you! How could I have been so stupid?"

With that, the existing veneer of ceremony fell away and the two men approached one another and embraced, much to the surprise of the remainder of the committee.

"Gentlemen, this man was the best gunner in the *Luftwaffe* and is responsible for saving the life of many crews and, might I add, of my life. The rear gun that he manned was vital to the safety of the Junkers 88 when we were under fighter attack. Unfortunately we had many losses due to the gun's jamming and such an occurrence often spelt death for our crew. When I heard the stutter from the rear cease, I used the controls to take evasive action - unless of course Klaus was the gunner; in which case swift immediate action on his part, based on a minute understanding of five or so reasons for a stoppage, always resulted in a continuation of the firing from the rear gun. He was awarded the Military Cross for his services between 1940 and '43. His capture by the enemy, having been shot down over Britain, was a loss to our efforts."

The professor addressed the meeting after this exciting interlude. The theme of his talk was based on research completed by a section of the Science Department in Innsbruck. One of the implications of accepting Marshall Aid from the Americans was based on a commitment to developing research into environmental impact in the Alps. For this reason the Environmental Section of the Science Department in the University of Innsbruck was established. Hans Peter Ipsen, who had served with the

Nazi military establishment in wartime Brussels, became West Germany's leading expert on European Community law, lectured in Innsbruck, and supported environmental research at Doctoral level.

Gerd Hissler had studied weather as a part of his science course in Berlin. His pre-war pilot training was confined to gliders because of post-First World War military restrictions. Glider training, however, was linked strongly to weather conditions and a macro study of weather so, having survived the war, he was chosen to head up this new section of research in Innsbruck. The Chancellor of the university had served as part of the air staff of General Major Hans Jeschonnek, *Luftwaffe* Chief of Air Staff, and was aware of Captain Hissler's leadership qualities and interest in the protection of the environment.

The Marshall Plan in Austria was used mostly to develop industry, both new and that partly destroyed by the war. The Tyrol had its chance to invest and it was obvious that tourist enhancement should have a high priority in this beautiful mountainous area of Austria. Some of the hotels in St Anton had received grants for extension and refurbishment, but it was in the area of getting the tourist population to the top of the mountains that most attention was given. The cable car to Galzig and Valluga was one such venture, but it was obvious that further development at the top station, to cater for restaurants and links with other villages, was an essential focus also. At this stage the only link by skis to another village with a return possibility was to St Christoph about five miles by road from St. Anton, plus a planned development to Zurs and Lech, a further five and ten miles away. The application of these developments in tourist terms would mean that increasing numbers of skiers would arrive daily in St Anton over what had been virgin mountainside.

The professor delivered his talk with military precision and some passion. The natural timberline, views and prospects, flora and fauna, wetlands and their function, wildlife and nature preserves were all dealt with and discussed. However, his bottom line was that the Alps were vulnerable despite their size and range, and were only capable of sustaining a certain level of human activity of the vigorous nature inherent in skiing and trekking. He cited the Matterhorn as an example of overuse and showed slides of approach routes decimated by parties of uncaring climbers. Not alone were these routes marked and worn by continuous boot marks, but discarded rubbish was evident everywhere and in particular close to campsites. On rock routes it was now acceptable to leave lairs of ropes and pitons still in position.

Klaus was particularly interested in detail about the dramatic reduction in the Alpine grouse, although the demise of wildlife in general, including the grouse, could not be blamed on the tourists alone. Hunting, which used to be a sport for the upper social levels, now was partaken by all and sundry.

"Unless care is taken, the Alps, which are considered to be the lungs of Europe, will die of pneumonia!"

Dr Hissler's eyes glittered behind his black-rimmed glasses as he emphasised the role of the regional committee and completed a visual circuit of the table members.

"Your committee has an important part to play in preventing the overuse of this wonderful God-given facility. Yes, we can play in this heaven on earth, but remember that we can also kill the goose that lays the golden egg!"

Some of the meeting sprang to attention, raising their hands in an enthusiastic military salute in support of *Oberst* Hissler's sentiments and the role of their committee. The professor returned their salute, but not everyone took part in this militaristic ritual and some even looked embarrassed.

At the end of the meeting a motion was passed, setting in print the local group's commitment to a continuing focus on the five principles of environmental protection and a structured link to the research centre in Innsbruck. Dr Hissler was identified as the committee's liaison with the rest of the country, bringing to fifty the number of committees all over Austria affiliated in the same way. As secretary general of the AIEPA, the Austrian International Environmental Protection Association, he controlled a very powerful and influential non-governmental association. He told the committee that, the following month in Hawaii, he was to attend an international conference and read a paper on local developments in Austria. He promised to send a copy of the conference report to each area representative, including that of the St Anton region, on his return.

Klaus and Hans were delighted that their committee was part of this important movement and both looked forward to seeing the results of the meeting printed in the local papers. They were also interviewed by *Der Speigel* reporters and had some pictures taken.

J ack and Louis skied through the day, but at about three o'clock Jack was having difficulties with the skis. The bindings were not releasing when he fell and, as his mood of discontent grew, he noted other problems.

"Look, Louis, when I hold them together base-to-base, there's no gap in the centre."

"Is that necessary?"

"Of course it is. If the ski is flat, without an arch, there's no purchase at the tips and the back when the skier puts his weight in the centre. Look at yours; they're completely different. No wonder I can't ski!"

Jack's searching disconcertion put Louis on the back foot, but without an immediate visible solution he put an emphasis on pushing on.

"Okay, nevertheless, the play must go on. As your hero in '*Homo Ludens*' would say - let's have another run."

Louis led the way to the chair lift at speed to get away from Jack's complaints. He could see, however, that a solution had to be found if the holiday was to survive. Jack meanwhile cribbed his way up to Gampen and joined the many sitting out in the afternoon sun in front of the restaurant. He sat on the wall, watched the skiers as they left the restaurant and took off down the mountain. The local photographer, 'Photo Rio', had set up about fifty yards down the slope close to a ridge in the snow. His clients, young guys mostly, were involved in being captured on camera in mid-air as they left the ridge at speed. They were having fun and most of the shots taken were of uncoordinated bundles of humanity heading towards a crash landing. However, it was fun and 'Photo Rio' was making money. Jack lay back, listened to the background music and soaked in the sun.

"Hello Jack, you look like you're enjoying yourself."

Just below him a gaggle of girls had gathered, Heidi among them. She looked different from how he remembered her. The best of gear he noticed, boots, skis, anorak, the lot. He was conscious that his old leather boots were hanging to within a foot of her gaze and the dud skis on the wall were obviously his. He jumped down quickly and was introduced to the other nurses and another local friend of Heidi's.

"We're going down to my home for a break, will you come?"

He nearly used Louis as an excuse, but the group was so friendly and he, being the only male, was the centre of attention, which he liked. They were obviously champing at the bit, skis being slid quickly to and fro, poles punching holes in the snow, so he delayed any long conversation with Heidi and pulled on his skis. Could those girls ski! In jig time they were off, heading to the right side of the slopes where Heidi's house was located. The snow was well packed by this time of the day, so he had no difficulty in keeping up. One of them, however, was less than his standard, giving him an excuse to play tail-end-Charlie. He even had an opportunity to help her up when she fell, an act which gained profuse thanks from the group. It didn't take long to reach what he figured was the house. A sign outside advertised food and board, and Jack was impressed that access to and from the house was by foot or skis only. About a quarter mile of steep hill had to be negotiated before reaching level ground on the Bahnhof side of the village. The girls went straight into the yard, took off their skis, and placed them in a corner, chattering all the while in German. He joined in the camaraderie, using body language and an odd word of English to Heidi, as they entered the Glos kitchen. It was warm and smelt of cooking - *Apfelstrudel*, he figured.

'The way to a man's heart is through his *Apfelstrudel*,' were his thoughts.

Heidi excitedly introduced him to her mother and explained that she had met him in the hospital.

"Is this the hero we heard about? Congratulations, I believe you saved that young man's life."

"Well I helped, but the local rescue team did most of the work."

"That's not what Doctor Flunger's wife told me. According to her, your first aid was critical."

Jack accepted the accolades and watched Heidi as she moved around the kitchen helping her mother lay the table for afternoon tea. In a domestic situation she was different, unlike in the romantic social setting in Innsbruck. She was still very attractive and her occasional glance in his direction gave him a surge of pleasure. He couldn't understand all they were saying; mostly they discussed family matters. He gathered that the father was attending an important meeting that day. The meal was conducted in English mostly and of course the conversation included skiing. Jack told of his *Pistenhelfer* experiences and also his accident on the Osthang where he broke the Attenhoffers. The skiers among them had never heard of Attenhoffers and Jack could see that Chris had probably taken him for a ride, as far as the skis were concerned.

'At least I got a room at a good price,' he thought, trying not to feel done.

The conversation then switched to his skis, the ones he had borrowed from the Trittkopf. When Jack expressed dissatisfaction with them, the group slid out from the table and trooped as one out to the yard to carry out an inspection. Heidi looked at the skis and then at Jack. He could see that she was figuring if he would be offended by any criticism of his gear, but the skier in her came to the fore and she let fly.

"Jack, they're terrible, how on earth could you work on those things? You deserve a medal for being able to stand up, let alone ski. If you continue with them you'll break something and I don't mean ski gear." The bossy nurse in her emerged and she pushed the offending articles back on the ski rack in the yard. She placed her little clenched fists on her hips as she faced up to the much taller, but somewhat abashed, Jack. His 'little bold boy lost look', however, prompted her to place her hand kindly on his arm as she led the way into the house.

Back in the kitchen the mother joined in the conversation and suggested that Heidi bring Jack down to Josef's shop to get a new pair of skis and boots. This suggestion was okay by Jack, but Heidi blushed and was quiet. All right, she felt a warm glow in her breast when she thought about Josef, but Jack was fun and needed looking after, in ways. Jack had asked her out for a drink that evening in St Anton so, like Scarlett O'Hara, she decided to think about the problem, including Jack's skis, 'tomorrow'.

Anyway, the gathering was disrupted by the vigorous barking of the dog, a stamping at the door, a flurry of snow and cold, and the arrival of Klaus. He was in good form and had had a few. He greeted each girl with a bear hug and a litany of wellness incantations. Jack said hello and they all sat down again as Frau Glos opened the door and banished the excited dog to his shed in the yard with a word and a flick of the dishcloth.

"Was the skiing okay this morning?"

Eventually the conversation got around to Jack's involvement in the skiing accident and his trip to Innsbruck.

"Do you have many accidents? Is the *Pistenhelfer* work dangerous?" Monika Glos was playing out her concerned mother role.

"The slopes are high mountains and we humans are small fry." Jack tried to put the *Pistenhelfer* work into perspective.

Heidi's father's period in England had prepared him well to engage in the conversation in English and he enjoyed himself. Jack wasn't sure when exactly the penny dropped, but he and Klaus both had a simultaneous moment of recognition about the hay sledge accident. Before Klaus could form a question, Jack blurted out his version of the sledge epic.

"Yes, we met earlier on the slopes - in a physical sense as well as the other."

"You're the fella who ran into the sledge; well, this is a double coincidence!"

Klaus described the incident to the open-mouthed audience. He explained how close Jack was to going over the edge with the sledge, and how lucky he was that a tree stopped his path.

"You seem to be accident-prone, Jack; perhaps you should take out more insurance?" said a serious-looking Heidi.

She didn't realise that Jack, apart from the life policy bought by his father with which he used to barter for spending money and had made this trip possible, had no insurance except for his rude good health.

"So this is the man who ran into the back of your sledge. Are you a priest on holidays?"

Jack jumped to correct Klaus's wife's impression, but before he could form a reply to smooth the shocked, confused faces of Heidi's friends, Klaus responded.

"No, there was another skier on the path up beside the Osthang. I saw him going to say mass the other morning. Is that correct Jack, was that him I saw - it was about seven o'clock?"

Jack explained that he and Father Louis were friends, that Louis was staying in the Trittkopf and had permission from Father Stremitzer to say mass every morning.

"It was late and Louis and I were flying down the cat-walk. To tell the truth, my speed was more to do with my inability to short swing the Attenhoffers on the narrow *piste* than anything else. I think they might have been a bit long for me at two meters twenty."

"They sound ancient, Jack; it's a wonder you could ski on them at all. You need a new pair of skis." Heidi used a very sympathetic tone and risked being tumbled by her mother.

"I know, but events have moved on. The Attenhoffers came to grief on the Osthang." Jack's ski life had achieved full attention from all present.

The conversation progressed and Monika suggested again that Heidi bring Jack down to Josef's shop to buy new skis. Heidi agreed with her mother that Josef would be able to help at the right price. She saw the gates close somewhat; her position vis-a-vie the relationship with Josef became more and more an inter-family arrangement. Her mother never missed a chance to pour some more cement.

That evening Jack turned up at the house on time and dressed in his new blazer, white shirt and tie. Frau Glos let him in.

"They're very nice girls, Heidi's friends. Which of them have you your eye on?"

Jack played the part of the young embarrassed male and changed the conversation.

"Your husband's a wonderful man for his age. Carrying all that hay from the top of the mountain is some feat."

"Well he's not that old and…"

"Oh, I didn't mean that he's very old, I'm sorry. It's just that a load like that takes great strength and control. I know that Louis or I would have great difficulty getting it down - even together."

The mention of Louis got him off the hook, and Monika was at once interested in hearing more. Her experience of priests in the village was mostly confined to the very old parish priest. He was a fine man, but light years away from a young priest like Louis, of whom she heard great things from her daily mass-going friends. She went on about how important it was to have young priests in the Church. Recruitment to the Church during the war in Austria was difficult, if not impossible, and as a result most of the priests were old and unable to understand the falling off of young people's involvement in church practises, particularly in the fleshpots that were the ski centres. She went on a bit about what a bad example the ski instructors were.

"They almost never go to mass, would you believe it?" she said looking Jack straight in the face with wide, incredulous eyes.

Jack just nodded and wished that the birds would arrive. He had called for Heidi but obviously the others were acting as a cover. Eventually they arrived, just in time as it turned out because Frau Glos was fringing on the subject of Heidi's strong line with Josef, the tailor cum shopkeeper.

L ouis and the American had met again, this time by appointment. He was wearing his usual black ski gear, including glasses on a string around his neck. Avis, in contrast, was a bit dolled up, so much so that he hardly recognised her. She stood up in the anteroom of the Hotel Post as soon as he entered and called out.

"You hoo, Louis, over here!"

He walked quickly to her group of armchairs in case she might dance out to meet him. There was the possibility that she might have done a 'Rick and Ingrid' there in the middle of the floor - one leg arched up at the rear showing a nice ankle and a high-heeled shoe and all that. Why he thought that she might overreact he didn't know, perhaps the dress and make-up change, or the light in her eyes. He got to her while she was still in the nest of chairs and they greeted one another with a double peck and a handshake. His aftershave got to her.

"It's great to see you again Louis. I found our meeting in the Bahnhof very helpful. You won't believe it, but last night was the first real sleep I've had in ages and I put it all down to our conversation." Breathless and wide-eyed with excitement, and elegant legs tucked to one side, she sat forward on the edge of the leather settee and looked deep into his eyes.

Despite the focus, Louis remained calm and let her talk for a while. He called the waiter and asked for the menu from the restaurant. She recommended that they take the set menu; she had found it reliable on the occasions she had eaten there. Her conversation was about all the issues surrounding her departure for Europe. Louis was concerned about the isolation from the friends she talked about, and he also saw that a depth of a relationship with any of them seemed very shallow. In a way she was a social butterfly following the break up of her marriage and, worse still, the loss of her womb and child. He also knew that he was walking on very thin ice!

Although Louis lived a celibate life, because of his social involvement at flying club level and with the many upper crust individuals in and around his parish, he was fully aware of the benefits of having a female life companion. He felt that the church was being pushed towards married status for priests by the writings of some high level Jesuits in Universities in the United States, particularly the French Jesuit Jacques Maritain. John Courtney Murray's beliefs and writings about religious freedom attracted Louis also, and he spent some time contemplating the import of the many writings of these two religious academics.

At a practical level and during his work in Canada, Louis had admired the joint work of a young married couple. In his opinion their work as medical doctors was very professional but, more than that, he saw the value of having a soul mate in that cold and lonely tundra environment, during work time and in the long leisure hours. Jack was often regaled with Louis's account of the happiness that was born of the relationship between these two married people and the positive effect it had on the rest of the group.

He was a different man on his return from Canada and displayed an enhanced ease with women from that time onwards; less in keeping perhaps with the mode of the traditional priest in Ireland and Britain. During dinner conversations, Louis's favourite leisure occupation at home and abroad, he voiced support for the work of lay volunteers and looked forward to the time a priest could be married. He realised that, as yet, his vow of celibacy stood, but he guessed that dramatic change within the Church was just around the corner.

The bottle of local wine fuelled them both and the conversation at the meal transcended the ordinary: her problems, ski life, or life in America and Britain. Avis had majored in philosophy in Brooklyn College, the City University of New York, and when Louis summed up her account of hard times in New York business with the phrase 'c'est la vie', she immediately latched on to the idea of issues in daily living.

"Despite the problems in my life, I still have one little corner in my mind that somehow or another is secure, and it is from there that I start the journey back to some form of quiet and happiness. Even as a little girl, that light always glowed in the dark of my mind. I'd like to think that the light was my real parents, as I was adopted from an institute when I was twelve. That lighted corner had been dimmed by life in the convent, yet it always survived; it must have been God. If that light had been extinguished by my tormentors I wouldn't be talking to you today."

Louis felt somewhat of a cheat as he listened and reacted to her account of the difficult times that she had survived, but just, and with serious trauma. It was his job to explain how a Supreme Being is present in our lives and His role in making life have meaning, despite difficult times. He was about to declare his hand when she began to describe life in the orphanage and the happenings that created the foundation for her stumblings through life.

Avis didn't remember her real parents; life had begun for her in a convent with a lot of other girls. Being beaten because she wet the bed was one of her first memories; they were beaten a lot, but that wasn't the worst part of her young life. When she was eight she was moved from the children's house to the laundry and this in her memory was a real hellhole. The work was hard: steam and heat and the weight of wet clothes, long hours and poor food. More in keeping with Dickinson-England than that of the 1940s in 'the land of the free'.

At that period, however, one of the sisters, Brigid, came to her aid and from then on Avis's path was directed towards getting a good academic education. She graduated at junior level and it was during the graduation ceremonies that Sister Brigid introduced her to Jacqueline and Stephen.

They became friends, in as much as a damaged child and two adults can, and in the following year was adopted by them.

The change of lifestyle was dramatic, but Avis always maintained contact with Sister Brigid in the orphanage. The education base facilitated by Brigid bore fruit and she flew through second level college and got a scholarship to Brooklyn University. She could have moved out of her immediate environment; she was offered a place in the business college upstate but, despite her bad experiences in New York, she felt tied to the path prepared for her by her new parents and Brigid. She accepted a post-graduate course and went back to Brooklyn to lecture, met her future husband there, joined his business, and then they were married.

Avis didn't offer all this information at the meal. Bit by bit over a number of conversations however, Louis began to see that her trials in recent times had had a traumatic effect on her mind, but her complete breakdown came as a result of the layering of recent problems on an already badly damaged ego. Although his first attraction to her was as a result of seeing her beauty and her smile across the crowded bar in the Bahnhof, Louis became more involved because of her courageous fight back in very difficult circumstances.

'She's a wonderful person,' he thought. 'It's amazing the way she's emerged as a beauty in person and personality despite all her troubles.'

As a priest he was used to getting involved, but in this case it was more than that. His spine tingled when their knees touched under the table and when she reached over and placed her hand on his, in reaction to his sympathetic words to one of her problems, he fell into her dark brown eyes. He knew then that he must come clean and tell her he was a priest, 'but not just yet - wait until coffee and brandy'.

"Do you believe in Eternity?" he asked her, hoping to find a way to explain that he was a professional religious.

She surprised him with her answer and he realised then that he was dealing with a person with an exceptional grasp of the principles of life.

"It's the only thing I believe in, Louis. I believe that time will destroy you and for that reason, Eternity is the only reason for living. Slight exaggerations perhaps, because there is love in the meeting of two souls."

In her enthusiasm she allowed unrelated wave to follow wave. Remembering a significant research paper, she reverted to her college studies.

"I believe Freud was more religious than Jung," she posited.

Louis was thrown back to his own philosophical training in Maynooth but found that she had studied and read outside his lecture parameters. He had of course studied philosophy; but his studies were mostly confined to Christian philosophers such as Newman, the more controversial Jacques Maritain and the disgraced John Courtney Murray S.J. - the latter of his own volition.

She voiced simple but complex versions of life and living.

"At night I work through my dreams to understand my inner self. In the morning I have to decide whether I want to live or not; morning is a rebirth," she stated simply.

"Are you happy to live in that world?" he asked, being led by curiosity rather then academic endeavour.

"I'm not able to channel anger," she said. "Friendship for me is very beautiful and important and I feel, having met you Louis, that something wonderful has happened in this small, simple place. In New York there are too many attractions and degradations - I have seen my friends wither and die there. As Socrates said, you must be a gadfly to survive, and in New York it is difficult to combine your soul and the city. Modern society professes to be supportive of individualism, yet civic control is authoritarian and the individual is dominated. None of these controls allow the love ethic to prevail and so the people who live in New York, for example, are controlled by a political philosophy and a political theology that is not a love ethic and is therefore flawed."

Louis could have quoted Murray S.J. and his view that the paternal state was to inform, correct and direct the masses, but figured that personal holiness and its importance might be a safer platform. He knew that she was close to a belief in God, but somehow he felt that there was an invisible barrier between their philosophies.

"I believe," he said, "in the importance of personal holiness and in the importance of work. Doing it very well, for love of God, contributing to the common good, being a genuine friend and loyal work colleague, someone who readily works with others, listens to them and when the opportunity arises serves others willingly."

"Oh Louis, that's beautiful. Did you know that Socrates never wrote a word and yet he said so many beautiful and wonderful truths? Your words are simple but important also and it makes me very happy to be here with you tonight. What you say is fundamental to life and living and reminds me somewhat of what Socrates once said: '*the soul must grow feathers to return to God*' - I do hope that we're growing feathers as we communicate here tonight."

He still hadn't mentioned that he was a priest, but her next move pushed him on to the back foot.

"Would you like a joint, Louis? She took a package from her bag and offered him one. Louis had never smoked a cigarette let alone taken a joint. He didn't say no immediately; the truth was, he had accepted one in Canada while in the company of the young married couple whom he so admired. They had smoked and he made excuses not to light up. She explained that everyone in New York smoked marijuana and that she found through the experience an intensification of her emotions, making them hyper real. Yet she was cautious, and only took marijuana with a friend in a controlled situation.

"I learned from the experience and it helped me to become intellectually promiscuous. However, I need to share my life with someone, a friend. It was this void that brought me down before, Louis, although I do realise that we are just passing ships. However, can we expand this meeting of two souls to be a psychological meeting?"

He didn't pursue this slightly fragmented conversation nor fully understand it, and wondered if she had already been smoking. Nevertheless he accepted the joint and lit up in the spirit in which it was offered. They were alone in the dining room by this time. Their table was in a secluded position close to a window; the waiter had been excused and so they felt close and unobserved. The conversation continued and about ten minutes after starting to smoke, Louis coughed.

"Avis, I haven't talked about my work and you haven't asked. I mentioned that I counsel at times, but there is a serious significance attached to that."

"I know Louis, you're a priest, I've known from almost the start, but I wanted to wait until you were ready to tell me. We may not have much time, you have a career in the Church and I wouldn't wish to divert you in any way. We talk of killing time and yet time is quietly killing us."

"However, Louis," she continued, feeling that she had to give him time to prepare a reaction to the changed relationship that his declaring himself a priest had achieved. "Relativity is perhaps our saviour. Einstein once quipped, 'When a man sits beside a pretty girl for an hour, it seems like a minute. But let him sit on a stove for a minute and it feels like an hour' - that's relativity!"

They both laughed and Louis wished he had his front incisor capped. He could see that the smoke had an effect so he decided to play the game.

"Well, sitting with you and having this conversation is support for that remark of Einstein's, which he no doubt made in jest, and leads me to quote James Joyce," Louis drew on a remark of Jack's before the sledge incident. "Look to the here, the now, through which all the morrows rush to the past. And do you know Avis, I can't think of a more appropriate motto at this time - if it weren't for my Roman collar."

She reacted as if he had thrown a cup of water into her face. He felt sad and tried to lighten the moment by introducing the possibility of their skiing together the next day. He knew that this evening had been a close run thing. For him forming a relationship with the opposite sex was always a possibility and he had slipped once before. Yet he knew that this occasion was different and he applied the brakes before becoming involved in a physical as well as an emotional way. He knew he'd formed a strong attachment with Avis in the four days since their chance meeting. He wondered if the sympathy he felt for her was the driving force and yet there was more. They simply got on well together; a bit like the young couple he had met in Canada. He should have realised that he was a victim of the liberal writings of Maritain by perceiving that the door was slightly open. However, this was a process of action and interaction, involution and evolution, making change forever. This creature is alive, she has a head on her shoulders native to her body and she cannot be aggregated as chattel property - not that that was ever his considered intention.

Even in four days Avis had made her mind up. The only competitor for this man's heart was in heaven but she felt equipped with a superior weapon. She wanted him, and this in her belief was a meeting of two souls. She knew that lovemaking was never a simple pleasure, but the first step for her was to consummate their love. This was pure love, she had lost her womb, she felt only part a woman, but he being a priest placed him somehow equal. She knew they were perfectly matched.

And so they talked on the surface, he not realising that he had been weakened by circumstances, she spinning a web hoping that he would eventually tire and succumb, yet wishing him no harm. 'Perhaps I should walk away,' she thought, 'and yet it's life before death that is attractive to me.'

They met next day and skied. For Louis the sun was warmer and the sky bluer and he bathed in her praise of his less than adequate skiing. They took the cable to Valluga, skied to the Ulmer Hütte, had a drink at the outdoor snow bar there, and met a group of American tourists who invited them to take part in a toboggan run. Everyone in the group, it seemed, was having a meal in St Christoph that evening and they planned to toboggan back to St Anton on the road. Avis and Louis agreed to take part, and met at the Hotel Post where the others had ordered a taxi to take them and the toboggans to St Christoph, only about five miles away. The road was covered with snow and ice and was very steep in parts, and as the traffic was little or none, tobogganing down was not a problem. Most cars going north went by train, and local traffic was reduced after dark because of the ice on the steep road. Anyway, the lights of the odd car could be seen well in advance.

Louis had rented a toboggan for two. "Is one toboggan big enough for two?" she asked. She wore a well-fitting cat suit with a fur trimmed hood and calfskin boots. Her face was radiant, her eyes shining with excitement and, framed in fur, her head made a very pretty picture. She greeted him in continental style, changing cheeks three times. Her perfume was a subtle Chanel and yet it attacked his nostrils and permeated into his olfactory senses at all levels. For some strange reason he thought about his mother.

They laughed and talked their way up to the famous 'Hotel Arlberg' in St Christoph. The owner, dressed in traditional dress, met the party. The windows blazed shafts of light out on the pretty snow-covered front and the sounds of zither music from inside completed the picture. Louis slid his arm around Avis's waist and escorted her gently into the hotel. Coats taken, the party was guided to a beautifully set corner table for ten. The typical green-bubbled stem glasses glistened and as they took their seats four waitresses in local-style dresses attacked them. Their brown, healthy faces glistened with perspiration, brought on by an almost demented approach to serving the guests. Elfriede served Louis's side of the table and, having poured the local wine from the red jugs on the table, began to serve their meal.

Halfway through, a musical trio, two violins and an accordion, came to their table and serenaded the group - a romantic serenade and beautifully done. As their dessert course was being served, the conversational sounds were silenced by the entrance shrieks of a group of local dancers - leatherhosen, strong legs, thumbs tucked in the shoulder straps, they performed a variety of local dance routines. The six-man slapping and kicking dance routine brought the house down. Finally the folk dancers kicked one another out of the restaurant, and the coffee and brandy or Schnapps was served.

"How are we going to manage the trip down, Louis?" Avis guessed that sitting on a toboggan and guiding it down by controlling the turns and the speed with the heels of the pilot was no big deal. But Louis was large, she wasn't small and both had to fit on the one vehicle.

"Don't worry, all you have to do is sit on my shoulders."

"You're joking."

"Yes, I pull you behind with a piece of rope tied around your feet."

Teasing her made him feel good. Eventually, however, he explained the plan for the descent. She in front and he with both legs apart, using his heels to guide the toboggan.

"Simple really, but will you be able to control the speed? Some of those hills are very steep and the turns are sharp. Supposing we run off the edge?"

"Have you a good insurance policy?" Louis jested confidently.

Not drunk but well on, their party coated up and stepped out into a starry night where the reflected moonlight on the white snow made seeing easy. Louis had planned ahead and was wearing ski boots. He noticed that some of the other pilots were wearing city shoes and slacks, and knew from experience that they would have difficulty in controlling their toboggan. Not alone that, but they could expect a continuous shower of snow and ice up the legs of their trousers.

'Ah well, never send a boy on a man's errand,' he thought.

The romantic setting was reduced when they arrived at the start point. It was freezing and the surface hoar protested bitterly at being stepped into dust. Some of the others got going, and the sight of them disappearing rapidly into the evening gloom was a sobering sight. There was a bend about fifty meters on and the first two negotiated at speed without any trouble. Not so the next couple, however. They were full of drink and good spirits and there was no way the driver could have negotiated the bend at his speed. Their momentum was such that they demolished the bank of snow and disappeared. Their friends rushed down and gaped over the edge. After a few seconds of focus time by the would-be rescuers, the two were spotted spread-eagled in a field. The heaving of the two bodies was fortunately not the death throes, but the result of senseless hysterical laughter. Eventually they rescued the sledge from a snow-bank further down and the start ceremony for the remainder continued. From then on the initial take off speed was reduced and all managed to negotiate the first bend. For no reason Louis and Avis were last. She sat down gingerly.

"Where do I put my legs?" Her brown eyes hit Louis where it was intended.

He persisted in being flippant in a manly way, although he badly wanted to wrap her in his arms.

"In your pockets - no, just tuck them up and hold on to the timber side of the yoke. My legs will be one each side of you, so you'll be well supported. Now this is the good part. I have to hold on to you - my arms will be around you; try to secure us both to the sledge by gripping the timber tightly. On the straight this is not a problem but torque on the bends could dislodge us both."

"Torque?" She nearly overdid the saucer-eyed business.

"Don't worry; I'll keep us on an even keel."

"Keel?" Another effort on her part to play the girly role.

Without more ado they were off. Louis worked the heel job on the bends well, but found when he lifted his heels clear the speed increased dramatically. The night air whistled past and in Avis's case it buffeted into her chest. It was so cold that she ducked down to form a slipstream, but Louis's arms held her tightly and getting her head sufficiently down was impossible.

"To Hell with appearances, I should have worn the winter woollies," she muttered through chattering teeth.

It was a wonderful experience for them both - the crisp, clean air, the speed, the near misses, but most of all the feeling of closeness. On one bad bend Louis was doing his right heel thing when he noticed a hole in the snow bank at a tangent to the bend, just about where an errant sledge would go. He slewed to a halt and in so doing they overturned and rolled like rag dolls to the edge of the road. Avis thought it was just an unscheduled stop, but took an immediate interest when she saw Louis peering through the gap in the bank.

"Has somebody gone through?"

No answer because Louis had followed through and when she looked in, he was up to his armpits in snow. He searched around and at last he touched on something with his feet. There they were lying together asleep in deep snow, with just a face-size of hole allowing air down.

"Help me get them out, I think the drink has taken its toll."

"If they stayed asleep in the freezing snow they'd wake up in the morning and find themselves dead," he muttered.

The rescued pair was sent on their way while Louis and Avis stayed close behind them to supervise the rest of their decent to the village. They were the same mad couple that had missed the very first turn earlier.

They stopped at Avis's hotel and went into the bar for a nightcap. Louis said goodnight and headed up to his room in the Trittkopf. He checked his musculature again in the mirror, before going happily to bed. Avis checked her happiness index and figured that this was the 'now' she wanted to live for.

Heidi, Jack, and the two nurses from Innsbruck left the Glos household on foot. In winter the path down from the house usually required a new set of footprints and on this occasion Jack led, dug his heels well in and made a negotiable zigzag path. When they reached the level ground just in front of the cable car, Heidi linked with him arm in arm. Their plan was to walk down the village to the 'Hotel Nasserein' where a nice bar, music, and an indoor skittle alley were available. It began to snow lightly as they made their way past Hotel Schwarzer Adler and the church.

Jack introduced Heidi to the crazy concept of viewing the church steeple from a supine position. Lying on one's back, head towards the building and looking upwards, with the sky as a background, changed the view dramatically. The height of the steeple was accentuated and the snowflakes made a pretty picture, appearing in the light and fluttering down like wheat dust on threshing day.

An army friend had introduced him to the concept. Lying on his back at a cliff edge near the Cliffs of Moher, he had watched with great fascination the Aurora Borealis performing its multicolour dance on a skyline stage stretching all the way across the wide Atlantic Ocean to the United States of America.

Heidi accepted the strange behaviour without fuss and slipped her hand quietly into his as they lay shoulder to shoulder, blinking as the feather-light snowflakes landed on their eyelashes.

When they arrived in the Nasserein they headed for the bar. The skittle court was a simple country version, nothing like the sophisticated American game, yet the essence of concentration and eye-hand co-ordination were present.

'Heidi is such a beautiful creature,' thought Jack. He noticed her ease of movement, her ability to switch from stern concentration to flashing an odd bright-eyed glance in his direction. It made him feel good to know they were connected.

On the way home they played the lying-on-your-back game at the church steeple again, threw snowballs and talked. Heidi brought up the subject of skis for Jack, and so the group gathered around Josef's shop and gazed at the brightly lit window.

"Typical," said Heidi, "he must be still in there, and the lights in the fitting room are on."

Jack knew that a relationship with Heidi was written in the stars, 'what a load of shit - get a grip on yourself; the swing to her hips when she delivered the skittles; they don't make girls like that nowadays,' the thoughts in his drink-influenced mind revolved and displayed like the globe in a Pathé film newsreel. 'I would drown peacefully in those brown eyes.'

Reality struck when Heidi whispered, "there he is," and the smiling face of Josef appeared and walked swiftly towards the front door. Heidi met him and they embraced; introductions followed and when it came to Jack's turn, Josef brightened even further.

"Hello Jack, I heard about your good deed on the slopes. Heidi's mother told me the whole story."

Jack muttered his usual deprecatory responses and took time to study the young Austrian. He was friendly and relaxed and Jack knew that he was the sort of guy that he could get along with. Jack wasn't what you'd call deeply involved with Heidi, but yet he knew from her responses, both in St Anton and in Innsbruck, that he and Josef were sailing on the same course in a very narrow channel!

"It was a coincidence that you and Heidi met in the hospital. She loves her work there, especially her involvement in the baby unit. I've never visited her there - is the hospital in a nice part of the town? I'd love to get over there some time and take her out - I should have done so before now. She says I work too hard. The thing is that when the work arrives here, needs must."

Somebody mentioned that Jack needed a pair of skis, "and a new pair of ski-pants," said Heidi. The worn-out pair of golf pull-ups had not gone unnoticed. Before he realised what was happening, Josef was measuring him for a new pair of ski-pants. There was no mention of filthy lucre while he was being measured, or even before that. In the meantime the girls were excitedly pouring over stretch cloth.

"What do you think about this colour, Jack?"

"Look at the stretch, isn't it great!"

"Stay steady," muttered Josef through a mouthful of pins.

"Which type of zip do you want? I like the chain on this one."

"How much will they cost?"

"Don't worry, Josef will give you a good deal."

Jack did a mental calculation on the possible cost and what money he had hidden in the mattress. He knew the price of the skis, at least the price in the shop window, and knew that he could just about make it, if he got a good deal on the pants. Without this pressure he probably would have struggled on, perhaps even on borrowed skis, but there was no going back now and he even began to look forward to the new Muldoon.

Two days later he was to be fitted into the trousers, and the Kneissl Combi fitted with the most up to date Marker bindings. As they walked up the road, Heidi snuggled her hand into his and leaned her head on his shoulder. Somehow they became separated from the others and at her request they went to have a look at the location of his room. She pointed out where her father's cattle were housed, next door to Frau Gasper. As she drew back the large bolt and creaked open the door, they were immediately overcome by the strong smell of cattle and hay. The cows were mostly lying down in their stalls and some of these *Fleckvich* ladies of the milk world turned their heads in Jack's and Heidi's direction and wiggled their giant ears.

"Your room is up there?"

"Yes, I knew the cows were here, but didn't realise that there were so many."

As his eyes became accustomed to the dark he saw a large bale of hay stacked by the wall in readiness for feeding to the cattle later.

"This is probably the bale I hit on the way down the mountain."

He walked over and sat down, as if renewing his relationship with the dry grass. Heidi sat beside him and they kissed. The hay was soft and they were able to stretch out in comfort.

"I should sleep down here." Jack also thought that if the money for the ski-pants and skis was more than he had, he might have no choice!

They stayed and talked awhile in the sweet smelling hay. Things were getting a bit hot between them and Heidi put on the brakes, voicing a worry about her parents expecting her home. He knew that the others would probably be there already so he reluctantly agreed to begin the journey home; her scent and presence was causing him no end of sexual difficulties but his conversation with Josef loomed large.

He left her in the hall inside her front door and scrambled back to his home in the attic. He checked his money and saw that he was about eight pounds short. Louis had already offered to lend him enough to bridge whatever gap there might be and so he fell into bed with a plan of action decided. 'Heidi was another issue - what was he going to do about Josef? Happy is the dealer in the big ace pot; fortune favours the brave; *ni thig leis an gobadain an dha tra a fhreastail*; everyone cheats a little,' were some of the thoughts that finally closed his eyes and brought on the dreams. However, a new pair of Kneissl Combi skis figured largely in his nocturnal thoughts.

Heidi returned to her hospital job with her friends but, before she did, Josef had been briefed on the service he was to provide for the pants and skis. The price was a major reduction and although Jack did borrow from Louis, the money wasn't necessary to pay Josef, but used instead as a support for Jack's social life. Four days and two fittings later Jack Muldoon stepped self-consciously from Kerber's shop wearing a tight-fitting pair of blue pants and carrying a shining new pair of 190 Kneissl Combi skis. It supposedly was the radical change in gear that caused the *Pistenhelfer* friends he met on his way up the village to stop and whistle.

T he skis still had to be tested and he purposely used the borrowed ones at work that morning. The Kneissls looked great and he could see these beautiful blue boards carving their way down the slopes. He wanted to be alone on this initiation ceremony and it suited that Louis was off skiing with the American bird.

Maureen Flanagan's knitted blue sweater, the new pale blue pants, and Kneissl skis completed the picture.

"I've got the colours of the kingfisher - all I've to do now is fly like one."

As he fitted the old leather boots into the Marker bindings and stepped on to the new snow at the Kapall station, he was landed in the immediate. He snow-ploughed around the chair station with ease. That wasn't really a test; it was the run down to Gampen on the Kandahar race route that would tell the story. He wanted everything to be perfect, and he knew that the start and the first ten or so turns would form the basis for what was to come.

Just like snooker, the grooving of the cue action at the start is critical. In this case, the weight distribution and the carving action of the skis needed to be grooved. 'Slowly, slowly, catchee monkey,' he said to himself, as he leaned forward and started moving, leaving a clean line in the virgin snow. It seemed like a miracle as effortlessly he glided down. Just to be sure, he made a small stem, Arlberg-ski-style, on each turn and let the rhythm take over as he weighted and unweighted and edged to a stop. Looking back at his marks he could see that he'd moved into a new realm, thanks to the new skis and the metamorphosis.

And then the ski spirit moved further and Jack, despite his poor grounding, became a moving part of the essence of skiing. Nocoli's 'Merry Wives of Windsor' became his instrument and as the music came through his heart to his brain, the staccato, crescendo and pizzicato sounds were translated into movement and the Kneissl edges listened and answered. Jack became a different being and, on his path down from Gampen, he interpreted the music in checks; cheeky stems, long, rhythmic sideslips, and aggressive, clipped short swings. He pulled up at the village and felt he had created something, but then again it could have been wishful thinking. If he had had the flexibility he would have leaned forward and kissed the skis that had taken him way beyond what was his right to expect.

He knew the moment was special, perhaps never to be exactly repeated; he had stepped up to another plateau, destined perhaps to be his new ski domain? His alter ego muttered one word - 'bullshit,' but his was a very faint voice without influence and was easily pushed into the abyss where all the forces of negative self-image lurk, awaiting a chance to apply their power.

In that euphoric moment he thought of Heidi. At times of great intensity it is natural to think of those you love, and Heidi for Jack was the nearest he had to a relationship outside men and family. There were others of course, but each one had replaced the former. The encounter in the hay had laid a foundation, although Josef the tailor was a major obstacle.

As he walked through the village parading his Kneissls he bumped into Louis. Since the American woman came on the scene, their one-to-one encounters had been reduced.

"Great, Jack. The skis look good but what about the boots? Perhaps when we meet at Mama Pangratz this afternoon, we should look at what they have in the line of boots."

He realised that the boots needed replacement, but he was trying to make do and keep some shekels for social activity. Events played their part in Jack's skiing life, however, and when on a run from Galzig that very day, he felt a draft and looked down to see that the upper had departed from the sole of the right boot. If it weren't so serious it would have been funny. His big toe protruding from the hole in the sock presented a picture probably never seen before or since on that route. The die was cast. He changed into his visiting clothes and met Louis at the Trittkopf for the weekly visit to Mama Pangratz, carrying a pair of laughing leather ski boots, well past their sell-by date.

"Well, you've no choice now - as they say in my business, the soul has departed from the body! New boots are expensive, but you can look at what old Mr Pangratz has to offer." Louis's chest heaved with suppressed laughter.

And so Jack was taken under Louis's arm and the chase for the final piece of equipment in the jigsaw began. The weather was much colder and the crunch down the main street was exhilarating.

As usual, Mama Pangratz saw Father Louis coming. She fluttered around the door of the shop, getting rid of her apron, smoothing her hair and fussing over the already-set table in the lounge. The boss was his usual immense quiet self at the workbench, adjusting skis, repairing boots, and serving customers. Jack went straight to him with the leather boots he had bought earlier, at which time they were already somewhat out of date.

"I bought these boots from you recently - they must have been from bad stock; look, the sole has departed from the body."

"They were already dead when you bought them for next to nothing," joked the man of the house - keeping in tune with Jack's approach.

Anyway, a deal was done and Jack got a much more up-to-date pair of boots for 200 schilling. A great price and he couldn't help showing his deal to Tony, the Pangratzs' son.

"You got a good deal, if you don't mind the story that goes with them."

"What story?"

"Well," said Tony Pangratz, and looked Jack straight in the eyes with serious intent. "He'd hired those boots as new to an American pilot last year and when he was killed, his wife returned the boots and skis before she left for home with her husband in a coffin."

"Good God! How was he killed?" Jack wiped a fleck of saliva from the side of his mouth.

"Believe it or not, but he ran into a tree after a stop off with a few locals for a drink in Gampen. He'd been drinking all day and the final one took him into the dark of the evening. It was especially gloomy among the trees, but he was still trying to keep up with the local lads in skiing as well as drinking. Anyway, just as those in front emerged from the tree line, he made a serious effort to pass the leaders and hit a tree head on. He was dead, it seems, before he hit the ground."

Jack's eyes bulged. "Nothing to do with the boots?" he stuttered.

"No not at all," said Tony, "but I thought you should know."

Jack's romantic frame of mind and his recent ski and boot debacles easily facilitated a negative link with the dramatic history of the boots.

When he made it to the table, Louis was talking to a delighted Mama Pangratz and tucking into the ham salad and tea. Although shocked by Tony's revelation, the sight of the spread of meats and bread played some part in having him revert to being a post-adolescent male-eating machine. He ignored Louis's queries about the new boots and chewed his way through an amount of Austrian pig, dressed in a variety of fashions, mostly with a hint, or a lot, of garlic. When his stomach allowed, he told Louis about the boots, but without the macabre addendum. Jack also showed respect for the efforts of Mama Pangratz by way of pleasant recognition, hand shaking and the like. She didn't speak English so conversation was out of the question, and her pleasures in the visit mostly rested in watching young men, and particularly Father Louis, eat. She had spent a lifetime feeding men in this rural outback.

They talked about the boots on the way home. Louis didn't know what to make of Tony relaying the history of the boots. He figured that in some way Tony resented Jack's freedom, he being tied to the daily grind of the ski and boot-hire business and being supervised by his father and mother.

"How did the new skis work today?"

"Great," said Jack, lighting up at the mention of his new skis. "Will you be free in the afternoon?"

"I'm sorry, but I promised Avis that we would go skiing. I'm learning a lot from her about skiing and in particular about short swings." Jack was aware that short swings were not what one would attribute to what Louis did on skis. He would unweight all right, but the push out right and left didn't happen. He had fond hopes of a reaction to the unweight action, but his version was limited to some upper body emphasis, which mostly didn't make it to the skis. Avis wasn't geared to manage Louis the skier; she confined her reactions to ones of loving acceptance of his displays of affection for her on the slopes. In a way, they both skied into one another's hearts.

Avis had messages from her friends in New York. Naturally, they were concerned about her health and about the possibility of her return to the Bronx. She was recovering and her letters reflected that, but leaving Europe was another matter. She mentioned Louis a few times, linking him as a priest and adviser. They were happy that she was in good hands, but her women friends read between the lines and expected more as days passed and Louis remained in the picture. For Avis, living between the lines was just what the doctor ordered. She had been told to try to forget the past and build a new future, and that's what she was doing.

She had moved past the philosophical reasons for linking with Louis and now her emotions were those of a woman in love. The physical was lurking beneath the veneer of play as they met each day - daily encounters now, to which Jack could bear testament. Louis had played a blinder, if playing avoidance of full physical contact was what he was doing, but Avis was more focused now and considered the introductory discussions at an end. She had counted the times they had kissed and knew that one of these goodnight kisses would lead to what she wanted - not just a sexual encounter but total commitment between them both. The thought of lying with Louis took her breath away.

"Hello Avis, great snow. Let's head up to Galzig and down to St Christoph. We can eat there again and take a taxi back to St Anton. We could even take the lift up to Valluga. Are you on?"

If Louis had suggested a lift to the moon, Avis would have agreed. In this case, she smiled and nodded enthusiastically.

Louis knew that Avis and he had become more than adviser and client. He heard her talk of going home and thought that whatever happened, the separation after the holiday would allow events to settle. He pushed his responsibilities, both priestly and with Avis, to the back of his mind.

The lift from Galzig was full and the pressure increased as the last few passengers were pushed into the cabin by the lift attendant. Avis allowed her body to be pushed into Louis's large frame. Their eyes met and she placed her head on his chest and heard his heartbeat.

They clumped their way out of the cabin at 2,811 metres, inhaled the thin air and, exposed to the vertigo effect at this altitude, tightened their muscles in anticipation of heading down the precipitous slope in the direction of the Ulmer Hütte and on to St Christoph. The usual necessary preparation routine for the trip took place; gloves, check cap, glasses, sun cream, but mostly the boots and bindings. For the ordinary skiing partners, there is a code of support, and items such as ski wax, cream, and lipstick are shared with scant regard for cross-contamination. If there's a boy-girl, or even a man-woman element involved, then the support is often extended lovingly. Louis helped Avis with her boots and when the boots tightened she made the required stress sounds. She placed her hands on Louis's kneeling figure as support and felt the tightening of his back muscles as he pressed down the binding lever. Fitting the left boot to the binding involved her holding the boot up on bended leg at the rear, as Louis beat the collected snow and ice from the groves in the soles of the boots with sharp taps of his ski pole.

"Thanks. Look, the weather seems to be changing; is it going to snow?"

Dark, angry clouds had gathered higher up and a look at the weather gage showed a drop in temperature of three degrees, to minus two. Minus two degrees at that altitude wasn't low and even in the village, given certain weather conditions, indicated snow.

Looking down the steep descent from the Valluga station Louis remembered a poem he had written as he studied a wild summer sky over his native Donegal. 'How does the screeching seagull feel, floating inland from the storm?' For one moment he longed to be in the land of his mother - only for a second, however.

Avis sped off, her pink scarf flying, and Louis followed. They played in the fresh snow on the edges of the *piste* and Louis moved into the mogul field to practise his newly acquired way of negotiating the deadly bumps. Over the brow of the hill they sped, chased by dropping light and flurries of swirling snow. Yes, the wind had decided to join in the action and by the time they arrived at the open-air snow bar near the Ulmer Hütte, it was blowing hard, but as yet not certain of direction. The barmen were closing up in preparation for the run home and there was just time for a brace of eggnogs, before they too skied down to St Christoph. The good thing about the outdoor snow bar was that skiers could pull in, have a drink, and head off without having to loosen the safety bindings or get out of the skis. By leaning back on the poles and propping up the skis one at a time, they were able to wax each other's skis. This exercise was a cause of laughter and fun because of the fine balance needed.

Louis suddenly realised that he'd never been so happy. All the dark clouds were weather ones, which added to his sense of protectiveness and her joy. The storm gathered strength as they skied down the valley and by the time they arrived in St Christoph, snow was pelting down. The gathering darkness was a bowl into which white pellets shot, steadied in the light, and floated down to form banks of snow against doors and windows. It chased them into the door of the Hotel Arlberg, pretending it was a part of their party, until the solid door slammed shut, the curtain was drawn, and soft music, heat, and the babble of conversation took over.

"We'd better order the taxi before we eat," said Louis.

"I'm afraid, *mein Herr*," explained the receptionist, "that the weather has worsened further down the valley. It's bad here, but there's about a half metre of snow on the road to St Anton. The snow-plough will of course clear the road during the night, but as yet they haven't started and the taxies are confined to base until the plough has done its work."

"We'll have to stay the night," gasped Avis. She looked up at Louis with no trace of disappointment in her voice. The hotel book was thrown open.

"We've only one double room left; you're very lucky."

"We'll take it," said Avis, looking at Louis and using the phrase more as a question than a statement. In what seemed to her an eternity, Louis's acquiescence came and the clerk presented the registration documents and shouted instructions to Adolph to prepare room number 12 for Herr McCormac and his Frau. No baggage, but the hotel would provide toiletries and pyjamas.

"I hope they have your colour in pyjamas," sniggered Avis to a scarlet-faced Louis.

"Will you visit your room before you eat?"

"Yes," answered Avis, already linking Louis to the stairs with the key for number 12 in her hand.

"What about our skis and boots?" muttered Louis, realising that they were both in ski-gear and socks.

"Don't worry," said Adolph, the hotel janitor. "This happens a few times a year and we've arranged a selection of slippers on the first landing. I'll leave your skis and boots in the cellar; they'll be safe there until morning."

Off they went up the stairs, led by Adolph. On reaching number 12 he opened the door and revealed a pretty Tyrol-type bedroom, complete with wooden carved mirrors and a window looking out on the by-now howling tempest. The large bed was carved timber also and displayed an array of winged cupids on the headboard. The brilliant white eiderdown was piled high on the bed. Louis and Avis stood at the door while Adolph strode across, pulled the curtains, and explained that he would book a table for them in the dining room. Louis gave him a tip.

"We'll be down shortly."

The door closed and they looked at one another in silence. Rather than rush into his arms, which she felt like doing, Avis excitedly inspected the room and bathroom, smoothed the bed covers, and peeped out the window, but before she could continue her intervention tactics, Louis wrapped her in his arms and held her tightly. She looked up and Louis kissed her lips, tenderly at first, but then with passion. Avis responded; she slipped her tongue between his teeth into a warm and welcoming mouth. They were saved from a '*moment de force*' when Avis spotted their hotel slippers reflected in the wardrobe mirror.

"You've got red slippers, like the Pope," she giggled. The moment was arrested and they sat on the edge of the bed, talking and kissing. They were both at ease now and Louis realised that he was in love and there was no going back. Avis was happy also but her crowning moment was to be, she thought, when they lay together later that night in this lovely bed.

They were met downstairs in the restaurant by the beaming, sweating face of Herr Ober.

"Your table is ready. Adolph selected this spot for you."

Adolph grinned as he rushed to the kitchen with a pile of crockery from another table. Their table was perched on a little raised section in an alcove, close to the window and screened to some degree by a palm in a large brass tub.

"This is lovely," said Avis and Louis nodded his approval. He held her chair and stepped around to his place, taking a look around the crowded dining room before settling in. He realised that his arrival in this situation was sequential and logical, although some doubts existed. 'Perhaps this is just a theatrical re-enactment of what I observed in Canada,' he thought. 'When the curtain comes down there'll be applause and I'll slip into the wings.'

Avis's cool hand on his emphasised the reality of the situation. He looked at her and thought of the difficult times she'd had. Perhaps this was part of the readjustment process and he was expected to play his part. Immediately, however, he pictured the bedroom in his mind, and knew that his role as a Catholic priest and adviser had been eroded and what was happening would change his life.

'Drink,' he thought, 'I need a drink.' A tray of Schnapps and lemonade arrived and he launched the fiery liquid into his stomach on a mission.

Dinnertime flew and before long it was the coffee and brandy course. They had by then drunk two bottles of wine; well, one half-bottle of white and a full bottle of red, and the conversation flowed. Louis was in great form and gave vent to his personality by allowing the conversation to overflow to the next table. The English couple there talked about skiing and occasionally broke into song. The man had a good voice and on realising that Louis was Irish, tried to outdo John McCormack. Avis looked on in admiration as Louis joined in the chorus.

"Oh the days of the Kerry dancing

Oh for one of those hours of gladness.

When the boys began to gather in the glen of a summer's night,

Oh to think of it. Oh to dream of it."

Avis was dreaming, but not of dancing in Kerry!

The song took hold and before long the complete room was on the floor, dancing an Irish set under Louis's direction. He tried to get the accordion player to play Irish dance music and succeeded in getting the rhythm right, although the tune was a local one.

Aon, do, tri, ceathar, cuig, se, seacht, aon do tri, aon do tri.

Louis led, pulled, sang, directed and, more by dint of overwhelming personality than attention to the detail, got everyone to stagger a version of *Baint an Fheir*. Great applause and they all happily collapsed into seats.

"I didn't know you were a choreographer."

"I'm surely not, but sometimes the spirit moves me."

With support from Adolph, Avis had arranged that their coffee and brandies be moved to a quiet bar on the other side of the entrance. They sat on high stools and sipped their drinks.

"It's a pity I didn't bring my party dress."

"I think a track suit would be more appropriate to that dance session," said Louis.

"I didn't mean then, I was thinking of our sitting in this little bar. It's so romantic here - look at the snow falling through the light from the window." Adolph increased his pace of glass cleaning, avidly squinting through a wine glass held up to the light.

"I remember a couple sitting like this when I was in Canada. She had the most beautiful high heel shoes. They were partly see-through, made of a glass-like material, and mostly impossibly void of any method of being fixed to the foot."

Avis looked at her slippers. She kicked them off when Louis wasn't looking and rubbed a tissue over her dainty painted toenails. When he looked back, her knees were crossed and one elegant foot was seeking recognition. She leaned across and kissed him gently on the lips. Words weren't necessary, and anyway Louis hadn't the right combination of words; his eyes poured into hers by way of compensation. It was a simple yet sophisticated moment and their two souls were one in joyous celebration.

Avis took Louis's hand, said goodnight to Adolph and joined Louis out of the bar and up the stairs to their room. Suddenly they were alone and Avis played her part. She knew what to do and guessed that Louis would have difficulties in lovemaking. With his quiet help she tenderly took his clothes off and soon they were in bed naked.

"I love you Avis." She was released, and under the bedclothes made love to his body and then to him. Louis showed remarkable strength and went to the well again and again.

'Perhaps the more human I am, the more God-like I am,' he thought.

Later in the night Avis felt a void. She patted where Louis should have been and frantically turned to see his side of the bed. He wasn't there! She looked around the room - no sign of her lover. She slipped on a dressing gown and walked to the bathroom - 'he wasn't there - but where?' She had no intention of rushing out of the room with the message that her Louis had disappeared! Without clearing the thoughts in her mind, her American experience flooded back and she felt deserted and exposed.

On instinct she opened the door slightly and peered out. There he was. Louis was walking up and down the corridor reading his offertory. This was a daily prayer for priests. He must have awoken and realised that he had missed saying his office the day before. Whether or not this reversion to his consecrated role involved a cry for forgiveness she didn't know, but unable to make sense of Louis the priest and Louis the man, she slumped back on her hunkers and closed the door quietly.

"Man the Viceroy of God
How great is your name, O Lord our God?
Through all the earth!
When I see the Heavens, the work of your hands,
The moon and the stars, which you arranged,
What is man that you should keep him in mind?
Mortal man that you should care for him?"

Jack felt like a new man as he headed up to work the morning after his spending spree. The ski-pants were perfect, but it was his new Kneissl skis that made the difference. He realised now that the length of the Attenhoffers and the uneven edges had been a big drawback. Even working with the team of *Pistenhelfers* was easier and of course his status with the rest of the workers had risen. The locals insisted on inspecting them carefully and his nickname, Romeo, now had a new dimension, more in respect for his gear than his suspected prowess with the ladies.

He had an opportunity during fittings for the ski-pants to get to know Josef, and he now fully sensed that there was a greater force to reckon with than his own feelings for Heidi. He hadn't made any firm decisions, but then he didn't have to.

The team of eight men and four women swooped down from Kapall to a fairly bumpy spot on the *piste* and started levelling out the area. Heinrich was happy with the way his team had learned, and noted some leaders, like Jennie the American girl, providing guidance to the newly-arrived. They dug out the soft interior of each bump and smoothed the area with deft steps on skis. Jack was careful to ensure that those stepping near him didn't step on or mark his new skis. The work was hard and they all sweated, but there was a sense of joy in activity. Regular bursts of song helped keep the team spirit alive. Not involved in treading new snow and its extreme physical pressure meant that a playful group chase to the next section on a given word from Heinrich was eagerly awaited.

Down they sped to the next target area. Jack was delighted and as a result of added confidence he nearly always arrived in the leading group. Heinrich told him his skiing was improving and even gave him a few hints. Jack figured that skiing beyond a certain level was mostly about having the confidence to attack the fall line. Sitting back was a common cause of disaster and he knew that his clash with the bumps on the Osthang could have planted nervousness about attacking the slope.

The weather deteriorated before they reached the village.

"More feckin' *treten* tomorrow." Jack unloaded his anticipation of the chin-high knee-lifting action that was required when treading new snow, and thereby touched a nerve ending with one of his fellow *Pistenhelfers*.

"I expect I'll be feeling sick tomorrow," his colleague replied. He was well versed in the ways of ski bums!

The work finished; there was the required dash up to Gampen for breakfast and Schnapps, and Jack as usual enjoyed this part of the day. It was a chance to swap stories of the morning's work and get to know one's workmates. Sometimes they paired off to ski for the rest of the day, but Jack usually went back to the Trittkopf to arrange the day with Louis. Since Avis arrived on the scene, however, Louis was occupied and when he did join him it wasn't the same.

'Women can do that sort of thing to a man,' Jack thought. The others seemed to be organised, so he figured that it might be a good idea to ski alone and practise some of the latest adjustments to his ski technique.

Events flowed by dint of his Muldoon attitude; nothing was planned and when a light of opportunity appeared, he dived in and to hell with the angels! He was like a 13-year-old boy in a sweetshop; he wanted it all and he wanted it now. Whenever he felt unattached, like now on the slopes, he sometimes unreasonably blamed father figure Louis for having a life of his own. Working alone on his ski technique, while beneficial to some degree, sometimes exposed the frightened boy within the manly frame.

His practise went well. Forcing himself forward on the fall line he carved his track easily. On the extreme slopes at the top of Kapall he figured that edging on the ice was essential. Although his feet were receiving the message to edge on icy patches, sometimes he felt that the leather boots were too slow to relay the necessary action to the Kneissls. Making sure that the laces and clips were tight was a part solution.

Not having to queue with the paying customers at the bottom of the chairlift however, as well as being a convenience, lifted his ego. He dipped under the chain and on this occasion only one person occupied the chair in line, leaving a space for him. Without looking at the occupant of the left side he grabbed a *mantel* and settled in. They jerked off and experienced the usual process of gliding between stations and rattling over the pylons.

"They are new skis, *ja?*"

He could have responded briefly and remained anonymous all the way to the top, but he figured that in his role as *Pistenhelfer* he should be friendly to the paying patrons. He lowered the hood and looked to his left. A good-looking woman dressed in a Scandinavian sweater and green slacks sat by his side. He bade her the time of day in English and accepted the compliment about his Kneissl Combis. She smiled in recognition of the young man's obvious obsession with his new ski equipment and her casual social remark became a discussion about the plusses and minuses of skis. She burst into laughter; showing her strong white teeth, as Jack described the new American Head metal skis, as 'cheaters'. She turned in the seat to face him and Jack blushed. Basking in her womanly personality and not inconsiderable sexuality, they discussed the weather, the snow, and skiing, but mostly he gazed calf-like into her laughing eyes. He discovered that she was much more conversant with the skiing environment than he, and in particular she was familiar with skiing as a sport. She pointed out the original route of the famous Alpine/Kandahar race and identified a few of the crux points.

The word 'sport' came much into the conversation and she mentioned that she had made a film about sport. At this moment he gulped and realised that he was in the presence of someone really famous.

Jack, as a member that summer at the 'Loughborough Summer School of Athletics' in Leicestershire, had seen the 1936 Olympic Games film, played for the course as an example of the relationship between sport and politics.

"You're Leni Riefenstahl the film-maker! I saw your Olympic film just this summer." In the sports' world, of which Jack was a part, there was only one Olympic film and Leni Riefenstahl had made it. Jack didn't know much about film-making in general, but in this environment, her approximate age and her statement left him in no doubt about her identity.

She seemed flattered at being recognised. They conversed for the remainder of the journey and when they got to the top he joined her for a few runs. She skied very well and they had fun playing on the *piste* and among the trees. It wasn't that she was skiing to a very high standard or very fast, but she was very smooth and obviously enjoyed joining a variety of types of skiing into a pattern without stop from top to bottom. It was this flow that separated her from the rest of the recreational skiers. Jack tried to keep pace and when he succeeded somewhat she smiled approvingly. He could see that she was very confident, very experienced. He expected her to move away to join her friends but that didn't happen. Completing an immaculate parallel turn she pushed out her heels, and playfully faced him.

"Care to join me for a drink?"

Jack should have been dumbfounded, but somehow the flow of events set in this Alpine dreamland had been normalised and he just nodded and grinned. He took her skis and stacked them with his own at the wall outside the Gampen restaurant. She linked his arm easily as they pushed open the doors and moved to a table overlooking the slopes.

Having settled in, she listened intently to his description of the occasion when he had seen her film. She insisted on buying her round and as she moved across the floor from the window seat he noted the gentle sway of her movements and basked in the smile she relayed to him over her shoulder from the service area. There were many others seated around but Leni had the ability to focus on Jack, making him feel special.

He explained that the film he had seen had been taken by the British army from a film archive in Berlin at the end of the war and copied. Her face showed intense concern at this news and she watched his face as she asked him about the number of copies of which he was aware. The information he had was mostly casual rememberences, but she reeled in the information, her lips repeating some of the key words in his story.

"I know there's one in the Film Institute in Leeson Street also."

Jack had used the Film Institute as support for his courses.

"Leeson Street?" Leni Riefenstahl absorbed every detail.

"Yes, Leeson Street in Dublin. The National Film Institute is there."

She mentioned that once she had been involved in making German propaganda films about Ireland. Since the end of the war however, she had spent much time trying to clear her name of being a Nazi propagandist, so that she could get into the film business again. She'd been to America but the response from the film people there had been very cold. Because of her close association with Hitler and other leading Nazis, there appeared little or no chance of her being employed in the West Coast studios and their mainly Jewish directorships. She was now trying to start up in Europe, but was interrupted by committees investigating war crimes and had attended a number of start-up meetings. Nevertheless she'd set up a business in Munich, called 'Riefenstahl Productions' and through this company she sought co-operation from Jack.

"Do you think you could secure the Irish and British copies of the Olympic film and return them to me in Munich? If I could recall the film, I could reissue a new copy of the original with a different dialogue."

Jack felt a bit out of his depth and also reckoned that she was clutching at straws. She didn't identify how many films had been issued and obviously had no idea of their whereabouts. Nevertheless he showed keen interest, nodded his head, and promised to stay in touch when he returned to Ireland. He could see that the glorification of the German team in the film and the many close-up shots of Herr Hitler and the other German leaders, were very much to the detriment of a wide circulation of a reissue of the film. There wasn't anything concrete they could do at that point, so she changed the subject.

"Where are you eating tonight? Perhaps we could meet?" She placed her hand on his sleeve as she asked the question.

He explained that he usually ate in the Bahnhof Restaurant with his friend.

"You'll be my guest tonight in the Hotel Post." Her hand squeezed slightly and her brown eyes smiled.

It wasn't so much an invitation, but an order, and Jack was not offended; he was thrilled by the quiet confidence with which she dealt with the situation. He identified the time, said goodbye and left.

"Best get the good clobber on," he muttered as he headed back to base. As he passed the cowshed, the doors were open and he saw the back of Heidi's father as he sat milking a cow. Still floating from his encounter with Leni Riefenstahl, he light-heartedly entered the barn and addressed him in traditional form. He sensed his significant integration into the Arlberg environment in such a short time and it made him happy.

"*Grüss Gott, mein Herr.*"

Klaus must have been miles away in his mind, because he kicked the pail as he turned. Some of the milk spilled over, but fortunately he managed to grab the handle just in time.

"Ah Jack, *servus*. Josef told me that you're all kitted out and I see he did a good job."

"Yes, the ski-pants are great, too good for my standard of skiing I think."

"Not at all; Heidi says you have the makings of a very good skier."

"Potential perhaps, yes, but you'll know that there's a distance between the cup and the lip."

They chatted while Klaus finished the milking; the conversation was about nothing in particular at the start, but Jack was naturally interested in the war. Allowing a discreet introduction, he broached the subject of Klaus's part in the *Luftwaffe*. The old soldier started slowly, but as he described his love of the machine gun his face lit up and he launched into stories about its use even before joining the *Luftwaffe*, and about his role as a gunner in the Junkers 88.

"I got to know that gun like it was one of my family. I could sense the slightest weakness in the 'gas return' and many times I'd prevent a stoppage by making a gas adjustment before it happened. I served with Captain Gerd Hissler in the *Luftwaffe* and that was my best experience of the war. He's now a professor in the University of Innsbruck and he spoke to our local environmental committee just this week. Unfortunately for me, he was promoted early in the war and my next captain was probably responsible for us being shot down. I managed to parachute to safety, but the rest of the crew was shot in the sky by the Home Guard. I fell into a hen house. And I still can't stand the smell of hens!"

During their conversation, apart from the remark about Josef and the ski-pants, there was no mention of Heidi. Jack thought it best, however, to ask about her welfare. He discovered then that there was a certain amount of tension in her relationship with Josef. Her father wanted what was best for her, whatever that was, while her mother, as Jack already knew, wanted the joining to be about property and land. Of course Jack's relationship with Heidi was totally romantic and accidental, and unrelated to the needs of her mother.

One of the ski lift people had relayed information about the family relationships. Jack, it seems, would be to Heidi's mother a threat that would require squashing in order to create order. This, according to his informant, had happened to others, but luckily for Jack he had as yet not been identified as a serious danger, and probably would be considered but a seasonal feature of life during the ski season. The other blips on the life screen, which had been efficiently dealt with by Heidi's mother, had, it seems, been local and without resources.

From what Klaus had said and reading between the lines, Jack, rightly or wrongly, figured that Heidi was complicit to some degree in this cleaning operation and expected to finish in the arms of Josef, if not physically, at least contract-wise. Heidi, he figured, was in love with the potential of life, not with any person or thing.

Josef, the tailor, saw life in very simple terms, as a way in which Heidi's family and his could survive. The place for physical love for him was not measured in realistic terms. If he had to say, "I love you", it would mean, "I will support you and you will never again be exposed to survival dangers of any sort." Jack figured that although she was complicit, her occasional sorties away from security, like her attraction to Jack, were just a dash for liberty as the noose tightened. Eventually, she would be landed like a salmon, and perhaps have children with strong freedom genes.

Fortunately for Jack, his visit to Josef, his meeting with Klaus, and his local *Pistenhelfer* informants had warned him of the dangers of 'getting serious' with Heidi and yet, as he looked at the hay in the corner of the barn as it was being closed, he realised that they had nearly consummated a love that didn't exist.

He was happy in his little room which, since his arrival, he had made home. For some reason he felt that this dinner appointment in the Hotel Post was a threat to the simple life potential above the cow barn. With some degree of trepidation he put on his best shirt, a tie, and the *piece de resistance*, his Agar of Trinity Street creation, the blazer. A blast of smellies, out the door, down the steps to the road and away. The evening had darkened and the snow continued to fall as he made his way up the village to the Hotel Post. He felt good physically, a combination of the almost continuous exercise in the open air since he arrived and the excitement of meeting this beautiful and famous older woman. Not that he was considering her as a woman, female that is. She was famous, had made the 1936 Olympic film that included shots of Jesse Owens and Hitler. Jack, above all, advanced in social terms and despite a certain amount of trepidation, moved on to where, perhaps, angels fear to tread.

When he arrived at the Hotel Post, which lay just at the back of the railway station, an angry engine puffed its way on to the Arlberg tunnel.

As was typical in snowy weather, it pulled a long line of rail cars loaded with motorcars, plus the usual number of people-carrying carriages. He heard the new arrivals at the station laughing and talking as friends greeted them, or they made their way to their hotels or into the Bahnhof restaurant. For a moment he wished he were up there, rather than entering the cold stately entrance of this three-star hotel. It wasn't cold inside the doors, but for him the formality and décor, plus his appointment with Leni Riefenstahl, an erstwhile colleague of Hitler's, caused him to shiver. However, remembering their ski fun on the slopes that afternoon, his spirits lifted and he lightly approached the desk.

"I have an appointment with Miss Riefenstahl. Could you tell her that Jack Muldoon is here please?"

"*Jawohl Mein Herr*, she has booked a room for dinner, Reinhold will show you up."

Jack nearly did a runner, but the porter was on him like a flash and ushered him to the marble stairway leading from the foyer. They chatted on the way to number 12 Zimmer. Leni Riefenstahl had a suite of rooms in the Hotel Trittkopf, the same place Louis was staying, but she nearly always ate in the Post.

"*Kommen Sie herein.*"

Leni opened the door. She wore a long pink gown, adorned on the left shoulder by a red silk rose.

"Welcome, Jack, great to see you! May I introduce you to Gerd Hissler, a professor in Innsbruck University and an old friend of mine."

Professor Hissler stepped forward, clicked his heels, and shook Jack warmly by the hand. Behind both, Jack could see a table set for dinner and four chairs. The room was part of a suite which included an anteroom and a spacious bedroom, dignified by two tall elegantly curtained windows, numerous mirrors and typical twenty's wall light fixtures.

"You'll have some champagne." Without waiting for a response Leni poured champagne into a long-stemmed glass from the magnum of French Champagne - not that he would have said no. A number of thoughts ran through his mind. Firstly, the dress and behaviour of his two companions reminded him of how he figured life in the higher social level was in the 1920s or thereabouts. He made this judgement based on the wedding photographs of his mother and father, and some romantic films of that time. Music from 'The Merry Widow' played on a tall radiogram in the corner, adding to the scene. The conversation was casual to begin: the weather, snow conditions and inevitably, developments in the area and protection of the environment. The professor had a clear picture of the issues that needed attention in order to protect the natural environment. "Take one example," he said. "The Capercaillie is one of the most beautiful birds in the Alps. It's a part of folklore, mentioned in children's stories, but because of man's incursion into its domain, it is being pushed higher and higher up the mountain. It lives in the pine trees and only there, and now that skiers are skiing more and more off *piste* and in the trees, the birds are really under pressure. Of the five pairs between here and St Christoph registered in 1946, only two remain and we're looking at a reduction in those numbers if some measures are not taken. I don't think the fact that the male is polygamous and takes no part in the domestic duties of the brood is significant in their demise, but you never know." Hissler couldn't resist adding a bit of techno nature information to impress.

"But what's the solution?"

"Well, we have tried telling skiers to keep away from certain areas, but they don't seem to care and so I have recommended to the local committee that nature reserves be established without delay. The funding that is made available for environmental reasons and tied to the Marshall Plan can be used for this purpose."

Leni showed her skill as a hostess and was able to redirect the conversation away from the hobbyhorse of the professor from Innsbruck University. She poured more champagne and started a conversation about tourists and the range of nationalities represented in St Anton.

"Every nationality is represented here, except perhaps the Germans; South America, New Zealand, Australia, and dominated in numbers by the British."

Jack was able to confirm that that was so and especially the Americans from the USA.

"There are a group of American pilots stationed in Munich who come up here regularly to ski. I believe some of them have Irish backgrounds," said Jack.

"How do you know if an American has an Irish background?" asked Herr Hissler.

"Well, in fact, we consider that all Americans have Irish blood in them somewhere and we start from there. Secondly, their names are a real giveaway."

"How is that?" Herr Hissler liked having his students on the back foot.

"In Ireland we're still somewhat tribal. The O'Reillys come from Cavan, the O'Sullivans from Cork and so on. When we meet an American with an Irish name, he or she is amazed and excited when we can tell him from where their antecedents came from. Not just the county but where exactly in the county. For example, your father is Irish and probably came from Cork and possibly from west Cork - all from a name! We had a Famine, which started a great emigration. We were eight million in 1798 and after the Famine about two million had immigrated to America to compete for a living with the Germans, the Swedes and the Italians."

The two Germans were somewhat bemused and obviously had a different vision of how the world was developing. Considering the proximity of the war and its tragic completion for them, they seemed still in a state of social shock.

Leni brought things back to the present with a polished hostess move in which the music was changed and a new drink suggested. She did however refer back to Ireland during this transition. While working on the Olympic film she had fallen foul of Herman Goebbels, mostly because as propaganda minister he considered the Olympics should have been his responsibility. Hitler however had admired Riefenstahl and her work in the film world, and had given her direct responsibility for the '36 Olympic project. On one occasion while in Goebbels's office, as a result of an angry summons by him to report progress, she met the Irish ambassador Mr Bewley, accompanied on this occasion by a Mr Murray, an Irish Department of Education inspector. They were discussing the '*Kraft durch Freude*' - 'Strength Through Joy' programme and its connection with Physical Education in the state. The daily radio fitness programme was also discussed and she heard mention of an important 1936 Irish report which they were intending to use to establish physical education in Ireland.

She said that the Irish group was very friendly with Goebbels and appeared enthusiastic about all things German. She also described her involvement in the making of German propaganda films about Ireland, under directions from the Minister of Propaganda. "Olga Checkova played a very beautiful part in 'My Life for Ireland', directed by Kinnich," she explained, "and 'The Fox of Glenavon', made in 1940, was very popular in Germany."

"But we must not forget the famous Irishman who worked for Herman Goebbels and was completely supportive of National Socialism."

"Who was that?" Jack enquired, immediately interested and quite perplexed. Hissler chipped in, unable to resist identifying whom they considered being the most famous Irishman of the war, William Joyce. The British hanged him for treason on the 3rd of January 1946.

Leni saw that Jack was not fully briefed on the life of Joyce and his support of Germany, so she sought to protect her investment in collecting her film by a complete change of subject.

"I'll play some Schubert, okay? Jack, tell me which variation you like best."

"I must say, Leni, that it's the early variations close to the theme that I like best. I find the latter variations exciting, but a bit contrived." Jack hoped that he was not opening a complete conversation piece.

"That's typical of the solid way you ski, Jack. What do you think, Gerd?"

Gerd refused to be drawn into the conversation and, rather rudely Jack thought, asked if he could have a beer. She produced an *Erdinger Weisbier* which was just what he needed, judging from his reaction.

The fourth guest arrived. He was a distinguished-looking, rather stout man with a wide moustache and a monocle. He handed his coat to Leni and before she could hang it up he was at the drinks table. No champagne, no white wine, no red wine.

"Haben Sie Pils bier, bitte."

He recognised from the selection shown to him by Gerd a Pils bier that suited his taste.

"Jawohl - Paulaner München."

Jack studied the new entrant. He was a legal 'bod' it seemed, and reflected an image of the profession he represented. 'His *pince-nez* was somewhat of a giveaway,' Jack thought.

"This is my legal representative, Herr Emmerheichs. He will, I hope, lead me from my present situation to a new position in life. One day I will have a future!"

Jack wasn't briefed any further and although he realised that the dinner party had moved from being a discussion about nothing to something else, he held his position and sought to identify who was going where and with whom. Who's being represented and why, he wondered?

Leni Riefenstahl was an important figure in German theatrical life. She trained as a dancer and specialised in dancing to ballet music, but barefoot. Her work in the theatre gave her the chance to study stage management and she travelled throughout Europe. Unfortunately, she had had a series of accidents while dancing, the worst being a knee injury before three thousand spectators in Prague, in her role as the 'Dying Swan'. This was the beginning of the end of her career as a dancer and the beginning of her interest in filmmaking. Her films, 'The Triumph of the Will', 'The Blue Light', and 'Olympia', the film about the 1936 Olympics in Berlin, had all won gold medals at the Paris World Fair. Many artists considered French Vichy censors as their enemies, while the Germans were the staunchest allies of many artists in Paris during the war.

It was claimed that The Triumph of the Will, which included the famous 1934 Nuremberg rally of the Nazi Party, was purely a propaganda film and this, added to her years of co-operation with Hitler and the propaganda minister Goebbels, paved the way for legal investigations by the Allies into the war life of Leni Riefenstahl.

Jack figured that this dinner meeting was an opportunity for her to discuss tactics with her solicitor in defence of her position as an artist and not a Nazi party worker, despite her involvement in filmmaking in the Third Reich. Jack's knowledge of the whereabouts of copies of the Olympic film qualified him to be present.

Leni and Herr Emmerheichs sat apart for about an hour after the meal, while Jack and Dr Gerd Hissler sipped their port and talked.

"I joined Air Field Marshall Kesserling's *Luftflotte*, established in northern France in 1940. I discovered later that we were to support the invasion of England, but as you know it never took place. We had Junkers 87 dive-bombers - they had been very successful in Spain and in the invasion of France as part of the *blitzkrieg*. I liked the ME 108 fighter best and we had fun over the Channel before I was transferred. While stationed in Brest, Leni came to the camp as part of a show for the troops and danced for us. We all fell in love with her and later in the officers' mess, she had to make some tough decisions. I still love her."

Professor Hissler smiled and cast a shy glance in her direction as she listened intently to her solicitor, he seated, she with her bottom propped against the back of a dining chair, rocking gently backwards and forwards. She caught his glance and her face lit up for a second, just like a furtive sunbeam on a cloudy day. In that second Jack could feel the heat of her personality and knew that she was special in so many respects.

"It was said that even the *Fuehrer* fell for her, but I don't think so. During the '36 Olympics in Berlin she met Glen Morris, the American decathlon gold medal winner. They had a torrid affair; she really loved him but still kept her work focus. She is, after all, the consummate professional. Anyway, after the Olympics he went back to a ticker tape welcome in New York and later married his hometown childhood sweetheart. From there he moved to Hollywood, got the part of Tarzan in the films, took to drugs and drink, divorced his wife and died a young man. I know she felt that their meeting in Berlin had been designed by the gods and still regrets that they had such a short time together and that her work came between them."

Jack looked over again and admired the cameo that was Leni

Riefenstahl, the use of the chair and the perfect Orpenese-like reflection in the mirror. Her pose and the information he had gleaned left him breathless.

Over dinner the possibility of getting the Olympic film reissued by Riefenstahl Productions was discussed. The solicitor was preparing a submission to the 'Voluntary Self-Supervision Board of the Film Industry' in Wiesbaden, to have Riefenstahl Productions established as an official film company. A submission had been made in January of that year but only the second part (less propaganda-oriented) of the film had been approved. Leni and her helpers hoped that eventually the censors would agree to have all her films re-released. In that case an effort would be made to regain control of the copies 'stolen' by the British army. Jack Muldoon agreed to help in this latter exercise, although he knew of the exact location of only two copies: one in Ireland and one in England.

The evening moved on and when the required alcohol-induced level of spirit was achieved, songs were sung and Leni was persuaded to dance. Despite her protestations and old injury claims, she eventually agreed to try the part of the Dying Swan made famous by the Russian dancer Anna Pavlova at the Kirov in Moscow.

"When last I danced this I wore a leotard of silver lamé. This evening dress is hardly suitable."

There was no direct response from the two men or Jack. Everyone moved back to the wall and cleared a space in the middle of the room. Leni turned off the centre lights, and the wall lights cast a glow up to the ceiling which reflected evenly but lightly over the room. Saint-Saëns' Swan music welled up and from behind the curtain Leni made her appearance. She had freed her hair and carried a chiffon scarf lightly in both hands, so that as she floated into the centre of the room, the fluttering scarf and the flowing hair enhanced the sense of movement and attracted her audience's attention. Suddenly Jack felt as if he had been punched in the stomach. His sharp intake of breath was a reaction to the fact that the dancer was naked. Leni flowed and flitted around the room, behind their chairs and between them like an Alpine stream dancing down the valley. She quietly pivoted, stretched, and rolled, displaying a complete understanding of time, weight, space, and flow. Once or twice Jack looked at her face, but mostly he admired the perfect body, moving so expertly on bare feet. None of her movements were gauche or overtly sexual and yet there was no denying that she exuded sexuality and used it in co-operation with the rhythm of the violin and piano music, to tell a story of a woman in love and tormented. 'Maybe,' thought Jack, because of the story he had heard from Herr Hissler about Glen Morris, 'her dance, which finished like the dying swan, was an illumination of her real story of disappointed love.'

Walter Raleigh-style, Jack rushed forward with his English barathea blazer and slipped it over her glistening body. She thanked him with a kiss while the others applauded and came forward to congratulate her again and again.

"She is the embodiment of Strength Through Joy."

Jack had the ear of Herr Hissler and sought to get as much background information as he could.

"Yes, members of *Kraft durch Freude* are shown in the opening of Leni's Olympic film. Most of them naked also, I should add. The British Army must have been starved for sexual pleasures if they considered the opening of 'Olympia' as extremely exciting. I believe that her Strength Through Joy introduction was the main reason why nearly all copies of the film were stolen after the war."

Hissler tried to speak in reasoning terms but Jack could feel the venom in his voice about the actions of the Allied forces.

It was Herr Hissler's turn next. He moved quickly to the boudoir grand, lifted the lid, and warmed up. Obviously he was a very proficient performer and before he announced what he was going to play, he ran up and down a few scales and glanced confidently at his audience. He eventually announced the Sonata No. 11 by Mozart and when there was quiet, began. Leni tucked up on the couch, still wrapped in Jack's blazer. The cascade of notes in the piece created a sentimental atmosphere, but there was something missing in the interpretation of the piece. He played with great confidence, but somehow failed to convert this percussion instrument into something it was not, and thereby inject real feeling into this wonderful piece of music.

The last note was followed by polite applause.

"How about you Jack, have you a turn?"

There was no escape - not that Jack wasn't ready to contribute. The problem was that the classical standard of the first two artists was so high that if he sang, and singing was his only option, he would have needed to be Paul Robeson to survive. He could play the violin, but was thankful that there wasn't one available.

As a contrast he decided the occasion called for a spirited song that had humour.

"She's a fine big lump of an Irish agricultural girl,
She needs no paint or powder and her figure is all her own,

If she hit you a kick you'd swear 'twas a kick of a mule you got,
The full of your arms of Irish love is Peggy Ann Malone.
I like to wander down the old bowereen
When the hawthorn blossoms are in bloom,
And to sit by the gate on the old mossy seat,
Whispering to Kate Muldoon."

Enough of the *comaille*, he thought, I think they're ready for the rebel song.

"When all beside the vigil keep
The West's asleep, the West's asleep."

He gave the 'West speaking like thunder' and 'being awake' his best shot. His father's favourite song seemed to go down well and even prompted a discussion about Irish whiskey. Dr Hissler led the main reaction and showed his knowledge of the role of Irish mercenaries in the armies of the French during the reign of Louis XIV. He lauded the spirit of the Irish soldier of that period.

Later a knock came to the door. It was Reinhold with the news that a car was waiting for the solicitor to bring him to Innsbruck. Jack saw his opportunity to leave also and bade goodbye to Dr Hissler and to Leni.

"Thank you very much. I'll do all I can when I get back to Ireland."

"I'm leaving tomorrow morning, otherwise we could have skied together again." Jack understood that she had work to do for the Military Tribunal in Munich.

The evening had given Jack an opportunity to see her in a wider social setting, but he realised that their ski meeting that afternoon for him was special. And so as he headed home to his room he knew he'd had a once in a life experience and wondered if he'd ever meet Leni Riefenstahl again. He felt her hand on his arm and smelt her perfume as he headed down the snow-packed street to his room. He'd be working next day when she left her suite in the Trittkopf. Perhaps Louis would see her when he returned from mass. He made a mental note to try and meet with him as he went to the church - he had a story to tell his friend. His room, which earlier had lifted his spirits, now seemed quiet and lonely.

Next morning he grouched his way up the main street towards the station and the chair lift. The usual roll of bread from the same bread shop. His new skis, boots, and pants made a difference and there was a swing in his stride by the time he rounded the bend at the church. No sign of Louis. It was half six in the morning and he had hoped to see him on his way to seven o'clock mass. He needed a friend with whom to share his experience.

Jack sat in the chairlift and again absorbed the beauty of the timberline. After the storm of the night before, the snow had combined with the wind to fashion the most beautiful shapes on the trees and in ridges along the ground. He felt a link with the war through Leni Riefenstahl; it wasn't only the war - somehow he'd become part of the Leni Riefenstahl story and she'd involved him in her quest to be seen as a professional artiste without any Nazi Party stain. She hoped to use the fact that Propaganda Minister Goebbels didn't like her, and other independent actions on her part, as a sign that she was separate from the Party. However, the close links she had had with Herr Hitler and Herr Goebbels weighed the scales somewhat, as would the fact that she used work-camp internees for crowd scenes in her films and then returned them to the camps.

'Anyway,' thought Jack, 'it's a long way from the Curragh to Berlin!'

'Who would have thought that there'd be a link between Agar, the Jewish tailor of Trinity Street, and the Nazi Party? Certainly the blazer will never be the same again!'

Jack mused, but mostly admired, his new skis as the lift floated high over the pine trees and deposited *Pistenhelfer* No. 516-1955 on the ski slopes above St Anton am Arlberg. The young locals hadn't much money and certainly new skis were a rarity among the seasonal workers. Jack could however trust their ability to have a go on his new Kneissl Combis without incurring any damage; moreover his path was made much easier if he included local lads. Up until now, and similar to the other foreigners, he had been given the rough end of the stick, the butt of the many jokes that made life bearable for the locals, but tough for the visiting *Pistenhelfer*.

After work the usual retinue retreated to the restaurant in Gampen. A bit of difficulty in getting a table to themselves meant that they had to split up. Jack finished up at a table of American pilots from the air force base in Munich. One guy, Harley D. Wright, was a senior among the group and seated beside him, Jack almost immediately got into conversation. When he discovered that Jack was Irish he explained that two of his group were Irish also.

"Mc Loughlin over there never stops going on about his Irish roots and Mulvey says that his family came from a place called Carrickonshannon

- is there such a place?"

"Sure there is, it's a town in County Leitrim on the Shannon."

Their conversation must have been overheard because a raucous version of '*Where the River Shannon Meets the Sea*' burst out. It was Mulvey and in jig time an animated conversation, well more of a shouting/singing match, burst out, and Jack found himself fully involved. He had some catching up to do.

This group had started late, taken a pit stop in Gampen even before the skiing started and for no reason got into the beer and Schnapps chaser rounds. There were six pilots in all, so that meant that six rounds of drinks were bought before they left. In fact it was seven because Jack became involved, although Harley said he didn't have to. Being a real 'indigenous Irishman', he was soon popular with the group and there were many requests for Irish rebel songs, of which Jack had a wide repertoire. Mc Loughlin blinked the tears away when Jack sang five verses of 'Kevin Barry'.

"British Tommies tortured Kevin just because he would not tell,

The names of his brave comrades and other things they wished to know."

Anyway, when the drink ran out - Harley wouldn't let another round start - they all poured out of the restaurant and focused on the job of getting the skis on. Bending over the bindings placed one's centre of gravity off plum, and with a raft of drink on board, falling forward on one's snot was a possibility. There were about four such collapses, making complex readjustments necessary. However, eventually, and with much laughter and Texas whoops, they were ready to take off.

"The B47 flies at twenty thousand feet, the B47 flies at twenty thousand feet, and it carries just a teeeeeny weeeeenie bomb." Final piece was sung in a squeaky voice.

To the tune of 'John Brown's Body', they skied in file and sang this mock of their brothers in bomber command. They were all fighter pilots and considered themselves above the bomber crews in status.

'A bit like Cavalry and Infantry in our crowd,' thought Jack.

They could ski, but with more courage than expertise. Harley was the best, but also the most restrained. Up to Gampen and down at speed, yahoos and crazy falls, but fun for all. When they decided to call it a day, they headed off to their accommodation, having made the afternoon tea dance rendezvous downstairs in the Post. This was where all the boys and girls eyed up the talent. It wasn't necessary to be dressed and normally the clients arrived straight from their post-skiing drinking session, although those seeking to dance would nip home and grab a pair of shoes. The girls nearly always got home for a change and a face job.

They arrived an hour later and the boy-girl thing began. The Americans were popular and in quick time had created a table group at one end of the dance floor. The girls were mostly English and one or two Jack had met previously. One girl, Susan, was a member of the British equestrian team and had worked for Inghams. Unfortunately for the girls, however, the Americans seemed obsessed with the idea of meeting an Irishman in St Anton and their focus was mostly centred on drink and the Irish. By the time the dance had finished, the group target was on where the closing drink binge could take place.

"Jack ole man, it's important that we celebrate the final hours of the night with a few drinks."

"Yes," said Harley, "a drink in the Bahnhof is a required part of this operation."

The rest of the air force group liked the idea, but hated the disciplined part of the operation order as issued by Harley.

"Harley. You're not the senior rank here; Jack is an infantryman and a Lieutenant. You may be senior in the air but here on skis, Jack, as *Pistenhelfer*, is without doubt the senior rank."

The conversation continued in this vein and it was agreed that a meal and more drink in their hotel was required. Jack seized the opportunity to scarper off to the Trittkopf, and collected a brace of Jameson stashed for just such an occasion. They all met again in the 'Hotel Alpenrose'. Harley was staying there and had arranged a table in the restaurant, and Jack was to be their guest. He protested somewhat but Harley was adamant. The conversation flowed and although Jack was an outsider, the social gap was bridged by the fact that he was military and Irish.

"I can't believe it," said Kevin Mc Loughlin, "my father, if he were alive, would be delighted to think that the Irish had eventually arrived to take their place among the nations of the earth."

Mc Loughlin's father had been a member of the IRB and an active member of the old IRA in the Clare region. He had served with Colonel Brennan, Chief of Staff, before and after the civil war and had taken part in a famous ambush outside Milltown Malbay.

When he arrived in America he became involved in the construction industry; he had been a carpenter in Killaspuglornane and served his apprenticeship with a master carpenter near Ennistymon. Anyway, to cut a long story short, he moved up the management scale in New York and finished up owning a floor of the prestigious 'Waldorf Towers' and was a multimillionaire to boot!

At the right moment Jack emptied the water jugs and filled them with Jameson Ten Year Old Whiskey. The fumes arose from the jugs and permeated the breathing facilities of everyone. Jack poured, toasts were made to the presidents of America and Ireland, to Caitlin Ni hUallachain, Roisin Dubh, Biddy Mulligan, the Rose of Tralee, the Yellow Rose of Texas, Kevin Barry, Johnny Fortycoats, Parnell, Arthur Griffith, Patrick Pearse, 'poor' Willie Pearse, Michael Collins, Cu Chullain, Ferdia, General Grant, Mickey Drippin, and Johnny Fortycoats again. By this time some of our American brothers had slipped under the table 'incablocked'!

"Jack, this was a great night. I'm sorry that some of our combatants weren't able for the Irish fare. However, one week from tonight we will, with your co-operation, have a rematch and provide the drink: American bourbon."

Jack accepted the challenge. He had no experience of American whiskey, but had been told that it was easier to drink than the Irish version. He had seen John Wayne and others lower the stuff no bother.

"Leave the bottle barman!"

Next morning wasn't Jack's best hour, but he managed to make the grade and arrived at the chair lift ready for duty. There was a lot of snow to shift and on the route down the *treten* was furious. The leaders exerted the pressure because with such deep snow, a *piste* had to be formed before nine if a route was to be available for the beginners and classes at half nine. In some situations, where the slope was very steep, it was possible to side slip and level the run, but in general it was a knees up to the chin sweat and curses job.

The week flew and on Saturday morning after work, Jack was hailed by his American friends.

"Hello there Jack, how are things?" It was Harley D. Wright and his team from Munich. "We have a plan of action for tonight, and this time 'the American Eagle' is providing the ammunition."

And so the arrangement was made. Jack had an embellishment which he thought might grab their interest. He had taken a bomb from the Curragh - well not a bomb really, more of a firecracker. These were designed to give a touch of reality to the obstacle course and when lit and thrown close to a tunnel where a soldier was in the crawl mode, the cracker would explode and, although not causing damage, would scare the recruit soldier and provide realistic training. The firecrackers came in a variety of sizes, and the one brought by Jack to St Anton was of the larger type. The tubular-shaped explosive carried a written warning to the effect that if exploded nearer than six feet, it could cause damage to the soldier. Why Jack had brought it on holiday wasn't clear. He'd thought vaguely that it might provide the opportunity for a bit of excitement and this was such an opportunity. An Irish bomb in St Anton!

They skied the day out and, as planned, gathered in the hotel for the American drink session and afterwards for the planting of the Irish bomb.

"I'll buy you a Horse's Neck, Jack, if you manage the controlled explosion."

"A Horse's Neck?"

"Sure, it's a popular cocktail in the States."

The bourbon was indeed easier to drink but the effects were the same or worse. When Jack left the hotel en route to collect the bomb in Louis's room in the Trittkopf, he was okay until hit by the cold. Stars other than those in the sky or on the American flag lit up his vision and he felt weak.

"Okay fella, help is at hand." It was Harley, who knew that action and reaction are equal and opposite. In this case a half bottle of whiskey was designed to have its effect and it did. Jack accepted the help and by the time they had reached the railway crossing, twenty yards from the Trittkopf, he was coming round.

"Louis is in bed, he had a bit of an accident today."

It was Johan, one of the Strauss family.

"Is he bad?"

"No, it's very little, a bit of a knock to the knee, but as he has a big trip planned for tomorrow he decided to rest."

"Where's he going?" Jack knew that the American lady would be involved, but couldn't resist seeking more information on his friend's movements.

"They have planned an off route descent from Valluga, led by one of the ski instructors. He and the American lady and a few others are leaving early tomorrow morning." Jack could see that Johan was acting as 'guard dog' to protect Louis from Jack and his ilk.

"I've been skiing with a group of American pilots from Munich for the past few days and we, Louis and I, have lost touch. However, I'm taking part in a midnight operation tonight and I thought he should be involved."

Johan eyed him curiously and thought God knows what, as Jack and Harley made their way to 'the Father's room' and knocked on the door.

"Come in."

Louis lay with a mountain of pillows stacked behind his back, quietly reading.

"This is Harley D. Wright, Louis. We have a project to complete tonight

- a co-operative effort between the Irish Army and the United States Air Force. Harley and his colleagues are up for the weekend from the base in Munich. I'm afraid that you'll have to become involved in a controlled explosion tonight - you're the time control officer."

Louis could see that Jack and Harley had a few drinks on board and was apprehensive when Jack took the package, which he knew to be a bomb of some sort, from the bottom of the wardrobe. He tried to delay and perhaps abort the escapade. He launched into a story of his recent meeting with a pub owner from Glasgow who had crossed his path. He had spent the previous year in St Anton on his honeymoon but, unfortunately, his new wife died and here he was a year later with his wife's ashes in an urn.

"Her last wish was to have her ashes poured from the Vallugabahn lift at the second pylon."

He had acceded to her wishes in detail that very day and told Father Louis of his feelings, while pondering the empty casket. Shortly afterwards Louis saw the same widower with a few on board, chatting up the dentist's secretary.

Jack had met the same guy earlier and knew of his aspirations for carnal knowledge of the same pretty secretary, ashes or no ashes!

Despite Louis intentions the story didn't delay the plans for the explosion.

"Let's synchronise our watches. The explosion is timed to go off at 23.59 hours, okay?" Jack signalled the off before Louis became maudlin about the pub owner and his poor late wife. Louis apprehensively played his part, but couldn't resist making cautionary sounds, which as far as he could see fell on deaf ears. Harley was too much in awe of the priest-Jack relationship to make any contribution. He would have liked to tell Louis that he would keep an eye on things and to some degree his steady demeanour did just that.

Anyway, away they went with the precious bundle, down the stairs out the door and down to the Bahnhof to gather the crew.

"Ole Jack is going to set off an Irish bomb in front of the Valluga lift."

Because he was aware that Louis was monitoring events from his bed, Jack tried to keep to the time schedule.

"Don't forget Jack, a Horse's Neck."

Although he hadn't a clue what a Horse's Neck was, he had an evocative picture in his mind of how it would taste and what it would look like. As time went by this image increased, until a picture of a Carmen Miranda hat - tropical fruit and prominent bananas, and a taste like a perfect Irish

Coffee formed in his mind; but first the bomb. He read the directions carefully, especially the bit about how far away one had to be for safety. Anyway there was a fuse which would burn for at least seven seconds, which gave the lighter an opportunity to be well out of distance. His plan was to light it in the snow about fifty paces from the protective wall of the Valluga lift station. At a rate of one step per second he would be well out of harm's way and around the corner of the lift station when the explosive went off.

Harley and the rest of the Americans were behind the wall as Jack uncovered the bomb. There were gasps of awe from the onlookers.

"Hey Jack, that's a serious piece of merchandise, the best of luck."

Jack shook hands with the group for effect, as he set off on that first fifty pace walk. Forty-eight, forty-nine, fifty at fifty paces he placed the bomb, fuse up, in the snow. He had made a small hole in the snow with his heel and, having planted the bomb, wrapped the snow around so that the blast would be absorbed. That done, he looked around at a clear frosty night like a general surveying the battlefield, drew a deep breath, took the matches out of his pocket, selected one, closed the box and prepared to light the match and the fuse. One more look at his watch to verify the time.

"Just right, 23.56; three minutes to go."

At exactly the agreed time minus one, he lit the match, the fuse, and when he was sure that it was indeed lit, turned on his heel and walked back to safety. Forty-eight, forty-nine, fifty, he walked at one pace per second; officers never run or show any sign of fear. At fifty he stepped behind the wall and listened for the explosion.

"Good ole Jack - the Horse's Neck controlled explosion."

They waited and listened and peeped around the corner and peeped and listened, but nothing.

"The fuse must have gone out; I'll go out and have a look. Shit! Louis's deadline for the explosion has passed."

"Be careful," whispered Harley, always the careful one.

Jack knew as he walked out for a second time that the eyes of the international world were upon him. 'Fuck, fuck, fuck,' with each step. 'At least the bloody thing hasn't moved.' There, as innocent as you like, sticking up like a rampant mickey in the snow, was the blue-and-gold, one-foot long cylinder. When he reached the spot the military mind clicked into action again and assessment was quickly followed by decisions, with no room for levity. The fuse had burned to the halfway mark.

'Must have gotten damp in the wardrobe.'

Immediate action: light another 'Friendly' and start the fuse burn again.

His hands were steady as he broke off the piece that had burned.

When the fuse started spitting sparks for the second time, Jack turned and strode back to cover; slightly quicker this time but still in control. His American support team welcomed him again and they all ducked and waited expectantly for the Irish explosion. Bang! No, not the bomb, it was Mc Loughlin doing his version of a bomb going off - still no sound. Jack wasn't embarrassed this time, he was angry and all protocol went out the window. With the cautionary cries of Harley trailing in his ears, he ran out to the spot where the bomb lay still inert.

'You're going up this time!'

What to do, though? He had reacted quickly because he couldn't stand to be within earshot of the questioning Americans. Suddenly he really was thrust into a national image issue.

'I must, for Caitlin Ni hUallachain's sake, get this bomb to explode, but how?'

Failure was out of the question, but the fuse had burned almost to the point of entry - no point lighting it again as before. Then, throwing all caution to the wind, he cast the final die. He opened the box of matches until all the red tops were visible and stuck what remained of the fuse on top of the matches. Then he lit the box and ran. His supporters were excited by the urgency he showed in getting out of the danger zone. This really is it, they thought - but no. The matches were seen to burn by Harley, but then died out in a cloud of black smoke, not even a cloud, more of a puff!

Jack looked defeat and total loss of prestige in the face and then he saw a possible out. It was the sound of singing that first attracted his attention. A large group of skiers had descended from Gampen in the dark, but lighting their way with torches. When they arrived at the chairlift station they planted the torches in the snow in a large circle. They sang a number of Austrian folk songs to the accompaniment of a lone accordion player standing in the centre of the illuminated circle.

"A ganze Weil habn heut g'sunga und g'spielt"

Leaving cautionary thought trailing in his wake, Jack ran to the circle of singers, slipped through the line from the dark side and, unnoticed, grabbed two torches and headed back to the reluctant bomb. At that moment he felt like a Kamikaze pilot on duty for the Emperor, no fear, just 'a man's gotta do what a man's gotta do'. The American observers, who had decided to decamp and head back to the bar, were suddenly galvanised by the sight of a heroic figure running from the site of the torch-lit singing, carrying two torches aloft. Harley thought, "Oh No!" but was too slow by far to do anything as he realised what was about to unfold.

Jack had it figured out before he reached the explosion site. Torches planted in the snow to form an 'x' and the bomb placed across the apex. This he did.

Blam! The explosion happened. Jack saw the bomb being introduced to the flames of the torches and the rest was a mixture of pain and mixed colours. Red, yellow, green, and blue; he was colour blind, but the colours rotated as his body did a back flip and landed.

From Harley's perspective things were the same but different. He saw Jack place the bomb across the torches and then the explosion. The body did a flip-flop worthy of an Olympic gymnast. The landing left a lot to be desired; no triumph with hand raised, just an inert pancake.

When he came to, the first thing Jack saw was the round face of a woman who appeared to be in control of the circle of faces gathered around him.

"Don't worry, you're all right, I'm the local nurse, how do you feel?"

He put his hands up to his face to see if it was still there. Just about, he knew from feeling that he had taken a hit. The nurse, on duty at the torchlight ski festival, reassured him. "There's nothing broken, as far as I can figure, and little bleeding. I presume you had eyebrows, well now you don't." Jack peed a little in his trousers, but held on and began a check of bodily movement.

"Jack, ole man, what a show, you deserve the Horse's Neck."

He was the centre of attention, all concerned about his welfare and thankfully no sign of the police. As he stumbled away from the explosion he marked the size of the hole left in the snow - impressive!

The remainder of the evening was somewhat blurred for Jack and when he awoke next morning the mirror revealed the excesses on two fronts. For once the demon drink played second fiddle and it was the nitro glycerine, dynamite or amatol or a combination of the explosives that did most damage to his face. The eyebrows weren't totally gone, but where visible they were sparse. Most of the space over his eyes was covered with patches of medical plaster. He experimented a bit by pulling off sections and found that the grazes and small cuts revealed were less offensive to the eye. When he was satisfied that he didn't look too grotesque, he plastered the lot with sun cream donated by the secretary in the lift office. She had hundreds of creams and lip gel picked up from under the chairs by the *piste* workers and deposited in the lost and found office.

'At least I have two eyes and a nose of sorts. Things could have been a lot worse.'

He didn't question the motivation for the whole exercise, but deep in his self-conscious a guilt gremlin lurked. A good morning's work and a day's skiing made a difference, so that by four o'clock his attention was refocused on getting his short swings right. On one occasion, however, the shock of seeing the large black patch on the snow near the Valluga cable lift jolted his system. He called to talk to Louis, to discover that he had fully recovered and was on his planned day trip on the non-prepared *piste* between Valluga and St Anton.

Louis and Avis met for breakfast immediately after mass. Avis didn't attend, but she was waiting in the front porch as he left the church. This had happened before, and Louis had come to accept that this was the way he and she should be. After all they were in love, he was doing God's work and somehow or another solutions would be found. Louis knew of priests who were married and who continued to say mass and work as priests. True, they had been married before and in some other cases, married priests from the Anglican Church had become Catholic and after some training had continued as priests in the Catholic Church. He also knew of married priests on the missions, but in those cases they were *incognito* and there was only a general knowledge of their existence. So why not he and Avis - he knew why, but hoped that the theologians would provide arguments based on scripture for priests to officially marry. And so he tried to avoid any break in his attitude to his work as a priest.

Any sense of regret, any misgivings about their love for one another, was swept under the carpet. He tried, and succeeded, in rationalising the pleasure he took from their being together, particularly in bed, and saw any creeping feeling of guilt as a weakness, and a disloyalty on his part towards Avis the perfect partner.

Avis was fully in love with the man Louis; his being a priest, rather than cause her problems, was a pleasurable risk. She believed him when he explained his attitude, and as long as he was happy, that was all that mattered. For her there was no tomorrow; every day was a part of the great now. For Avis, it was as if the world held its breath while they played out a sequence of loving.

There were no clouds in the sky as they headed off with Robert the ski instructor that morning. Again they stood together in the cable car as it made its way from gantry to gantry up to 2811m Valluga.

'Looking big and masterful while she was looking small;' the words of the 'Pride of Petravore' suited as he looked down on his love. Louis realised that responsibility went with his liaison and he would need to be masterful in more ways than one. What of the future? Avis snuggled in and wallowed in his aftershave and manly smells. All her bad experiences and memories had been truly exorcised in the past week.

The cabin hovered, steadied, and neatly docked. The man in charge spoke into the phone, flipped the door lever, and slid the door open. The passengers stepped out, their boots clumping on the well-worn timber floor. Using their skis as support they walked over the abyss below, highlighted by the swinging crows moving from crag to crag and no doubt feeding on the refuse from the mountain outpost. They headed out to the snow platform overlooking the descent from Valluga down to the Mattunjoch and via the Shindler Spitz to the Ulmer Hütte. Louis and Avis and the two others in their group had little to think about but focus on getting into their gear. The instructor, Robert, stood to one side talking in a strong local dialect to the lift attendant.

Louis and Avis had by now a well-rehearsed mode of getting boots and skis in order. They stood quietly by, with an occasional glance in the direction of the instructor, like gun dogs waiting for their master.

The pair with them was from London, Miriam and Tom. Miriam was a qualified doctor, a Harley Street specialist, in fact, and her husband Tom was in stocks and shares. Making money was his speciality, although judging from the way they spoke they had old money in the mattress!

Robert called everyone to heel and off he sped, ignoring the routes taken by the majority of other skiers. He skied out at a tangent, heading towards a large unmarked area of snow. When they arrived at the end of the long traverse, he explained that he was going to introduce them to the art of deep snow skiing.

"I know some of you have skied in deep snow before. Nevertheless, I'm going to ask everyone to follow my instructions exactly and repeat what I demonstrate. What is the most important part of short swings in deep snow?"

There were a few versions of what they thought it was.

"You have to sit back a bit so that the tips are above the snow," said Louis. He had heard some of the veteran skiers from the hotel discuss deep snow skiing and although he understood some fundamentals, the once or twice he had sought to put the concepts into practise, he went arse over tip!

"Good, but that's not all. This is the most beautiful part of skiing and as well as a number of individual skills, like weighting on flat skis on each turn and keeping the tips in the fall-line, and a good plant of course - the most important characteristic is courage. You mustn't panic or chicken out, because if you do you'll become a ball of snow and it's good night Vienna! Remember again, don't edge your skis on the turn, keep them flat."

"If he says 'concentrate on one thing' after that diatribe, I'll puke," whispered Avis.

"Okay, enough talking, I'll do twenty turns and when I call for the next person, get into position one at a time and take off."

Away he went, red cap tassel tossing from side to side as he danced down, leaving a perfect set of marks in the snow. He looked back admiringly at his trail and called for the first skier. They looked at one another and although Louis had sent a message to his moving parts, Miriam jumped in first, set her skis and away she went. Left, right, plant, left, right.

"By God she's good!"

"She should be, she skied for her finishing school in Switzerland in competitions."

"I want to go home," whispered Avis.

Louis moved a bit closer to her as a support signal while Tom edged forward, got into a heels high position, bent his knees and kicked off. He was steady, but not spectacular like his wife. He chickened out on one or two of the turns, but started again after a short traverse on each occasion. He got down, although his marks were rough and not joined like the first two. He finished, breathing heavily, and Louis could see his chest heaving and knew that this wasn't easy. He would have liked to set off just then, but he couldn't leave Avis alone on the slope. She set off showing the courage asked for by Robert in his opening spiel. About half way however, one ski took off on its own path and she had a split second decision to make. Either lift it and bring it back on path if possible, or join in its rush to freedom. She chose the latter and found herself making a wide curve back to where the rest were waiting. She had acted just in time; one second later and she was a ball of snow. Robert praised her immediate action.

"Most people in that situation don't take any definite action and their centre of gravity would move between their legs like a snow-plough. You took a quick decision and survived. Well done!"

Louis had a good start. He had an image of himself from the onlooker's eyes and thought that the first four or five turns were impressive, until he lost concentration and then it all went pear-shaped. His explosion was like a re-entry from space, bits of snow, ice, and skis dancing in the sky. Shit! Feck! God! Hell! Each time he landed, mostly on his back, the breath was forced from his lungs and he tried to keep control by mouthing words. His vocabulary wasn't wide enough to impress the onlookers, but what he lost in verbal presentation was more than compensated for by his physical twists and turns.

Poor Avis was in bits. Louis stopped halfway down and they all started sidestepping up to him to help. By the time they got there, Robert first, Louis had sorted out which part was which and was making a snow platform to put the skis on again. Robert thought it wise not to try to analyse the part of his technique that had let him down, but concentrated instead on getting him organised to continue. Louis could see that Avis was making heavy weather of sidestepping up.

"I'm okay, Avis, don't come any further, I'll be down in a tick."

The rest of those slogging their way upwards gratefully turned around and skied back to the bottom of the slope. Conversation continued as normal between them, but Avis waited at the halfway point to talk to Louis.

"Are you sure you're all right?"

Louis was disgusted with his performance, particularly in front of Avis. It was a new experience for him, having someone care for him; it was a support, yes, but also a pressure. Without her there, the fall was just a fall.

That little episode over, the party set off to join the main run down to the Ulmer Hütte at 2,288 metres above sea level. By this stage they had sorted out who was who in skiing terms. As well as reacting to the directions of the leader they each supported one another.

"Try that way, it's a nice run down the gully."

"The snow is very heavy over there, don't bother turning 'til you get onto the ridge."

They had lunch in the Ulmer Hütte - poor Louis had downed a glass of white before he felt able to communicate. The hut was warm, heated by a boiler stove in the centre of the room and soon they all felt relaxed and comfortable. Some of the talk was about the morning's ski, but gradually they chatted about their homes and their work. Miriam explained that she and Tom lived in the Channel Islands, but ran their business and lived in Harley Street for most of the year. Louis didn't say much, apart from the fact that he was Irish and living in Yorkshire. He was interested in why Miriam and Tom lived in the Channel Islands but worked in London.

"Well, we used to live in Sussex with Daddy. Mummy had died earlier and we moved in with him. He was very concerned that when he died, the British Government would tax his property and bank account at a very high rate. Literally, this went between him and his sleep so, believe it or not, we decided, for his peace of mind mostly, to move lock, stock and barrel to the Channel Islands, where taxes were almost nil. One snag however, Daddy had to live for three years before the new tax rate would click in. Will I continue?"

"You can hardly stop now," said Tom. Louis, Avis, and Robert nodded furiously.

"Well," said Miriam, taking a large breath and registering with each set of eyes. "Believe it or not, but Daddy, who wasn't well from the beginning of the move to the Islands, died before the third year was complete. You can imagine our dilemma. I mean the whole bloody exercise was to ensure that Daddy's small fortune, earned by the sweat of his brow, wasn't forfeit to the Crown. Not that I have anything against the Crown mind you, but poor Daddy had so wished that we should benefit from his inheritance. I was his only daughter, only child, for that matter."

"Anyway," she said, and from her demeanour her onlookers knew that this was the climax of the story. "We decided to put Daddy in the deep freeze and leave him there until the three years was up."

"But was that possible, would the doctor certifying the death not know that he had been frozen?"

"Maybe so, but that's where we tried to be clever. I had a friend a doctor with whom I had worked in the Maudlsey in London for a while. He, like us, had moved to Jersey and was treating Daddy in his capacity as a general practitioner."

"So!" She drew a deep breath and eyed her rapt audience. "We arranged that he would certify Daddy dead by natural causes, but not date or sign the certificate until four months later, at the end of the three-year term. And so Daddy would have served his term and we would be 'in the money'!"

She paused again and by this time everyone was agog.

"So you got the money and now you live in the Channel Islands?"

"Well, not exactly. It was very funny. Whenever we had friends in, and I used Daddy's freezer as an overflow, I chatted with him when taking out a bag of frozen peas or whatever."

"You'll never guess, Daddy, who's coming. That ole French bat that you hate! She would be amazed if she knew you were here, instead of in the hospital in London."

"I digress. You'll never guess what happened then." All eyes were fixed on Miriam. "The doctor friend with whom we had made the arrangement died before the four months were up."

"Died?" Almost everyone mouthed the 'D' word.

"Yes, it's not that unusual, he died."

"But how did you manage?" Even confessional hardened Louis was sucked in at this stage.

"Well, there wasn't much we could do except defreeze Daddy and call in another doctor. Because he hadn't treated him for an illness, he had to carry out a post-mortem. Anyway, that done, the doctor returned one evening to give us the result. I'll never forget the moment."

"I'll sign the certificate," he said, "your father died of old age; there is no other sign of disease except what's in his medical history. One thing strikes me as strange, however," at this stage he paused dramatically at the door just before his departure, "how could he have fresh strawberries in his stomach at this time of year?"

The story ended there and Louis and the rest were left hanging, wondering was the whole story a fabrication, or was it true in part but with embellishments.

After lunch the pace of skiing increased and it took concentration and effort on the part of the weaker skiers to keep with the group. At about five o'clock Robert announced one more run down without pause to St Anton. They were given the opportunity to drop out, but nobody did.

Avis was looking forward to Louis's promised visit to her hotel room. She looked at his handsome good looks and promised herself and him, an enjoyable but sometimes torrid evening. Louis looked at her and felt a great sense of pride, tinged with the anticipation. Was it possible…and yet it had to be? Avis had become a part of his very being. He flushed a bit as he remembered the words of the psalm he had read that morning after mass.

'But the Lord sits enthroned forever. He has set up his throne for judgment; he will judge the world with justice, he will judge the peoples with his truth.'

'I should know what the truth is,' he thought, 'surely it wouldn't be true justice to desert her now after all she'd been through?' He realised, however, that dipping in this font of human love had perhaps made it difficult for him to see the truth.

The group took off as a team, yet each one serving an inner instinct. Skiing and its complexities overcame any thoughts they had about life and living. The beauty of the environment and the needs of a sound skiing technique were in themselves sufficient to concentrate the mind, and provide the satisfaction they all sought.

At one point Avis sidled up to Louis.

"Louis, this is the most beautiful moment of my life. Thank you for making my life worth living."

The group, led by Robert the *skilehrer*, were near the end of their day. The final *schuss* took them past the path around the Steisbachtal that had such memories for Jack and Louis. Just as they entered the gully a loud crack rang out. The sound was like a cannon shot, a bit like the start of a boat race. Louis was at the back of the group and he saw that suddenly their group had become part of a river of snow and pine trees. It was as quick as that.

The avalanche had started in a gully further up the valley and by the time it had funnelled into the path on which their group were skiing, it had eaten about a mile of countryside and now consisted of a fast-flowing river of slabs of ice, snow, trees, and even a few mountain huts. Louis was at the back of the avalanche enveloping his group, and he saw Avis floating down in front of him like a scarlet speck of flotsam in a boiling sea of confusion.

Before he himself was snatched into the maelstrom, he got a glimpse of her face and a mouth, which seemed to say, "Louis!" He then tried to sort of swim towards where she had disappeared, and succeeded to some degree. Just as he reached the spot where she had been eaten up by the avalanche, a large tree trunk caught his body and swept him downwards. Strange as it may seem, he did manage to reach her, at least the red jacket tumbling just within reach was hers. Suddenly the monster ground to a halt with just an occasional settling growl.

Louis had carried out a number of immediate actions as soon as he saw the arm of the avalanche reach up sideways in the gully to snatch him. He had reached down quickly and pushed forward the binding levers thus releasing his feet from the skis. When he stopped moving he had one hand and his legs free to move and kick clear of the rubble that surrounded him. He hadn't as yet made enough space even to turn his head fully, but he had some movement and as far as he knew nothing was broken, although he had a sharp pain in his left leg and his head hurt.

"Avis, Avis, can you hear me?" In the tumultuous final settling of the avalanche he had done his best to close the distance between himself and where he had seen Avis's red jacket disappear. She was almost within touching distance when he and she were swallowed up by another wave of the avalanche.

No sound, but the effort to call out made him realise that if he was to continue breathing he needed access to air. He guessed that up was in a particular direction. Looking that way it was slightly brighter and he raised his free hand and poked into a second cavity. Beside his hand he saw a piece of pine branch, which he figured would be a help to poke through to the surface, if that were possible. He took hold of the stick and pushed and pulled. At first he couldn't anchor his body for the effort needed, and then he realised how necessary it was that he had opened the binding and freed himself from the skis. If he had left them in position, part of his foot or leg would be wherever the skis were now; the pain in his left knee was however increasing. Using his right foot to form a base, he began to poke upwards and eventually broke through. He couldn't free his body from the grip of the snow and ice, but at least he could now breathe freely.

He also tried to make a way in the direction he figured Avis lay. He used the pine branch to poke through the snow and rubble. He felt something warm like a wound and blood as he spread his left hand to provide support. "Oh no Jesus please," Louis realised that he even now feared the worst and was ashamed of his lack of confidence and then he wriggled his fingers and felt the surrounds. It was the fur of some dead animal perhaps. He kept working and calling, making progress but hearing no response. 'What about the others? They were further down. The village will be setting up a rescue but in the dark?'

'If I am to be judged,' he thought, 'I want it to be as part of our love, our being'. He had a vision of the sterile love for a God that had controlled his life until he met her. Avis had said that Eternity was the only thing in which she believed. 'Not just a set of smart words,' he thought. 'I want to be a part of her Eternity.'

He shook himself into action, accepting that the cold was numbing his senses; only then realising that cold was a serious factor to be taken into consideration. 'I want to survive, but without Avis?' Somehow he managed to stop the mind games associated with Avis, and existence with and without her. Galvanised into action, he used all his physical strength to clear a way to his left where he figured Avis lay. He picked his way with care in order to avoid causing a collapse. As he cleared a path, like deadheading in a sea of floribunda, he eventually touched a hand and realised that it must be her.

Avis felt an influence outside her world of pain and silence. When her slide to a halt in the grinding chaos happened, she endured wave after wave of nauseous pain. The only movement she could manage as a test of physical competence, apart from the continued beating of her heart, was finger movement with her right hand. She had sent cerebral messages along other nerve tracts but to no end. Her dribbles eventually melted the snow around her mouth and she moved her lips in prayer, for her friends and for Louis.

'Oh God, Louis is yours, we were only ships in the night and I love him, but he's really yours. Please don't let him die. Don't punish him because of me.'

The mention of the word die was another shock to her already battered system and then she felt a touch to her only moving parts, her right fingers. She thought she was mistaken - but there it was again!

The tips of the fingers touched and there was instant recognition.

"I love you, Louis."

"I love you, Avis."

J ack was in the Bahnhof when he got the call.

"All *Pistenhelfers* are wanted immediately for avalanche duty." The Ski Club of Great Britain members were to the fore, although few of them worked on the slopes. This was an 'all hands to the pumps' call. Jack ran to the service station and joined a stream of others. Already a trailer loaded with sets of lights and other equipment was pulling out towards the valley high above the Vallugabahn lift station.

"Get into this sledge quickly," shouted Wolfgang, the leader of the rescue team responsible for a probe search of the avalanche area. Their job would be to walk shoulder to shoulder up the valley with two metre long steel poles, which would be used to probe into the snow in the hope that avalanche victims would be detected and dug out. The police arrived in their own transport with the all important Alsatian search dogs. The dogs barked excitedly and pulled on their leads.

Above all, they were told speed was of the essence.

"The people under the avalanche, and as far as we know there are five, may only have a very short time to live - if they are alive - unless we act quickly. Find them and dig them out!"

The rescuers loaded in a variety of transport, including horses and tractors, made their way to the avalanche site. As they passed the house of Klaus and Heidi, Jack's group pulled in and Klaus jumped on to the trailer.

"My Frau and I have arranged to feed the relief effort. Monika will have refreshments ready when we require it. All we have to do is send a detail down to collect it."

Wolfgang nodded his head in acceptance and Jack spoke to Heidi's father as they made their way upwards. It seemed that an avalanche was a regular feature of life in their part of the Alps and it was normal for everyone to join in the search in a form best suited to their position. The doctor, the police, and the workers all became part of the life saving services and were happy to do so.

"Your friend Father Louis is one of this group?"

In the back of Jack's mind lurked the possibility that the avalanche had in fact taken Louis's group, but this was his first definite challenge in this regard. Hearing that Robert was the leader of the group confirmed that Louis was one of the people they were seeking under the snow.

When the probers got to the avalanche site, the lights exposed the devastation that was the avalanche. For about a half-mile the gully was full of broken slabs of frozen snow, splintered pine trees, and parts of mountain huts. Rocks and soil oozed like streaks of dark chocolate from its innards. 'Louis and Avis hadn't as yet returned from their deep snow outing in this area. Could the avalanche have hit them?' It was cold and the thought chilled Jack to his marrow. The excitement of the rescue project was no longer an adventure, as the cold acceptance that his friend Louis could be a victim consumed his mind and body.

It didn't seem possible that anyone could survive this monster and yet even before they could start probing, the dogs had identified the smell of humans near the surface. With the efficiency of well-practised experts, a group surrounded the dog and began to clear the space while they frantically clawed at the snow, barking furiously.

"Line up right to left and take your signals from me."

Jack was shocked back into cold reality and action by the call of the rescue leader.

Wolfgang got straight down to the main job, although most were riveted on the possibility of getting someone out where the dog were scratching. Waving a torch as a signal, he marshalled his team over the complete width of the avalanche, and guided them to move forward one step at a time and slide the thin steel poles down between their feet until it sank to the bottom, or touched some obstacle. If it did stop, the rescuers were instructed to keep searching for the type of resistance a body would provide and slide past obstacles like trees or rocks. The probes were strong enough to push through slabs of frozen snow and eventually the *Pistenhelfers*, Jack included, became expert at identifying the type of object they had encountered.

"Wolfgang, Wolfgang, I've hit something."

Just as the person discovered by the dog was lifted clear and on to the waiting stretcher, one of the *Pistenhelfers* held one arm high in the prescribed manner and shouted in excitement.

The person on the stretcher was a male, an English man according to his papers. He was dead; his chest cage had been crushed to a pulp and half his head was missing; brain matter oozed on to the stretcher and left a trail in the snow.

As the helpers rushed to the new discovery, that stretcher was carried away and placed on the sledge used to take injured skiers down from the mountain. The local workers were relieved that the body was not that of the ski instructor. His mother and father were standing apart at the back of the relief effort, being comforted by other members of their family. Everyone now knew that Robert's group were involved - likewise Jack knew that Louis was probably covered by the avalanche.

The rest of the group was signalled to move forward. It was getting darker outside the perimeter of the lights and all knew that it was only minutes, even less, that made saving the remainder a possibility. Jack felt a chill stab of fear run through his system as he shuffled forward in line in the semi dark, probing again and again, seeking to find, but hoping against hope that Louis would not be found in a similar state to the mangled Englishman.

The second person was alive. It was Miriam the English storyteller, who had been trapped in a cavity below a giant slab of ice. As she was lifted out she cried for Tom, her husband, and nobody had the courage to tell her that he was dead. She was led away to the adapted hospital in the village, where the distraught lady received the tragic news.

Robert the ski instructor was taken out badly injured, but alive. It was obvious that he would never ski again; that is, on two legs. His parents were happy to have him alive to bring home.

And that left two, Louis and Avis. On and on they went, probe, move forward, stop, check the alignment, probe and move forward again. The nearness of the probes on the surface made it seem impossible that anyone could be missed, but Jack was aware of the needle and haystack relationship between their efforts and those in the grips of the avalanche. There were so many obstacles, not alone on the surface but also beneath. Once or twice Jack's heart jumped into his mouth as his probe caught, a few exploratory jabs and eventually broke through - nothing! There were about ten signalled moves forward when a hand went up and the support team moved to that point with the dogs. They dug the spot and the dogs were let into the hole again. They still showed an interest and the soft top of the probe still indicated a body or something like it. One more session of digging and out it came - a dead fox!

Louis heard the noise, the dogs barking, and an odd shout. Avis had stopped talking and he wasn't sure that he wanted to be rescued. Right next to his left arm it happened. He saw the fox being pulled out, but the movement upset the snow around that area and there was a partial collapse, pinning him more firmly under the debris than before. He shouted, but his voice seemed to stall in the area around him. He began to doubt his mind, and he wondered if he was really shouting. The wound in his head, which had been but a trickle of blood, now grew in intensity and he could feel the blood strongly running down his back.

On the surface there was great disappointment as the fox was dragged clear.

"I could have sworn…"

Avis also heard the sounds but her reaction was that of a flickering candle waiting to be extinguished. She was at peace now and slowly her eyes began to close. Louis, however, knew what had happened and realised that help was close by. He took the stick and tried to push the tip above the surface.

'Surely they'll see the movement.'

The fact was that many twigs were moving. In the increasing wind and snow, they were being whipped up to join the snow already beginning to fall. On and on the workers went and Jack was shocked to see that there was only about 200 yards of surface to be investigated.

"What happens when we get to the end?"

"Turn around and start down again, we keep going until the two are found; at least until the leaders call off the search and that could be at first light tomorrow. Their chances of surviving after that are slight to nil."

He continued moving with the group and eventually they reached the apparent end and turned around. A sledge loaded with food and drink was pulled into the centre of the work group and, much to Jack's consternation, they all downed tools and started to eat. He didn't want to stop, but was assured by Wolfgang that a short break for food was normal practice and an essential part of keeping the team's senses, touch, smell and sight, in top condition; the time was also normally used by the rescue managers to assess and plan. Reassured somewhat, but in conflict with their early principle that speed was of the essence, he dived in with the rest.

When they started again, Jack took a renewed and more intense interest in the work of the probe. He saw himself as an extension of this eye that he was pushing into the bowels of the avalanche. It was a growling beast and with each push of the probe he pierced its interior in search of his friends.

On the surface, the detached nature of the snow covering, and the 'tumbleweed' type of flotsam that blew across it, nearly succeeded in blinding his mind to the serious workings of the steel tips spread right across and sinking to about five feet every two feet. He remained in focus, however, and took pleasure in sending each probe deep into the workings of this terror; finger tips tingling at the prospect of it being stopped by a human mass.

"I think I see something moving."

Just for a second Jack had lifted his head from the immediate task of lifting and striking again. His eyes had detected, about twenty feet ahead, something blue waving on the surface. Louis had at last managed to fix his glove to the piece of stick and force it through his air hole. Luckily, Jack had lifted his eyes, just as with a superhuman effort Louis had pushed it clear of the surface. Jack ran forward to the spot and pulled at the stick, which now protruded clearly from the snow.

"Louis, are you there?"

He heard a muffled sound that was like music to his ears. Scratching away at the surface he managed to widen the hole, looked down and saw the face of his friend far below. At that point the experts arrived and made a careful study of the layers that supported the area around where Louis lay buried. Gently they removed the rubble from about six feet wide around the spot, and gradually made their way safely down to him. Jack helped, but the avalanche team kept him back. The paramedics hovered with their medicines and equipment, ready to move in and administer as soon as there was space for them. Louis was speaking, but the words were a mumble, as bits of snow kept falling down. As soon as a worker reached him and cleared his face, he gave vent to the message that was welling up inside him.

"Avis is just over there. She's badly injured I think. Please help her."

And so one group remained to give first aid to the injured and almost incoherent priest, and the others set about identifying where the other person was, if there was another person. It didn't take much looking to reveal what he had been talking about. She was there all right. Having cleared the way above her they could see that she was either unconscious or dead. Some timber fragment appeared to have pierced her lower body and it was with extreme care that they probed further down the length of her body. Below the left knee there was nothing. The medics gave her pain-killing injections as she was uncovered. And at one point her eyes opened.

Louis was being patched up on one side; although he protested, the medics insisted in splinting his left tibia and bandaging his head. He continuously asked about Avis, and eventually he was guided to the hole where she was being treated. Before he reached the point, however, Dr Victor Flunger told him of the predicament.

"She's alive but just. She's held down by a piece of timber, which if removed will kill her and if we don't try, she will die here in the snow. Unfortunately, she has become conscious. I say unfortunately; although we have reduced the pain, the next few minutes will be excruciating for her. That's not the worst part; no matter what we do she'll probably die. You're a priest and probably have a more important role here than we do..."

Louis's conflict of emotions was intense. He loved this woman and yet he was expected to perform the last rites in this hole in the snow. He stepped down the path created by rescuers in the hole where she was. She broke his heart with her first glance. She must have known that it was all over and looked at him like an injured collie dog about to be put down.

"Hello Avis sweetheart," Louis whispered.

The poignancy of Louis's simple greeting must have reached her, because a tear began its long journey down her cheek.

She wished to say many things, but knew that she had little time and strength. Her few words tore into Louis's consciousness. They were intended as a tender statement of her belief in Eternity - the Eternity they had discussed just two weeks before.

"Louis, I will always love you!"

That was all there was between them. From that point Louis reverted to his role as priest and prepared her to meet her God.

"Dominus qui liberat te á peccatis te salvet et suscitet. Amen."

Jack and the others stood in a circle around Avis in her final moments. The lanterns in the hole cast a glow that lit the immediate scene and bathed the faces of some of the group of onlookers, Caravaggio like. More than onlookers really because each knew what was happening, although few, if any, understood the relationship that existed between Avis and Louis.

Louis became the lover one last time. He leaned forward and kissed her lightly on the lips.

"Good-bye Avis - until we meet again."

The past two weeks had been a total lifetime for Louis. He had arrived for the holiday in a peculiar frame of mind, and Avis had opened the door to the possibilities of a new life. The young couple in Canada had made a strong impression on him, but Avis was the catalyst that facilitated his next step. And now! A return to the celibate, rigid life of a priest seemed more like a sentence than a calling. He could still hear her, feel her, and smell her womanliness, and wished that he also had been taken. With her gone and the dent she had delivered to his position as a priest, he was placed him in psychological freefall. If he left the priesthood, which he thought of doing because of his commitment to Avis, where would he find a life so coherent and comprehensive? He questioned other aspects of his faith and shuddered at the prospect of becoming the 'a la carte' Catholic that he had so often criticised.

"You must get your leg properly treated," said a concerned Dr Flunger to Louis, following the transportation of Avis's body to the mortuary in St Anton. "I'm sure that you have an ankle problem, but judging from your reaction to weight bearing on that side I believe that an X-ray and treatment in a hospital is essential." Louis protested vigorously. He knew that a nun from America was on her way to collect Avis's body and that the transference would take place after the mass ceremony in St Anton, and he wanted to be with Avis until she was taken away for burial in New York. He had plans for the mass ceremony in St Anton, in which he hoped to be the main celebrant and thus bid her good bye in this world.

In fact Louis became more of an invalid as the night wore on, and he was barely aware of events as he was transported by ambulance to Innsbruck Hospital. His leg was broken, but what caused him to be placed in intensive care was the irregularity of his heartbeat and his raised blood pressure. For the next two days he was on heavy medication and on the third day when Jack visited, he appeared okay and was in a recovery ward. He heard then of the transference of Avis to the airport and thence to Amsterdam and New York. Jack tried to give him some detail, but it wasn't the same Louis, and Jack confined his conversation to return plans.

Jack had a loose end that needed attention. He had met Jane the film starlet from the Elstree Studios in Boreham Wood, London. They had agreed to meet again in St Anton but with one thing and another that hadn't happened. Jane was a lovely natural girl and when she met Jack they had a connection, in that Jack's brother had pretended that Jane was his partner at a dance in the Gresham Hotel. She was in Dublin to promote Rank Films and had signed photographs for everyone that evening including Jack's brother. 'What a coincidence that we should meet like this so soon afterwards,' thought Jack.

Before leaving St Anton Jack made an arrangement to meet Jane in Dublin at another planned promotional event. He was prepared to follow wherever this link with the film world led - perhaps!

As Jack and Louis boarded the train at the end of the holiday in St Anton am Arlberg, much had changed in their lives. Jack had had a taste of adventure in an environment very different from the Curragh of Kildare. The hole in the snow, still visible, reminded him of his contacts with the American pilots, and of course there was Heidi, Leni Riefenstahl and the Inghams's girls.

Louis had stepped over the brink, and even though Avis had died, he was still on the other side and very vulnerable. 'Was all this part of the plan and what is the message for me?' Louis was open and wounded and needed closure from his St Anton experiences.

"**Y**es, we have a long weekend and I could take a day's special leave. I'd be there by Saturday morning - is that okay?"

Jane Thornly had invited Jack to come to the Elstree film studios in Boreham Wood, London. She'd played many small parts in Rank films and had been invited to play the female lead with John Gregson in an Irish film called 'Rooney O'. Parts were to be shot in Dublin and for that, co-operation with a range of Irish people and organisations was required. Croke Park was to be used in a hurling scene and the GAA had already given their permission. The film director felt that Jack could help in other support areas and Jane had convinced him that Jack would suit the bit part of an Irish man in a pub scene.

He just missed sending an officer's mess waiter and a laden tray into the air as he rushed back to his place at the dinner table. For about two minutes Jack resisted telling the other officers about his offer, but it was too much to hold and, with some embellishments, he outlined how this entrée into the film world had happened. Some listened and viewed the project as another harebrained idea, which would lead nowhere. There were others who couldn't resist slight pangs of jealousy, while some of his friends were just as excited as Jack and promised to cover for him if there was any overlap in time.

"Jesus, imagine getting out of here and not alone that, but - a film star!"

There was however a lot of planning to be done; debts paid and an arrangement about duties, but as time has a habit of doing, it went by, and on the Friday in question Lieutenant Jack Muldoon set off for London.

Jane met him at Waterloo railway station. She drove a Mini and with Jack ensconced they sped through the London traffic north to Boreham Wood and Elstree Studios. Once through the gates reality ended - this was the Rank centre of make-believe and sets of all description abounded.

"See over there," whispered Jane. It was the mighty figure of Errol Flynn standing in front of a set, chatting to a group of young women.

"It's time for his trip to the Red Lion over the road - perhaps we can join them later."

Jack nodded; mostly his thoughts were about the tales he would have to tell on his return to the Curragh. He had not achieved a metamorphosis, and half his mind was still with his army friends despite the attentions of the beautiful creature beside him. And yet the few days in St Anton had created a bond, and helped to make him feel at ease in this strange environment, supported by her friendship.

"Mr Stifield, this is Jack Muldoon, the Irish man I was telling you about. He is prepared to help us on location and, as you suggested, he could play a part. He has done some work in Ireland in advertising and is a member of Actors' Equity over there."

Jack could see that some preparatory work had been done on his behalf and all he had to do was agree, and stay with it when filming started.

"We have taken Ardmore near Bray for the period and we'll be shooting on location some of the time. I'd like you to have a word with our locations manager as soon as you get a chance; you may be able to help him."

Jack wasn't sure whether or not he should be pleased. He was out of his normal environment by a long chalk, yet there was a relationship between the film outfit and army practices. Their world was theatre and his army was something of the same, in that they were preparing for a war with God knows whom. He recognised the elements of play that existed in both. One was pure theatre and the other was theatre but as yet not recognised.

The people Jack met, including Jane and stars like Errol Flynn, were being paid megabucks to do what they did and yet the link between work and play for them was fragile. Although their work was play of sorts, they also felt a need to play furiously outside the theatre. Jack was either a plaything of Jane's or perhaps part of her effort to link with the real world.

Luckily, the weekend for Jack seemed easily routed into areas of competence with which he was happy. Drinking in the Red Lion in Elstree wasn't a challenge, although Errol Flynn did set a standard hard to equal. He never left the film part really and his swashbuckling approach to drinking left the rest of the company in his wake. He had an account in the pub, a bit like the mess, Jack thought; but in this case the studio paid the bill. He frequently involved the public bar by sticking his head around the partition and inviting one and all to join him. On this occasion Jack recognised a group of Irish, John Laing building workers, who had already imbibed and were only too delighted to join the well heeled and articulate on the other side of the social fence.

"Oh Mary this London's a wonderful sight,
With the people here working by day and by night.
They don't grow potatoes nor barley nor wheat,
But there's gangs of them digging for gold in the street.
At least when I asked them that's what I was told,
So I just took a hand in this digging for gold.
But for all that I found there I might as well be,
Where the mountains of Mourne sweep down to the sea."

Flynn joined in with gusto, as did everyone else, especially the Irish workers who managed a tear or two as part of the exercise. After all, they were away from their homes in Mayo or Cavan or wherever, and as the years rolled on they recognised that they were exiled. Jack felt an affinity with them, but mostly he was ashamed that while he was living in comfort in the Irish State, they would probably remain exiled.

There was much drink consumed by all, including Jack, and later Jane tucked him into bed - she had a room made available close to her apartment where she could 'keep an eye on him'.

Next morning, Saturday, he was fully involved as an extra in the film. He had three parts in crowd scenes and each was rehearsed a number of times. He didn't know the whole story as yet and the bits and pieces he saw appeared very disjointed. He had discussions with the locations manager and it was agreed that he would seek support from Army Headquarters to get some recruits or soldiers participate in the crowd scenes.

He really enjoyed himself and in double quick time the weekend came to a close. He hadn't seen much of Jane because she was fully involved with John Gregson in rehearsals.

On their way to Paddington she apologised.

"Not at all, I enjoyed myself very much - what an experience! You'll be coming over to Ireland soon I suppose?"

"Yes of course, I'm attending a film festival in Dublin in two weeks' time. Maybe we could meet then?" She crunched the gears of the Mini as she looked in his direction and vigorously pushed the gear stick home.

Back in Ireland Jack went about clearing his commitments for the film production. He touched base with Camp Headquarters and handed over the official letters from the director in Elstree. Work in the Army for Jack consisted of both instruction and administration in the Army School of Physical Culture. The British had left a school of Physical Training, but the first Irish Minister of Defence had changed the name to Physical Culture in deference to a friend who happened to be Czech ambassador and an advocate of the Sokol System of Czechoslovakia.

A Standard PT course had just begun consisting of twenty-five students - twenty NCOs and five officers. The aim of the twenty-two-week course was to train physical training instructors for the various units around the Army. Thus, the course consisted of personnel from a variety of units: Cavalry, Infantry, Signals, Artillery, the Air Corps, and the Navy. Initially the course members would socialise mostly with others from their own unit or corps, but as the days passed and an involvement in Olympic gymnastics, track and field athletics, swimming and lifesaving, and a variety of military activities like the obstacle course, the course members became a very close-knit unit regardless of rank or unit specialisation. This was one of the few Army courses where non-commissioned and commissioned ranks worked together on an equal footing. Jack lectured on management and coaching in sport and taught some practical courses.

It was their function also to run the annual 'All-Army Athletic Championships' and preparation for this was at the initial stages.

Although Jack loved his work and the life associated with sport in the Army, his head had been turned by the trip to Elstree and by Jane. After all, she was a film star; living in the Curragh didn't seem to compete. Her visit in a couple of weeks' time was anticipated and the damaged insurance policy was revisited.

'I'll need a car for starters, and then the 'civvies' clothes will have to be right.'

His plan was based on a two-pronged attack. Firstly, the one-pound dinner dance in the airport at Collinstown airport and secondly, a visit to the Curragh and a meal in one of the messes. They had a visitor's room in McDonagh Mess, so she could stay there overnight. All the details had been attended to by the time of Jane's arrival, even the film arrangements. The army was very helpful and following Jack's intervention in the Curragh Camp Headquarters, the army PRO officer in GHQ, Parkgate Street, took a personal interest in the project.

Most decisions at top level in the army really did go to the top, including clearance by civil servants. One would have thought that operations personnel at Camp, or at least at General Headquarters level, would have had enough clout to take responsibility for issues such as what Jack sought, but in the Irish Army everything involving civilian issues had to get top level clearance.

J ane was staying in the Gresham Hotel and by the time Jack met her she had completed her work for the studio. They embraced in the foyer of the hotel and he outlined the programme for the weekend. He had hired a car. The car hire firm didn't pay much attention to his credentials, all they wanted was the money, seven pounds for the three days.

Jane was as excited as he about going to the dinner dance. Jack hadn't been to many upper crust civilian dances before, and was looking forward to another step into a world devoid of soldier waiters, orderlies, and non-'sir' types. He had a double whammy in mind; Jane would be his escort at the airport and, more importantly, she would be on show in the Curragh. They both changed in her room in the hotel and when she stepped out of the bathroom in her pink wraparound dress she was stunning! The creation was extravagant but Jane wore it with great simplicity, perched as she was on her high-heeled court shoes. As they sped out to the airport, Jack was very happy and wished he could share this moment with his friends and particularly with Louis. He had been on the phone to him shortly after St Anton and he appeared to be surviving - just.

He parked in Collinstown and they made their way up the winding staircase to the restaurant. Jane attracted a lot of attention from males at other tables and Jack accepted that as par for the course and enjoyed the attention she got.

"You put your right hand in, your right hand out,
Your right hand in and you shake it all about.
You do the Hokey Pokey and you turn around
That's what it's all about."

They buck-leaped their way through the 'Hokey Pokey', down the room, out on the balcony, in and down the stairs and up again. Jane's face was flushed and her eyes bright as she and Jack Muldoon danced to the traditional last dance music.

'Good night sweetheart, see you in the morning.'

Jane had friends in Foxrock in south Dublin who were anxious to entertain her. A party had been arranged in their house, and as they headed across the city they were way behind time. She had explained to them that she was on her way to the Curragh and about the dinner dance, but that she would call about ten-thirty. It was now eleven-thirty. 'That's not so bad,' thought Jack. They were expected in the Curragh at twelve thirty and they would no doubt be late for that also.

A few drinks at the party, a chat to the hosts and up and away. Jane had changed into 'something more comfortable', which for her was almost always a polo neck of some sort and jeans. She giggled like a schoolgirl on a school outing as she slipped into the passenger seat and shouted goodbyes through the car window. Down the canal and out on the Naas road; the last bus to Kildare was parked outside the Red Cow Inn. This was the regular retreat mode for soldiers of all ranks, escaping the civilian regime en route for the Curragh or the Artillery Barracks in Kildare. It always stopped at the Red Cow Inn for refreshments for *bone fide* customers. Jack couldn't resist a quick visit, so he and Jane sidled in through the smoke and bodies and shouted an order over the heads of a few at the counter. To know the barman's name is almost essential if you are to get a drink in an Irish bar at all, at all, at all.

"A pint and a G and T, Jimmie, please."

The drinks were passed back.

"How's she cutting, Sir."

The clients at the bar were from the camp and Jack was recognised by almost all. He introduced Jane around.

"Excuse me miss, but didn't I see you in a film in the camp recently?"

"Perhaps, what was the name of the film?"

The cat was out of the bag and in quick time Jane and a gaggle of military males were engaged in conversation. One or two knew their films and were able to quote chapter and verse - Jack of course basked in the reflected glory.

The car wheezed a bit before it started, but eventually they were on their way again, having made a call to the mess to explain that there had been a slight delay. It happened near Johnstown. Suddenly the car began to chug and at the hill beyond the Johnstown Inn, which was closed, the engine gave up the ghost. It was long after midnight and before Jack could think, the Kildare bus passed, leaving a cloud of blue smoke and the image of a row of faces. Jack stepped out of the car and tried to look efficient as he opened the bonnet and peered in. There were some streetlights outside the building on the left-hand side of the road. He peered at the building for a second and saw that it was a garage, but of course long closed.

Back to the engine and on first glance he could see that there were no major wires adrift. That's about all he could handle and he had hoped that a significant wire would have said, 'Please put me back in my place at the battery' or whatever - but no, everything appeared pristine except for the normal heat arising from the cylinders. Jane was no pressure and spent her time having a look around the village. Time passed and Jack, in the two hours they spent there, fussed around, knocked a few doors to try and get to a phone, but without success. Just as despair was about to set in, he saw a milk van come down the road and stop at a shop in the village.

"Where is your next stop and could you give us a lift?"

The milkman was doing his early rounds and his next stop was Mrs Lawlor's hotel in the countryside nearby. In they got and jammed close in the cab with the driver; Jane and Jack sang their way to Lawlor's 'Osberstown House Hotel'.

The next day was Sunday. Jack wondered where he would get mass, and of course there was the question of the car. He had been in touch with his friends in the Curragh the night before and had acquainted them of his plight. He hoped that one of the Cavalry lads, who knew all about cars, would come to his aid. Sunday being what it was - matches away and other social events - the possibility of aid coming his way was slim to slight. He needn't have worried however. Just as he stepped out of the front door of the hotel, his hired car crunched into the gravel forecourt driven by Mick Flynn and alongside, Bernard Smith of the Cavalry Corps.

"Jesus! Mick, how did you manage - without the keys?"

"Keep the faith baby. When the convenience of a film star is in question the impossible is not a barrier to the Cavalry Corps." Mick Flynn was proud of his army corps.

"Feck off! But how - was there much wrong?"

The object of the discussion was ticking over like a Singer sewing machine beside them.

"Very simple really, the points were stuck. Happens a lot in the Hillman."

Jack discovered that his friends had opened the car with bits and pieces and wired up the ignition in the dash. 'Easy as pie, really,' thought Jack. 'When you know how!'

He invited his two friends into the hotel for breakfast.

"Are you sure we won't be getting in the way of you two lovebirds?"

"Shut up, you can wash your hands over there in the toilets."

Jane arrived in the dining room just as the rashers, eggs, sausages, and black pudding were being served. They stood up to be introduced. It was a rather open-mouthed occasion as Jane, by dint of professional training and indigenous benefits, presented herself in as perfect a female form as any of the three had ever seen or envisaged.

"Hello Jack, please don't let me interrupt your breakfast. Thank you for a wonderful evening. I enjoyed the dance and the party, and the car breakdown. In fact that was the part I enjoyed most - I see we have a set of wheels under us again?"

"Thanks to these two experts." Jack introduced Mick Flynn and Bernard Smith and apologised quietly to Jane for having absented himself to check the car.

After breakfast the grand tour of the Curragh area began. Leaving Osberstown, the group - Jack and Jane and one of the rescuers in the hired car and the other cavalry chap in a car behind, set out for Donnelly's Hollow. It was a beautiful morning. They stopped and parked at the Hollow close to the golf club. The scene was a symphony of sound and vision: gorse bushes, the chirping of blue tits, the baying of newborn lambs and the measured clip-clop of a string of thoroughbreds from the training stables nearby. It's enjoyable to introduce a visitor to places that are special and for Jack this morning was a series of magic moments.

Jane laughed as she was led up the steps left by Dan Donnelly to the highest point in the Hollow, overlooking where he had eventually beaten Henry Cooper in a bloody, bare-fist prize-fight the century before. They ran down the hill, always one step away from falling arse over tip on the dewy morning grass. She reached for his hand for support on one or two occasions and Jack tingled to her touch. From there they sped out to Kilcullen to look at Dan Donnelly's arm, which was on display in a glass case in a pub called 'The Hideout'. There was about two hours to go to the lunch arrangement, so a tour of the camp to identify possible sites for the film 'Rooney O' was on. Jane described the potential of the camp from film peoples' point of view.

"It's secure and private and, if available, there are plenty of men on site to play the crowd scenes."

Jack had already participated in some scenes shot in Elstree, but it was planned that he would also be in street scenes when they were shot in Dublin, and might even get a short speaking part. Because of his friendship with Jane, events were developing apace and he wondered if he would be able to slow or even stop the horse. His army work however was still important to him, and especially his work in the gymnasium.

Their tour of the Camp took them to each barracks, the rifle ranges, and the prison, and a visit to the Artillery barracks in Kildare. The square there seemed to be particularly suited to some part of the film. Then back to Pearse Officers' Mess for lunch, which was indeed a splendid affair. All the officers were delighted to have such a distinguished visitor and she was regaled with mess stories and bombarded with questions about the film. Jane was full of praise for Jack, who had provided the opportunity to link easily with the Army.

At last her time came to leave and the taxi arrived to take her, and some of the film officials who had been working in Dublin, to the airport.

"I have a surprise for you, Jack. Now, you don't have to make an instant decision, but next week is an important time in your life."

Jack looked at her in amazement. Up to now his relationship with Jane and the film was a spin-off the ski holiday, and he wasn't ready for an enhancement of his present role which her words seemed to indicate.

"The director is pleased with your contribution so far and would like you to become seriously involved, both now and later this year in the South Seas, where he is making a pirate film in which your Irish actor Noel Purcell, and me of course, will star. Apart from the director I would love you to come on board." Jane placed her hand on Jack's and looked pleadingly into his eyes.

The car sped off, leaving Jack open-mouthed with a lipstick mark on his right cheek.

That evening while lying on his bed, Jack indulged his senses by looking again at the photograph of Jane the film star and realised that he had big decisions to make. 'Whether 'tis nobler in the mind to suffer the slings and arrows of outrageous fortune' - and this was outrageous fortune indeed. He had a noble call for Leni Riefenstahl also, to find and secure the copies of Olympia. Heidi had passed to another realm but she was still a part of his consciousness; at least he wished her well and looked forward to visiting her and Josef in different circumstances.

When Louis returned home he wasn't the same person. Well, under the circumstances being a fully 'normal' priest wasn't to be expected. He was neither a parish priest, nor a residue of the love Avis and he had generated. He didn't even know if her parents knew about him. He heard that they hadn't come to the funeral - what would their feelings be towards him - did they even know about his relationship with Avis? Imagine being told that your daughter was having an affair with a priest!

Some of the damage that remained in his mind related to the boss man God, and what Louis should do to pull together the strands of his life. How could it be the same? There was so much sameness when he returned, but he couldn't see a way to exist, at least not the way he was before he met Avis. His religious reflections were locked into circumstances surrounding the last week of their lives together. 'It would have been easy,' he thought, 'if I were not a priest of God.' How simple and noble to end his life in St Anton and wing his way to join her, but then, decisions like that were not his to make.

It wasn't the end of Louis's affair with Avis. The conclusion in St Anton was swift and brutal and yet he would always remember their last days together and their dramatic finish. The candle was burning at full strength at that final moment and even though it was extinguished, the force that fed the light was still there, and returning to his parish tasks had not reduced it in any way. As days went by his feeling of loss strengthened rather than diminished. He realised that he needed more time for closure and figured that it could happen only in the environment in which she had lived. Yes, a visit to New York was a necessity, not only to meet her parents, but more to breathe in the air that had created the woman he had grown to love.

His physical condition had improved greatly since his return. He checked in at London Airport and almost immediately felt a sense of relief. It was as if he were re-creating Avis's desire to escape from the pain of her New York experiences. From what she had told him, life in New York previous to her departure for St Anton had many pressures. In some weird manner he sensed that he was rewinding her experiences in a way that her poor dead body never could. She wasn't there in person but Louis felt that he wasn't alone on his journey of reconstruction.

He had previously been in New York, so he knew his way about. Without much difficulty he made his way to Brooklyn to find her parents. He was surprised that they hadn't come to bring her body back from St Anton, leaving that role to a nun acquaintance.

'The number of the building in Ponsenby Street in Brooklyn is 156 - mostly offices - yes, 156, St Mary's Orphanage. That couldn't be - must be the wrong street.'

He walked back a block, but there was no mistake. He thought for a moment about what she had told him of her life in New York. She had been in care, and according to her account, life there had been bad and good. There was a Sister Brigid who had taken her under her wing and arranged her education, which had culminated in a master's degree in Brooklyn College. He thought that he might have gotten the addresses mixed up and that her parent's address was somewhere else.

'This could be the home where she was reared before being adopted.'

He walked up the steep red sandstone steps to the door and pressed the well-worn bell. There was no doubt about the ring; the sound outside was like a fire brigade. He tried to feel Avis's presence but nothing came through; he realised he was just grasping at straws. He wondered if coming to America had been such a good idea after all.

"Hello, may I help you?"

Louis looked at the person at the door. He was about fifty and was dressed in some form of uniform; it could have been a religious outfit but he wasn't sure.

"My name's McCormac, I'm looking for Mr and Mrs Maxwell. I have their address and thought it was here."

"I'll get Sister Brigid for you. I'm sure she'll be able to help. Please come with me into the parlour."

A typical institution, thought Louis as he looked about. The building looked and smelt of what it was - parquet floors and timber-panelled walls throughout. There was a strong smell of floor polish but mostly kitchen smells.

'How, even in America, do they get the smell of boiling cabbage to permeate throughout?' thought Louis.

One window of the parlour overlooked a playground, in which about thirty children were playing basketball, and in their midst a referee in nun's garb. She could move and appeared to be a member of one team as well as being referee. At one juncture the man who let him in approached her, spoke, and took charge of the whistle, while she smoothed her garb, looked up at the window and headed in his direction.

"I'm Sister Brigid, can I help you? I believe you're looking for the parents of Avis Maxwell? By any chance are you Louis?"

He could see that the nun facing him knew about their relationship in Europe. He didn't know however, whether she was aware that he was a priest.

"Come with me down to the graveyard."

She led briskly and he followed. He felt that she was in charge; and destined to make a significant contribution to his life. He questioned why he should have any sense of misgiving, 'had not he reached the bottom of the pit, as far as feelings about Avis and he were concerned?' Down a brown lino-clad corridor to an exit which led to a flight of wrought iron steps to a garden, and on to a gate in the garden wall. She led and he followed without a word passing between them. He figured that she had total understanding of the situation and his reason for being there. As the gate squealed open she turned, and with her back to lines of little white crosses on a green lawn she addressed him in a compassionate tone.

"This is Avis's last resting place. I know all about her relationship with you, and I am glad that at least her last days were happy ones."

She had a short conversation with Louis about how Avis died. Details of the requiem mass had been passed on by Sister Wolfram who had returned to St Anton and accompanied the body back to New York and was now back on a visit to her home in Austria.

Louis walked down the line of crosses to the last one; the cross with the freshest paint and signs of sods having been recently laid - he read the inscription.

'In fond memory of Avis Maxwell'

He looked and thought and thought and looked, but it was all too much for him to absorb.

"Is this Avis's grave? What about her parents and her husband? She wasn't a sister - why is she here?"

Sister Brigid guided him to a nearby seat and sat with him. She explained that in fact Avis had stayed in the orphanage and never had a mother and father or a husband. She was about to continue the story, but she was needed to support Louis. He collapsed like a punctured balloon and when he came round he was prone on the seat and his collar and tie had been loosened.

"But she told me she was married and had lost a child."

Eventually he heard the whole story about Avis. Yes, she had had an operation for cancer but there never was a husband or parents or a child. The sisters, particularly Sister Brigid, were concerned that Avis had been kind of hijacked, in that she had begun working, clerical work, with the order, straight from school. She had never experienced life outside, except on her trips to Brooklyn College during her graduate and post-graduate years. She was recommended by her GP to visit a psychiatrist and was treated for a manic disorder. When she began to recover they planned a trip for her to St Anton, to put her in the way of experiencing life away from New York in a healthy Alpine environment.

"The trip took a bit of engineering, but one of our sisters is Austrian and from that general area, so with her help we managed."

It took some taking in and Louis pondered the situation. The sequel to her going took some understanding. Why the affair? Why me? Was she genuine in her relationship - but how could she? She knew I was a priest - is that why she loved me - did she love me?

He realised that instead of having questions answered, he had inherited a range of new, unanswerable ones. But what now? He was in America and had leave for another two weeks. He had no other reason to pursue bits of Avis, like parents or husband, because they didn't exist, but he liked the idea of staying close to the grave for a while and maybe he could see inside her head and identify her personality traits.

He spent the next week in and around the orphanage and got to understand the milieu in which Avis had grown to womanhood. Some people in the area, who knew her and had worked on certain projects with her, heard about his presence, approached him and gave him some insights. A man who had studied with her in Brooklyn College made a special contribution.

"Avis was searching for a mode of escape from the religious connection. There was one lecturer in particular with whom she was friendly, but rather than trying to enhance her own academic position she sought to make gains for the rest of us."

"What about her social life in the College?"

"She was a member of the college Theatre Company and as well as taking part and having a hand in production, she travelled all over and made quite a name for the company. She got to know the rest of the students in theatre real well and in particular Father Kelly. He was moved upstate by the bishop, however. She was shattered by the suddenness of that move and quit the theatre company soon afterwards. Her health deteriorated from then and in particular her mental health."

Louis didn't ask any more questions. He was afraid to unravel the layers of Avis's life experiences any further and decided to say one last prayer at her grave and go back.

"Good-bye, Avis. I'm sorry if I've disturbed you here in the place from whence you flew to my side. We were in love for a short time and that will always be a bijou in my memory store. I still love you and always will, but I wanted more from you."

Louis shed a tear, closed the door to the graveyard, and went home.

Jack couldn't see that he had much of a decision to make about whether to stay in the army or become a film star.

"I mean, my application to go to the FCA in Bailieborough was turned down by the commanding officer - he said I was too young!" He snorted to one of his pals over a pint.

"If I hear about your Bailieborough experience again I'll get sick. However, it's a difficult one all right, a film star in a film being shot in the South Seas in close proximity to the lovely Jane, or orderly officer in this shithole?"

Jack also considered the idea of having a secure job and pension, as championed by his father.

"Look, you've only one life to live. This is the chance of a lifetime; you should be upstairs packing your bag. Will you be able to bring your orderly? Forget that, I jest." Jack's fellow officers enjoyed making a contribution to the flotsam and jetsam that was Muldoon's life without having to take any risks themselves.

Jack moped through the next week or so and one day it happened.

"This is the Adjutant speaking. We've been asked by the United Nations to send a battalion to the Belgian Congo. Will I put your name down? We'll be sending a series of units out over the next few years and the CO wants a list of commissioned officers and NCOs. There's no guarantee that you'll go out with the first group the month after next, but once you're listed you'll go into training of some sort. There'll be a lot of physical training to be done, both here and in Africa, so your crowd in the gym will have lots to do - for a change," he added tersely.

"Africa." Jack's eyes lit up and he straight away had visions of cutting his way through dense jungles and doing land deals with Zulu warrior chieftains. In less than a second he weighed the two options, the film bit and the United Nations peacekeeper with his own unit of soldiers, and spat out the words, "Put me down."

He contacted London and spoke to Jane, explaining that he really had no option and that this was a call to duty. She understood but sounded disappointed.

"We would have had great times together, Jack, but I understand and wish you well. We can meet up now and again and if you're around next ski season in St Anton, we could meet up."

Jack was relieved that there were no more great decisions about lifestyle to be made. The film job sounded romantic, but how it would have panned out in the long-term was another question. He knew from his brief experiences in the Curragh Theatre Group that acting was a special skill that few had in terms of natural talent.

'But then films are not really acting,' he thought, 'it's different from acting in a theatre. That stuff that Errol Flynn does is just about 'buck lepping' around, sword fighting and the like. I'm sure I could do that, but how do I know? I could finish up a square peg in a round hole!'

Jack put film acting and film actresses on the back burner and became involved in the normal duties of a lieutenant posted to the 'big gyms', and a possible link with fitness training for a trip to Africa with the United Nations. He kept a keen eye on the postings for the first battalion to leave. There was a bit of pulling and pushing in order to get an appointment, because as well as getting away on overseas service and all that it meant professionally, the money side of the operation was not unsubstantial for officers and men, who although well catered for in their messes, seldom had what they considered to be adequate leisure money.

At last the decisions were made and Jack was disappointed. He didn't make the cut for the first group, but he was happy; he was a definite starter with the next battalion the following year. Jack kept a close eye on how the preparation was done for the Curragh contingent with this Battalion.

The main group were gathering in Connolly Barracks and training with the 3rd Battalion. Their enthusiasm and equipment was a giveaway. He had expected that they would have new uniforms suited to the tropics, but right up to their departure date they were still in 'bull's wool', the usual army issue. They left in a blaze of flags and cheers.

"The list's in the Adjutant's office!"

About a year later Jack made his way down to breakfast in McDonagh Officer's Mess. Peter Murphy, one of his fellow officers, gave him the news. A list of officers destined for the Congo with the UN contingent had arrived from Camp Headquarters.

"Is my name on it?"

"Yes, you're attached to A Company from the Eastern Command. There isn't a Curragh Company as such, although there are quite a few officers and NCOs from the Camp."

Jack saluted as he stepped into the Adjutant's office. The CO and the Adjutant were still in overcoats as they pored over a printed list of personnel detailed to prepare for the UN mission. They obviously had personal interests. Everyone, without exception, wanted to be a part of the exercise and money was a significant factor; they were after all, professional soldiers.

"You're on the list all right - provided Camp HQ don't change things around."

With the CO present in the office, it wasn't possible to discuss things further, so Jack left and made his way down to the Army School of Physical Culture.

"Did you hear about Joe Purser?" One of his fellow officers had a story about UN participation and its vagaries.

"What was that?"

Joe lived in Newbridge and was stationed just a mile away in the

Curragh Camp and had an account in the bank in Newbridge. Joe was one of Ireland's great economic adventurers, and the bane of his bank manager's life. He stumbled from month to month and only survived by borrowing from his family, from friends, and from the old reliable, the bank, of course. He celebrated the arrival of the annual uniform allowance without spending on a new uniform. He was listed to go to the Congo at a particularly bad time in his money misadventures. When his selection was made known he floated down the main street in Newbridge and presented at the bank.

"May I speak to Mr Gleeson, please?"

The staff, from cashier down to doorman, smirked and anticipated another amusing interlude, with an irate manager and a bruised customer as the principal protagonists. It always started civilly. They thought Joe was more confident than usual, wearing a new tweed jacket, creased grey slacks and he seemed taller than his portly five-feet-six frame.

"Ah good morning, Joe." They were on first name terms. "I was going to send for you." A serious manager ushered Joe into his office and sent a 'get back to your work' body language signal to the gawking staff.

That was a bad sign from Joe's point of view. The staff recognised the signal for a row and as the door closed the younger members eyed the two blurs visible through the opaque glass and grew their ears in the direction of the expected contretemps. Even the darkly suited cashier found an excuse to work at the office end of his desk. They were surprised, however, as on this occasion the raised voices from within were ones of loud relaxed talk and laughter, and as the two emerged, still in good form, cigars were being lit.

"Maybe he's had a baby - no that couldn't be, Sybil wasn't pregnant."

Everyone knew everything about everyone in Newbridge.

"Maybe he won the Sweep?"

"I know - his horse has come in." Joe was a big gambler, as was the manager. This meeting between difficult customers and the manager was a break from the normal boredom of bank work. For the junior members it was a break from totting arm lengths of figures, and the chance perhaps to pass on embellished stories to their peers in the pub later.

Joe was unlucky by nature. He was a risk-taker with a big personality, whereas the manager was nearly the opposite and couldn't understand Joe's approach to life. All he wanted was to retire without having Joe as a big black mark on his record, and the news he had heard that morning made that possible.

Joe had explained in detail how his trip to the Congo was an economic boon, signalling the end of his financial worries.

"From now on I'll be a good example to all your customers."

Harry, that was the manager's name to his friends, including his wife, should have pointed his antenna in the danger direction at this extravagant claim by Joe. He had however been sucked into a feel-good lacuna by the cigar and Joe's verbal manipulation of the money figures.

"I'm throwing a party up at the house, Harry. Of course you and your good lady wife are invited."

You would have thought that a manager of Harry's experience in a gambling town like Newbridge would have been on his guard.

"I'll need a few bob to fund my going-away arrangements. I suppose that's okay?"

Harry felt his head nodding and the deal was done!

It was a great sending off party, plenty of drink, food, and music. Harry enjoyed himself, but he had a slight sense of foreboding.

"Don't be an eejit," his wife said, when at some stage he voiced concern to her about the cost of everything.

"Did he have to push the boat out so far - I mean Mrs Lawler's for the catering!"

The *piece de resistance* was Joe's going-away speech. It would have done credit to Livingston at the Royal Society in London on his departure to search for the source of the Nile. Joe mentioned that event indeed and even went so far as to place his historic sequel in context, with the Bank of Ireland as one of his sponsors. Harry nearly choked on a cocktail sausage, but nevertheless he was the last to leave and celebrated the pending voyage with a couple of Napoleon brandies and smokes; best Cuban, of course, rolled on Cuban ladies' thighs and all provided by Joe - not the thighs, the cigars!

The birds were singing as the bank manager and his wife made their way home to Lumville Cross.

Joe was over the moon literally and metaphorically. To tell the truth the moon was fading somewhat as he made it to his bedroom. "A great frigin' night," he said, as he did a Leo Lynch jump into his half of the bed, sending his wife almost ceiling high. Poor Sybil pretended not to notice the experience, despite landing heavily on her mouth and nose.

The battalion left from the army airport in Baldonnell on American Globemaster planes. They arrived via Tripoli and Kano in Nigeria to a fairly warm welcome. They had to fight their way out of Leopoldville airport, with the help of a few Indian UN units, to reach their base in Leopold Farm on the outskirts of Elizabethville.

Although the Belgians had left the country, intending that it should remain one united country, as it had been while they were in charge, a dissident group of mercenary soldiers and local militia attempted to set up a separate state known as Katanga. Katanga province was situated in the south of the Congo next to Northern Rhodesia. Like the rest of the Congo it was French-speaking mostly, although in some cases a local Swahili dialect prevailed.

An essential difference between Katanga province and the rest, with the exception of Kivu perhaps, was the giant copper deposits there, being mined by Union Minière. This and other mineral deposits, made Katanga attractive economically to a ménage of agencies from Belgium and the United States of America. American strategic military planning relied on nuclear defence, and the Shinkolobwe mine in Katanga was a main source of uranium through the 1950s. There was also a leftist element, headed by Patrice Lumumba, who was flitting here and there in the Congo seeking support for their political aims.

When Joe and the Irish UN contingent arrived at Battalion Headquarters, they were stationed at Leopold Farm on the outskirts of Elizabethville. Mortars from the adjacent railway marshalling yards were shelling them - it was only spasmodic, however, and they were, with care, able to move to and from the airport and live within the farm buildings. On the first day they dug trenches in the main yard and set up mortar positions, protected by the requisite infantry units.

Joe had responsibility for liasing with the other Irish units in the farm area. Although it was dangerous, he moved freely between positions and spoke to officers, NCOs, and men, as required. He had just arranged a relay of men to bring food to the trenches when he felt in need of a smoke. A flush of well being ran through him as he realised that life in Newbridge would be better from then on.

"No more boot licking in the office of that auld shit Harry Gleeson."
He sang a little ditty as he walked from point to point.
"O Eileen a leanna, I hear someone talking,
T'is the ivy dear mother against the glass knocking."
A mortar bomb crashed through the parapet that surrounded the farmyard. As the explosion sent bits of stone and slivers of timber all over the yard, everyone dived for cover, including Joe. It wasn't the bits of stone that were the main cause of worry. The sinister crack of a mortar bomb explosion saw pieces of metal rush at speed in search of a bonding with human flesh. They showed their potential as they slapped dramatically into timber posts, walls, and pieces of equipment.

"You'll have to give up that old singing, Sir."

Joe was out of the trench at this stage and the smoke urge was even stronger. He was pleased that his hand didn't shake as he selected a fag and offered one to Corporal Jameson. He patted his uniform pockets but discovered that his lighter was missing. In typical quick fashion the Corporal observed and reached up with a lighter. As Joe took the lighter it happened again. Bang! Before he could dive in any direction a mortar bomb exploded in the middle of the yard. When the dust cleared he was still standing, and amazingly, uninjured.

"Feck this!" he said. "This fag is going to get lit despite the efforts of the mercenaries over there in the train station. As he lifted his right hand with the lighter and flicked it open, his eyes widened in disbelief. His hands were still steady as a rock, but one of the fingers of his right hand was missing. He saw the stump beginning to ooze blood; he felt no pain and wondered if he should continue lighting the cigarette.

When he awoke he was in the hospital room of the medical centre. He looked down at his hand and saw it wasn't a dream; a large bandage covered his hand and he could see the gap. "We searched for the finger but couldn't find it anywhere," the nurse said.

"Don't worry," said Doctor O'Callaghan. "You're okay and we'll have you home in a week."

The manager of the Bank in Newbridge, Harry Gleeson, was a happy man. The weather outside was sunny and there were other reasons for his positive feelings. There had been an inspection of his branch the week before and he was complimented on his management skills, not alone in the bank itself, but also with his customers. He looked out into his garden and admired the flowers and the lawn as he tucked into a breakfast fry. The lawn was his responsibility, on which he lavished loving attention. No weeds. It was just like the putting green in the Curragh Golf Club. He was a member there and planned to get a game in this afternoon.

"Good-bye, darling, I won't be up for lunch, I might break off early and go up for a game."

He had decided to walk. It wasn't far, but he would get his friend Peter, a teacher in Newbridge College, to collect him at the bank for the trip to the golf club. He eased out the drive past the cars and strode in the direction of the main street. He practised the golf swing in his mind as he walked. Back, chin on shoulder, eye on the ball, cock the wrists, strike, keep the head down and follow through. He visualised the flight of the ball from the first tee down the fairway to within a five iron of the green. Follow through with the back of the hand on the putts - that's important.

He crossed the road at Mickey Pat's Grand Hotel, heading down to the bank.

"It couldn't be, it's not possible, I'm dreaming!"

Harry's world began to shatter as he reluctantly recognised the figure coming towards him. Joe wasn't happy either. He had hoped to avoid meeting anyone in Newbridge and particularly the manager. He hadn't ever seen Harry walk anywhere before, except on the golf course.

"Bloody hell." When they did meet he had prepared some sort of explanation, but in the short rehearsal time he had, it wouldn't be adequate or even credible. It didn't strike him to tell the truth; there was no activity in his stunned brain.

"Good morning, Joe, this is a surprise. I presume you are home on some errand. You'll be going back again?"

"I had an active service injury, but I hope to get back again when I recover. At least it's not my trigger finger!" Joe spoke to the wilting bank manager with the confidence of a war hero.

Harry found out about the injury bit by bit and as soon as he heard about the loss of the finger, he knew that Joe's active service life was probably at an end.

Joe never returned to the Congo, or any other UN duties, and his story didn't influence Jack or his colleagues about the risks of going to Africa. Harry played the worst golf of his life that afternoon and retired from the bank a year later.

Time flew and about six months later Jack and his group were called for training. Jack had contact with a colonel in the Director of Training's office through athletics training, coaching and CISM, the international army organisation for sport. As training started, he was summoned to the Director of Training's office in Parkgate Street to discuss how physical training would help acclimatisation in the tropics, and how sports management would assist the maintenance of morale.

"I want every man on active service to be in peak condition both physically and mentally; I consider both to be linked, '*mens sana in corpore sano*', and all that."

Jack was delighted to have this extra role, but noted that his posting was as part of a company from the Eastern Command and he knew that the officer commanding that company, a commandant, would require him to play his part in the normal sense of company duties. Without a special appointment within Headquarters Company, he couldn't see a way to meet the colonel in Training Branch's instructions. He wouldn't have a chance to work with the battalion as a whole before departure, because each Company worked alone and there were no plans to bring them together until just before departure. He knew also that each company commander would want to run his own show and apart from common weaponry and management systems, each unit was independent. Certainly the units from Cork and Dublin would have their own development programme. Interventions from Headquarters were limited to a not-too-deep study of Swahili and common inoculation procedures.

From the time he heard of his appointment Jack had been living his life in a kind of time bubble. Although work in the Army School of Physical Culture went on apace, his main thoughts were about going to Africa. His image was of the Zulu Wars; young subalterns from English public schools, standing in breeches and leggings, red tunic and pit helmet, facing hundreds of Zulu warriors, naked except for head feathers, anklets, and loincloths. This was the image put forward by supporters of the British Empire and published in many annuals and comic books.

The nearest Jack had gotten to a foreign posting was a near miss to the FCA in Bailieborough, Co. Cavan! Many young infantry officers aspired to go out to the FCA, a volunteer reserve organisation, where you were more or less independent and the important point, you got subsistence, travelling allowances, and for those leaving the Curragh, a chance to meet civilian 'birds'. Anyway, that was water under the bridge. On receiving his official briefing, including a booklet on the Swahili language, Jack became focused.

"*Jambo bwana, habari zenu.*"

"Would you ever get stuffed."

He didn't always get a supportive response from his brother officers, particularly those who were not on the departure list.

The call to arms began in earnest when the company commander, Commandant Stephen McCoy, summoned officers and NCOs to Cathal Brugha Barracks for briefing. It took place on a Monday morning in Dublin and Jack took the opportunity to go to a dance at the 'Four Provinces' and stay overnight in the mess. A few officers from the Curragh and two from the Eastern Command joined him on the sortie, and it was with a feeling of excitement and almost breathless anticipation that they had a few in the mess and struck for a pub close to the dance emporium.

Part of their conversation in the pub was about how things were going for the present battalion in the Congo. They all knew some of those killed in the ambush in Niemba, and were aware that there was shooting in Katanga as they spoke.

"Getting killed isn't much fun."

"This present crowd are up to their ears in it - I suppose we'll have to prove our worth."

"First things first, let's pull a few birds and see how we perform in active service in the Four Provinces ballroom."

As usual, there were a few black Nigerian medical students at the dance and Jack opted to try his Swahili out on one of them. Harry Jenkins reminded him that not all Africans spoke Swahili and that these guys were probably oil-rich Nigerian chieftain's sons, educated in England and now in the College of Surgeons in Dublin. Later, however, Jack, subsumed by demon drink, approached a six-feet-five, well-dressed black man and tried out his few words of Swahili.

"Fuck off 'ourada'."

The tall African smiled and said nothing, but his dancing partner from the inner city lit the space around with language embellished with cupla focle, bequeathed to her and hers by a succession of Dublin based Hussar units and their Irish successors.

Commandant McCoy went for his usual jog that morning. His wife was still in bed and as he tiptoed out he made sure not to slam the door and, very important, not to let the dog out. Poppy, like most Jack Russells, made a racket as soon as she was released from her kennel in the garage and rushed up to the back of the garden to stake her claim. That was one of Patricia McCoy's pet hates; she didn't like dogs very much. She was a country girl and when at home before her marriage to Stephen, dogs knew their place and the house wasn't it. In fact, she wasn't sure that the house was the most suitable place for smelly husbands, stamping all over the place in dirty shoes. A bit like Mrs Organ Morgan in 'Under Milkwood' - 'put your pyjamas in the drawer marked pyjamas'. Stephen valued a quiet life above all, and keeping 'herself' happy was high on his agenda.

'I'll have to set a good example to my Unit,' he thought, as he ran through Dundrum village. Some of his officers were not in the full flush of youth and he was aware that for one or two, a brisk walk would be best effort. 'That makes my example all the more important,' he reasoned, 'although I know most have volunteered for the money and don't expect to have a fitness regime imposed on them. Loyalty, that's the word I'll use in making this company the best in the bloody Battalion.'

"Oh sorry!"

In his excitement he ran into a dreaded buggy being pushed from a terraced door. His momentum carried him onwards down the path and as he looked back to identify the nature of the obstacle, he ran into a 'Victoria Regina' letterbox. This wasn't unusual for Stephen. He often had accidents, but mercifully not of a serious nature - at least up to this point - although a stint in an African environment might offer a greater range of opportunities. He was small and muscular and was easily a match for the child's buggy and the letterbox; and although slightly winded he offered the experience up to the god of military training.

Commandant McCoy considered the value of loyalty in the army code and immediately saw its place. Loyalty to the Battalion, loyalty to officers and men, loyalty to the country, loyalty to A Company and its commanding officer. He considered the range of applications of the concept, with a view to using the word as a core element in his first statement to his officers. If he had their loyalty, then it was each officer's responsibility to build a sense of loyalty through the non-commissioned officers down to the men. He'd been a boy scout in his young days, and remembered the list of characteristics that each scout was supposed to follow: loyal, trustworthy, helpful, obedient, cheerful, thrifty, brave, pure, and God's glory in mind.

"All the rest go without saying, it's the loyalty bit I have to concentrate on." He voiced the sentiments out loud as he rounded the telegraph pole at the far end of the village.

When he arrived home he shared his thoughts with 'the wife'.

"That's all very well, but how do you expect to keep those lot pure in the Congo when they're not pure to start with?" Patricia was happy with her contribution, realising the need to downgrade the 'playing at soldiers' elements in his lifestyle, to help maintain a focus on her and the home.

"I'm concentrating on loyalty. The simple truth is I only mention the rest because they are the Scout's code. I was thinking of developing morale by focusing on loyalty and perhaps introducing a name like 'McCoy's Colts'."

"You can try, but I can't see Brendan playing a part in McCoy's whatever. Anyway the truth is never pure, and rarely simple."

Stephen recognized a bit of Oscar Wilde lore from her University College Dublin extramural course and refused the bait.

Brendan was one of the officers appointed to travel with Stephen's company. He was about forty years of age and saw the army as an opportunity to play out his role as a dug-in *wallah* in the ordnance stores in Cathal Brugha. He had a brother-in-law in Saggart who ran a meat packing business of some sorts, and Brendan used to help him out on occasions and thereby make a few bob. He was thinking of leaving the army and working with the wife's brother full-time, but the army was a '*cushy*' number and it seemed worthwhile struggling on to pension time, in another ten years or so.

A trip to Africa with the UN sounded like a good way to get a few shekels in the bank and he was an advocate of the old 'double tap'. Apart from the money, he saw at least one trip abroad as essential to preserve professional status and keep the young 'whippersnappers' in their place. Brendan's wife and Stephen's had been to a boarding school together and were still friends, so Patricia understood Brendan's thoughts about being controlled by anybody.

'I have trouble with Stephen, but Brendan's not an easy mark,' she thought.

Stephen had, however, sorted a number of items out in his mind. He found running a good way to clarify and identify essentials in any of his life strategies. He got into his uniform; perhaps he'd wear the UN blue beret instead of his officer's cap. It certainly looked good in the bedroom mirror and he marched down the stairs to show herself. She thought he looked good, but it wasn't in her nature to flatter him, especially about his dress.

"You look silly; you're like a full moon in a fog!"

Patricia didn't reveal that she thought all his army goings-on were silly and a blue beret only made things worse. Anyway, he prepared for the meeting in Cathal Brugha and off they went in their Ford Escort. She went because the mess had invited all the wives as a precursor to their being alone for the six months of the UN mandate in the Belgian Congo.

Stephen had spent some time in support of the social life of his soldiers by managing and coaching soccer football at inner city league level. He figured that his experiences with the league were as relevant to peacekeeping as a large portion of his army experience and training.

The Ford Escort was recognised at the gate, the sentry saluted and

Commandant McCoy and wife drove into the barracks, around to the right as the signs indicated, and around the square to the officers' mess.

The first square in Cathal Brugha was apart from the main square and was used mostly by the FCA - the voluntary part-time defence forces, for drill exercises. The men's canteen was situated at the top of this square and soldiers often went across for tea and wads, and back to their billets. Squares were sacred areas, not to be crossed except by a formed unit under command, but for some reason the ethic of this first square had been undermined. The main square remained sacrosanct, however, used only for parades and drill practise.

"Look, Stephen, those men! Why are they walking across the square?" Patricia McCoy remained comfortably seated as she asked a question. Stephen was caught off guard and without thinking, reacted to the problem of men with the mugs on the square. He knew full well that men, recruits particularly, always carried their mugs of tea across that square to their billets. It irked him that they did so, because he was a stickler for regulations, but he realised also that common practice eventually became law - he resented this sort of progress. Patricia's objection was founded on his oft-repeated attitude to such misdemeanours and he had no choice but to react to her observation. The high military significance of his visit to the barracks was an added incentive. He dismounted from the car.

"You men, what are you doing? You can't walk willy-nilly across the square."

Those who could hear him were perplexed. "Something about Willy somebody!"

Those who couldn't hear stood still. They saw an officer standing beside a civilian car, his mouth was moving and their tea was getting cold.

"Get in, Stephen, they're stupid, don't waste your time."

"Carry on," said Stephen in his most authoritative voice, as he slid into the well-worn driving seat of the Escort. He was glad that he'd put his foot down on this occasion.

"Things are slipping, someone needs to take a stand." Patricia nodded in agreement, but by this stage she had moved on and was thinking about the reception food in the officers' mess.

When he arrived in the Adjutant's office it was empty.

"The Adjutant and the CO are up in the gymnasium with the shooting team, sir. They won the all-army Bren gun championships and there's a presentation ceremony there today." The message was delivered through the hatch between the orderly room and the Adjutant's office by one of the Orderly room staff.

"Thank you, Corporal, there's a get-together of the Congo unit here this morning. I'm Commandant McCoy."

"Oh yes sir, a billet has been prepared for you on the other side of the square. The Adjutant left word."

Typical Eastern Command," he muttered as he left the office. "They never get their priorities right - bloody Bren guns." He had expected a welcome from the CO - not a garbled message through a hatch in the Adjutant's office from the beer-bloated head of one of the orderly room staff.

Patricia had deposited herself in the mess, so off he strode in the direction of the billet. He began to feel better, fed on a number of individual salutes from soldiers and an 'eyes right' from a passing recruit platoon. When he reached his destination he saw a sign on the wall beside the billet, indicating that this was the domain of A Company UN Battalion. The barrack's Sergeant Major was waiting in ambush inside the door. He came loudly to attention, saluted, and introduced himself. He had made an extra effort this morning, and all leather and brass in his uniform sizzled in gleaming perfection.

Sgt Major Morgan had two functions; he was the barracks sergeant major, but more importantly he was travelling with the battalion to the Congo. He was somewhat uneasy, never having travelled abroad, and most of his work at home was in the administration of the barracks. Forty years of age, but on the plus side he was physically fit, had played all games in the army and was all-army rifle champion four years in a row. He was respected by all ranks and feared by most. Commandant McCoy looked forward to working with him, although the Sergeant Major's position would be with Battalion Headquarters - his links with the various company sergeants was a vital part of the operation of the battalion.

The room was set up with tables and chairs in rows for the meeting.

"Do you think you could lay your hands on a rostrum, Sergeant Major?"

"I tried this morning, sir, but discovered that the CO was using it up in the gymnasium. There's a platform next door however and I've planned to set a small table on it, at the top of the room there. Would that be okay, sir?"

Stephen needed to get a bit of physical elevation from the rest of the meeting for more than one reason. He wanted above all to look imposing and, sensibly, to be in a position to see all his officers.

'I can tell a lot when I see the whites of a man's eyes,' he thought.

Above all he didn't want big shits like Brendan McGonnigle superciliously looking down on him from his six-foot-four frame. Anyway, the platform was carried in and placed in position. He tried it out and decided that the two-foot elevation it gave was certainly adequate. Another advantage was that he had room to move around at this level, despite the presence of a table and display board. He quickly got his charts in position, pinning up the opening chart displaying the word 'Loyalty' so that it couldn't be seen until the pin was knocked away.

'There are some things you have to do yourself. You can only trust some of the people some of the time.' He was beginning to feel good and smiled to himself as he anticipated the exercise.

The meeting was due to start at 09.45 hrs and with about 45 minutes to go he informed the sergeant major that he would return at zero hour minus two minutes. His first thought was to go up to the mess and check that the women were being looked after, but the idea of getting involved with Patricia before his presentation wasn't attractive to him.

Early the same morning Jack and his brother officers awoke in 'Charlie Burgess' barracks. The light poured in from a tall window facing east. It had been a good night, and they had all finished up in a flat in Rathmines.

"Where's Mick?"

Mick Keane was a bit of an individualist, and where he saw people swimming in a certain direction he generally chose to swim against the tide. This tendency in an officer begs the question 'was he wisely chosen to be a soldier'? Mick's bloody-mindedness was manifest in many ways and Jack, and in particular the company commander, were to experience the cutting edge of Mick Keane's contrary nature in Africa.

It seemed that one lonely transport plane, with a load of Monaghan mushrooms and Carlingford mussels for Paris, had droned across the sky over Cathal Brugha Barracks. Mick leaped out of bed and announced, "the noise in this shithole is terrible".

"I'm out of here to somewhere quiet. That's one good thing about the

Curragh Camp."

"What about the sheep?" Jack spat the words from under the army issue blankets.

"It's fucking engines I'm talking about, dickhead!" The door and doorframe shook in response to Mick's venomous exit.

Where he went nobody knew, but it couldn't have been very far on a bicycle. A few seconds later:

"Can I have a lend of the loan of your bicycle pump?"

He was met with a litany of obscenities from almost all, but he got the pump from Harry Jenkins who had everything; even a full set of the 'housewife mending kit' he was issued with in the Military College while a Cadet five years previously. At four in the morning Jack and the rest discussed the event. It's reassuring to talk about someone else's problems or idiosyncrasies, when warm in bed hugging your genitals.

First light and Mick is back shaving and whistling.

"I'll take you back again Kathleen,

Across the ocean wild and wide.

To where your heart has ever been, since…"

"This is too much! I wish you and 'Kathleen' were stuffed into a cell in the glasshouse prison."

"You're not in the Curragh now, old flick. They don't have a glasshouse here."

Anyway, Mick was effective in getting most of the officer corps for A Company out of bed on this morning of their introduction to Commandant Stephen McCoy. They were the young set while the rest of the officers were married, mostly from the Eastern Command and living in Dublin. An orderly called, cleaned the brasses, polished the leather, and briefed the officers on the hot water and showering arrangement, and by about 08.00 hrs they all trooped into the dining room for breakfast. The resident officers weren't surprised at the influx of strangers, because since the start of the UN exercise in the Congo, groups of others had been appearing for meals and then heading off, leaving a single feather to settle. The banter was good and at about half eight they made their way to the rooms to ready for the meeting with the commandant and his staff.

"Commandant McCoy's in barracks since eight o'clock. He was seen checking recruits crossing the square about that time."

"Checking what?"

"Checking recruits coming from the canteen with mugs of tea."

"Wow, that's a good start, I heard he was keen, but this beats Banaher and Banaher beat the devil!"

Anyway, at about 09.05 hrs this group of officers made their way to the billet allocated to the UN contingent. The NCOs, controlled by the Sergeant Major, formed a welcoming party at the entrance and showed them to their seats. Just as Jack and his crowd arrived, an older group made their way in and settled in the front seats. They seemed to know one another, but made no effort to establish relationships with the junior ranks. Captain Brendan McGonnigle seemed to be the social leader and most of their discussion was routed through him. When he cracked a joke they all laughed. Eventually everyone was seated and the conversation settled to a low hum and an occasional guffaw. There was a general feeling that the mundane chores of their life in Ireland were to be jettisoned for an exotic participation in military peacekeeping in sub-Saharan Africa, whatever that might turn out to be.

A shuffling at the back and like Herr Hitler striding into a Bier-keller in Munich, Commandant Stephen McCoy, flanked by his Adjutant, strode down the centre aisle and bound on to the platform. Stephen stood legs apart and cast a steely gaze around the seated officers. There was silence but for the continued low buzz of conversation from the group close to Captain Brendan McGonnigle. It wasn't that they were intentionally rude; Brendan, and Jack Fortune, a machine gun officer who had served during the Emergency, hadn't seen one another for yonks and were catching up - Stephen McCoy wasn't high on their agenda. However, curiosity got the better of them, and they eventually focused on the Commandant.

Stephen knew his magnetic personality would eventually grab their attention and as soon as he had quiet he started.

"Gentlemen, for those of you who are not from this Command, I'm Commandant Stephen McCoy, Officer Commanding A Company of the UN Battalion. This is our first meeting and I take the opportunity to introduce myself, explain the modus operandi of this unit and give you all an opportunity to become acquainted with the officer corps in 'McCoy's Colts'."

"The wha?"

Everybody turned their heads in the direction of the intervention. It was easy to identify who'd spoken, because Brendan McGonnigle was on his feet.

"Sir, with the greatest respect, I wish to object most strongly to this demeaning term to describe what I hope will be the best bloody company in this Battalion."

The Commandant and the Captain stood like two antlered stags, face to face, although Stephen McCoy was standing on a platform at least two feet high. In fact McCoy may have had a slight height advantage and it was partly this that gave him the courage to tackle the problem head on. He realised in a flash that this encounter was his opportunity to establish his position in management terms, and to illustrate beyond doubt that he was in charge. Brendan was showing his cards; it was up to him to trump him, and the time was now. He said nothing for at least five seconds and when he saw the blood rise to the Captain's face he struck.

"I realise, Captain McGonnigle, that you're an officer of vast experience who will no doubt achieve senior rank, given the right time and circumstance. This trip to the African theatre may in fact be that time. Your opinion of my light hearted effort to boost the morale of the troops and younger officers I value, but I request you to see the big picture, rather than react in such a way that you may undermine the morale of the officer corps and create dissention. I'm sure that's not your intention?"

Brendan said nothing, at least nothing audible. He sort of mumbled his way down to the sitting position.

"What the hell is he talking about…senior officer, right time…"

He had a gripe about promotion, in that he had been passed over by officers from De Valera's Volunteer Corps during the Emergency; but this wasn't the time or the place to discuss that. He'd been in touch with politicians over the years to seek redress, but unfortunately his contacts were seldom in power, although they and he lived in hope.

Stephen knew all this and he used the occasion now to stamp his authority on Brendan and his friends. Brendan's crowd thought Stephen a bit of a shit, but they needed this trip so they would keep their powder dry.

McCoy smiled around the room and made support sounds like, "there are seats up here, come on up," etc. When everyone was settled, he started his talk in earnest. He firstly asked the Adjutant to brief everyone on the logistics: estimated time of departure, transport, equipment, supplies, and training. The Battalion was planned to assemble in Cathal Brugha five weeks from then, train as a unit for three weeks before departing from Baldonnell Airport aboard two American Globemaster transport planes. A buzz of excited conversation spread around the room. This was what they were waiting for.

'Loyalty.' The word appeared as if by magic. Commandant McCoy knocked the holding pin out of position with his pointer and the paper dramatically rolled open. Now that he had Brendan under control, Stephen could enjoy the presentation he had prepared so carefully.

"Gentlemen, this is the most important word in the English language and it is central to what this unit will be. Loyalty to your unit, to your superior officers, and of course to your country. We are going to make a name for this battalion with the concept loyalty as a foundation block."

He couldn't resist looking into Brendan's eyes as he spoke the words in ringing tones.

"I remember when I was young and in the Boy Scouts. We met in Rathmines Town Hall, and in a way I consider that to be the beginning of my army career. The structures of the scouts gave young boys the opportunity to take responsibility and to develop the ability to lead. It comes as no surprise to realise I suppose, that Baden-Powell, founder of the scouting movement, was a retired army officer of senior rank. The scouts are taught a code which begins with loyalty and goes on to include the following: trustworthy, helpful, obedient, cheerful, thrifty, brave, pure, and God's glory in mind. All are important and worthy of inclusion in our consideration of and preparation for the great project on which we are embarking."

"Did you ever hear such shit?" whispered Mick Keane. "Do we have to listen to this for much longer?"

When the meeting was over Commandant McCoy ceremoniously removed his peaked cap and replaced it with the UN blue beret. Descending from his lofty perch and with his Adjutant in tow, he walked up each row of officers, shook each by the hand and addressed them by name and rank. This was a surprise to many who had never met Stephen and hadn't expected him to know their names.

Outside, the reaction to the address was mixed. Brendan and his brood saw the whole thing as a replay of what they thought of him anyway.

"He still thinks he's in the boy scouts and we're the Beaver patrol."

The junior officers enjoyed the session, all except Mick Keane of course. Jack had some scout's experience himself, but just couldn't marry army life to the code as proposed by the Commandant.

"Loyalty, I suppose, okay, but the rest…two in particular stick in my craw: 'thrifty and pure'." Jack got support from Mick Keane whether or not he wanted it.

"I believe that the chaplain posted to the battalion has a thing about purity, and I don't mean the whiskey. He was notorious in his last posting abroad for not allowing French letters to be issued to the men."

"That's one way to make sure they stay pure - but remember, good people do good things and bad people do bad things, but it takes religion to make good people do bad things." Harry Jenkins felt that he had trumped the conversation.

"Who the hell said that?" Mick was ready to chew the fat but the others moved on. They all agreed, however, that Stephen was enthusiastic, would probably be supportive of them and his researching the names of the twenty officers in the company impressed them.

"Fair dues to him, I say." Jack was beginning to feel the call from the Company Commander for loyalty.

"I figure loyalty's a very emotive word. I'd prefer something more in keeping with planning and tactics. Is McCoy a thinker or a feeler?"

Jack was about to respond to Mick's unusual contribution, but wondered if he had the verbal firepower to argue the point.

And so the events of the day began to settle into reality. The junior officers ignored their older colleagues and made their way to the anteroom for coffee. A pit stop to the toilets at the bottom of the stairs, a bit of horseplay - fair shoulders and side steps - and up the brass-edged stairs two at a time and left into the anteroom. They were hit by a blast of heat from the fires, one at each end of the room, and the smell of Bewley's coffee.

'Jeeze, I can't believe it,' thought Jack, 'four weeks and I'll be swinging from tree to tree in the upper canopy searching for Jane'.

"Come in for your four bananas and five passion fruit!"

"What's that about passion?" said Harry Jenkins.

"Oh nothing, just dreaming about being called in for my tea by the lovely Jane. You know, Tarzan's wife," said Jack.

"Your dreams could get you into trouble." Harry was a mite more conservative than Jack Muldoon.

At the other end of the anteroom, at the other fire, the ladies, the wives that is, and their husbands, were ensconced. Jack could see the face of Commandant McCoy, beaming like a lighthouse as he sucked heat from the fire through the seat of his pants. Tipping back and forward from heel to toe he listened attentively to the conversation. The wives were seriously engaged in conversation more suited to their interests.

The morning passed off without any more excitement. Commandant McCoy had made his mark and the rest of the company officers spent some time getting to know one another and planning the training for the next two weeks, before the units from the west and south arrived. The junior officers, Jack included, were led by Brendan McGonnigle to a committee room off the anteroom. The planning continued and notebooks and pencils were used to good effect. By the time they broke for lunch, a training plan had been agreed. The Adjutant was to relay the results of their meeting to the commandant in his office that afternoon.

Weapons training, drill on the square, NCO training, and fitness work were identified for attention. These and other areas of the soldiers' work were to form A Company training schedule for the next two weeks, whereupon battalion exercises would have priority. Jack, in keeping with his position in the Army School of Physical Culture and his meeting with the Director of Training's man, was given the responsibility for physical fitness and introducing a fitness schedule. He was familiar with the Canadian Air Force 5BX system, which included an assessment programme suited to all levels of fitness. He knew that some of the older officers would have difficulty with intense physical exercise. Anything containing a strong element of endurance was out of the question for this group in the short period available.

Jack decided to get to work with the 'men' and spent a week building up their endurance and morale. Down the canal to Kilmainham and to the Phoenix Park became a daily run. A one-hour run took them to the magazine hill just inside the gate and the exact spot was chalk-marked on the road. Each day they made an effort to get the last man more quickly over that mark made on that first day. They rested one day in three and gradually the company of men became united in the effort to beat the target. Towards the end of the two weeks the weakest men were placed in the front of the group so that the pressure of attainment came from the fit men at the back.

"Okay, men, this is it. We're going to beat the target today by at least fifteen yards. That means that we must turn the corner at the end of the canal in twenty-five minutes. The rest will be built on that foundation."

They made the turn by twenty-two minutes, broke the record by twenty yards, and sang all the way home!

The programme for the officers was a slow burn and apart from a daily 5BX set of exercise repetitions in the gymnasium, each officer followed the remainder of the fitness programme in his own time. Commandant McCoy never missed the morning sessions in the gym with the officers of 'McCoy's Colts'!

The obstacle course in Cathal Brugha was in regular use and this part of the programme was extended to river crossings at the Strawberry Beds and hill walks in the Glen of Imaal in Wicklow. Apart from the fitness and morale benefits of the training, it was recognised that acclimatisation in a tropical or sub-tropical climate happened more easily as the level of fitness was raised and particularly when similar training was done in Africa. A continuation of the programme was therefore planned for physical as well as morale reasons. A swimming programme, including endurance swim tests and lifesaving, was arranged in the Curragh and Terenure pools on a regular basis. The conclusion to this programme was a night swim in the Liffey with full kit, using swimming aids, jackets with trapped air, timber rafts and the like.

There was emphasis on communication with the local people in the Congo. Headquarters had prepared an issue of Swahili phrases to which officers and men were introduced to this non-written language. This session added to the romance of the overall operation but, funnily enough, the national language of the Belgians and the Congolese, French, received no attention, nor did the languages of the most numerous residents of the Congo - Luba and Mongo, who spoke Kikongo, Tshiluba and Linguala; languages that had national status and were taught in primary schools.

The buzz rose to fever pitch when the companies from the West and

Cork arrived. The Cork contingent had been billeted in the Curragh for training and accommodation reasons, but many training exercises brought all three together - on the firing ranges in the Curragh Camp for example. A large proportion of soldiers were not well travelled, and moving all over the country was excitement in itself, let alone going to Africa by plane. A group of smart-assed Dubliners were heard to remark that some of those from Cork thought they were in Africa when four hours later they got to the Curragh plains!

Being issued with lightweight UN uniforms was a thrill, especially when they first paraded in complete kit, including scarf and blue beret.

Eventually the big day arrived and in typical army fashion everyone was prepared to move well in advance. The week before had been used to get the equipment and supplies to Baldonnell and on the morning of departure, the Globemasters were due in at 15.00 hrs and due to leave at 18.00 hrs. This was, however, a big operation for a country like Ireland, where the military had only just evolved to be sufficiently independent of the Civil Service in Parkgate Street to make decisions of any real portent. For officers like Jack, the presence of ranks up to Lieut Colonel was a normal experience, but on this occasion a full Colonel from GHQ, with scrambled egg on his cap, was regularly in charge of the operations at the departure airport.

"**W**hat about civilian clothes?" Jack asked a general question of his colleagues. He figured that, like duty at home, there would be work times and opportunities to do your own thing.

"Well, the word from the crowd ahead of us is that free time is available, but in a semi-conflict situation; areas around the post are mostly off limits. The government in Leopoldville has control, but things in the south, in Katanga Province, are a bit hot. There's a residue of armed Belgians and mercenaries attached to Union Minière in Elizabethville, who are holding out for a separate Katanga province with their puppet Moise Tshombe as president. Since going out there we've had about twenty casualties, so, first things first, keeping yourself alive is more important than having civilian clothes." The solid Harry Jenkins pouring cold water on Jacks 'way out' ideas again!

Nevertheless, Jack couldn't get away from the Casablanca Rick image and saw the value of civilian clothes in the climate prevailing in sub-Saharan Africa. He had a word with the only Army group who regularly travelled abroad - members of the Army Riding School, his contacts for the Agar blazer of ski fame.

"What do you think, Brendan?" Jack posed the question to Captain Cullitan who had been a regular member of the Army Equitation Team.

"Of course, Jack. There'll always be opportunities to recreate. What about playing golf or visiting resident civilians? We had a team in Leopoldville once and had a great time downtown, as well as winning the Leopold University Challenge Cup."

"But the Belgians have left."

"That may be so, but I'll bet life goes on. I know a place where you'll get a good lightweight suit."

"A lightweight suit, I like the sound of that, where do I go - it's in Dublin I suppose?"

"Siberries of Dame Street, tell them I sent you."

Jack knew that Brendan was a natty dresser and that his advice would be good. Anyway, he went along with a suit-length of lightweight material, bought at the right price from a civilian friend who had contacts everywhere for whatever you wanted. He got the usual personal attention from the tailor of 'gentlemen's suits'. Three fittings later, he emerged from Siberries carrying the two-piece suit under his oxter. He spent some time parading in front of a mirror in his room and had to admit that he was well satisfied. The material did crease easily but he figured that this characteristic went with this type of suit.

Jack was impressed by Commandant McCoy's approach to company morale and, when on a home visit, he called to a local yarn factory that made up items of clothing to contract. Jack had family connections with the owner and when it was discovered that Jack had volunteered to serve in the Congo with the United Nations, he was offered free swimming togs for each member of A Company.

A staff car containing the Commanding Officer, the Adjutant and the Chaplain led the departure to the airport. The battalion CO and the chaplain, Father Knightly, were close associates and had discussed many aspects of the operation.

"You have a great responsibility for the moral behaviour of the men, Colonel, and any way I can help I will. I believe there are many risks to their welfare and rest assured, I'll be on watch from the time we leave the airport."

As they arrived at the turn off the main Dublin-Naas road, the Globemasters became visible. They were huge, and grew in size in relation to buildings and other aircraft as the convoy got closer to Baldonnell. Army engineers were loading supplies through the rear entrance doors, into what looked like giant pelicans gobbling up all and sundry.

The equipment and ammunition had a special store place and within that space the weighting placement was carefully graded. Jack was surprised that there wasn't an American to whom they could relate. All decisions about positioning were made by a sergeant who was a bit laconic and left the nuts and bolts of the work to a lesser non-commissioned officer.

As the day progressed and afternoon light faded into evening, floodlights were switched on. Immediately an atmosphere was created which added drama and mystery to the area around the parked Globemasters. Orders were shouted and vehicles buzzed around like bees coming to and from the nest. Jack's job completed, he had an opportunity to relish the scene and try to link the present bustle with their future role in Africa.

"This is the most exciting time of my life. Did you hear anything about how things are out there?"

Brendan McGonnigle was nearby. Being the most senior of the captains in the company, he had been appointed second in command; another bridge building exercise by Commandant McCoy.

"The word I have, Jack, is that things have settled down and that the UN is supervising a period of negotiations between Tshombe in Katanga and the President in Leopoldville. The negotiations are somewhat of a window dressing because Katanga is not going to be allowed to cede it seems. As you know, there has been trouble, but I believe that the UN has sufficient firepower in the variety of contingents in place."

"What units are there?" asked Jack.

"About four Indian contingents, a Malayan unit - Signals, I think, Swedes, Italian medics, oh, and a contingent from Ghana and Tunisia. Anyway, if there's more trouble, we should be able to handle things."

Brendan smiled and hoped that his opinion would stack up.

The final moments arrived and, with everyone aboard, the colonel in charge of loading shook hands with the Officer Commanding the Battalion, and indicated to the crew that all was well and they could leave.

"Oh no, this ship ain't going nowhere 'til I say so!"

The objector was a private first class whose function, Jack thought, was to supervise the load aft in the Globemasters. True, he'd been around telling all ranks where items should be situated, but nobody fully understood his role and function. In the Irish Army, senior ranks above sergeant, even up to top commissioned ranks, took responsibility, which was reduced below the rank of sergeant. In this case a private first class was telling all ranks, including a scrambled-egg-on-cap colonel, that he had a job to do and until he was satisfied "nobody was going nowhere". For those who were within earshot the situation caused some surprise.

"What's the problem?" It was the captain of the first Globemaster.

"My triptych hasn't been signed, Sir."

The pilot solved the problem and everyone shook hands. The private first class saluted the Irish Army colonel and scampered off to his position on board.

'There's something familiar about that American pilot.'

Jack wasn't sure in the light that prevailed - 'but hadn't he seen him somewhere before'?

The doors were closed, the floodlights doused and the mighty engines whined, spluttered, and then roared into life. The trembling airframes edged their way on to the runway while, inside, the tumult of engine life had its effect in a number of ways. There was the vibration of the airframe that could be felt by all, and which added to the excitement of the moment. Secondly, the noise caused stomachs to tighten, pushing sensations up through the body, while one's head became a part ration of engine power. Jack could see that the soldiers were impressed, better than impressed really, because, as the plane taxied up the runway, all talk and bravado body language ceased. Protruding rotating eyeballs were the only indication of the young soldiers' excitement profile.

The seats in the Globemasters were a rough example of body support, consisting of straps slung along the side of the giant plane. This form of seating and the lack of any 'home comforts' made the whole experience even stranger.

The plane had two levels, both barn-like spaces, joined by a plain aluminium ladder. Just before take-off, Jack made his way down from the upper deck where his platoon were and joined a group of officers, some from his company and others from Headquarters Company. Reggie Morrison was close by. Jack knew him as the master of the beagle pack in the Curragh and their only meeting until now had been on Sunday mornings when the hunt gathered at the stables near Plunkett Barracks, before taking off for the hunt somewhere in the Kildare countryside.

Reggie was a Signals officer, but army life allowed plenty of free time to officers and men. The more enterprising officers spent their time fruitfully, organising sport and leisure activity and enriching the lives of the rest of the camp. Thus, Reggie was almost invisible during the week, but turned out on Sundays resplendent in breeches, hunting jacket, hunting cap, horn and whip, to lead the hounds. It wasn't a simple exercise; the Master had to recruit assistants, care for the hounds, communicate with the farmers, arrange the rebuilding of damaged fences and plan the hunting programme.

Jack couldn't figure out why Reggie would bother to move away from his country life and dinners with well-off landowners in Kildare, to be a part of the UN operation. He looked like a fish out of water and appeared to be having difficulty in remaining seated in the plane.

"These seats are desperate," he muttered as he strove to find an at ease position.

"Can I change with you?"

"No Jack, thanks, it's my back."

It appeared that Reggie had been suffering from a sore back; the result of jumping ditches and carrying injured hounds. He had wondered about going to the Congo. His wife was against it, but he figured that this was his one and only chance to get overseas as part of an official operation and he needed the money. He didn't give the impression of being hard up; in fact the opposite appeared to be true. In the horsy, tweed environment of County Kildare, he slotted in well. On an officer's salary, however, it was hard to keep up, and again the oversensitive Newbridge bank manager may have accrued grey hairs because of Reggie's overdraft. Like everyone else however, Reggie was a professional soldier and a signals expert and couldn't refuse the call to arms.

The wind was nor-west, so the Globemasters queued up on the tarmac at the southern end of the runway. When the roar of the four Pratt and

Whitney turboprop engines reached their maximum, or so those inside thought, they switched to a higher pitch, and as the brakes were released, the giant airframe jumped forward and sped up the runway, eating up the perimeter lights with gusto. Jack peered out a porthole and figured that the length of the runway and the full load might be significant. His flashback was of some RAF type in a war film, finishing up in an old lady's orchard and being invited in for tea and scones.

'Not with this yoke - get your feet off the ground quick.' Jack willed the giant airframe into a greater effort.

It was a laboured swan-like take-off and it appeared to all that they just made it. There was a babble of voices immediately after taking to the air and some of the young soldiers, who had never been on a plane before, clapped, before they were quietened by the steely gaze of the NCOs.

Things were worse for Reggie during the early part of the journey. The route to Leopoldville was to take them down the Irish Sea, across southern England, over France and the Mediterranean to Whellus, the American base in Libya. They would overnight there, then across the Sahara to Kano in northern Nigeria and on to Leopoldville, a journey of 2,000 miles in two days. Poor Reggie couldn't sit still; the pain was too severe. He spent most of the time lying on the floor and Jack could see that he was unlikely to survive the journey and be in a position to be an active member of the battalion. And yet the Master of Hounds refused to have treatment or tell the medics. His plan, it seemed, was to try to survive until they got to Africa and then to recover without being discovered. Painful as it was for him, the sight of his poor body in spasm was a cause of trauma for his colleagues, who should have been enjoying this adventure.

"Hi Jack, I hope you've brought your skis."

"Harley, I don't believe it - are you the pilot?"

"Sure thing, you didn't think I'd let you fly American with anyone else!"

The pilot was indeed Jack's friend from St Anton am Arlberg, Harley D. Wright. He and his friends had left Munich shortly after their encounter with Jack. Harley had opted for a desk job, but the UN trip had come up and he was asked to fill in for some other guy. Even transport was better than the dreaded desk! If he passed the physical he hoped to make active fighter pilot status.

"I suppose you have a few bombs stashed away in your kit, Jack?"

"If you can produce the Horse's Neck, my Yankee friend, I'll produce the bombs!"

Harley brought him up to the flight deck, where he introduced Jack to the co-pilot and they talked of their ski encounter and about life in general.

"How long will you be on this project?" Jack tried to converse normally, but in reality he was in a state of shock at the level of coincidence involved.

"I don't expect to be flying for more than another six months. You know that my promotion on one hand involves being chained to a desk back home, but I hope to pass the fitness test for fighter status."

Jack, somehow or another, saw Harley as being more suited to the desk job, but he didn't say so.

From the flight deck, Jack had a bird's-eye view of the flight. The plane flew at about twenty thousand feet, so city by city were easily visible. He couldn't rest, however, with the thought of poor Reggie in pain on the lower deck. After a brief discussion with Harley it emerged that there was a spare crew bunk available at the back of the flight deck; without any fuss Reggie was secreted into bed.

"Do you want me to tell you a bedtime story?"

"Feck off and thanks," said a weary Reggie.

Harley pointed out the various lights of interest and he and Jack drank coffee, delivered without request by a staff sergeant loadmaster called Pete. Pete announced himself as Irish even though he or his parents had never been to Ireland.

"I'm from McDonough County in Illinois. We were given the county after the Civil War."

"You were given a county - that's like what happened in Ireland, probably why your forbearers left Ireland. Who lived there before you arrived?"

"It was Illiniwek Indian country and they're still there. My great grandfather married a relation of Pah Me Cow ee Tah, The Man Who Tracks, which no doubt accounts for my instinct for finding our way."

Pete was essential to the running of the giant craft. He acted as loadmaster of the 585,000-pound plane. When loaded, as well as part-time navigator and cook/manager, although Harley and the co-pilot drove the plane and got called 'Sir', Staff Sergeant McDonough was the lynch pin around which everything rotated. Jack Muldoon enjoyed their clipt conversations.

The Staff Sergeant had been on a number of the trips to the Congo and some of their deliveries were accomplished under small arms fire and sometimes mortar bombs. He described dropping a previous Irish battalion who, after the planes left, had to fight their way off the runway to join an Indian Gurkha group, dug in around the airport.

"Those Gurkhas sure are some soldiers. We collected them from Dar es Salaam on the east coast, where all the Indians come by ship. They are very organised, but I think it was a first for this group to be transported by plane - certainly on this type of aircraft. I was on my rounds about an hour into the journey when I thought I smelt smoke. Sometimes we do have electrical faults and a bit of smoke, which we can handle - but this was different. It reminded me of the smell at home when my father lit the garden fire. Nothing on the top deck, so I made for the gangway to the lower deck and there was my problem. Five or six little Gurkhas sat cross-legged around a fire of broken timber boxes with sausages on their bayonets, cooking; I nearly shit myself. They looked dazed when I read the riot act, 'after all, it was only a little fire'!"

"On the way back to the port we sometimes notice that the luggage is a bit over the top. It's not my business, but on one occasion an Indian battalion was loaded to the gunnels. It was discovered by a UN person at Dar es Salaam that they were bringing home the stripping of complete houses. I'm not talking about loose items, like ornaments or even furniture. These guys, including the officers, had crates of tiles, light fittings, bidets, toilets, phones, and God knows what else. One engineer group had a complete Peugeot 404, stripped and packed for transport home! The Indian unit was billeted in Belgian houses vacated when their owners fled. In a lot of cases they left their cars, keys and all, at the airport. Anyway, that particular group of Indians did make it home with all their stuff, but I wonder if there might not be a bidet or a toilet or a phone in a prominent position in the living room of some unplumbed shack in a village near Nagpur!"

"I suppose it's hard to blame them."

"If you saw some of the living conditions there, you'd certainly believe it," said the much-travelled Pete McDonough.

"Who was Whellus anyway?"

Jack was referring to the American airbase to which they were headed, about ten miles due east of Tripoli in Libya. Harley explained that Whellus was named after Lieut Richard Whellus, USAAF, who had been killed in a plane crash in early '45, just before the end of the war. It had been an

Italian air base, Mellaha, since 1923 and was captured by Montgomery's Eighth Army during its battles with Erwin Rommel's '*Wehrmacht* Africa Korps'.

"It was used as a base for our B17 and B24 bomb missions to Italy and southern Germany."

Eventually the Mediterranean appeared and Harley soon recognised the lights of Tripoli, just beyond the airbase.

"We have to be careful of the weather here, y'all. This is where 1,000 miles of North African desert on three sides and 500 miles of the 'Med' meet to produce temperatures of 110 to 120 degrees. Have you brought your Arab dress with you? You might need it when what they call the 'ghiblis' sand storm rolls in. I was here for a stint and my eyes dried up, and the top of my head was like a boiling pot!" Harley was obviously talking truth, maybe slightly in excess, to get Jack wound up.

"Check 32/53 North-13/16 East. Stand by for landing."

All the Irish Battalion found their original places and strapped in. A bleary-eyed Reggie managed to do the same, although he still looked a bit twisted and sore.

"At least I can rest without pain now. The bed was hard and helped a lot. I must make sure I have a few boards to slip under the mattress when we get wherever we're going."

'If there is a mattress,' Jack thought, but he couldn't see much hope for the survival of the damaged signals officer. 'That's what comes from being a member of a group; it's impossible to concentrate on your own enjoyment.'

Jack looked at the lights and thought, 'Africa; we're on our way!'

Under the control of the NCOs, the battalion personnel disembarked and headed into Whellus. Jack and the junior officers stayed with the men and when they had been billeted, saw them begin their meal. The food was different but enjoyable. At this stage and having eaten only pack food since morning, anything would have tasted good, but this was the Irish soldiers' first taste of McDonald's-type food and they enjoyed it.

After dinner, Jack and a few of his friends went for a walk-about. The camp was obviously a piece of America on the edge of the Sahara. They saw houses and gardens just like in the films, and the fact that about fifty per cent of the people they saw were black was an eye-opener for the Irish, some of whom had never seen a black person except in the films. The cars that drove around the neat rows of houses kept to a speed limit; not one drove at over thirty miles an hour. Jack stood on the edge of the compound and looked out at the endless sand. He thought of the Sahara, Arab horses, nomad tribes, camel trains loaded with goods from Persia or slabs of salt from the Red Sea, Rommel and Montgomery. He pictured Kathryn Grayson being carried by the Red Shadow on his pure bred Arab stallion to his tent in the desert - all this fed by Jack's romantic notions of the Sahara.

"What are you looking at?" Jack's friend, Lieutenant Harry Jenkins asked as he appeared out of the dimming evening light.

"Apart from looking out there at the biggest beach in the world, I was thinking of what lies in front of us from tomorrow onwards. Do you realise that we will travel about 2,000 miles, to a land where everyone is black and some not so friendly? This is the 'Dark Continent' that we have been reading about in our schoolbooks. This isn't a joke, this is the real thing!"

They started next morning well before dawn and roared south over the Sahara into the darkness. Jack was surprised to see Sgt McDonough open a porthole in the roof of the Globemaster, produce a sextant and take a bearing from the stars. This was considered an important check in this low flying type of craft. When Jack mentioned the sextant to Harley, he told him that in fact the camel tracks leading from oasis to oasis were another navigation guide. Looking down Jack could see the shadow of the plane flitting over the sand dunes as on and on they droned over the desert. Gradually the darkness lifted; most were asleep, but Jack stayed with Harley, talked about past ski adventures, and was briefed by him on the changing terrain below.

"Niger, those lakes are on the border of Nigeria, pick up the river Gashua and south west to Kano. There are some Americans living close to Kano and they usually call out to the airport when we touchdown."

A small building, a bit like Collinstown in Dublin, a few camels, sand, and as the Irish walked out of the planes, the searing heat hit them with the message 'welcome to Africa'. Jack's eye caught a few people kneeling on the platform overlooking the runway, facing east and obviously saying prayers to their Muslim God.

Jack took the opportunity to get in a bit of training and A Company stripped to the waist and did some light rifle exercises. He could see that the other company commanders were impressed and Stephen McCoy could hardly contain his enthusiasm.

"A fine body of men," he ventured to some of the other commanders, who tried to look everywhere but at A Company! Jack could see that his men were happy to take part in soldiering activity. Before they started the training session however, one section, complete with Bren gun, took positions at the edge of the runway. There were trenches already *in situ*, the residue from another passing unit no doubt. A Company having led the way, the other units also placed defence elements on the surrounds of the runway, while a beaten up oil tanker and a strange looking local in full Nigerian dress refuelled the planes.

They slept on the floor of the airport building; the mosquitoes had a field day. It wasn't that they hadn't been told and advised about the dangers and precautions, but here they were on the floor, no glass in the windows, no nets. These creatures didn't play by the rules of the game; they attacked in numbers but usually gave the traditional warning; a high-pitched whine in the ear by a designated member of the attack flotilla. Slapping the ear with a fierce intensity may have killed the offending whiner, but her mates were most likely finishing dessert by this stage. The medieval plague bubers were probably a nasty business, but the swellings left on this sweet white flesh must have been a close second.

"**D**id you rub the cream on before lying down, Sir?"

Jack had been sharing his mosquito miseries with Corporal Denis Larkin, a corporal from Cork who had served before with an earlier battalion.

"I got some stuff all right but I didn't use it. I will the next time," admitted Jack ruefully.

Corporal Larkin had volunteered for service with the United Nations as soon as he heard about the Congo expedition. His was the first group of Irish troops to go to the Congo, and their proposed departure caused quite a stir in the country. They left Cork to join the rest of the battalion in Dublin. They were a mirror image of First World War British troops heading for the trenches; standard issue of uniform at that time, bull's wool, and Lee Enfield bolt action rifles. This was before the modern, lightweight or camouflage uniform was on issue. Bull's wool was a very coarse cloth, green of course and warm to suit the Irish climate. Ideal for night exercises on the Curragh in winter, but even in summer in Ireland it was sometimes considered unsuitable. There was a superfine version called 'walking out uniforms' but on this operation the coarse original version was worn.

"When we were on the way out some of the other units thought we were Korean!" Corporal Larkin never missed a chance to embellish a story.

Before leaving Dublin they paraded down O'Connell Street and were greeted by thousands. Larkin's account, told sitting on the edge of a defensive trench on the runway in Kano, Northern Nigeria, eased the boredom of the wait and kept Jack amused and not a little concerned for what could happen when they got to their base.

"Auld ones kept shaking our hands and giving us Miraculous Medals and even Rosary beads. One or two shouted 'remember Casement'."

The Irish patriot Sir Roger Casement had served in the Congo earlier in the century and had complained to the League of Nations about the atrocities perpetrated in the rubber plantations.

"God, we were a simple lot. As well as the bull's wool, our image of Africa was a combination of black babies with wobbly heads and snakes that could kill at twenty yards with a spit. I'll tell you, sir, how simple we were and some of the guys here now as well."

Denis Larkin adopted his storytelling pose, honed in his favourite bar off Patrick Street in Cork city.

"An Irish guy's sitting in the sun at a roadblock for two days. It's high noon and he's sweating like a pig. A local Baluba passes by and he asks him, like he would at the crossroads at home, 'where, in the name of God, could he get a drink?' Would you believe it but the Congolese takes him down to the nearest tap, and yer man can't believe it. I mean water! Sir."

Jack became more and more interested in the stories of the corporal from Cork. It wasn't only tales of the Congo and the part he had played but, being from Cork, the wonderful way he told them. The trip from Kano was delayed due to a shortage of fuel, so there was plenty of time to hear about previous trips, from the mouth of someone who had lived through some serious encounters. Jack wondered why these accounts, warts and all, were not a part of their training. They had been given very little historical information and nothing about previous difficulties - a little Swahili, a bit about anti-malaria drills, weapon training, fitness work, purity and loyalty lectures, drills, etc, but nothing about the position on the ground, the black inhabitants, their attitudes, and why not a bit of French?

"When we arrived in Leopoldville, which was our next stop," said Denis, "I remember, just like here today, the heat, but then we were in bull's wool so it was even worse than now. Funnily enough, not funny really when you think about it, the first thought in my mind was, 'we won't all come out of here'. I hadn't myself included in this statistic mind you, but looking around at the airport and the Gurkhas dug into the surrounds, I had a premonition that something was going to happen. We had been told that the Belgians had up and left, that the Congolese army wasn't up to the task of protecting the people, and that whatever law the Belgians had, had broken down."

The headquarters of Corporal Denis Larkin's battalion was near Buchavu in Kivu province. His company bivouacked at Kindu, about fifty kilometres from Battalion Headquarters. On their very first morning there, a takeover ceremony took place. The lowering of the Belgian flag and the raising of the UN flag was a central feature of the parade.

One of their first jobs involved visiting a group of missionaries under threat in the jungle nearby. Two sections of the company were sent out one morning to check and take whatever protective measures were necessary. The first patrol task was to get across the local river, which was about 300 yards wide. They boarded their open Land Rover, drove down to the makeshift ferry - a rope and a floating barge, and made their way to the mission station. They had travelled about eight hours through a jungle path, and across many small river crossings, and by the time they reached the missionaries they discovered that in fact all was well. The Belgian clerics were afraid to be seen having too close a relationship with the Irish forces and asked them to leave.

"Not even a cup of tea or have you a mouth on you. Welcome to Africa!"

Denis was warming up on his account of life in Africa and his next story flowed without pause. His section was performing military chores in the local school building in Kindu, filling Bren gun magazines, priming grenades, and weapons cleaning.

"Denis, Corporal, Corporal Henry Cassidy has disappeared."

"What do you mean?"

"Well he's missing."

Anyway, they had a look around, talked to the other NCOs and there was still no sign of him. 'Where the hell had Henry gone?'

Denis Larkin drew breath and engaged Jack with enthusiastic determination.

"Again, we were like chickens in a coop - we fluttered and squawked, couldn't find him and were afraid to tell any officers in case Henry got in the shit. Anyway, we waited for an hour, reported him missing and organised a search around the place; no sign of Henry. About twelve o'clock at night we heard a commotion out on the road. There was the brave Henry, rotten drunk with two bottles of Simba beer sticking out of his pockets, marching a couple of drunken Congolese soldiers up and down the road, using Swahili and Irish as words of command."

"*Aire, go mear marshail, gwenda mingi gwenda mingi.*"

"The funny thing was that the Congolese were playing the game and despite their peals of laughter, they came to attention and did whatever else they thought Henry wanted."

The Company Sergeant, an older, more sensible country man, wasn't amused; he went out, took the bottles out of Henry's pocket, smashed them, and manhandled him up to the billets where he was locked into a classroom which acted as a cell for the night. The two Congolese had disappeared into the village, leaving the sounds of their drunken laughter as an echo.

"Henry was outraged at his treatment," explained Denis, "and he engaged in a shouting barrage out the window in what he considered to be Swahili, with intermittent verses of that well-known Cork favourite, 'The Snowy Breasted Pearl'."

The following morning Corporal Cassidy was up on orders; the charge - absent without leave while drunk during active service. The commanding officer of the company was more or less unknown to the company NCOs and men. They didn't know what to expect from him and especially when it came to discipline. In other words, Captain Des Hardy had no record in the company, and that spelt trouble. How would one know how to behave, without knowing how army laws might be interpreted?

Corporal Larkin was surprised and even shocked when he saw the charge.

"That frightened the shit out of me - Henry as well! I mean, absent on active service!"

Corporal Larkin acted as escort as Corporal Cassidy, without cap or belt, was marched into the CO's office by the Company Sergeant.

"Go mear marshail, stad."

"Sir, Corporal, 29353 Cassidy, charged with being drunk and absent without leave on active service."

Captain Hardy eyed the man on charge.

"How do you plead?"

"Guilty, Sir."

"Have you anything to say for yourself?"

"Well Sir, I was walking along the path beside the school when this Congolese soldier came up to me and said, 'Are you coming for a drink?' You know how it is Sir?"

"I don't know how it is, Corporal." Captain Hardy's words dropped coldly, like water on a stone.

"We went in Sir, and they gave me one drink after another. There was a load of people in there, and they were all shaking hands with me. I couldn't walk out without buying them a drink; you know how it is sir?"

"I don't know how it is, Corporal. Listen to me; this is the most serious charge anyone could face outside of deserting in the face of the enemy. I intend to make an example of you so that every soldier who comes to the Congo will know - you'll be remembered!" Capt Hardy spoke with deadly emphasis.

"The atmosphere was tense," explained Denis.

"I sentence you to be shot at dawn tomorrow. March him out."

"What'd he say?" Cassidy didn't believe what he was hearing.

"I think you're going to be shot tomorrow," said Denis, matter of factly.

"But he couldn't do that, could he?" The corporal eyed Denis intensely, seeking a glimpse of hope.

"I don't know; we're an independent unit, a bit like a captain at sea." Corporal Larkin didn't for the life of him know why he was being sucked in to give an expert opinion.

Poor Henry turned as white as a sheet and said, "the wife'll kill me!"

Larkin knew that Henry's wife had a bit of a reputation, developed no doubt by trying to survive with Cassidy and his flawed bread winning skills. His family of ten children, all under twelve, was an added complication in their fraught lives.

Henry was shaking like a leaf as he lit a fag outside the room. The unreal feeling was strengthened by the sounds of local children at play. There Corporal Cassidy stood, barely able to breathe and not fully believing what had just happened. Before any further conversation started, the Company Sergeant fell them in again and marched the shocked pair into the Commanding Officer, still sitting behind the company office table.

"I've had a word with the Company Sergeant and he feels that up to now you haven't been too bad. Not good but not too bad. He has pleaded with me to give you a chance and I've decided to take a risk with you. I commute the death sentence and I fine you a pound instead. Do you accept my punishment?"

Cassidy's mouth opened, but only a fleck of saliva came from within and hung from his lower lip.

"March him out." The grey file sheets were slapped closed.

The Company Sergeant stopped them outside the 'courthouse'. "Cassidy, you're a waster, a waste of space, and if I catch you drinking one more time we'll re-constitute the death penalty. Get out of here!"

They went outside and Henry sheepishly put his UN blue beret back on.

"Would you like to go for a cup of tea, Henry?" Corporal Larkin sought to offer friendly advice to his friend and colleague.

"A cup of tea after being sentenced to death - are you crazy? I'm going for a drink, are you coming?" Cassidy had already changed to adopt his usual level of belligerence, and the metamorphosis happened as quickly as a local chameleon changing colour, when coming from the shade into the sunlight.

"I will, but be ready to be paraded again tomorrow morning." Denis felt the onset of anxious dread, the normal feeling when in Cassidy's company.

"Shift my arse; I knew he was only bluffing!"

The Globemasters were well on their way to Leopoldville, capital of the Congo Republic. Jack had introduced his company commander, Commandant McCoy, to his ski friend and captain of the plane. McCoy only needed *gaoth an fhocaill*, wind of the word, and he was ensconced in the cockpit with his feet on the dash, deep in conversation with Harley. He discovered that there had been a bit of shooting at the airport, but that the Gurkhas were well dug in and had the area under control. Apart from getting his load to the airport in Leopoldville, Harley had the responsibility of getting the planes safely airborne again. On one previous occasion they just managed to get airborne - the bullets were flying and mortars were landing on the runway as they took off.

"I remember the shock on the faces of the incoming units as we revved away while they were still on the tarmac. However, the Gurkhas did their job and I'm sure they will this time as well."

"I haven't been briefed about hostile fire on landing." Stephen McCoy felt a shot of cold realism flow through his veins.

"Oh neither have I, but it's best to be prepared." Harley glanced at

McCoy's face in a bid to assess the level of control in the Irish officer.

Father Knightly, resplendent in UN blue and Roman collar, had spent most of his journey with the commanding officer, but as they prepared to land he felt it best to have a few words with the men. The officer commanding the battalion was the biggest ace in his pack; he and the CO were cheek to jowl on most issues. Knightly's training was slightly unusual; rather than go to Maynooth or one of the other diocesan seminaries, he had trained especially for the missions as a member of the Fathers of African Missions in County Cavan. He had begun religious life as a brother, straight from secondary school, and joined the priesthood later. His order's mission was to spread the Word in Africa and when ordained he spent a year in Kenya. He taught religion in a secondary school and, following an uneventful year, he returned to Dublin to attend university. There he met some officers from the army attending extra-mural courses and saw another life in another uniform, which he figured was for him. His deductions were simple: life in the army is structured and authority is respected.

His visit to the Curragh Camp was evidence for him that there was a role waiting, in which the men would respectfully listen to him as one of the officer class, with authority to ensure that religious observances were respected. The idea of marching men to mass of a Sunday was an exciting prospect; after all, the brutal and licentious were a challenge, just as much as the heathens abroad. He didn't think it strange that he was an officer and received salutes from all lower ranks, lived in the officer's mess, and had an orderly. Civilians saluted all priests in the street anyway.

Parish priest to peasant, "Hold my horse while I go into the shop."

Peasant to parish priest, "Hold him yourself."

"Hold the horse or I'll stick you to the ground."

"If you're that powerful, why don't you stick your horse to the ground?"

Going abroad presented challenges for Father Knightly. The usual masses and confessional duties, of course, and whatever religious help he could provide to the natives. On reading UN literature, he realised that it was expected that the men would be sexually active and, for that reason, condoms were provided to the Battalion medics for general issue. He spoke to the CO about the dangers to the moral health of the soldiers and got his support in banning the issue of 'French letters', in spite of objections by the Commandant Medical Officer.

"It's not just their souls that we have to protect, Father; there are variations of sexual disease in the Congo that could be carried home to roost in married quarters. Are you prepared to take responsibility for such a situation?" The Medical Officer pulled no punches and started as he intended continuing.

However, although medical staff handed out condoms, there was no official issue by the Battalion as such.

Harley touched down the giant aircraft with the same skill as he had skied through new snow in St. Anton - a little better than on skis, if truth were told! Jack enjoyed the reverse thrust of the four 5,000-horsepower Whitney engines and realised that this was the real beginning of what he and his colleagues had anticipated for the past year. He saw the hunt master wince slightly as the reverse thrust had its effect, but Reggie had come through the trauma of damaged lumbar vertebrae and knew that he would survive with the judicious placement of his body and an avoidance of stress.

Mick Keane, Harry Jenkins and Jack eyed one another as they organised their platoons to disembark. The sergeants and corporals picked up on the increased tension as each man positioned himself as detailed and with his full complement of equipment. On hitting the ground each company was ready to deploy in active formation and this meant getting off the tarmac at speed. The heat and the smell of aviation fuel hit the nostrils as they ran down the ramp and adopted defensive positions at the side of the runway.

'So this is Africa,' thought Jack, as he studied the countryside around. Airport building, like any other, but on the perimeter, foliage and trees, set in a haze of heat, unlike anything he had seen before. He smelt burning of vegetation or perhaps rubbish, and this was the precursor to that burning smell that seemed always to exist in populated areas of this mission field.

'Something rich like plum pudding,' he thought, as he viewed the richness of the natural surrounds and smelt the smells. Certainly the heat coaxed this image from the red African soil. His closeness to the ground, as they dug in or readjusted the existing trenches, revealed a myriad of insects and small animals new to his experience. Some of the spiders were the size of mice.

"Watch out for the spitting cobra."

"Feck off, Mick."

There were a few words with the departing troops that they were relieving. Jack noted their obvious happiness at leaving, in contrast to their own gaping interest. They watched as their precedents quickly boarded; they had obviously spent some time planning the loading of their equipment and baggage, and loaded with incredible speed - most of their arms and ammunition had been moved into storage in the transit camp, and this was a significant factor in reducing the time of their departure operation.

A moment's comparative quiet, the engines revved, one Globemaster used its unique three-wheel pivot facility to turn on the narrow runway, inched forward, picked up speed, and sought the freedom of the sky. Harley waved from the cockpit and aircraft number two followed and wheeled north.

Jack wasn't ready for the eerie silence that prevailed afterwards. A lone Coca-Cola can careered across the tarmac. Its rattle was easily heard; he realised then that a dry north wind was blowing from the Sahara, dusting his eyes, but not effective in reducing the heat to any degree. His musings and sense of loss following the departure of the planes were interrupted by a relay of words of command. The shouts of the NCOs were both effective and reassuring, and before very long the battalion was loaded on transport. Out past the Gurkha camp and they were on their way to the Martini transit camp in Leopoldville.

More sights and sounds assailed their senses as they convoyed their way along the concrete road. In particular, the line of near-naked black people, carrying foodstuffs into town for the markets, was new and strange. This was Africa of the films come to life. The files of men and women, mostly with loads on their heads, carried on conversations with words and songs thrown sideways to the wind for consumption by the remainder of the group. Jack Muldoon for one was happily lost in the initial experience of this strange world, which was to be their home for the next six months.

Camp Martini was a mixture of buildings and tents. The mess hall for the officers and men, a large marquee, was their first port of call. The food consisted mostly of tinned rations packed by Irish firms, and they were to learn that the Irish pack rations were much appreciated by all UN units. Clover Meats, Bachelors tinned foods and in particular the current cake by Gateaux, developed a very high reputation and were even sought by other contingents on a barter basis. The Irish pack rations were seen as quality food, in comparison to the rather indiscriminate platter of quasi-international offerings, which tasted just okay, but in which the actual source materials couldn't be identified by sight or taste.

"What the hell is this?"

"Owl shit."

"Oh, I thought it was something I couldn't eat."

The first night was an experience. The mosquitoes came out after sundown mostly. They were everywhere and because the doors and windows were either nonexistent or broken, they flew around and settled with ease in the nooks and dusty shelves in the bedrooms. Thus, the Irishmen going to bed were at the mercy of the female mosquito in search of blood.

There were a number of ways in which skin can be protected. One was a cream which when rubbed on acted as a repellent. Unfortunately, it smelt awful and mostly just shifted the point of attack to places missed by inexperienced application. The spray was effective provided it was available; cover the space off and spray every nook and cranny until you have killed all flying creatures and half-smothered yourself. Mostly the spray was used in bed: cover the complete space with a mosquito net well tucked in, to be reapplied at the first sound of a recovering mosquito that perhaps had lain dogo in the folds of a blanket.

Mosquito bites were to be avoided because of the danger of malaria, and daily malaria tablets were a required habit. There were many stagnant pools in the area where the female mosquitoes laid their eggs, begat on a feed of Irish blood, thus creating the malarial cycle.

On this first night, just south of the Equator, Jack and his fellow officers took great care.

"This isn't so bad."

"I suppose not, but a bit hot."

Jack could see the lighted end of Mick and Harry's fags through the gloom and the nets. All was quiet and he was happy that he had beaten the early onslaught of winged weirdoes. A series of "good nights", quiet, and suddenly Jack heard a victory shriek in his right ear. There are high pitches and high pitches, but this was brain penetrating in its cold-steel level of decibels. He hit the ear in question, exploded into the net and scattered the makings of his bed all over the floor. He might have killed the offending insect and squashed his ear, but they out there had achieved their objective and he could feel insertions in all the soft places on his wrists and ankles. The other three in the room tried to see the humorous side of the event! Mosquito battles were a feature of the remainder of their stay in Leopoldville and it was as normal as talking about the weather in Ireland to discuss, compare and contrast, lumps and bite marks.

L uckily the Battalion's term of office was to be spent mostly further south in Katanga. The province of Katanga, and its capital Elizabethville, was situated in high country with a glorious climate and almost none of the high humidity and heat that was a feature of Leopoldville.

The main industrial feature of Katanga was the very rich mine deposits of copper and uranium, controlled almost fully by Union Minière, a Belgian company. There was some American involvement also, and atomic bomb research in the States contained Katangan uranium in its gene pool.

The stay in Leopoldville, however, was spent training and getting accustomed to the new environment, but it was a relief to everyone when the transit camp was deserted and the Battalion headed by plane to Elizabethville. The rather shaky old Douglas DC-3s, which were used for this exercise, were the air transport workhorse in Africa of that time. They stopped for a refuel in Kamina airbase en route to Elizabethville.

The airport in Elizabethville was tightly controlled. The Gurkhas, the little Nepalese that took soldiering so seriously, were in charge and carefully supervised off-loading and transportation to UN Headquarters in Leopold Farm on the northern suburbs of the city. Not that the battalion didn't take its security seriously and control their movements independently, but the Gurkhas mirrored every move and as Jack's transport swept past their tented camp, infantry men were seen practising their bayonet drill on a series of human-like sack figures. They looked as if they were enjoying the simulated penetration of human bodies. Elizabethville had reason to remember the bayoneting skills of the Gurkhas. Within the last twelve months a local Gendarmarie group had been offered surrender terms, hadn't accepted quickly enough or at all, whereupon the Gurkhas sent them over the top of the three-story town-hall building at the sharp end of a bayonet. The local radio from then on referred to the area as Martyr's Square.

Jack was aware that the Irish army's ventures in the domain of Leopold of Belgium were a chequered experience. Officers and soldiers had recently been killed in classic pitched battles with determined mercenaries leading local troops. Some deaths may have been as a result of a vague peacekeeping brief. The stories told by the soldiers showed that, as well as being under equipped initially, they were obsessed with the idea that they must not fire first under any circumstance.

However Jack's battalion arrived at a particularly quiet time, when Tshombe was negotiating Katangan succession with the powers that be in Leopoldville, but conducting a low-key propaganda war in the province.

"Hello, this is Elaine Doyle speaking on behalf of Radio Katanga, where President Tshombe is fighting to protect the existence of the small nations of Africa against the United Nations and their lackeys, the Irish and the Swedes."

"Dah da da da dah, dah da da da da dah, - Katanga-da da dah."

Katangan National Anthem.

The anthem was intended to support the idea of action against the UN in all its forms. Elaine Doyle was full of patriotic fervour in support of a Katanga separate from Congo. Her Irishness, a bit like Tokyo Rose during the war in the Pacific, was a psychological difficulty for the Irish involved in competing with the Katangan mercenaries.

The early groups seemed to have taken the brunt of the settling-in period, which had been dramatic and traumatic. A French-language competence amongst NCOs and men would have facilitated direct contact with Armee National Congolese members, with whom the Irish were meant to co-operate. Having Swedish interpreters acting as liaison officers may have complicated some important relief operations.

The Battalion's work consisted mainly of patrols in the Elizabethville area, with particular reference to the four-mile-square camp in which the Baluba Katanga resided - if the term could be applied to the living accommodation afforded by a maelstrom of straw and timber huts, and the inevitable corrugated galvanised sheeting.

The area, in which about 10,000 Balubas lived, was intended as a holding operation. These tribesmen had been used by the Belgians as servants and factory workers and were now vulnerable, out of their own homeland in southeastern Katanga, and awaiting transportation home. It was 'get your own back' time for the locals, who were deemed by the Belgians not to be sufficiently enthusiastic to meet the needs of the 'maitre d'maison' or the Belgian businessmen. At least that's the story as understood by Jack and his officer friends.

The Baluba Camp was given a character beyond its miserable inhabitants and shanty style, by the emergence at intervals of about twenty-feet high defunct anthills. These sandcastle-like mounds offered an amount of cover between the various conclaves and were used as lookout posts by the local young wild men, known as Les Jeunesse. They didn't see going back to a desolated jungle area in the southeast as career advancement and created as much diversionary activity as they could. When they became organised this resistance became quietly effective. It was an unwritten rule that if by some chance you were to hit and, God forbid, kill a child from these areas, you kept going. The backdrop to this operational practice was founded on an incident when two Swedes in a jeep killed a child, stopped, and carried the dead child into the camp. The Swedish soldiers were killed and eaten!

One of Jack's first duties was to supervise two Irish security posts on the outskirts of the camp. The posts were manned by Irish and Tunisian troops to prevent egress or ingress without paper permission. The process of moving the Balubas back to their homes in the east had started, but a number of those wishing to remain in Katanga returned, hence the UN security posts around the camp.

In the Congo of that time, a stamped piece of paper with a signature, and if possible a photograph, was worth its weight in gold. However, any tatty piece of paper was preferable to nothing. Shortly after the UN had set up the camp posts, it was reported that an example of rough justice in comings and goings was seen being applied at a Tunisian post close to an Irish checkpoint.

Jack felt good as he drove the jeep to this particular Irish post. His company was established in a series of bungalows on Avenue du Tullipiers on the outskirts of Elizabethville. All the streets in this area were named after flowers and it was obvious that, before the Belgians left, this was a delightful area in which to live. Beautiful streets and modern well-finished bungalows, each with its own swimming pool, were the norm, as were a small group of servants' outbuildings at the bottom of each garden. Jack's particular house had a split-level feature, with a short stairs leading from the ground floor to the kitchen and dining area overlooking the garden and pool.

The realisation that they were preserving the buildings for their owners, should they return, helped reduce the guilt of living in someone's family home. Buildings in non-UN-occupied areas were usually stripped of anything of value, and that included fixtures and floors.

As Jack parked his jeep at the Irish roadblock on the perimeter of the Baluba camp, the corporal in charge came to attention and saluted.

"Good morning, Sir, a great day."

"Good morning, Corporal, how are things?"

Corporal Tracy, a Dublin man, was on his second trip to the Congo but still hadn't realised that, unlike Ireland, talking about the weather in this part of Africa was a futile exercise. Here it was possible to plan a picnic with a degree of certainty! Jack and the corporal had a close relationship through the sports programme, Tracy as a member of the football team and one of the few Eastern Command soldiers to make the mostly Munster-dominated panel. John Tracy was also a good athlete and would be one of the Battalion representatives at the upcoming inter-contingent athletic meeting. They spoke about the track and field meeting until their attention was drawn to a truck approaching the Tunisian post about 200 yards away. It was halted of course, but the next sequence really stuck. The back doors of the truck swung open to reveal a steaming heap of offal - animal's heads, guts and entrails. The opening of the doors in themselves allowed portions of pink flesh to fall out on the road, whereupon the guts were wiped on the trouser leg of the driver and thrown back to join the other animal innards.

"What are they doing with that stuff?"

"It's for eating, Sir - there's a regular traffic into the camp."

Before they could continue voicing their abhorrence of the truck's contents, events progressed somewhat.

"My God, look at that!" Jack was shocked at what he saw.

The Tunisian soldier reached into the truck and pulled an animal's head by one of the horns on to the road, and in so doing dislodged a number of pieces of offal. Out it tumbled piece after piece, like the movement of the 'Quartermasse Experiment', and lay steaming and trembling on the red dust road. Later Jack was to learn that the truck's content was the offal residue of the 'bushmeat' industry, serving large cities such as Elizabethville and Leopoldville. Chimpanzees, water buffalo and gorilla were slaughtered in the game reserves where the system of preservation and supervised control had broken down.

That wasn't all, however, because the clearance from within the truck revealed something more. The red and pink of the inside was dotted with a row of white eyes and black faces. Five Congolese were ordered out and as they slid from the stinking heap they were kicked and beaten unmercifully. One was a woman; the guards pushed her into their hut and chased the others down the roadway from the camp. Most left, helping the injured along the way, but one man kept coming back waving a piece of paper; that magic piece of paper. All to no avail, because his words and gestures only provoked the Tunisians to further acts of violence and one soldier was prompted to fire a burst of automatic fire at the feet of the Congolese. Despite the threats he bravely kept coming back, until eventually the woman was released. She joined him carrying parts of her clothing and they both disappeared.

The driver and his helper loaded up the truck and headed into the camp. Jack's main emotion was respect for the woman's man, who showed great courage and persistence. Another rotting dead body in the red dust of Katanga would not have caused any investigation or trouble for the soldier, and the Congolese knew it.

"It's the first time I've seen that truck, but taking women into the hut for jig a jig is nothing new." Tracy was becoming a hardened observer.

Jack drove back to Leopold Farm, Battalion Headquarters, and joined the rest of the officers for coffee. He told his story, but the fact that the Battalion had been put on alert to accompany Tshombe to Leopoldville for negotiations with the government had priority, and was the main interest that morning.

"We'll need to leave a small holding unit here to look after stores and equipment, and Commandant McCoy has agreed to provide a section of men under your control, Jack."

Jack wasn't sure if this was an acceptable posting, but of course he hadn't a choice. His brief included linking with the Rajputana Rifles and the Tunisians, the other UN units in the area close to the Headquarters.

"There's no chance we could leave McCoy here?"

Brendan McGonnigle was still smarting from the verbal battle that he had lost with Stephen McCoy in 'Charlie Burgess'. His use of the English translation of 'Cathal Brugha' was his attempt to downgrade the Company Commander's adherence to customary military speech. He'd been appointed second in command of the Company and rather than peacefully accepting the senior post as a sop or peace gesture, he simmered under the tight rein imposed by Stephen. This aside was directed at his buddy Jack Fortune, his personal sounding board, but available to all.

McCoy was having a ball, handing out instructions right and left, whether they were needed or not. His small frame was a reduced shadow beside the six-feet-four Company Sergeant, whom he used as a direction finder and personal conduit to company pulses. His morning 'al fresco' meetings with company officers, around a table at the entrance to the company headquarters in Avenue du Tullipiers, gave him enormous pleasure.

'We had another very successful planning meeting this morning. I'm proud of my officers and, should the balloon go up, we'll be well prepared. Bren is a powerhouse and I rely on his opinion above all.'

This extract from a letter to his wife glowed with good news and in his opinion the letters would provide a historical backdrop to life in the Congo. He warned Patricia to keep them safe. His pet name for Brendan McGonnigle was a continuous cause of annoyance to Brendan, who was slipped odd pieces of information passed from McCoy's Patricia to his wife. Because of his company role as second in command Brendan kept a tight lip, but there was a volcanic prompt in his gut, which would vent, he vowed, as soon as he left the army and joined the brother-in-law in business.

Jack got himself organised for the departure of the Battalion. He had no choice about the members of the section to be left behind, but he insisted on having the services of Corporal Mickey Callaghan, a one-time army and national flyweight-boxing champion. Mickey was from Newbridge and was known as 'a sound man'. In the ring he was a punching machine that never stopped, and on duty he was quiet and completely reliable. Jack needed a wingman and they didn't come any better than Mickey. Jack also arranged to have his personal gear, including the unused lightweight suit, housed in a bungalow close to the Indian HQ and even briefed the Indian Colonel in charge.

The Baluba Camp contained about 10,000 individuals of all ages. One of the Irish officers, Murt O'Brien, had linked up with a core contingent in the camp and was working with them almost since his arrival. Murt, aged about forty, had a strong social conscience and provided food and medical services to those in need in the camp. Even in this transient situation, the Baluba Katanga were planning their return to their homeland carefully and had formed a government consisting of a president and ministers, all of whom took their role and functions very seriously.

The Jeunesse, although extreme in some of their activities, could be seen as the noncompliant youth wing of their society.

The meetings of the Baluba 'Government' discussed affairs based on reports from the various ministers of finance, health, education, etc., and at one of the meetings attended by Murt O'Brien, Jack was introduced as a UN representative to their government. Murt broached the issue of control of the wilder elements in the society and proposed that an education programme be introduced in order to give the young a raison d'être, and to introduce work and living skills.

There was a ripple of interest when Murt, much to Jack's surprise, invited the 'Government' to select a track and field team for the forthcoming athletic meeting. The fact that the local police would be involved was an added incentive for them. Jack wondered if perhaps Murt had overstepped the mark; public acceptance of this 'Government' by the locals might be a step too far.

"I thought you might have introduced the idea of cookery courses!" murmured Jack, tongue in cheek. "A Swedish menu perhaps?"

Murt didn't respond to Jack's inappropriate attempt at black humour; he felt too excited to be flippant about what he considered a very serious matter. The athletics meeting was to take place two days later, and just one day before the Battalion left for Leopoldville with Tshombe.

"We have an extra team for the meeting, Sergeant."

Sergeant Higgins was A Company orderly room sergeant but, more than that, he was Jack's administrative support and was therefore a kingpin in planning for sport in the Battalion. One of the central supports for sport was the weekly Sports Bulletin, which reported on events that had taken place and indicating what was next on the sports programme. A copy of the Bulletin was sent back to sports section in Army Headquarters each week.

"What do you mean, an extra team?" asked Higgins.

"Well the Balubas in the camp have been invited to enter a team and they've accepted."

"Will that not cause problems with the Gendarmarie?" The orderly room Sergeant was used to putting plans in place and could easily spot a weakness.

"It might do, but they have been invited and the die is cast. I suppose we'll have to meet the local lot and test the water. Anyway Capt O'Brien is most anxious to have them involved, so the negotiations are up to him."

Despite their attempts to push the onus on Murt, events moved ahead of any structured talk of difficulties in having the Balubas involved. A final planning meeting, with representatives from the UN units and the Gendarmarie, was to take place in downtown Elizabethville that very afternoon. Jack had attended most of the other meetings and knew the representatives from the other contingents. He had even practiced his French on the local police representative and hoped that the same guy would be there this time.

"Good afternoon, Captain."

It was Major Kapoor of the Madras Rifles. They had become friends at an early stage and met every couple of days. The Major arrived at the meeting, his jeep driven by a sergeant wearing a beautifully coloured red and green turban. The Rajputana Rifles were also there, as was a Tunisian, a Malayan, and an Italian, all representing their units.

The local Gendarmarie was last to arrive, almost at the same time as the Baluba Camp representatives. The police pulled in, three jeeps abreast and screeched to a halt, while the Baluba government officials walked briskly into the foyer of the hotel, dressed in their usual business clobber, and carrying shiny briefcases and notebooks. Jack could see the arrivals from the window of the meeting room and sighed with relief that both elements seemed to be on different tracks and didn't pay attention to one another. He walked down the stairs to the foyer, to be met by a delegation of the Gendarmarie on the way up. A cursory '*bonjour*' and he continued down, pulse racing, to welcome the Baluba contingent.

He had spoken to significant others from the various contingents, but not the local Gendarmarie, about allowing the Balubas to be a part of the competition; a decision had still to be taken by the committee however. Major Kapoor was to chair the meeting, with an Italian doctor as secretary.

The meeting got started and one of the first items on the agenda was the application by the Baluba Katanga to be allowed take part.

"This sports meeting and all other organised sports events, including the Soccer Championships next month, have a very valuable aim. The *esprit de corps* of our various units is part of this aim, but on a more macro level and closer to the operational brief of the UN perhaps is the creation of a high level of communication between the Congolese people and us. Nothing is more effective in that area I believe, than a well planned, inclusive sports and recreation programme. Competition yes, but friendly participation must lie at the core of our efforts. Nobody, or group, should feel excluded and this brings me to the next point."

Jack watched the faces of the Gendarmarie representatives, as it was explained that there was an application for involvement in the sports meeting from the Congolese in the Baluba Camp. There were four Gendarmarie at the meeting; the rest of the group had headed into the hotel bar. They partially understood what had been said, but when one of them exploded in French mixed with Swahili, the full message, and particularly their negative response, got home.

"Ce n'est pas possible. Ce group ne represente ni notre region, ni une organization officielle. Si on les acceuille on insulte notre Président Maoise Tshombe." The Gendarmarie nailed their flag to the mast! The inclusion of the Balubas was considered an insult.

Jack was shocked - this was an international incident. They saw the acceptance of this group as an insult to their president, although Tshombe wasn't official either, unless Katanga was allowed to secede and that was highly unlikely. Stalemate!

Major Kapoor was unruffled by their reaction and with utmost dignity and certainty in his voice he referred to his own country and some similar situation in Kashmir, which had been solved to the acceptance of all and without rancour. He explained that they had a responsibility to allow everyone participate in a sporting event regardless of their position in society. Kapoor had already completed an assessment of the possibility of the Balubas being accepted by the local police. His Colonel and the Irish Colonel had agreed that the idea was good and the Irish quartermaster at Battalion level had arranged a number of green vests just in case.

"Unlike the Olympic games, which has deteriorated to becoming a sports war with national flags taking pride of place, we are different, dear Colonel, and I propose that we fly no national flags and take part in this competition as children of mother earth. As Dean Swift said in his immortal story, Gulliver's Travels, and with respect to our Irish friends in attendance here today, let's consider ourselves as equines and a step above humans. Finally, I am able to confirm that these new entrants to our play ceremony will wear green sports vests similar to the Irish."

There was a silence as the portent of the Major's speech was explained. Gradually facial expressions changed from obstinacy, to surprise, to bemusement, to curiosity, to dumb acceptance. Jack figured that they were neutralised beyond reply by the contribution of this 'Bangalore torpedo'.

"How did he come up with this package in such a short time and especially the idea of competing in green kit? Murt will be delighted; I hope the Baluba Camp people are happy with the arrangement." Jack enthusiastically shared his feeling about the sports arrangements with

Mickey Callaghan his driver.

Meeting over, everyone trooped out and when the various transports had squealed away, Jack and Major Kapoor approached the Government 'in waiting', drinking tea in the foyer.

"Mr. President, gentlemen. We have had our meeting and although there was some opposition to your participation we were able to get agreement on certain conditions."

The Baluba camp contingent behaved as though they were surprised that there should be any opposition to their participation.

"The local Gendarmarie felt that their position would be undermined in some way, but the Chairman convinced them that sport and politics should be separate - a binding force rather than the opposite."

"And so it is agreed?"

"Yes, but with one modification, we proposed - and I hope that you agree - that no national flags would be flown and that your team would wear vests similar to the Irish."

There was a long silence and then the group began to converse in a low tone at first and finally in full voice, with obvious sides being taken. The loss of their traditional yellow and blue vests was a sticking point. Jack and the Major could see their plans melting away, but they stood back and allowed a full debate to take place. Eventually the president wiped his brow with a red handkerchief, stood up and made a final statement. At least that's what it sounded like, because the rest of the group became silent and looked at Major Kapoor with a respectful demeanour.

"*Oui. Nous acceptons les conditions de participation - mais avec une seule exception. Serait - il possible de porter notre propre marque sur nos maillots.*"

Kapoor glanced at Jack, read his face and accepted that the Baluba badge could be attached to the green vest for purposes of identification.

"Could we see the badge that you will affix, please?" Jack asked.

He figured that if the badge was more than two feet square the object of the condition might be undermined, with resultant disharmony on the day.

"*Bien súr. C'est, de la méme taille que celle sur votre casquette, Lieutenent.*"

They all shook hands and made arrangements to have their entrants in the athletic events supplied with vests next day at a sub-committee meeting at Leopold Farm and with cap-badge size badges attached. The numbers from the Baluba camp would be small, a few sprinters and a javelin thrower.

Jessie Jesus Van Dam was born to a Belgian missionary family in Kivu, close to the Baluba heartland in eastern Katanga. His father was white, his mother black and daughter of a local chieftain. Jessie, an only child, unusual in the Congo, was given a good education. He even spent some time after missionary school, in Louvain in Belgium, at a secondary school in his father's home area. He was tall and not as black as his mother's people. This gave him an advantage in Africa, as even among Africans to be less than black had a social advantage.

Jack had been surprised at how a pecking order of posts of responsibility among the Africans was applied. In the Irish Battalion for example, his peers placed an albino man high on the list. He had total responsibility for the allocation of jobs and control of payment at Leopold Farm headquarters. Jack was told that respect for whiteness was the norm and he could see the pride with which their black African mothers carried European white children.

Jessie came under the influence of an Irish Jesuit post-graduate student in Louvain University, who was also a qualified javelin coach. He progressed in strength and technique and in the one year he spent there, became school champion, competed for Louvain University and won with a throw of 215 feet. He even learned a few words of Irish from his Irish Jesuit coach!

Jessie Van Dam returned to his home in the mission in Kivu Province - the same mission visited by the Irish patrol, and approximately the same time as the Niemba ambush in which five Irish were killed. Any one with Belgian connections was in danger at that time and his father was no exception. The mission was ambushed, his father killed, and he and his mother taken back to the tribal village from which they both escaped. They finished up, having moved to Katanga, in the Baluba camp in Elizabethville and now awaited return to the south east again.

On one of his visits with Murt, Jack had seen Jessie Jesus and noted his fine looks and athletic walk. He stood out in a compound in which medical services were practically non-existent and sickness and malformations abounded. The inhabitants tried to make life bearable, but the start was from a very low base. Water taps, attended by an endless stream of camp residents, stood out as the high point of basic physical necessity and top of the social scene for women and children.

There was a number of drink *sheebens* however, frequented by men only. There they drank Simba beer and performed social niceties; meeting and shaking hands Belgian-style and polite conversation around half-barrel tables. These were the high points. The level of disease and deprivation was shocking. Little children, whose belly buttons had not been properly sealed, performed ruptured gut balloon frog-like displays when they sneezed or coughed. These were common enough, but there were other more grotesque manifestations of illness, such as the poor man who suffered from elephantiasis and carried his swollen testicles around in a wheelbarrow!

Because of the possibility that the Jeunesse might seek amusement in the form of European mutilation, visits to the camp were never taken without armed support. Jack looked forward to completing his promise to organise some recreation in the camp, but the anticipation was laced with more than a hint of danger.

The meeting next day was arranged with an eye to controlling the Camp people and the Gendarmarie, at least until the parade of athletes the following day. Again, although there was a broad range of applications for almost all the events, priority for both of these groups was based on the javelin throw and the sprint relay.

There were some exciting possibilities from the Indian battalions; a Madras rifleman who had taken part in the Asian Games in the long and triple jump; two under-even-time sprinters from the Rajputana Rifles and a Tunisian long distance runner of some repute; and finally, a 12-foot pole vaulter from Malaya, who had come second in the Commonwealth Games. The Irish had a sprinkling of runners, army cross-country champions, and one or two throwers of some repute. Two Swedish javelin throwers were entered and this caused excitement among the javelin throwing fraternity.

The opportunity to talk about the proposed football championship wasn't missed. This was to be an inter-contingent event sponsored by the UN. The six teams would play in a league form and the top three in a play-off. Jack could see that there was a great enthusiasm for this event, planned to begin in about two months' time.

"That means that we'll be back from Leopoldville in time," said Jack to Sergeant Higgins.

"*Bonjour*, Mr. President." The camp people had two entrants, the javelin thrower and a sprinter of not much consequence. Being a part of the international event was, however, the most important issue for the leadership of the Balubas. Jack handed over a batch of green athletic vests in a shack at the corner of the camp used as the government office.

"*Merci beaucoup, vous et tre gentile messieurs, go raibh maith agat.*"

Jack looked up quickly to see the voice and noted the tall figure of Jessie approaching from outside. They shook hands and began to talk in English about the forthcoming contest.

"I had you in mind when I choose the sizes, I hope they're okay?"

Jessie's eyes lit up as he quickly stripped and tried on the green vest.

"You look the part, it's a pity you don't qualify for Ireland."

"Maybe some day, but firstly we must leave here and go back to our homeland and try to re-establish our provincial government there. The Government officials and others are due to leave by train shortly. Are you free to see me throw - I have arranged also for a few of our problem Jeunesse to meet you?"

Jack hadn't planned anything in the nature of a programme for the youngsters, but he was excited by the prospect of at least coming face to face with these teens with such a terrible record. There was a space in the middle of the camp and here Jessie planned to have a couple of practice throws. While he was getting ready Jack saw a group of rakishly dressed youngsters sidle in. They appeared to defer to one guy with a bandana on his head and it was he who approached Jack, followed by what could be interpreted as a group of courtiers. Jessie introduced Jack.

"*Bonjour mes amis, Monsieur Jacques est un ami, ici san visite officielle avec notre Président. Ai avant notre depart il va nous prepare le retour dan notre patrie.*"

The Jeunesse behaved like lambs and questioned Jack about how training for their group might be arranged. Although not fully prepared, he explained his ideas about literacy and numeracy, limited as it was, but he emphasised the need for health and physical education if they were to survive to be in a position to avail of opportunities for life and living.

Jessie had a very fast arm, which he used to launch the javelin to good effect. His run-up wasn't great, a bit slow, but then he did get into a strong throwing position, shoulders and hips rotated, palm supinated, left foot jammed into the earth, and the explosion was dynamic. His follow-through was unusual in that he launched forward over the left foot and took the weight of the forward momentum on both hands just before the line. The javelin sailed through the air and plunged tip first into the red earth about 190 feet away.

'This isn't the sort of technique that you mess around with, and particularly so close to the competition,' thought Jack.

"Well done, will you be using this javelin on the day?" This was an important issue because there was always a possibility that the javelins would be provided by the organisers.

"I don't mind, I'm used to throwing all aerodynamic types."

'Okay,' thought Jack, 'he seems to know what he's about.'

The Jeunesse watched the throwing and showed an interest in what happened. They were prepared to take part. A bit of stick became a relay baton and they were coached in teams of four. Some of the hards stood back but as soon as two teams got going, the enthusiastic participation by the others acted as a magnet and they all became involved.

Session over, arrangements were made to meet at the sports arena in the centre of town.

The meeting with the Gendarmarie took place that afternoon. There was a certain worry that they might feel that the wool was being pulled over their eyes. Their status vis-à-vis their political position, but especially their jobs in the police, was of great importance to them and they viewed taking part in the accredited sports meeting as significant. They were not pleased, to put it mildly, that the occasion would not include a parade of athletes with flags, just like the Olympic Games. Tshombe had agreed to attend and present some of the prizes, but now, because of the intervention by the Balubas from the camp, there was a certain reluctance on his part.

Despite these setbacks the Police were sure that they could dominate the sports meeting. True, the Indians and the Malayans, and perhaps the Irish, would have some trump cards, but they saw that they would win overall on points, win the relay - which had double points, and especially the javelin.

Sgt Mohamed Salonka was African javelin champion, his medal still new from the Championships in Addis Ababa just the year before. They were determined to parade their flags and medals after the meeting in the

Stad de Liberation to their camp, regardless of agreements made with the UN. The stadium originally named Stad Leopold II was changed, in common with the renaming of other public buildings by the Tshombe administration.

Jack pulled into the stadium with a group from the battalion. This wasn't a case of marking a green grass pitch as in the Curragh; here everything was *in situ*. The *Stad de Liberation*, a 400-metre synthetic track, was a copy of the Atomium Stadium in Brussels and perfect in every aspect. Changing and showering facilities were an excellent standard, as were track and field markings. A warm-up track with a special access tunnel was a feature of the set-up, and the store in which all the athletic equipment was managed was under the control of a staff of two. Jack noted a selection of about twenty javelins, most still in their cellophane packing.

The Gendarmarie javelin thrower was having a training session. He was indeed very impressive and not only in stature. His technique was simple and powerful, in keeping with his bulk. He relied on a strong throwing position also to achieve terminal velocity. His slow run-up but dynamic wind-up and unleashing of the implement, caused Jack to take a sharp intake of breath.

"Get a load of that!"

The javelin soared into the air and plunged almost perpendicular into the dusty surface, well beyond the 200 feet mark. The intensity of the throw was accentuated by the savage yell of the athlete at the moment of delivery and then by his reverse run back from the line, as if in retreat from the enemy at the receiving end.

"He looks the part," said Sgt Kiely from A Company, a bit of a thrower himself. "We don't have anyone in his league."

"He's impressive all right, but a competition is about what you do on the day. It's easy here on your own in training, but you know what a difference there is between training and the real thing. We'll see how he fares tomorrow against the young Baluba Irishman," said Jack seriously.

"Irish?" Sergeant Kiely intended taking part and was interested in all aspects of the competition.

"Yes the Balubas are to wear green vests with their own badge."

They stayed and watched the Gendarmarie relay team practice. They were very good also and had obviously had international-level coaching. Their baton changes were very slick.

Jack was going to get the Irish relay team some practice in the stadium but decided to return to the field close to the Farm, where they could practice in peace. Anyway, they were short of running shoes and the running togs weren't up to standard. They were hoping to be supplied with gear from the UN stores later that evening; hoping that is. The official issue of training gear to Irish soldiers was fairly basic.

B ack in Avenue du Tullipiers at A Company Headquarters, Elizabethville, the sports meeting played second fiddle to escort preparations for the move to Leopoldville with Tshombe. There was also planning to assist in the movement of the Baluba in the Camp back to the eastern region by train.

McCoy and his second in command were discussing the details of the move and the Company's responsibility.

"Our role is to assist two companies of the Gurkhas. I've had a meeting with their Officer Commanding and he'd like us to act as sweeper and move through the camp to unearth any defectors. He, with assistance from us, will control the mounting of the train and the move out."

"One train will hardly take them all. There are at least 1,000 designated to move." Brendan was quick to identify weaknesses in the military brief.

"I know that, but the exercise will take about two weeks, using two trains and a plane and shuttling between here and their homeland will take another five weeks before the camp is cleared."

"If they're not all gone, how do we act as sweeper?" Brendan was still not satisfied.

"I asked that question and the answer was that the operation was taking place section by section, using bulldozers to level the cleared area. They said that they had the co-operation of the 'Government' in the camp."

"Even if they have, I can see problems. Thanks be to God we're on our way to Leopoldville for most of the operation. What about food and drink and accommodation at the other end?" Another snag!

"The UN officials are looking after that - I think. The whole exercise and its lack of concern for the travellers, smacks of the movement of refugees to work camps during the last war."

The other major movement at this time was the battalion move to Leopoldville. Jack discovered that Lieutenant Harry Jenkins was already transferred to Headquarters, to join a team preparing the logistics for the move to Leopoldville by DC-3. Through Harry, he was able to identify what his role would be during the Battalion's absence.

"You'll be required to see us off at the airport and be there when we return. You'll communicate with Brendan McGonnigle by radio after takeoff and each day until our return."

"So it's just Mickey Callaghan and me and a few others until you come back?" Jack knew the situation but needed to emphasise his isolation and high level of responsibility.

"You'll have to visit each of the Companies' accommodation daily and of course supervise the Guard mounting and dismounting at the Battalion Headquarters in the farm."

All this was next week; in the meantime the athletics meeting and the movement of the Balubas from the Camp.

The training session went okay and the Rajputana Rifles, thanks to Major Kapoor, made some togs available. Jack reported to the Adjutant and briefed him on the lead-up to the participation ruling for the inclusion for the Balubas in the athletics meeting. Naturally, because they were not involved in the decision about participation, there was concern amongst the upper echelon in the Battalion.

"If there's any trouble about the arrangement, you'd better be ready to join the Balubas on their trip back home!" said the Battalion Adjutant.

"I'm not the only one involved in this," muttered Jack.

Jack knew that Murt and he were the facilitators of this plan, with the support of Major Kapoor of the Madras Rifles. They felt that the outcome in terms of human dignity was much more important than their limited careers.

"What do you think, Harry? Is there a chance that we could be seen as responsible for a debacle?"

"Nothing ventured nothing gained I say. But then it's your neck that's on the block."

"Thanks a bunch - that makes me feel much better." Jack and Lieutenant Harry Jenkins often played a verbal game about responsibility and possible problems.

Next morning Jack awoke to the sound of the washing machine chugging away in the washroom. For a few twilight moments he let the sound play as a background screen to his thoughts of Jane the film star and life in the movie world. Looking through the mosquito gauze, he noticed that his slacks and uniform shirt were not on the chair beside his bed. He peered around and realised that all his clothes had gone.

" Patrice! Patrice, where are my clothes?"

He had this experience once before. Patrice, the manservant inherited from the previous Belgian owners, was a rabid clothes washer. Unless instructed specifically he was likely to come in, collect all the clothes he saw, and bung them into the washing machine.

"Take it easy, Jack, just let him get on with the job. Send him over to the mess to pick up breakfast and pray that the clothes will be dry and ironed by 09.00 hours. We're all in the same boat."

Patrice, like most Congolese working in Elizabethville, was a master of housework. As well as being immaculate in his own dress he expected a high standard from his officer charges and sought to achieve perfection by getting dirty clothes into the wash as often as possible - it got washed if you weren't wearing it. This was necessary with tropical gear because of the heat, sweat, and red dust, but not always fully appreciated by the officers from a very different climate. However, shortly after the breakfast had been eaten, Jack and Harry were presented with fully dry and perfectly ironed underclothes and uniform.

"Patrice *a stor*, you're a miracle man."

After the morning parade, Jack climbed aboard the sports officer's jeep and headed down to the Arena. Things were ticking over - the track was being swept, take-off boards replaced and plastercine in position, throwing nets adjusted, and groups of marking flags placed at the distance-marking semi-circles. Testing of the microphone was ongoing and the announcer's voice created an atmosphere conducive to raising competitors' blood pressure.

Jack was transported back in spirit to the sports in the Curragh, where Con and his plum voice expertly controlled the timing of each event through the microphone. He shivered in anticipation but this time there was more at stake than his own participation.

The discussion at lunch in the mess was about the move to Leopoldville and the athletics meeting.

"Have we many taking part?" asked Stephen McCoy.

"We have an entry in almost each event but, apart from the relay, I don't fancy our chances." Jack's answer was based on information from round and about.

"I thought you were a big-time hammer thrower," quipped Jack Fortune.

"Okay, go on and have a bit of fun. I was down at the stadium this morning and, take it from me, this is going to be one hell of an event. The UN support unit, under the control of the Egyptian, Colonel Hassam something or another, has pulled everything together and as well as having the stadium in tip-top condition, he has published the event all over. He expects a big crowd."

Bang on time the Sergeant Major, minus one company, on guard duty in the farm, paraded the Battalion for the march down to the stadium. The Commanding Officer took the parade and handed over to the second in command. The pipe band struck up, 'when boyhood's fire was in my blood', and away they went, followed by an array of locals both young and old, and all highly excited. The drummers attracted high attention from a plethora of snotty-nosed kids, agog with excitement. Somehow or another in Africa, snots were 'in' among under six year olds.

They arrived at the stadium at the same time as units from the Madras Rifles and the Tunisians. The Irish, dressed in neat tropical uniform, blue scarves and blue berets, looked the part, but as far as dress was concerned the Indian units stole the show. They had a pipe band as well, but were much more lavishly dressed and the soldiers wore very extravagant multicoloured headgear.

"Hi Jack."

Major Kapoor, dressed in his canonicals, addressed him. Jack handed the Battalion team over to Sgt Higgins and went with Kapoor to suss out the situation regarding the Baluba team from the camp and the Gendarmarie. Both had marked dressing rooms and the Balubas were set up and putting things in order. They looked good in their green gear, but there was no sign of Jessie.

"Pardon; mais ou est Jessie?"

It appeared that they had a bit of an ordeal on the way to the stadium. The Gendarmarie on traffic duty had refused to allow their parade through the town centre. There was a discussion and even an argument until finally one of the police officers that had attended the planning meeting, where the arrangement had been agreed, arrived and cleared their path. By this time however, Jessie had disappeared and was still missing.

"I hope nothing happened to him. Where could he have gone? I know he was worried and even wanted to call the whole thing off this morning," said one of the camp's government ministers. Jessie Jesus van Dam was a strong plank in the aims of the Baluba from east Katanga for political recognition on this day.

Events moved on. At a level above the dressing rooms of the athletes and their coaches, the *hoi polloi* arrived in posh cars and took their places in the stand. Moise Tshombe and his wife, met by a Guard of Honour of the Gendarmarie, received loud applause from those already seated and even from those scattered around the track. General Gandhi of the Rajputana Rifles and UN Commander in Chief and his wife received a similar reception, and he and President Tshombe exchanged greetings.

Gradually the spaces filled and it was noticeable that white mercenaries under the control of Irishman Major Mike Hoare filled a section of the stand close to Tshombe. It was they who led, on behalf of Union Minière, the resistance against the assimilation of Katanga into the Republic of Congo. Jack noted that Irishwoman Elaine Doyle, who worked for Radio Katanga, mixed easily with this group. It was a strange feeling for the UN Irish to be seen as aggressors against 'poor little Katanga'.

As agreed at the planning meeting, the UN flag was raised to a simple trumpet call. What would have taken place without this prior arrangement could only be imagined, but certainly the Katangan national anthem and flag would have played a central role. Anyway, from the Katangan point of view the games began with a whimper.

The microphone got things going and competitors for the sprints and 110-meter hurdles were called. This also had been a bone of contention. The locals, following the Belgian mode, were used to the metric system, but the majority, the Irish and the Indian units, wanted a feet and inches measurement. Unfortunately for them, the track measurements were already set out in metres - it was a 400-metre track. Re-marking wasn't on the cards for track events, but it was agreed as a compromise that field events would be measured in feet and inches.

Jack spoke to the sergeant in charge of the Irish team to discover that arrangements about the gear had not worked out. Central stores had sports equipment all right, but no personal togs or jock straps or anything like that. The togs offered by Kapoor were the standard gym issue to Indian troops and for some strange reason they were starched to look like uniform shorts, but white. Worse still, track shoes were not available and Larkin, the best Irish sprinter, decided to run in bare feet as gym shoes, he figured, didn't give any purchase on the cinder track. The only NCO properly equipped for athletics was Frank O'Sullivan from the gymnasium in the Curragh. All the hurling and football teams were okay of course, except the hurleys split easily during play unless stored in water.

Jessie Jesus Van Dam - his father's name - had been with the group in the camp that morning and had agreed to meet on the perimeter of the town. They decided to take an irregular route to the stadium. Rather than travel as a full group, the Baluba team decided for safety reasons to leave and arrive at the stadium in dribs and drabs. Jessie with his coach and friend decided to make their way together. As they moved towards the stadium they did on occasions catch a glimpse of some of the team, rounding a corner or turning into one of the avenues. Somehow, their routes parted even more and Jessie and Jean became isolated. The sky seemed to blacken as Jessie saw that their route was blocked at the end of the road by a Gendarmarie jeep and again on the left and behind. His heart jumped into his mouth and he hardly recognised his voice as he spoke to his companion.

"This is serious, Jean. These guys are here for a purpose and it's not to our advantage. What can we do?"

"Jessie - when I approach the jeep, you run through the houses on the side and escape. You must get to the stadium; don't pause once I start to run. I'll shout and try to get their attention. Hopefully they won't know which of us is which and so I'll draw their focus."

Jessie looked his older friend in the eyes and full realisation flowed between them. Jean the coach would without doubt be killed.

"Jean, we may be able to talk our way out."

Before Jessie could say another word, Jean turned and ran at full speed towards the Jeep about fifty yards away. His tribal shouts echoed from the buildings on each side of the road. It was clear he had taken the Gendarmarie by surprise, because they didn't react at once and he was within ten yards of them when their guns spoke.

Jessie Jesus only peripherally saw the smoke from the automatic weapons, because he had simultaneously dived to his left and into the first convenient house. He heard the stutter of the guns and even the ping of lead fired in his direction as it clipped into the walls around him. He should have kept going, but he couldn't resist looking down the road from the safety of the house towards the death dash of his friend. Jean, although hit many times by nine millimetre slugs, kept going and almost reached the jeep before his chest took a brace of bullets. Even then he made a dramatic effort to maintain momentum, but his legs folded and he hit the red dust almost at the wheels of the jeep.

Jessie had seen the Gendarmarie at work before, so he knew what the result of Jean's charge would be, as did the unfortunate Jean. He knew then that Jean's sacrifice deserved a maximum effort on his part. He must have been seen from both directions, but it was the group to his rear that caused him most concern.

The house was empty, obviously vacant since the Belgians left, vandalism evident by broken furniture, missing tiles, broken banisters. He ran up the stairs to the mezzanine dining area and, realising that there was no exit at that level, quickly leaped the banisters and headed out to the back garden through a broken door. He jumped over the narrow part of the kidney-shaped swimming pool.

'*Merde*', he was in the air when he spotted the body floating on the water. A group of rats were feeding busily on the bloated face and only flattened their ratty ears in recognition of the human interruption to their feast. He broke the world record garden run to the sheds at the end and ducked inside. This had been the living accommodation for the black servants.

'What now, they're on their way. I don't have much time,' thought a panic stricken Jessie Jesus.

Instead of getting across the next street and away from the immediate area, he wasted time transfixed in fear and when he did move it was all too cautious. As he inched through a hole in the flowering Bougainvillea he heard the click of a cocking hand automatic - the cold steel kiss of the weapon on his neck caused him to freeze - two seconds and he wondered why he wasn't dead.

"Why in so much of a hurry, black man?"

His immediate reaction was one of relief. He knew that if his capturer had been one of the Gendarmarie he would either be dead or on a longer journey of torture and indignity to the next world. To some degree the mutilation of Jean and the body in the pool had prepared him for his own demise. He recognised something in the voice of what he took to be a white man. Could he be Irish?

Tim Cope was from Carlow. His father was headmaster/warden of Kings Hospital College and his mother had taught there. He always had a thing about adventure, armies, danger, glory, and risk. He read avidly from a box of books his father had bought at an auction, about red uniformed soldiers fighting in the far-flung trouble spots of the Empire. He was a boarder in the college and brushed shoulders with other Protestant students who voiced stories of their grandparents fighting for king and country in the first and second world wars. He was aware that there was another tribe in Ireland who were warlike also, but who limited their forays to attacks against one another and against those who tried to settle and colonise Hibernia. His were the colonisers who had succeeded in dropping roots in Ireland and who now considered themselves more Irish than the Irish themselves. Tim figured that they could all have settled easily in time. Religion was now a line in the sand, however, and Carlow and its rich soil fringing the winding Barrow was home for Tim and his ilk.

Adventure of a serious nature was available, and so Tim became involved in canoe racing and rock-climbing. The people he met on the mountains were different from his friends in school. They were a philosophical lot and often talked about life and living while sitting on a ledge between pitches of the climb. He graduated from crags in Glendalough in Wicklow, to climbs in Kerry and Donegal. Tim decided to go to University College Cork, where he would have easy access to the crags in Kerry and West Cork. Four Professors of advanced vintage spent all of their weekends walking the mountains and occasionally rock climbing. They discovered that he was on outdoor activity person and invited him to accompany them to Sherkin Island. He accepted the invitation and enjoyed climbing cliff routes such as White Wall Corner and a dramatic sea stack all overlooking Roaring Water Bay.

Despite his extensive climbing and sailing experience in Baltimore, West Cork, Tim felt the need to search for adventure of a military nature. This meant joining an army, and although his family leanings would be towards the British Army, he went with a friend to the Curragh as a direct entry and survived a one-year training programme. He was commissioned as a second lieutenant and appointed to a newly formed education corps.

"Could I be transferred to an infantry unit, Sir?" Tim stood to attention in the office of the Commanding Officer in Ceannt Barracks, Curragh Camp.

Tall and angular with blue eyes and wispish fair hair, Tim gave the appearance of being a strong decision maker, which belied his perhaps childish attraction to the immediate.

"Your function in education is very important, Lieutenant Cope; you must see the big picture. After all, many of the recruits under your control desperately need to have their potential released, without which their lives in the army will be very limited." His Commanding Officer was understandably focused on the needs of his men.

"I understand that, Sir, but I joined the army for adventure and now that we have a role with the United Nations, I'd like to play a part."

"Ambition is all right, but there is also a matter of seniority." The senior officer liked the sound of what he'd said and reckoned that he'd solved the problem.

"Seniority?"

"Yes, seniority, there are many who have been in the army for years, some since the Emergency, and anxious to go abroad now that they have the opportunity."

Tim could see that the cards were indeed stacked against him and that his adventure for the immediate future was limited to walking young ones across the plains to Brownstown, not that that was all bad.

"Why didn't you join as a soldier?"

His girlfriend hadn't a clue about ranks and progress in the Army. She asked the question as they crossed the plains towards one of the hotels on its perimeter, and as they passed the firing ranges, the smell of cordite fuelled his adventure ambitions as did the tank track marks that crisscrossed the terrain between the plains and Brownstown. Even the occasional shimmy run of his female companion, in celebration of young life and sexual promise, wasn't enough to dislodge his attention.

"I know what I want, but I'm not so good at the planning bit. I guess I'll have to make a serious decision and this time get it right."

"Like what?"

"I was thinking of the French Foreign Legion."

He did resign from the Irish Army and straight away joined the Legion at their office on Avenue Picpus near Place Nation in Paris. He spent a year in the Legion's training post near Poitiers in southeast France. His platoon was a mixed lot, primarily from England, Germany, and France, and one other Irishman who had been a private in the Eastern Command in Dublin. He had done a runner, mostly to get away from his social circumstances.

The majority of the recruit platoon was getting away from something boring, illegal, or downright against the law of their country of origin. Many of the conversations in his billet were a competition to establish who was the hardest man. He didn't always join in and was considered the odd one out by the most vociferous in the group. His officers saw his potential as an officer and even broached the possibility of Tim taking up an administrative post, but he saw that move coming and stated clearly his position about active service.

After recruit training and specialist weapons training in Marseilles, he was posted to the French Congo, across the river from the newly established ex-Belgian Congo. They were aware that the Belgians had returned to re-establish civil living and repatriate some countrymen who had tried to soldier it out, and thereby salvage some of their business or careers. The Katangan attempt at independent survival under President Tshombe was a much-discussed topic. Word had leaked out about the great money that was available to mercenaries employed by the Union Minière-backed cabal.

"Some of the guys over there are being paid thousands."

"What sort of money though, Congolese francs aren't worth much."

"They're being paid in American dollars and hard cash."

"What are the prospects though, if the UN come in they could be forced to stay with the Government in Leopoldville."

"That's not very likely. The Belgians and the Americans are keen to protect the uranium and copper. The first American nuclear bomb was made using uranium from there - it's an important source. I figure that anyone who helps hold the fort now will find himself in a pretty serious post when the dust settles, and rich to boot."

"What are we doing here then, are we missing the chance of a lifetime?"

"There is the little matter of the Legion. If we desert, all French areas of control or influence will be out of bounds. People with records escape to the Legion, but the reverse can present problems. There is also an inter-army thing, which might put a damper on movement to any sphere of influence afterwards."

Despite the reservations voiced in conversations with his Legion colleagues, most of the Legionnaires had dollar signs in their heads and for Tim the prospect added up to one word: adventure!

One year later, as a mercenary in President Tshombe's Katangan army, Tim was detailed to stop the Congolese in the Baluba Camp from taking part in the inter-contingent sports meeting. Tshombe and his advisors saw an opportunity to have Katanga represented in an international sports event. They didn't want the waters muddied by involving other aspirants to nationhood within their region.

The brief that morning was to take out the significant athletes before the event. The Balubas were spotted leaving the camp and although the plan didn't include killing anyone, Tim heard the firing, but was still unaware of the nature of the confrontation nearby. He and his fellow mercenaries, two other ex-Legionnaires, were in charge of this part of the exercise. He now realised that perhaps they should have divided up, one mercenary to each jeep - anyway, too late for that now.

J essie Jesus turned to face his capturer. He was taller by far than the white man facing him, but there was no question of confrontation. The blue-eyed mesamorphic type stood easily in his snake boots and pointed the pistol automatic as if it were an extension of his hand and arm. The barrel was without movement, with a focus at his entrails - a broad target should he move.

Tim Cope knew from what was on display, that this was one of the sports contestants.

"Manfred, check the list - what's your name?"

The first question was addressed to the mercenary behind the wheel of the jeep and the second to Jessie Jesus.

"Jessie Jesus Van Dam."

"Yes, he's on the list - he's a javelin thrower."

Jessie was bound and seated in the back of the Jeep. His handcuffs were tied to one of the uprights supporting the canvas cover and he relaxed in the knowledge that there was no possibility of escape.

"You are to be kept in the nearest police station until the sports meeting is over."

"An bhfuil cead agam dul amach?"

Tim nearly twisted his head off in excitement as he turned to face Jessie Jesus. Here in Africa, a black man speaks in Irish and uses one of the only phrases in the Irish language he, Tim, knew. An important phrase for an Irish schoolchild - 'have I permission to go out' - usually used in primary school if the child wished to go to the toilet. He got the jeep to screech to a stop.

"Where did you learn that?"

Jessie described his background and his meeting with the Irish Jesuit in Louvain. He saw a chink of light and realised that there was a chance of survival, at least. When he had finished, the three mercenaries went into a huddle about his fate.

"I want this guy saved from harm, guys." Tim carried his heart on his sleeve.

"Okay, but he can't be let throw at the event - that would mean our end one way or another." His mercenary colleague was careful to protect number 'one'.

"Sure, I also want to survive, until we get as much money as possible and then scarper across the border to Northern Rhodesia."

Tim could see his African tour continuing similarly, but he knew that Jessie 'whatever' had to be saved from harm if he was to live with his conscience or with his family whenever they met again.

"Okay, let's leave him in the nearest police station and retrieve him after the meeting. He's marked as a significant athlete on the list, so he must be kept under cover until the meeting is over." Tim made the decision quickly so that deadlier alternatives were not on the agenda.

And so Jessie was incarcerated in a police station nearby, but with a tap on the head from the sergeant's baton as a non-returnable extra. Jessie could feel the blood dripping from his eyebrow. Shortly after being arrested by Tim Cope he had a further more traditional interrogation by the Sergeant of the station. The sergeant wasn't prepared to just keep Jessie for 'safe keeping' as requested by the white mercenary Cope. He charged him with stealing a green UN singlet, and as Jessie didn't say yes or no to any of his questions it was interpreted as dumb insolence, or its equivalent in French or Swahili, by the Sergeant whose dull job was enhanced only by stiff resistance and the delivery of classical beatings. Luckily for Jessie Jesus the Sergeant had been satiated by a spate of summary justice to about five others, so he was content to seal Jessie's enclosure with a well place tap of the regulation baton over the left ear as he was pushed towards the cell.

"I'll help him to sleep more soundly later on," he muttered as he re-entered the dayroom and locked the main door. He and his colleague left for food and drink at the local across the road.

Jessie, taking in the sharp pain he felt in his head, squinted around and tried to penetrate the inky blackness of the cell. There was no window of any sort, but a half-inch gap under the door shed a sliver of light from the single bulb hanging in the corridor outside, and joined the other molecules in the cell to create a wave of light particles in which shapes could be seen and recognised.

The smells and groans from around the cell prepared him for the carnage he eventually saw. Some were obviously dead, but a few bodies still moved. One in particular gurgled blood from his open mouth, like an oil well at first, but gradually easing to a trickle. This was followed by a frantic coughing session. Although he could have wallowed in the realisation that he would probably receive similar treatment later, his basic humanity caused him to move closer and help if he could. It was then that he recognised the badly mutilated man beside him. Jean! Yes it was his coach, also dumped in this Gendarmarie station following his heroic run in an attempt to give Jessie an escape opportunity.

Jessie managed to make contact with his dying coach Jean, before he stopped breathing and accepted the silence of death, though his legs twitched once or twice more.

Jessie lay beside Jean and tried to make his friend's dying position more dignified. He held his eyes closed and placed his hands together on his stomach. Trying to help had provided him with a focus to ease, momentarily, his own predicament. As he lay beside Jean he noticed that his own arms and legs were working well. Poor consolation if he didn't make it to the Stadium, and he had no reason to believe that that would happen; he had reassured Jean that he would be competing before his coach died.

Tim Cope and his team drove to the stadium and checked in with the rest of the group detailed to ensure that no Baluba camp internees made it to the meeting.

Meanwhile, Jack spoke to Major Kapoor about the non-arrival of some of the Balubas from the camp. Again the major's experience stood the test and he offered an opinion based on a study of the Tshombe group settling down to view the meeting. They looked pleased with themselves even before proceedings had started; Kapoor suspected that they had arranged events in support of their efforts at the sports meeting.

"It would be worth your while, Jack, to mingle with the whites among them, to see if there is something afoot. I'll pick up one of their Gendarmarie blacks and see if we can't squeeze some information from him."

"How do you mean squeeze?" Jack more or less knew what Kapoor had in mind, but he needed to check.

"Come along and I'll show you another side of my diplomatic nature." A shadow passed over the major's face and Jack realised that his new friend probably wasn't just beer and skittles.

Kapoor spoke to a few turbaned NCOs and headed down to the dressing room, which had been delegated as a drinks room for the UN group. He moved a few tables to one side and placed a chair in the centre. He spoke to two innocent looking Gurkha soldiers, who stood to one side with their short Kukri knives in scabbards.

"Come in."

The Madras Rifles Military Police entered the room with a wide-eyed Gendarmarie between them. They placed him on the chair and Major Kapoor addressed him in French.

"Avez vous information de les Baluba de la camp. Nous somme triste pasce que les athlete arrive pas."

"Non, mon Major". The policeman claimed to be innocent of any plot to stop the Balubas from taking part.

Kapoor signalled to the Gurkhas, who moved into the centre of the room with their hands on their knives. It was explained to the prisoner that if they drew the Kukri they had to draw blood; it was a part of their culture. He looked distressed and increasingly so as the Gurkhas slowly drew their weapons.

"Unless you tell me what has happened to the Balubas, and particularly the javelin thrower Jessie Jesus Van Dam, I'll command them to cut off, firstly your ears and then your penis, which you will be forced to eat."

A stream of wet ran down the Gendarmarie's leg and pooled around his left boot.

"Tell me what I want to know, or that will be the last pee you'll ever do through that miserable, overused prick."

A short pull on the Gurkha sword and the torrent of words told all.

Unfortunately, only one white mercenary knew exactly where Jessie was kept. While Kapoor detailed a platoon to rescue the rest, Jack headed up to the stand and sought the mercenary who had been identified by the prisoner down below. He didn't approach him full frontal, but sidled into an adjacent seat quietly, listened to the conversation for a while and could hardly believe his ears. He recognised an Irish accent. To be truthful it wasn't a total surprise, because it was well known that there were some Irish among Tshombe's recruits.

"I don't believe it, you were in the Curragh for a while." Jack spoke to the white mercenary.

"Yes, I was stationed in Ceannt Barracks, setting up a new Education unit."

"I have a favour to ask, Tim. I know you took a thrower called Jessie Jesus into custody today. We're at this very minute releasing the rest of the team, but I'm very anxious that nothing happens to him particularly. I know that the Copes of Carlow wouldn't want to be labelled with responsibility for his death."

Tim swallowed hard and realised that he was between a rock and a hard place.

"Come with me and we'll release him." 'If the rest are out, then there's no political reason for keeping him in custody,' he thought.

Jack and Tim, plus Corporal Callaghan and his Gustaf machine gun, headed off in a UN jeep to Region 33 and the police barracks there.

"This could be a difficult one, Jack. These guys don't like releasing anyone and particularly the Balubas from the camp. I hope we're in time."

"For all our sakes I hope so, Tim. This is a special case and you should have seen that when you took him. I thought you said that you intended releasing him?"

Tim squirmed in his seat and avoided dealing with the significance of the question. They approached the barracks just as the sergeant and another were making their way back to the cells, full of Simba. They were feeling good and looking forward to interrogating the prisoner, before the two *manamucks* they had just met arrived to attend to their sexual needs. When they saw the UN jeep they stopped and checked their weaponry. This might mean trouble and on the other hand it could be an official visit of some kind. The sergeant spotted Tim and realised that the visit must be to do with the prisoner but why the UN transport?

"Come inside and be prepared to lock the door from the inside." He figured that Tim might be under some duress from the UN.

He wasn't the only one to make a plan. Before they left the jeep, Tim had advised that there was a back door leading straight to the corridor from the cells. Callaghan and his weapon and two primed hand grenades were therefore dispatched to the back, to await a signal.

Jessie Jesus had recovered completely from the baton blow, but when he heard the doors slam he knew that stage two of his interrogation was about to take place. He switched from his Florence Nightingale role and readied himself to make a desperate bid for freedom when the gaoler opened the door.

'Perhaps he might think that the blow on the head had been more effective and not be fully on guard.'

The cards fell quickly into place. Before Jack or Tim could move, the front door was slammed shut from the inside. Jack threw a grenade at the door, which blew it from the hinges and was the signal to Corporal Callaghan to go into action.

Inside the building the sergeant grabbed the keys and rushed down to the cell. In advance of gaining entry however, the back door, used mostly to vacate dead bodies from the cells area, burst open, and he accepted a full deposit of nine ml machine gun fire in his manly chest '*gratia a*' Swedish weaponry and Corporal Mickey Callaghan. He fell flat and hit his head and body off the cell door, causing it to collapse inwards. An amazed Jessie Jesus saw his likely executioner follow the door and fall flat and motionless among the dead and dying. Callaghan called Jessie Jesus by name just as Jack arrived post haste and they all three congratulated each other. Meanwhile, Tim was rooting out the other Gendarmarie from under the wall seats in the 'day room'. A neat hole in his head settled matters - 'No names no pack drill', he concluded, and thought sadly, 'Tim Cope, you've come a long way!'

They made their way carefully back to the stadium, placing Tim in his Katanga trappings well in view at the front of the jeep, particularly where groups of Gendarmarie plied their trade. They pulled in and went their own ways, Jessie to the team room of his crowd, Tim back to his group in the stands and Jack to report a successful completion of the mission to Kapoor.

"We had a little altercation, but all is now well and Jessie Jesus is ready for the javelin competition."

"Good, it would have been a pity to achieve so much and fail to deliver the icing on the cake; your Baluba thrower I mean."

The sports proceeded event by event and the Madras Rifles, the Katangan Gendarmarie, and the Irish were placed within a few points of each other. The final scores of the top three places on completion of all events, except javelin, were: Madras Rifles 45, Gendarmarie 40, and Ireland 33. The Baluba Camp, competing in their green vests, had scored 15 points, mostly by dint of Jessie Jesus's efforts in the long and triple jump. Thus, the javelin could decide the winning team and it looked almost certain that the Gendarmarie would win, because the Indian unit didn't have a thrower of any consequence. However, Jessie was the fly in the ointment; if he won, the Indians would win by one point.

There was a fair bit of choreography going on, no doubt orchestrated by Tshombe's crowd. His speech at the start, the crowd support, the placing of the javelin as a final, and now - yes, the Katangans had another trick up their sleeves.

The official loudspeaker commentator was pushed aside to allow the announcement that the African Games medal for javelin, won by Sgt Mohamed Salonka in Addis Ababa that month, was to be officially presented by President Tshombe of Katanga. The significance of the event, the presenter, and this special time in the birth of Katanga as a nation, was milked to the full. Fair dues, it was a real *coup*, well planned and executed. Tshombe strode out to the centre of the stadium surrounded by the trappings of nationhood, officials in tribal and European clothes, and bodyguards. Jack saw his Carlow friend Tim ensconced as one of the latter.

"President Tshombe of Katanga, champion of the rights of small nations in Africa, presents the African Games' gold medal for javelin to Sgt

Mohamed Salonka of the Gendarmarie National du Katanga, as a prelude to the final event of this international sports meeting."

She went on a bit in this vein. Yes, she, it was Elaine Doyle from Radio Katanga, another Irish piece in this game of political chess.

There was an effort to get a band on to the track, but from the stand Jack saw the turbans of an Indian unit as they clicked into place around the entrance to prevent any serious incursion of this nature. Kapoor, he noted, was close at hand also and was no doubt pulling strings to ensure that the sports event didn't deteriorate totally into a political meeting in support of the Katangans and their separatist aims.

The final scene was set and the whole focus of the meeting was on the javelin throwers. They began warming up: Jessie Jesus Van Dam, Sgt Frank O'Sullivan, and Sgt Mohamed Salonka. Even though the event hadn't started officially, each warm-up throw was greeted with cheers and shouts from supporters of each competitor. The Swedes didn't turn up, due to pressure of duties, it was said. Maybe they didn't think it worthwhile to travel from Leopoldville to the competition.

O'Sullivan had a beautiful throwing style but his distance was obviously about 25 feet short of Van Dam or Salonka. The 200-foot distance was marked out in an arc, and also with flags at the apex of the throwing arc within which each throw must land. This made it easy for the athletes, judges and the crowd to make instant decisions about who was throwing best. Even warming up, the Africans were close to the 200 mark while O'Sullivan was throwing about 180 feet.

At this point the officials took over. They were a mixture of experienced judges from each contingent under the control of a chief judge - an Egyptian officer. Of the range of javelins on a stand at the throwing end, some were new, in their cellophane wrappers, and some already used.

A javelin is aerodynamic in shape, which relates to the centre of gravity of the implement and the grip. The grip is a cord wrapped around the body of the javelin, held by the thrower along the palm of the hand, with a purchase for the throw by the index finger at the back of the cord grip. Javelin is really a pulling event, rather than a throwing one, because the javelin is released at the highest point over the throwers head. If held any longer the tail of the javelin is pulled down, thus decreasing the terminal velocity of the implement and presenting a retarding figure to the airflow. If at all possible, the event should take place into the wind and this factor is so important that it even determines which direction an arena is positioned in the planning stages.

So the throwing took place from right to left, viewed from the main stand, and with a slight breeze blowing directly from the left. Jessie chose a medium javelin, which would guarantee an almost perpendicular stick when the implement landed. Thus, he could launch from the throwing end and not have to worry about getting a tip first at the other end, which each thrower must achieve in order to have a throw registered by the judges. If any part of the javelin, apart from the tip, were to land first, then it's judged a 'no' throw and gets a red flag from the judge. Each competitor had only three throws in the preliminary and three in the final round.

"Competitor number 5, Van Dam." Jessie stood up, picked up his javelin and walked back to the start of his run-up. He had marked the first eleven paces to a check mark. He looked down the run-up, adjusted his grip and started. Left right, left right, nine, ten, eleven - yes, left foot at eleven on the check mark. He started his wind up - palm upwards, hip and hit, yes. His release shout was part of the delivery and follow-through and in his case, a unique two-hand plant check; his check to prevent a foul by crossing the line was a virtual handstand. The implement soared high, gyrating like a live thing and plunged almost perpendicular into the turf close to the 200 feet mark - about 195. It was, however, a safe first throw that merited a white 'good' throw signal from the judge. The competition was on.

Considering the circumstances that had prevailed earlier Jack felt proud of Jessie Jesus Van Dam, and Tim Cope felt better about his part in that morning's exercise.

"For you, Jean," muttered Jessie Jesus in deference to his dead coach, as he walked back and placed the javelin on the stand.

Next up was Frank O'Sullivan. Frank wasn't tall, or big enough to be a top athlete internationally. In Ireland he was a good gymnast and snooker player, and his ability in all the throws was above average. He had practised a bit since coming abroad and that, plus his high level of fitness, added to his ability in this athletic event. His throw was further back than that of the Congolese sergeant, but well up on his personal best, about 185 feet. Unfortunately he got a red flag, as the javelin didn't stick.

"What javelin did you use, Frank?"

Jack was hanging around the throwing area and could see that he probably used the wrong javelin for the distance he threw and the force of the wind. The wind force had dropped which made sticking the implement difficult. Anyway, next time around he could make corrections.

Then it was the turn of the African Games champion, Mohamed Solanka. He as yet had not spoken to either of his fellow competitors, but as he walked back and selected his javelin, he allowed a smile to crack his face in the direction of his two opponents. He seemed to be addressing them, so they both nodded and said hello with their eyes. His selection was slightly different from Jessie's, more suited to getting distance and a low landing. His run up was impressive and as he launched the missile he shouted a loud war cry and on instinct turned and ran back in the direction of his run-up, still keeping his eyes fixed on the writhing piece of metal winging its way toward an imaginary enemy. It seemed to be up there forever and when it landed its tip searched for a home and was sucked into the earth over 200 feet away. The white flag was raised and the crowd went wild. It was a dramatic event, the launch, the flight, and the landing, and the crowd's part in the drama. There was a more discreet, but enthusiastic applause from the Tshombe contingent in the stand.

Jack watched with interest as Jessie selected a javelin and walked back for his second throw. He stood quietly in his green vest on the edge of the track. There was absolute quiet in the stadium as he looked with furrowed face and intense eyes into the sun-drenched distance. Slowly, like a quality Leika lens, the pupils in his grey eyes dilated quietly, evenly, but with a silent intensity, until the focus achieved was mirrored in the muscles of his face. This muscle adjustment linked wave after wave down the Adonis like body, until perfect body-mind concentration was achieved. Again the same pattern, one to eleven, the step check, the coil release and two-hand resistance before the line. He stayed prone and watched as the javelin rejoiced at its release and split the afternoon air, to plunge perpendicular again directly on the 200 mark, just slightly behind the small flag which marked the throw of Sgt Salonka. There was a gasp at first, because it seemed that it was on its way beyond the leading mark, but no, it dived at the end to emulate the landing of his first throw.

Frank O'Sullivan had the throw of his life to land just over the 185 mark, but he accepted that he had no more, and allowed the two others to progress to the next round of three throws each. Yes, the third throw of Mohamed and Jessie Jesus were similar to their first and second; the Katangan still in the lead, but only just.

During the interval, as the Tunisian Bugle and Drum Band strutted their stuff, followed by the Irish Pipe Band and the Gurkha Pipe and Drums, Jack had a word with Jessie.

"Good throws, but you're going to have to pull out something special to win. You do want to win?"

"Before Jean died, I could have walked away and let them have their showpiece, but now!"

"Okay, listen up. There will be a time during the next three throws when you'll be able in the driving position. I'll stay in touch and at that special moment you must pull the plug out and hit him hard."

Jessie Jesus looked somewhat bewildered by Jack's abstruse language, but he nevertheless nodded and walked away looking grave but determined.

"*Nil cead agat dul amach,*" you haven't permission to go out, Jack shouted after him, and at last Jessie smiled in understanding of his task.

When the dust had settled and the dignitaries returned from their respective green rooms, the two athletes reappeared and began a stretch and warm-up session. There was great joviality among the Tshombe group; it was obvious they were expecting a positive outcome and another presentation ceremony.

"Are you going up to Leopoldville with the president?"

Tim chatted to Elaine Doyle about the visit and its significance. Elaine enjoyed her role on the local radio; she didn't write the scripts and felt a bit like Lord Haw-Haw as she castigated UN troops, including the Irish, for their efforts to undermine, as she saw it, the Katangan position.

"I'll be with him, all right. There's a chance that Lumumba might stage a *coup*, or that whore Mobutu might try to rub him out." The language sounded strange coming from this good-looking European blonde, girded in her Sunday best.

"You're beginning to sound like one of us," responded Tim.

"Well, am I not? Anyway, the Irish Battalion is coming with us, so it's their responsibility to make sure we get back."

"What are your plans if all of this goes pear-shaped?" Elaine had made her own plans for escape and guessed that the professional soldiers, including Tim, would have planned a bolthole.

"I plan to move on to Rhodesia. Mad Mike has a recruitment list up his sleeve and I plan to be on it," said Tim.

They had been to a series of cocktail parties in Elizabethville and had met members of the Irish Battalion. They were both invited to an Indian party the following month.

"I hope we'll both be around by then."

"Of course we will - this is a good do," she switched the conversation to the present and the athletic meeting. "But I thought that the Balubas from up in the camp were to be taken out."

"They were, but there was a fight back by that Indian guy from the Madras Rifles. Elaine, do you know what 'taken out' means?" Tim looked into her eyes and noticed that she avoided eye contact.

"I suppose it means, not being allowed to take part."

"Yes, but in some cases, they'll never be able to take part again." Tim again tried to see the effect of his words on her face.

Elaine Doyle paled and behaved a bit like Scarlett O'Hara - she would consider the issue at a later date, but not just now.

Jessie and Mohamed had three more throws and the first rounds don't count. The psychological advantage was with the sergeant, who was in front by about ten feet. He was to have first throw and as he walked back to the start, he stopped as if deep in thought. He seemed to be about to approach the bench where Jessie sat, but another change of mind intervened and he selected his javelin and headed down to the start. Jack could see he was following his instructions, and fraternising with the camp Balubas wasn't on the agenda. He'd been spoken to by one of the Katangan officials and told that when he won, fraternisation with Jessie or his lot was not to take place.

Mohamed knew the politics associated with this event, but he wasn't entirely happy with the restrictions imposed on him by the officials. His memories of Addis Ababa and the 'African Championships' were happy ones; serious competition, but good relationships all round. He still communicated with the friends he had made from the many countries taking part.

The breeze was slightly better, so he put the idea of a 'no throw' out of his mind and faced the run-up. He felt he was slightly off his check mark and thought of aborting, but kept going, although he probably had failed to concentrate and was still thinking about his friends in Addis Ababa when he launched the missile skywards. He felt he hit it well and ran away from the line as usual, with the shouts of his supporters in his ears. He waited a reaction to the landing and when it came it was muted. The javelin landed on the 200 mark, maybe slightly less.

"Must have taken a short first step," he muttered. "I was at least a foot short of the check mark. Concentration Mohamed!"

Jessie Jesus's supporters cheered him back to the run-up and then quiet. The same javelin, the same process and away it went. It seemed like it was heading all the way to Kano in Nigeria, but it ran out of fuel and dived like a doodlebug bomb. The momentum had carried it a long way however, and it landed - yes - well over the 200 mark and got the white flag - 210 feet! As he walked back to the bench he didn't look at his competitor, but there was an added tension in the air and everyone knew that the competition had reached its crux!

Mohamed's next throw was a good one: 215 feet; he had spent some time getting his run-up right. Jessie didn't improve and with one throw left and Mohamed leading by about five feet, the outcome of the competition seemed certain. A little ceremonial group fussed around President Tshombe in the stand, in preparation for the presentation of prizes.

Jack had a cunning plan, but the idea caused him some moral concern and he didn't even know if it would work. With one throw left, it was obvious that Mohamed would win unless Jessie added some extra dimension, but what? As it stood, he was at least five feet behind and had thrown a personal best of 210 feet. Judging from the results in Addis Ababa, Mohamed had slightly more in the tank, so one's money would have to go on him to win. Unless? Jessie had been throwing the medium javelin and getting a steep decent, thus losing out by at least five feet. The only way this could change was if he threw a more aerodynamic javelin and achieved more float and a less steep impact.

'The danger was that he mightn't stick - unless, that is, there was more breeze. Everyone at the end to blow - stupid idea! However, if the end gates of the stadium were opened and the breeze allowed blow in unhindered - perhaps - why not - against the rules - cheating?'

Certainly the extreme efforts by the Tshombeites to keep the Balubas out of the competition were a weighty positive factor that had no equal weight to tip the moral scales. Jack was an advocate of the utilitarian theory of morality, which supported the idea that the rightness and wrongness of human actions is to be explained by reference to their results or consequences, which are judged good or bad. Anyway, even this was not a guarantee of a win for Jessie; he still had to make up the five feet plus and Mohamed had another throw.

The plan was to open the end gates immediately after Mohamed's throw, and get Jessie to select and throw a more dynamic javelin - or close the gates and suffer the consequences no matter what. He felt an urge to involve Kapoor, but on mature consideration, including the relative ease with which the doors could be opened and closed without being observed, he decided to keep the plan to himself. It mightn't work anyway and of course he had to convince Jessie to choose a different javelin from what he had already thrown.

He ran up to Jessie as Mohamed made his way back for his last throw. Jessie could see from Jack's demeanour that something was afoot.

"Jessie, do you want to win this competition?"

"Sure I do."

"Well I have a plan. You must gain some advantage; a change of javelin is your only chance."

"Sure, but in training I only stuck about ten per cent of those throws."

"Suppose the breeze increased?"

Jack explained his plan as quickly as he could and when Jessie seemed to balk, he leaned down and whispered in his ear.

"You owe it to Jean, Jessie Jesus Van Dam."

Jessie reacted as though hit by a whiplash, as he was transported back in spirit to the hellhole in the police barracks where Jean had died. He nodded his head vigorously, without looking at Jack again.

Jack made his way down to the doors as Mohamed prepared to run up and throw. He stepped outside through a small side gate and felt the increased pressure of the warm northern breeze in his face. 'Thank you God!'

At the same time Mohamed looked skywards and prayed that he would win for the Prophet against the infidels.

'Give me power O Enlightened One, to overcome the weaknesses of my human form.'

Prayers over, he launched himself down the approach track, hit his check mark dead on and began to wind up, shoulders and hips turned, palm raised, head forward in the classic pre-throw position. He knew as he unwound that he had it right. His left foot stamped into its position and the long spikes groaned but held, and forward momentum was transferred from the foot to his massive thighs, as an angle of delivery was created. Allah!! He reversed and checked about two feet from the line and watched as this live thing headed on its way. His now-familiar retreat from the point of delivery was a celebratory dance, joined by the hundreds of supporters present. Even the Tshombe group in the stand went a bit over the top.

The steel tip whammed into the turf beyond his previous best. Measured at 218 feet, the announcement was a signal for continued celebrations.

And so, to win, Jessie had to pull over eight feet of an improvement out of the bag. The pieces began to fall into place and Jessie selected a different javelin, but with some trepidation. He didn't take an 'extreme', but the one he selected was two grades up from his normal choice. He took it out of its cellophane wrapping and that process caused an eyebrow or two to rise at that end of the track.

Mohamed had been carried shoulder high to the presentation area; it wasn't part of the plan that the Baluba would upset the apple cart. At this stage the official Katangan band did make their way into the centre of the stadium and even blew a warm-up note or two.

Jack tested the well-oiled large bolt that held the two massive doors together and was impressed at how easily the doors opened and, importantly, how little noise they made and their lack of visibility from the rest of the stadium. Four tiers of unoccupied seats provided an ideal cover for the gate and, more importantly, allowed the breeze to blow in. The increased air flow was significant for a thrower although evidence of the increase was not obvious in the stadium - except by a change in the flag pattern and particularly, as far as Jack was concerned, of the flags close to the main stand. Jack noticed an increased flutter in those flags, but not dramatically so. He nearly chickened out and closed the gates again, but by this time Jessie Jesus had chosen the more aerodynamic javelin and without an increased airflow, a no-throw was not just a possibility but likely!

'Anyway, he still has to throw further than ever before, so…'

Jack threw the doors fully open and allowed the airflow to have full effect.

Jessie Jesus fired the new javelin into the ground as he walked back to the start. It looked good but took a bit of getting used to. The grip was more pronounced, due to lack of use, but that was good as it provided an improved purchase for the thrower's hand allowing the purchase finger fit well in.

'*Nil cead agat dul amach*. This is for you Jean.'

His run-up was perfect. The javelin felt light and Jessie felt so relaxed and in control that he had ample time to whisper instructions at the penultimate moment.

'Wind up; keep it pointing in the right direction, not so high and hit.'

He shouted and sprang forward but kept his eyes on the object of all his effort. The flight was different, lower but with the same intensity. It left at much the same angle, but the arc flattened out and at the apex it floated. He was so entranced by this flight pattern that he stayed in the prone position transfixed. This time there was no descent to a perpendicular landing - instead the javelin floated in and touched down.

'Did the point fix first?'

The rest of the stadium, however, were watching the distance more than the landing, because as it floated in, the javelin appeared to pass the 220 mark and then dropped.

"Two-hundred-twenty-three feet, six inches," called the judge, reading from the steel tape.

Two flags were raised, one red and one white. This meant that the judges were split as to whether the throw was fair or not. In other words, did the point hit first?

Jessie and Jack watched in horror. Was it all to end in failure?

"Will the chief judge please come to the end of the throwing area?"

The announcement over the tannoy brought the Egyptian chief judge scurrying to where the javelin lay on the grass. He studied the situation, spoke to the judges, chased a few Katangan supporters away, lifted the javelin and made his way back to his desk in the centre of the track.

"Ladies and gentlemen, that was a good throw. The winner is Jessie Jesus Van Dam of the Baluba East Katanga Province; second place the African Champion Sgt Mohamed Salonka; third prize Sgt Frank O'Sullivan of Ireland. Will the athletes in question please report to the judges' desk?"

Jack switched his attention to the Katangan group. They were milling around but not in a celebratory fashion. Their band had left the field and President Tshombe was nowhere to be seen. Major Kapoor had reported to the UN Chief of Staff and arranged the presentation of prizes. The Madras Rifles, his unit, had won the intercontingent competition, partly due to the efforts of Jessie Jesus of the Baluba camp; second, the Gendarmarie du Katanga, and third, the Irish Battalion. Although the focus latterly was on the javelin, the day had been a social and athletic success.

"Congratulations, the day went well. It was well worth while having the people from the camp take part." Kapoor, despite his efforts to keep the ship on course, was as dapper in dress and demeanour as if he was on morning parade.

"I did very little," said Jack, feeling a little guilty about the door episode, "the organising committee and particularly the judges, played a blinder."

"That's all very well," stated Kapoor, shaking his head from side to side in typical Indian style, "but without yourself and Captain Murt O'Brien, the Balubas would not have been involved at all."

"And everyone would have been happier and no bones broken!" Jack was thinking of Jean but still suffering guilty pangs.

"Well maybe, but you certainly played your part." It took Jack a while to convince himself that opening the gates had probably only a psychological effect on the important last throw - probably!

After the prize giving the various contingents went their way. Jack had a word with the Baluba group and in particular with Jessie Jesus who had, it seems, spoken with Mohamed and even arranged to meet him for a throwing session before the Balubas moved out to their homeland in the east.

"It's a good idea, but be careful. You'll have reinforced enemies in that group now. We've arranged an Irish escort back to the camp when you're changed and ready." Jack didn't want anything to go wrong at this stage.

The return trip to camp went off without an incident and Murt increased his special supervision of the camp until the mass move by train back to East Katanga the following week.

Things returned to normal in the Irish Battalion and apart from the preparation to leave for Leopoldville with Tshombe, officers and men went about their daily tasks. There was a UN enquiry into the expenditure of ammunition and grenades, and Jack and Kapoor had to account for the recovery of Jessie Jesus, and place the rounds expended on record. Being the senior UN officer, Kapoor took the brunt of the questioning. The officers on the enquiry had difficulty in seeing why the Balubas had to be involved at all and a note was written on the file of Murt O'Brien. On a more positive note, the 'Government' of the Province of East Katanga convened a meeting in the Baluba camp and presented a citation to Commandant Murt O'Brien for his service to their people and cause. He had of course an open invitation to attend their meetings of government whenever he visited their homeland. Jessie Jesus Van Dam and Jean, his coach, were made Freemen of the Nation, a posthumous award in Jean's case of course.

All of this took place against a background of misery and deprivation in the Baluba Camp, but with great pride of cultural heritage and hope for the future.

"You were lucky to get out of that alive," said Harry Jenkins from the bed, "and I don't just mean the altercation with the Gendarmarie. McCoy and his lot thought that you left the brief and lost the plot."

"Maybe I did." Jack responded laconically but felt tense inside.

"Are you going to the Indian party tomorrow night?" Harry tried to steer their thoughts down a more pleasant route and Jack responded enthusiastically.

"Now you're talking - try to keep me away."

Tim Cope was part of the escort that led Tshombe away from the stadium to his palace on the north of the city. The de-brief by a member of the control group from Union Minière was short and to the point. The sports meeting, it was said, could have been a major support for the position of the President. But there was a missed opportunity; his departure before the presentation of prizes was a stupid mistake.

"He should have acted like a real President and presented the prizes with the UN General Ghandi, Commander in Chief, playing second fiddle. Instead he acted like a petty tribal chief and missed his chance. There will be other times, but we missed a special opportunity."

Tim understood the frustration that existed at management level in this operation. American and Union Minière money was heavily invested and it defeated the purpose when the chosen puppet acted without thinking. Mike Hoare and his cadre of mercenaries were not employed to think, as their job was to keep the military support manifest and effective. The more successful they were, the more strength would be brought to the bargaining table, and so naturally they also wanted to have an independent Katanga.

There was some merit in this position, because nobody believed that democratic government was possible from characters like President Kasavubu or the previous president Lumumba, nor from army chief Mobutu, who some people described as being a manifestation of *les politique du ventre*, politics of the belly. The neo-communist Lumumba, who didn't survive of course, represented a red influence spewing out from newly independent Ghana and being imported into the Congo. It wasn't just democracy; it was obvious that a culture of demagogy would prevail between the many tribes involved, who weren't ever asked by King Leopold of the Belgians during the carve up of colonial Africa, if they agreed to be under the control of one agency.

Tim had swallowed the conversation line being propagated by his paymasters, hook, line, and sinker. However, he and his comrade mercenary friends were not supposed to be idealistic, unless it married with their thirst for adventure and money.

A trail had been laid across Tim's path - yes, this Garden of Eden too had its serpents of temptation and also in the form of a woman. On one of his visits to Rhodesia to play a rugby match against the local whites, he saw her. They don't make bowls of temptation like this in heaven; to sup from this vessel would cause one to lose one's soul. This sounds like an exaggeration, but she seemed to Tim to be thus and he was led by her looks and spirit like a lamb to the slaughter.

Fleurabelle was beautiful and tender in appearance, but she had been forged in the white heat of African life in the period of transition from colonies to independence. She was Dutch, only because her father was a Boer, who had fought and cheated his way from South Africa to Northern Rhodesia with Rhodes. He had carved a living from the land, discovered copper mines and diamonds and malleable malachite. Her mother was a second-generation Rhodesian, carrying the genes and colouring of her Indian mother.

Mother nature had milked the most attractive aspects and talents of both roots and given them to Fleurabelle. She was tall, slim, and beautiful, was a talented dancer and could sing like an angel. Fleurabelle put men through her hands as easily as she could play the pianoforte - which she did with great virtuosity. Her skin was golden and even paler than most of the men living in this 2,000-foot-high retreat. Her breasts, amazing as they were, were not her best physical feature; she had legs and buttocks worthy of an Italian marble masterpiece, and her languid movements declared the magic of her womanhood.

She didn't take men seriously and had left a trail of wounded male egos in her wake. In one or two cases she seemed tender and close, but when the she-cat in her awoke, she let her claws have their way. Like her father, she was glad to be away from the apartheid divide of South Africa. Because he had been independent enough to marry a coloured, she had the coloured social status - the main reason why he had left with goods and chattels. Her toughness, take-all attitude and plans to escape to Europe and America, was partially forged by her apartheid experiences in Cape Town.

From their first encounter Tim dreamed of this exotic woman day and night, saw her as sacred and sensuous, and wanted to worship at her altar. From their meetings he forged dreams in his mind and his dreams became what the body longs for; more than food, images. Fleurabelle was that perfect image for Tim Cope from Carlow!

And so it began, he down with her each weekend in Rhodesia, and she in Elizabethville whenever an opportunity presented itself. Whenever the political environment in the Congo wasn't stable, the visits were reduced, but that didn't diminish the commitment of either.

A Company had settled well into Avenue du Tullipiers. Meetings were held outdoors every morning in front of the Company offices and Commandant McCoy liked everyone to be there. That wasn't always possible due to a number of issues: other duties, bloody-mindedness, drink, or a hangover. Duty free drink at a third of the price at home could be bought in the PX stores, and this was a significant influence on why some officers were not attending Company meetings.

On this particular occasion the duties to be done, and those completed, were to be discussed. Jack, Mick Keane, and Lieut Harry Jenkins sat at the six-foot table and chatted about this and that, as the reminder of the Company officers arrived.

"Why the hell wasn't I told about the javelin competition?"

"You had a chance to be involved, Mick, but you weren't around when the list was being submitted," said Jack. "Anyway, the standard was very high; one of those guys was African champion."

"African champion me arse, I'd have given any of them a run for their money." Mick's response was classical Mick Keane, and was expected and enjoyed by his colleagues.

"Dream on!"

Before the discussion got too hot, the senior members of the company arrived. Brendan McGonnigle second in command, Capt Jack Fortune, and last the Company Commander, Stephen McCoy, as ebullient as ever.

"Good morning, Benny".

Brendan McGonnigle presented his special McCoy scowl. He hated being called Benny and especially he hated naked enthusiasm. His sidekick, Jack Fortune, acted again as a sounding board and made the appropriate support sounds.

"Gentlemen, before we discuss our movement plan to 'Leo' with the Battalion, there is one other issue which came up the other day at the Battalion meeting. The CO, Colonel Byron, is most anxious that the men are fully briefed about the dangers of having sexual relationships with the local women and particularly the women in Leopoldville, when we get there. He has had discussions with Father Knightly, who wishes to talk to each company in turn."

"What's it got to do with the witch-doctor, surely this is a medical issue," said Mick Keane.

Stephen bristled even more than was his wont, and replied.

"I would ask you to show some respect for the cloth."

"That's right, take your dirty elbows off the table," said Fortune, sotto vocce, but loud enough to be heard.

"This is a serious issue and I won't stand for any levity from my officers. Father Knightly is coming here this morning and after coffee will address the men. I want him to get full support - any questions?" Commandant McCoy appreciated any opportunity to lay down the law to his officers.

There were no questions, but the conversation afterwards dwelt on fornication and its side effects. One or two of the officers had already indulged in Congolese sexual pleasure, so the debate wasn't totally removed from the officers' lives. The discussion centred on the responsibilities of the medical officer and the priest, but it was accepted by all that it wasn't simple gonorrhoea that was in question. It was known that syphilis was widespread in the Congo, carried down by Arab slave traders and exported via colonisers and missionaries. Word had it that some Swedes had been repatriated with an incurable sexual disease; whether this was true or just a deterrent was never known. What was true, however, was that there were a few blonde brown babies in families around, and their Congolese mothers held them in high esteem.

Mick Keane, who stressed what he considered to be the vital issue, hit

Captain Fortune's social contribution on the head.

"That doesn't matter a shit, what we're concerned about here is the implementation of the orders of the medical officer, that condoms should be issued. It's not for the CO or Knightly to decide - this is UN policy."

Harry Jenkins tried to defend the status quo. "But they're at loggerheads. One issues the condoms and the other has them withdrawn on orders from the CO."

"Who has authority in this, the Medical Officer with the backing of the UN, or the CO? The Chaplin has no power unless supported by the Commanding Officer."

"But he is, supported that is!" Harry held on to the bone and stressed the de facto element in the workings of the Irish Battalion.

And so the Company officers held a general discussion about what could be done, and apart from staying in contact with the Medical Officer, a solution wasn't evident. It was agreed that Brendan McGonnigle should communicate with the Medical Officer, Tim O'Flanagan, and also act as spokesman for this morning's session. This was a planned approach, but it was also a way of keeping Mick Keane from presenting his views on authority and religion in his usual forceful manner.

The morning meetings on the street outside Company Headquarters in Avenue du Tullipiers became a melting pot for many issues of a social and military nature, and were a way of keeping some of the more excessive officers from going off the rails. Beautiful sunshine and a street lined with sweet-smelling African flowering shrubs were a pleasant venue and well chosen by the Company Commander as a launching pad for policy progress.

Fr Knightly chirped his way into the gathering of officers. His uniform was similar to that of the other officers: beret, blue scarf, and lightweight shirt and slacks. The only difference accorded to the Chaplin was the ranking on his epaulettes, which included a Christian cross. He was entitled to be called Sir, and saluted by NCOs and other ranks, but in general, lay respect for the priesthood, normal in Ireland, was applied here also. He enjoyed the rank thing and perhaps over-diligently, returned salutes.

Knightly viewed his position on sexual activity very clearly. Sex was forbidden outside marriage on pain of mortal sin; a mortal sin was a major penalty point and unless cleansed by confession, could earn the individual an eternal incarceration in Hell, which was painted as a poor alternative to Heaven.

When Mick Keane saw an opening he was away like a rabbit into a burrow. While McCoy was having a briefing session with the Company Sergeant he let his brain dribble.

"Do you know that George Bernard Shaw considered that we should beware of the man whose god is in the skies, and that we should not do unto others, as you would that they should do unto you - your tastes may not be the same!"

'How does he dig them up,' thought Jack, 'he must have a notebook of interjections geared to make the mighty think.'

Mick and Father Knightly often chewed the rag over what was right and wrong, but naturally they never agreed. Although Father Knightly played at discussing the issues, in reality he was the antithesis of Shaw's Maxims for Revolutionists, which for Mick was a philosophical foundation and often quoted.

"The Golden Rule is that there is no Golden Rule."

Now in Africa, however, the religious issues became real, and instead of raising psychological arguments to identify right and wrong, Knightly was faced with reality. The men sought nothing ostensibly, but in reality they felt they needed carnal knowledge of the only available women. And the difficulty for Father Knightly was that compliant women were available, big time! In this situation he fell back to fundamentals and his support actions were to withdraw the issue of condoms and be as an inquisitor reading from the teachings of Thomas Aquinas. Having discussions with Mick Keane for fun was one thing, but this was real.

He had, however, a support team in the upper levels of the Battalion; the Commanding Officer and the Company Commander A Company were unreservedly on his side and so he used this authority to support his instructions; that all condoms issued by the medical officer should be withdrawn, immediately, before the move to Leopoldville.

Stephen McCoy considered the issue closed, and whisked the Reverend Father away for a walk around the Company to meet the men. The Sergeant Major and the Company Sergeant led the way, and ensured that the men's quarters were prepared for the visit. Fr Knightly dropped a word here and there about the importance of saying their prayers and religious duties.

"Did he say something about a paper chase?"

"No you dickhead, he was talking about being chaste."

"What tha?"

The real meaning of what he said arrived home when the corporals came around later to collect any condoms that had been issued by the Medical Officer. For the next few days this cat and mouse game went on, the

Medical Officer issued condoms on request, the priest's supporters confiscated them.

Quartermaster Quigley was foraging around and about as quartermasters do. Food and equipment is provided according to the requirement lists in Headquarters in Dublin, but as in all armies in the field since time immemorial, a bit of bartering on the side was common practice. Jim Quigley was adept at making contacts with other units, with exchange in mind. It was always possible to stock up from the UN supplies, but with a very high value placed on Irish food issues, particularly tinned Gateaux cakes and tinned beef and stew, barter at a good rate of return was possible and greatly added to the variety of food available to the Irish troops. This exercise was unofficial, but generally known by the Company catering officers and allowed to continue in support of a dietary variation for the men.

Jim Quigley enjoyed meeting the quartermasters from the Indian, Swedish, and Tunisian units and formed a close relationship with some of them. Sometimes they met in one or other of the messes at evening time and discussed sport, living in each other's country, and whatever else came up in conversation. In particular, he became close to a quartermaster from the Rajputana Rifles and he was advised on how to cook a good curry, a skill mostly unknown among Irish cooks.

The Raj quartermaster had a broad based view of the men's needs, including the availability of women for sex. He had difficulty in broaching the subject with Quigley and was forced to switch from innuendo and a wink to a definite proposal.

"Don't the men in your unit need to jig a jig now and again - with women I mean?"

"They do I suppose but our CO, and in particular the Chaplin, are very much against sexual activity, and have even withdrawn the issue of condoms."

The Indian Quartermaster blinked underneath a furrowed brow, searching for an inkling of understanding of the Irish army's attitude to sexual practice. In desperation, and with his own sweet tooth in mind, he offered to barter condoms for tins of Gateaux cake.

The conversation continued, but there was an advance on the question of the exchange of cake for condoms. A number of local women provided sexual favours to soldiers. The other units were aware of this and soldiers were being advised on how to engage in healthy sex. Despite advice, however, some indulged in unprotected sex and the dangers of this were a worry to those in charge.

"We have established a special place where sex can take place under supervision."

"How? Where?" A few bottles of Simba, the local beer, had made the discussion possible for the Irish Quartermaster.

Situated in a secluded area between the Irish and Indian unit, Jim was brought to see the brothel. With some trepidation he pushed the canvas aside and entered the dimly lit tent. The space was divided into cubicles with a small wash area off each; a bit like a field hospital. The women sat and chatted in a foyer area and the clients were introduced to the possibilities. Just like the range of activity described on the wall of the brothel in Pompeii, a selection of ways of having sex, and which woman was expert at which, was outlined on a stencilled page on the table, to facilitate different languages and allow selection of woman and sexual preference. According to the Indian Quartermaster, the soldiers became attached to one woman and usually stuck with her. A change of woman by the client, or two arriving at the one time for the same woman, caused the few occasions on which trouble broke out.

"And how about the finances?" asked Jim.

"We deal in Congolese francs and American dollars. We pay the women 30 per cent and the rest goes to maintenance and other expenses." The Indian Quartermaster had the details of the operation at his fingertips.

"What sort of other expenses?"

"Cleaning material, lighting, security - that's an important one."

"How do you mean?" Jim was now fully involved and wanted all the details.

"It's important that things are kept under control, both from the client's and the woman's point of view. If there's any trouble we work the old ton of bricks routine here; in other words, I have a few tough men who can deal with trouble in any form. In fairness, we don't have much need for them, but the fact that they are there and known to be there, works magic. One final security need is perhaps the most important of all; I have to pay some influential people in the battalion to ensure that we are not interfered with. The Sgt Major, for example, needs to be kept sweet."

This was an addition to the normal responsibilities of the Quartermaster and Jim could see how a breakdown in security would be disastrous for the operation. A quick mental calculation, however, provided him with an incentive; apart from that of keeping the men happy, the financial rewards were great.

Back on his own patch, he pondered the possibility of setting up a sexual facility. He considered the medical dangers that were inherent in the present seek-and-find system and of how a well-administered business would benefit the men. He also thought about the money. The Indian quartermaster had his medical officer in support and the women were examined regularly. He had promised to arrange the same medical attention for the four women or so who were to provide sex to the Irish soldiers.

At the time of the Chaplin's visit to A Company and the huha about the condoms, the Irish facility was *in situ* and the clients were getting in, getting it, and getting out, so to speak.

The women who provided the service were typical black *manamucks* who, outside of the time they spent in the Irish tent, lived a normal life rearing children and cooking for the family. Sianka was twenty-five years of age and lived in a hut near one of the houses vacated by departed Belgians. A foursome of officers from the Irish Battalion occupied the house itself now and her husband was employed by the UN to look after their needs and clean the house. Whatever other income there was came from her scavenging skills. There was a small plot of land attached to the house in which she planted *manioc* as a main part of the diet, used like potatoes or rice in other parts of the world. Vegetables such as cocajam, gari, tomatoes, onions, and garlic were used to flavour the *manioc*. They got at least two crops from the garden and used whatever human or animal manure they could find to fertilise the soil. Her trusty wooden mixing pot was used to pound a mixture of greens into an edible mass.

The provision of casual sex outside of the family was always an opportunity to make some extra money, especially when the woman was still young. The demands of the husband were nightly and sometimes also when he returned from a midday visit to the local pub. He often fell asleep on top, in which circumstances she would push him gently to one side and get on with her housekeeping. She considered the visit to the Irish tent as no burden therefore, and she even enjoyed the visits to the white man's environment.

She was able to hide a proportion of the money, and use the visible amount to provide children's clothes and other household needs. Jingo, her husband, was happy to receive a few francs for the pub every day, and she was content to offer her services for good money, unlike the service she had been forced to provide to the Belgian man of the house, and sometimes his friends, for the 'promise' of money.

Things were going well for Quartermaster Quigley and his business venture. He had a few local helpers among the women, one in particular; she kept the books, made sure the cubicles were clean, and acted as go-between the women and the men. He depended more and more on her and was surprised at her efficiency and honesty. She may have creamed off a little, like the part time barmen at Punchestown Races were reputed to do, but his percentages were about right and he didn't mind that she wasn't out of pocket. Once a nasty-looking gink made his appearance as if to work with her, but Quigley immediately stamped this attempted incursion out, with a few well-chosen words and the promise of a "bayonet up the arse" if he were seen around again. He even managed to scare off a delegation of husbands, at least they claimed to be such, with the threat of military action.

"They're like flies around the honey-pot."

The Quartermaster wasn't long in business when trouble of the home variety struck - not all of his colleagues were happy with the enterprise. He had a fair amount of supervision to do and this meant that his own work in stores had to be delegated. One of his staff in particular was very unhappy.

"All those mortal sins are on your soul as well, you know. How do you expect to get absolution when you go home? I can hear you say to the priest in Fermoy that you ran a knocking shop in Africa. That's not just one sin - he'll add up the days and you'll have to account for about 500 mortlars - and it's no use claiming that there was no increase in black babies!"

"Gimme a break. What's it got to do with you anyway?"

Private Murphy responded almost hysterically at the response of the Quartermaster.

"What's it got to do with me? Do you not know that by knowing about it I'm an accomplice; my soul is also being blackened?"

"Is it money you want?"

The offer of money only poured petrol on the fire.

"You don't understand anything, do you? If I took that black money I'd be like that poor fucker Judas and I'd have to go out and hang myself."

"If I give you a rope will you promise to do that?" Jim Quigley lost all semblance of diplomacy.

"**C**ould I speak to Father Knightly, please?"

The Chaplin had a bungalow to himself and the black housekeeper ushered the Irish private, three star, into the lounge. Nice furniture with an odd black mahogany head to create atmosphere. The French windows were open and the white lace curtains billowed slightly, like the breathing of the world.

Private Murphy was worried that he wouldn't be able to express his concerns about the sex shop. The longer he waited the more anxious he got. He was about to scarper when the Chaplin bounced in; he wore a dressing gown and spoke through the furious application of a towel on his hair.

"Sorry for keeping you, Private, but I was having a swim. Is there anything wrong - can I help?"

He saw the slightly embarrassed look from the soldier, so he quickly gave his hair a few rubs from a brush, threw it on one of the armchairs, and slipped into a pair of flip-flops. He wished he'd had more warning; he didn't have many incursions from the troops and this visit gave him a degree of pleasant anticipation. A personal matter perhaps - he knew that some of the wives at home had strayed from the path of virtue, but as yet he hadn't been called to assist.

"I don't know how to put this, Father..." Private Murphy twisted and twisted his unfortunate UN blue beret.

"Is this something you wish to tell in the confessional, or is there some other way I can help?"

"This is a big matter, Father, but I don't want to get anyone into trouble."

"Don't worry, anything you tell me will be treated with discretion. Please sit down."

The private wasn't sure what discretion was, but he knew that he was being encouraged to tell all. He explained how he had become involved in the episode and tried to verbalise the reservations he had had from the very beginning.

"I didn't know what it was going to be, and when it was eventually set up I knew it was a sin, a mortal sin, to be involved in any way. It should be stopped, but there are people much more senior to me involved. What can I do?"

The young soldier broke down and was comforted by the Chaplain.

"Don't worry; I'll take care of this issue. You can rest assured that behaviour like this will receive the full rigour of army regulations. This is disgraceful and I am indebted to you, Private, for coming here to unburden your conscience. Kneel down and I'll give you a full absolution."

A sideways glance at his reflection in the full-length window, made him aware that he presented a slightly incongruous picture, dressing gown, flip-flops, and woolly head. Nevertheless, he kissed the cross in the centre of the stole, put it over his head and, placing his hand on the soldier's curly locks, said the words of absolution.

"Absolvote ab omnibus peccatistuis. In nominee Patris et Filii et Spiritus Sancti. Amen."

"Thank you, Father."

The Reverend Knightly watched the retreating figure affix his crumpled blue beret, and hurry out of the Leopold Farm area towards A Company lines on Avenue du Tullipiers. He could scarcely believe what had unfolded in the last few minutes. Apart from abhorrence for the detail of the story, he felt almost breathless when he contemplated his future role as a priest and officer. He could hardly wait to get to the office of the commanding officer with this story of sin and corruption. That such a level of corruption should exist, with the connivance of soldiers from the Island of Saints and Scholars, was beyond belief. He was almost in full flight when a thought struck him.

"Is this true? How could such a story of depravity stand up? Is the Private for real?"

He felt the cold hand of reason calm his excitement, and at that moment he realised that he relished the idea of playing the inquisitor. The questions about the veracity of the statement poured over him, and he knew that much more research was required if the story was to be believed. A cold sweat broke over his body when he thought how close he had been to opening the floodgates of innuendo without all the details. The demeanour of the soldier now assumed a different aspect - was he fully corpus mentis? But what to do?

He realised early on that he was alone until he could get some real evidence of what was going on and where. Asking for details from the

Quartermaster was a useless exercise. The slightest hint of knowledge by anybody at his level would lead to the operation ending without trace, apart from the savage scars in the minds and souls of those who had participated. It became apparent that he must catch them in the act.

'The military police are another avenue. But then, they could be involved.'

The more he considered, the more he knew that verification rested with him alone, and God of course, so he prayed for an hour and prepared to visit the scene that evening after dark. He had identified the exact location, so he knew how his physical approach should be. He drew himself a map based on the private's description and his own knowledge of the area.

At tea that evening in the mess he could barely contain himself. The question of the withdrawal of the condoms came up and he gave a spirited defence of his actions on spiritual grounds. The Medical Officer, experienced in things African for many years, stood his ground.

"Will you take responsibility for the sexual diseases that comes about because of your actions?"

"If they don't do what is forbidden by God, they won't get into any trouble, Commandant."

He tried to ease the tingle of anticipation he felt at being able to unfold the tale of horror and profligacy that was his to uncover - but not just yet.

He felt like Moses arriving down from the mountain with the Ten Commandments in stone, to find the Golden Calf being adored. Old Testament words like 'the wrath of God' and 'Judgment Day' sprang to mind as he changed into civvies.

'This isn't me,' he thought, 'but then desperate issues require desperate measures.' He said a prayer to Our Lady of Lourdes.

He hadn't thought out his approach to visiting the brothel, apart from arriving down there and checking that it existed. When he reached the vicinity, however, logistics loomed large and he began to focus on detail.

'People going in and out aren't enough. I'll have to get detail, but how and how much?'

Cognisance that he would have to behave like a client if he were to identify the full implications was a shock. He remembered his mother telling him that he should look before he leaped - perhaps he had leaped prematurely.

'Into the valley of death rode the four hundred - and there's only God and me.'

He spoke to himself as he approached the cunningly concealed tent. He attempted to appear normal, but wasn't sure what normal in this circumstance was.

'How would a good Catholic Irish boy approach such a place?'

He watched for a while and got his answer. While he skulked in the shadows, 'young Catholic Irish boys' of all ages strode towards the tent with what seemed a sense of purpose and showing no evidence of embarrassment or shame. It was clear that he couldn't stay standing at the base of the mango tree in the dark without attracting attention, so he took his courage in his hands and moved carefully towards the tent opening. He wasn't sure what he expected to happen, apart from a bolt from heaven, but in fact his progress was painless and there he was. The foyer area was welcoming and as well as low lighting, which he expected, music played softly in the background. Frank Sinatra sang - he didn't stop to consider the appropriateness of the lyrics.

"Can I help you, Father?"

In a flood of panic and disenchantment, he looked at the smiling black lady in colourful African dress. 'How could she have known? Unless, that is, they were expecting him.' The answer was much simpler. Sianka was a staunch Roman Catholic, and apart from her work in the brothel, was a mother, and twice weekly attended mass. That very morning she had received the host from Father Knightly and recognised him as soon as he entered the tent.

"Are you looking for someone, Father?"

His presence for the Irish clients was of a different order, however.

"Did you see who's down there? It's Knightly."

"The Chaplain?"

"Yes!"

"I'm off."

One thing about a tent, as all Arabs know: they're easy to leave in an emergency and can be folded up and taken away quickly. In this instance the porous nature of the tent allowed all the Irish soldiers, regardless of stages of lovemaking, to wriggle to freedom in seconds.

There was another issue to be factored in however - a priest talking to the concierge in a knocking shop.

"Stand still everyone!"

Not the sort of admonition one would choose perhaps when raiding an establishment of this nature. The Irish Army *Poilini Airm*, Military Police, were not known for their delicate natures or for their ability to match events to actions. When informed of the sex exercise underway, they first salivated at doing their duty and secondly, saw that this was a historic opportunity to open a sex file that had lain dormant since the British left Ireland in the Twenties. Apart from closing the disgusting centre down, they had no aim other than to arrest all Irish clients and get details on the organiser. They had information on the work of this Quartermaster and expected to get evidence that would bring him to justice.

Anyway, there they were, but like a dandelion blown 'she loves me not', all the seeds were floating into the warm African night.

Fr Knightly was astounded and could only gaze open-mouthed at the portly PA Sergeant facing him. Not so with Sianka, however. While the Police Sergeant and the priest were looking at one another, she picked up the appointment book, money, assortment of condoms from the table, and secreted them quickly and smoothly into an open black hand, which had appeared like magic from under the tarpaulin. Job done, she moved down the line of rooms to join the other African ladies, some with small children on their backs, all moving quietly away despite the protestations of the police in and around the tent. Notwithstanding all the planning, the police were left with a tent, some basins and towels, some used condoms, but very little else to justify their night raid.

Well, not exactly true. They had one private soldier and a very confused and frightened Chaplain in custody. The soldier had been found moving away from the area of the tent without a pass for absence from his quarters, and the Chaplin found talking to a black African woman in the area where they reckoned the allocation of sexual partners took place.

"Sergeant, I'm glad you came and found this den of iniquity. I came down to find out if what I had heard was true and was astonished to find Irish soldiers taking part in base acts."

"How long were you here, Father - could you identify any of the soldiers?" Sergeant Considine was settling into his role as crime buster.

Yes, Father had been there for about ten minutes talking to the woman in charge, but he didn't talk to any of the ten or so soldiers who came and left. Most of them were in civvies, which made them difficult to recognise, on unit, rank, or name grounds.

About five minutes into the conversation Father Knightly realised that he was being interviewed, rather than involved in a one-to-one conversation. He felt his blood run cold as he began to understand that it might look as if he were involved in the activities. And yet it couldn't be

- he was the Unit Chaplin. How could this Sergeant be so stupid?

"I have to warn you Father, that what you are saying is being noted and may be used in…"

"Listen here Sergeant, I'm the Unit Chaplin with responsibility for the morals of this unit and an officer also, may I remind you. My role here is similar to yours and I intend reporting what I have seen to the Commanding Officer this very evening. Your absurd assumption and attempt to give me a legal warning will also be reported, and I expect the outcome to be serious for you."

"You must understand, Father, that your position here is obviously very suspicious. We will of course carry out further investigations, but at the moment I must ask you to be available if required."

Next day what had happened spread like wildfire. Nobody really believed that the Chaplin was involved as a customer and when the investigation deepened and the Quartermaster was charged, evidence sufficient to charge Father Knightly was not available, let alone a charge against him.

However, the news of the evening spread, and stories based on rumour gathered pace, making it difficult for the Commanding Officer and the Chaplin to have the same relationship ever again. The Quartermaster was returned to Ireland on the first available UN transport.

The women formerly employed on tent duties were still available, but in a variety of venues as before.

The famous record book, which Sianka had so expertly secreted, turned up and caused a flurry of excitement among the police. That was, until it was found that the clients written therein were not soldiers in the Battalion, but famous Irish saints and heroes.

St Patrick	21-2-65 - 12.30 hrs	Simona Balonca	40 francs
Fionn MacCumhail	21-2-65 - 11.15 hrs	Hennie Clarisol	40 francs
Eamon De Valera	21-2-65 - 01.00 hrs	Francine Clarisol	50 francs
Niall of the Nine Sausages	22-2-65	Geraldine Bakatus	45 francs

Sianka had recorded each transaction in detail. It was mischievously suggested by Mick Keane that St Patrick might be Father Knightly - it took a while for the story to abate!

Not long after the sex scandal, during the week before the departure of the Battalion to Leopoldville with Tshombe, another major issue imposed itself on Battalion life. They were to become involved in the movement of a contingent of the camp Balubas back to their homeland in East Katanga.

Commandant Murt O'Brien, a Cavalry officer, had no official role in supporting the movement of a whole nation from the Baluba camp to their home in the east. His relationship with them was purely on humanitarian terms. Soon after he arrived in Elizabethville, he identified the camp and the displaced Balubas as a special project and deserving of attention. Murt saw a need, and led in an area to be followed later by non-governmental aid agencies.

He unashamedly cornered Irish stores for allocation to the Baluba Katanga and had the support of NCO Quartermasters, who by this time had become a part of his supply network. While the plan to move thousands of men, women, and children was the responsibility of the UN offices in Elizabethville, the actual logistics, food transport, and medicine, was to be carried out by the army units in the area, including the Irish. Murt viewed the process of repatriation as flawed. This tribe of people was being moved without regard to the history of their presence or the administration of their re-establishment.

"They have been here in Katanga for fifty years, about two generations. The relocation of a group like this is not just about movement. Imagine the work at many levels that goes into setting up a new town in Europe. The work on infrastructural issues would be addressed for years in advance by social scientists, civil engineers, and God knows what other experts."

"I agree with you, Murt, but if what remains of this tribe are left where they are, they'll either die of disease or be killed by the locals!" Murt's colleagues continuously tried to protect him from his over-caring nature.

Murt could see the logic of this argument but 'make do' was never a part of his philosophy.

"This is a nation in transit and the story will be written into their history. I feel honoured to be a part and I have written to a number of governments, placing this exodus in context."

Jack had difficulty in matching Murt's verbal picture with the death and filth that was the Baluba Camp. He accepted that his meeting with Jessie Jesus and the Jeunesse had injected some dignity into the situation.

"I suppose Irishtown in Limerick, about four hundred years ago, was something like it is here?" Jack was in awe of the African style medieval living that prevailed in the camp and sought historical comparisons.

"Maybe so, but we know better than the English rulers of Ireland at the time. After all, it was a policy of *laisse faire* that increased the ravages of the famine," said Murt.

Comdt O'Brien seemed to have all the time in the world to spend advising the 'Cabinet' on developing a movement order at both ends of this exercise. Jack on the other hand had duties to perform at company level in preparation for the Battalion move to Leopoldville.

Father Knightly played a significant part in lending credibility to the camp based Baluba. He was friendly with Murt and regularly said mass in a clearing in the camp. The celebration of mass gave the residents in the squalid encampment the opportunity to receive the sacraments and thus regularise life to some degree. Government officials often used the sermon as an opportunity to outline social plans associated with going back to the East. The Chaplain, through his links with the leadership in the camp, became more and more enthusiastic about the well being of the Baluba camp residents.

T he area in East Katanga to which they planned to return bordered the Mélange Mountains and Lake Tanganyika. Their near neighbours were the Banyamulenge, a tribe originally from Rwanda who spoke a different language and who were their traditional enemies. Certainly the Banyamulenge would not like to see this large influx of Baluba Katanga into territory on the perimeters of their homeland.

Even before the arrival of Jack's unit in Katanga, the UN had set in train the job of moving groups of Balubas from the camp east. By degrees and in groups of about three hundred, they were moved by air and rail. This particular group, comprised as it was of Government officials, was seen to require special arrangements.

One of Jack's duties was to be a part of the security arrangements at the railhead, about two miles outside the town, so he would at least be there when the next movement took place. The railhead was originally designed to meet the needs of Union Minière rather than the citizens of Elizabethville, and was therefore situated not in the town but at a spot between the Katangese and Rhodesian mines, with a spur to Kamina and the rest of the Congo.

The Baluba Government move was to take place on Wednesday, just three days before the planned departure of President Tshombe to meet the government in Leopoldville, a thousand miles north on the banks of the mighty Congo River. There was little to compare in the two exercises; one was about international government and the other internal adjustment.

A meeting of the government of Baluba Katanga was taking place in the camp. The President was greeted with a respectful silence as he delivered his movement order.

"By this time tomorrow this government will be in position. Unfortunately our tribal lands have been divided by an arbitrary line through the jungle, leaving our ancestral home partly in Kivu Province and supposedly under the control of the Republic of Congo and President Mhobutu, but in the deadly focus of our enemy the Banyamulenge. The other half, or almost half, lies in what is being claimed by the Katanga State, under the control of President Tshombe. This position may not last, however, as Katanga will probably not be allowed to secede, in which case our provincial loyalties will be with General Mobutu. The people here in Elizabethville know well of our neutral position and see us as a potential weak point on their border between Katanga and the Congo. We must be prepared to defend ourselves tomorrow, brothers, in case of attack from the Gendarmarie of Tshombe. We have tried to talk to them, but our experiences at the sports meeting are an example of their respect for us."

He felt, as did some of his Government, that the perceived value of taking part in the sports meeting might have been misplaced - especially by the death of Jean and the dramatic win by Jessie Jesus Van Dam.

The Balubas in the camp had no army or arms and depended totally on the UN to protect them. They were a group of about 10,000 souls, mostly women, children, old and sick people.

Murt spoke. "I know that you have had difficulties with your young people. The Jeunesse, as they like to call themselves, may have been a problem for you in the past, but now that they have come of age, maybe it's time to establish your own national army - especially now, in this vulnerable time."

Jack and Jessie Jesus had been working together in an effort to give the

Jeunesse in the camp a level of dignity through recreation. Their attitude since the athletic meeting had changed and, as well as taking part enthusiastically in football and athletics training, some of them had begun to show qualities of leadership. One of them, Jansus, the strongest in many ways, had derived his power from dreams, not from ideas, but from images in his mind. Living as he was in abject squalor he, more than the self-appointed politicians, saw a future in his mind, where the fruits of their brave and heroic behaviour as a young elite would deliver the tribe to a new beginning. A mishmash of religion and religious belief, accrued from priests, holy men and witch doctors, caused him to encourage the practice of eating body parts of the fallen brave. He had a belief in the God, Dawa, who could turn bullets into water. If one was struck down in battle it was because he was a sinner: a thief, or a rapist. It was this philosophy, mostly, that struck fear into the hearts of the Europeans from the UN and others invading their territory.

Jessie Jesus and Jansus had followed separate paths within the camp but, as a result of contact during the sports preparation, their organisational abilities had improved and they eventually became elected leaders of a young aspiring military. Starting with sticks and stones and an assortment of knives and spears, gradually a small cache of rifles, pistols, and grenades became available. Small raiding parties on police barracks on the day of the sports and since, mostly at night, had succeeded in adding to their recent stockpile of arms.

The movement of a Government by train would be a moment of history and the danger of attacks by the Gendarmarie were considered likely. The UN was to supervise their movement, but as peacekeepers they could only be expected to react to whatever might happen if trouble erupted. To some degree UN personnel had co-operated with the police in certain civic duties in Katanga, and word had it that they weren't expecting any trouble on that day.

"We must be prepared for whatever the police might do to reduce our strength as a nation." Jessie Jesus shared his fears with Jansus.

The more the Jeunesse spoke of the possibilities, the more they saw the need for a plan. Jessie was concerned that they were planning without the knowledge or permission of the President and his cabinet, but was convinced by Jansus that one of their main obstacles to having an effective plan was the high level of 'action less' talk that would be a part of any involvement of the government.

The morning of the movement from the Baluba Camp arrived, and buses and trucks came in support of the overall operation. There was no tension; children, women and men lined up and mounted their designated transport easily, carrying their bits and pieces in a variety of containers. All five hundred taking part had been issued with blue UN stickers, which they wore proudly on their left shoulders.

All the mining companies rolling stock was to be made available on the day. In this way the 'Cabinet' and their families, and about 500 women and children, would be transported by rail. The UN were to transport the designated remainder by truck the same day to Elizabethville Airport firstly, and thence to Kamina, and on by truck to join the rest of the tribe. Because of the destitute nature of their living, all requirements, there and in the east, was to be carried. The president's upright piano and a portmanteau, in which the deeds and records of the 'government' were contained, were to be transported to the railhead by tractor and trailer.

Jessie and Jansus paraded their 'troops' the morning of the move. Despite the close-knit nature of living in the camp, they were able to gather without generating attention in a corner of what posed as a playing field in the camp. They were always grouped together, so the added level of their armament was easy to conceal. One or two elders knew they were up to something, but on this morning everyone was too busy preparing to move to take notice of the 'antics' of the ragbag Jeunesse.

The plan was based on the known positions of the UN contingents at the embarkation area and the surrounding terrain.

"If the Gendarmarie are to cause any trouble, they will strike before we get to the train. We'll need to shadow the route. It's about a mile of narrow road, flanked by fields and a house or two. We must clear the houses before the start, and set up positions in each house as our people move along the road."

There was an air of excitement as the Balubas awoke to a dawn that promised another hot African day. As soon as they had eaten and packed the essential cooking utensils, they made their way to the assembly areas. Toddlers trailed forlornly behind their laden mothers and fathers. Some families carried parts of beds and an occasional father proudly wheeled a bicycle, piled high with valuable possessions, leading his family to a new life. Some were more ambitious and tried to carry large household furniture; one woman perilously balanced a six-foot kitchen table on her head and there was evidence of other acquisitions from the Belgian houses, like curtain rails and pictures. Not all were looted, but given as gifts as the Belgian incumbents left hotfoot for Belgium.

Toddlers peered anxiously from under the brightly coloured dresses of their sometimes-pregnant mothers. The dogs came too. At about three minutes to five the signal was given by the leader in each assembly area and those intended for transport by train moved out.

Jessie and Jansus had by this stage occupied the houses along the route. Each section had an allocation of arms, including an automatic rifle of some description. Suddenly, as the significance of their responsibilities struck, fifteen to nineteen-year-olds became old heads on young shoulders. As they watched the stream of humanity move along the dust track, they recognised one of their family and had to resist calling out, or their role as defenders might be revealed to those who might also be viewing the passage of people and waiting their chance to strike.

One or two twelve-year-olds and younger, helping to carry family loads or herd younger ones along, did break rank and, knowing snippets of the defence plan, ran excitedly into the houses to be with their brothers. They were whooshed back to the road unceremoniously, sometimes accompanied by a clip on the ear.

Jessie watched from his post and wasn't sure whether he was relieved or sorry as the parade passed without incident. The final sorry image was that of the wretched creature with elephantiasis. He carried a few personal items and a tabby cat in the wheelbarrow, along with his swollen testicles. The wheelbarrow squeaked a sad dirge as it passed Jessie's spot, leaving a single, red-rutted wheel indentation and scuff marks on either side from the unlaced, outsize boots of the pathetic invalid as he followed in the vanguard of the tribal exodus.

A large picture of an antlered stag looked out of place in the red heat dust of Africa as it moved incongruously along, carried by two Congolese youngsters - saucer wide eyes set in glistening ebony faces. The unblinking gaze of the 'Monarch of the Glen', set by Sir Edwin Landseer among the cool lakes and regal mountains of Scotland, lent dignity to the parade, as its weary carriers rested and proceeded en route. They were motivated by the thought of this mighty stag lording it over their new home. Only six or seven years of age, but their exercise lent excitement and personal purpose to the journey they had heard their parents discuss and plan.

The Jeunesse followed, moving from house to house and eventually along the road, until they arrived at the corrugated iron building that acted as station for the railway. There they split, Jessie's group on the west end and Jansus's on the east side. Everything was proceeding as planned and there was a chatter of lively conversation and laughter as children began to play. A moment's inquisitive quiet, however, prompted by someone spotting the engine and carriages moving from the Union Minière mines in the distance; the tall piles of out-fill and lines of cranes could easily be seen even from two miles away. Ten minutes later the green and red engine hooted an over-enthusiastic arrival, in reaction to the cheers of the Balubas as it pulled alongside the platform and stopped.

This was the moment for which the Baluba government had waited and planned, and the members seriously supervised their records and the piano into the first carriage and its storage van. The official flag was opened and proudly planted, held in place from inside the carriage by a smiling official. He shouted greetings to the predominately yellow-and-blue clad smiling women and their cheering children. Little ones that had been herded along mother hen-like under the skirts of the women were released to join their older brothers and sisters in a play celebration.

The Irish/Gurkha meeting had taken place the previous day. Stephen McCoy considered that he had enough on his plate without the Baluba camp exercise; the Battalion was moving with Tshombe two days later and the logistics involved were a major pressure. The movement east of the Balubas should have been a simple operation, but their leaders were acting like a government in waiting and the UN wanted assurances that nothing would go wrong on this particular occasion.

"I want you to take control of this exercise, Brendan. It's only a matter of seeing them off. A bit like leaving your missus to the station in Newbridge."

Brendan McGonnigle bristled. He didn't need this sort of flippancy from McCoy and certainly not in front of the rest of the company officers.

"If it's that easy why not send a good corporal?"

The Company Commander realised that he was losing control and restated the needs of the operation in mechanistic terms.

"All right, Captain McGonnigle, when the operation has been completed report back to the Farm. I'll be there at a Battalion Commander's meeting."

He reminded himself that in future he should be clipt and clear with Brendan in front of the rest of the officers. It was bad enough that he had to explain his quartermaster's involvement in the sex affair.

"The Gurkhas are only sending a section of men to supervise the train departure. Do you think you could manage with the same, Jack?"

Because of his involvement with the Jeunesse in the camp, Jack was seen as the obvious person to co-operate with the Gurkhas, and so he was landed with the job of protecting one flank of the operation. He wasn't given any strong indication that there would be trouble, so he accepted Brendan's brief; he placed a Bren gun on an anthill on his flank, with a firing line to the front and rear of the train. He wasn't sure what to expect, nor was the officer in charge of the Gurkhas, but they both decided that apart from the three machine gunners, the rest of the section should be stationed to the flank also; but with fixed bayonets and ready to move in as required. From the anthill and the rising at the other side there was full visibility front and rear.

All went quietly enough until near the end of the operation. The politicians established themselves and their flag in the front carriages, one carriage closed and one open topped. Jack noticed that the Jeunesse were operating as a military support - and armed as well! Their positioning created a problem because they were not part of the military brief, and if anything happened their reaction could not be predicted. Having prepared the Sergeant, Jack moved from where he was and approached one of the Jeunesse to identify their role. The first boy - he looked about thirteen - spoke only French and rather than take time to form his sentences, Jack decided to look for Jessie Jesus.

"Since this morning we are the legal, armed wing of the Baluba Katanga; our job is to supervise the transfer of government from here to the east. We had word that the Gendarmarie was planning some sort of attack. Your friend among the mercenaries sent word that we should be careful. The code was '*an bhfuil cead agam dul amach*'. I got in touch with him after getting the code, and when he explained what his information implied, we set up our unit." Jessie Jesus looked the part, equipped as he was with a machine gun and Mill's hand grenades.

Jack felt a surge of pleasure at how Tim Cope had been supportive, but anxious that he had predicted trouble.

The Gurkhas, on the other hand, had decided that the operation was complete, as all the goods were on board and passengers had begun boarding. Their special religious festival had started, and so they called it a day and went back to barracks to get ready for the oncoming celebration. The 'Hindu Diwali Festival of Light' lasted five days and next day was special.

Although two units in the field of operation could co-operate, three were probably too complex. And so Jack found himself having to co-operate with a rabble army without training. There was little use in agreeing on codes of operation with the Jeunesse; they had become an extension of their weapons and wished only for a chance to operate - without the 'co' that is. Jessie Jesus was a plus all right, but his control was limited. Without the support of Jansus he had little chance of phasing a response, regardless of the challenge.

J ansus was seventeen years going on fifty. Unsure of his birthplace or parents he had latched on to a family in the camp, but in reality the Jeunesse were his brothers and family. When back east at the age of fourteen, he vaguely remembered a mother. In Africa the child belongs to the mother, because it is believed that blood comes from the mother and the spirit from the father. She came to an agreement with the local religious leader to have the devils exorcised from him. This resulted in semi-torture and starvation as a process, until he absconded and became a member of a local juvenile crime gang. The religious mumbo jumbo of his home had left its mark however, and many of the crimes of the Jeunesse there and in Elizabethville involved ceremonies with a religious undertone. It was during his days in Kivu that he came in touch with the Mai Mai tribe and their Dawa belief that turned bullets into water. Although centuries of disdain, humiliation, and suffering had given Africans an inferiority complex, Jansus's perverse upbringing had given him a certain belief in self; even a belligerent pride.

Things appeared to be progressing satisfactorily and Jack moved back to his section of men.

When the firing of automatic weapons broke out, it could have been celebratory in nature. However, in seconds both Jack and Jessie Jesus could see that killing was in progress. Six Gendarmarie had moved from secret positions in the fuel truck attached to the engine, and were in the process of executing the government of the Baluba Katanga. The protection measures, geared to meet a challenge from the exterior, were for naught, and the Jeunesse and the UN could only gaze open-mouthed as a terrified few jumped from the carriage. Judging from the sound of firing and the congested nature of the inside of the carriage, those who didn't jump must have been dead or badly wounded. Some of those who did jump landed on the ground and didn't move. It took only about a minute, or even less, and as the protectors moved in from both sides, keeping close to the carriages, the main event was over. Two Gendarmarie took positions at the windows and began firing on the hysterical crowd, as the main part of their group climbed aboard the decoupled engine and took up defensive positions.

Jack kept the Bren gun on the hill while a section moved in. When the Bren opened fire on the engine, it was obvious that the 303 ammunition was having a shattering effect on the partly covered engine cab. Nevertheless, the Gendarmarie, firing from the windows of the first carriage, created carnage among the defenceless women, children, and old people.

Women tried to insulate their young with their bodies, wrapping long African dresses around the little ones, as if that would provide protection. As the Irish soldiers moved in on their target, they had difficulty in taking their eyes from some mutilated heavily pregnant women. Just before the final assault, however, there was a commotion from the back of the rail car. The Jeunesse under Jansus had moved around the back and stormed the car from the rear. Throwing away their empty rifles, they reverted to their traditional panga and savoured the screams of the police as they were chopped down limb by limb. One tried to jump from the carriage to the ground and was torn apart by the crowd.

In the engine, a few gendarmaries were alive but wounded. They were carried out for ceremonial killing.

Jack and the UN soldiers regrouped and while the others were involved on the ground, they checked the situation in the carriage. Most of the leaders were dead, two survivors out of twenty, one the president and another council member. So much for the aspirations of the government in waiting; the crew of the engine had survived and were lucky not to have been deemed implicated in the ambush. Although Jessie Jesus and Jack agreed that the journey could go ahead, they didn't have official authority. Jack was on the radio to the company commander, who wanted the operation to stop until further military support was available.

"I'm afraid the damage has been done, sir. We are at the mopping-up stage now and there are a number of dead bodies to be attended to." The silence from the other end of the radio was not reassuring.

The killing over and the consequences visible, the Jeunesse stepped in and assumed a mature responsibility. Jessie and Jansus took control of the operation to attend to the wounded and dead. The Italian UN ambulances arrived and set up a field hospital until the logistics were in place to get the badly wounded into the regional hospital in Elizabethville.

The President, and those of his cabinet who survived, organised a special meeting amid the dead and chaos, and officially commissioned the Jeunesse as the armed wing of their government. Jessie Jesus was given the rank of major and appointed as the Minister of Education and Defence.

There was a makeshift graveyard in the camp and the dead Baluba Katanga were buried there. The burial ceremony was dignified despite the terrible circumstances of the killings. Eight mothers, six children and fourteen men were placed in a communal grave almost head to toe, each baby beside their mothers and wrapped in a white cloth. The men from the Government who died were dressed in suits, shirts and ties, and mostly laid in family groups.

The women mourners painted their faces white, and had to be restrained as they cried in desperate despair and tried to lie down with their dead family members.

It took a day to reorganise the movement east but, despite the terrible killings, the Balubas were ready to leave on the same transport next day. There was some senior UN officer interference, but the reorganised Balubas had the bit in their teeth and were making governmental decisions. The engine started up, and again the flag was flown from the first carriage. Jack could see Jessie and Jansus smiling and waving to the onlookers as the train jerked into movement and clattered east on its 400-mile journey. His last view was of the 'Monarch of the Glen', propped against an open window and staring defiantly from his highland home into the African distance.

Jack could still hear the screams of the dying on that terrible day. He moved slowly away from the scene, feeling cold in the hot midday sun. As they climbed aboard the jeep, one of the soldiers heard a cat cry in the undergrowth and, pulling aside the flowering Jacaranda bushes, he saw the handles of a wheelbarrow protruding from the tangle of undergrowth.

"The cat is somewhere there."

"Never mind the fucking cat, let's get out of here." Jack could hear the bluebottles giving tongue and knew what that meant.

"I can see him."

The wheelbarrow was pulled out with difficulty by the soldier cat-lover, and what they saw surpassed even the horror of the day before.

"Good shit sir, look at that."

Jack knew before he looked what would unfold. He had seen the man, the wheelbarrow and the cat make their weary way to the train. The same unfortunate man with the swollen testicles was there, but now it wasn't possible to see the humanity. A burst of machine gun fire had ended the grotesque union between man and disease, and there was but a steaming heap of flesh as testimony to the fact that once this was a human being. The man's head, however, gave some dignity to the barrow's contents. He seemed at last to be at rest, the eyes not staring in pain, but gazing into the distance and at peace. Somebody had thought it unnecessary to bring him back to the camp for burial.

Tim was glad he had passed information on about the plans to hijack the train. He was beginning to add up the facts about the reason behind the setting up of the Katanga regime. Tshombe was but a puppet of the businessmen that ran Union Minière, and sought to establish an independent state at the southern tip of the Belgian Congo. He had seen CIA agents moving between both camps and he realised that the group to which he belonged was also being used as a pawn in an international dirty game. People, and black locals in particular, didn't matter. Like most of the mercenaries, Tim Cope was keeping his powder dry and looking to the next adventure move. His links with home were through his mother's letters, but his contact with Fleurabelle over the border in Northern Rhodesia was becoming more significant.

Each time they met her appearance captivated him and on parting he felt tied to Fleurabelle and found it difficult to turn away and not look back. More often than not, a look over his shoulder revealed the young woman in question happily swinging her way along. He cursed this weakness in his character, and swore that next time he would equal her nonchalance.

Each meeting was a story in itself. They usually met in small hotels that abounded in the area around the railway station. The staff in Hotel de La Gare got to know them, and this time the room was already designated, although he hadn't bothered to check his booking. From a small balcony overlooking the square, he opened the window and stepped out to view the early morning food and clothing stalls. Gradually, as sound and colour were added, the impressionist picture took shape. Calls and songs, shouts and setting-up noises by busy traders, added to a cacophony worthy of the multi-coloured scene. The *mingie* stalls took time to arrange and the tall Ethiopian traders, black as coal, carefully placed the tusks and ivory carvings in regimental order. He worried for them because they never seemed to eat into their array of goods for sale, but on the other hand he trusted that their innate business sense was as astute as their ability to drive a hard bargain.

He prepared for Fleurabelle, uncorked a bottle of French champagne and lay open a small box of chocolates. He checked the letter to make sure that he had the right day - again! Over and back to the window and then, like a *sighe gaoith* - a fairy wind, she swept around the corner and swung towards the hotel. The beauty that was Fleurabelle overcame him; the sensuous body movement enhanced by the dancing bounce in her lovely hair; he could scarcely stop from shouting down. She moved easily through the crowded square and even stopped to view the goods on display in one of the stalls; he wished he could be so contained.

In what seemed an eternity she was knocking at the door. Close up her presence had an immediate impact; he said what came naturally.

"Fleurabelle, you look beautiful."

She reacted to his compliment with a little rising of her shoulders, a Bushman click with her tongue, and an opening of her hands in suppliant acceptance of her feminine influence. She knew she carried a punch, but it was without effort. They embraced and he drew her gently into the room. He had learned a lot about lovemaking from her, and was eager to practise his skills; it was well after lunch when they surfaced. They showered together and he used this time to explore her body under calmer conditions.

She laughed and played like a child, and it struck her that this was the button this young inexperienced Irishman had pushed. While she was with him she felt like a little girl again, able to play and have fun, almost like she was in the schoolyard with her friends.

'Maybe this is the love feeling - I've never felt like this before, although I did make love to others.'

He, on the other hand, didn't contemplate his position. Like a cat, he lapped up the cream because it was there, and he felt fulfilled in every respect. Work and adventure suddenly didn't matter; all he needed was packaged in this beautiful form and, miracle of miracles, she was his! If action and reaction are equal and opposite, then he should occasionally have felt very down - but it never happened. She became so much a part of his being that he wanted to step backwards and bring her to see what had made him what he was.

'Imagine bringing her home and showing her Ireland and Carlow.'

The places in Cork that had meant so much to him in his youth were lined up as a wished-for visit agenda for him and his lover. People were another consideration however, especially his family. He realised also that he didn't want to share her with his family members, and certainly not his mother. He figured that Fleurabelle and he was an isolated unit, and he wasn't ready as yet to share any part of her.

'If I brought her home to the family, the magic might disappear and we'd be like any other couple.'

Believe it or not, but Fleurabelle had never been out of Africa, and one reason she found Tim so attractive was that he was strange in the African environment. She listened intently as he spoke of Ireland, France, and other parts of Europe. Bubbling deep in her psyche, however, was a passionate interest in the USA. Once or twice she mentioned America in some context or other but, not getting a connecting response from him, moved on. She was employed by the Rhodesian American Mining Company, for whom she worked as communicator, as well as developing a photographic business of her own. She became familiar with American speech and places, mostly from meeting miners from the States.

They parted company next day, he having looked over his shoulder, again! She returned to her work and he headed back across the border to Katanga. The trip to Leopoldville with Tshombe was in his mind and he wondered about the outcome of the negotiations. The results would determine if he would have employment in an independent Katangan state. There was however a strong possibility that war between his group and the UN would break out and if it did, he and his friends, the white mercenaries, would have battles to fight, but also would need an escape plan if all went to all.

Festering in the back of his mind was the fact that he had absconded from the Legion. If picked up in France or any French colony, retribution was on the cards, retribution by him to the system that is. In that event would he be sent to prison or serve his time in the Legion itself? He shuddered at the prospect of the latter - Wicklow Goal-type torture: carrying buckets of stones from one heap to another, but in mind-sapping heat and terrible isolation.

'The Bastille would be the easy option.'

Thinking out his future life, which to a large degree was determined by past actions, he was eased by the thought of Fleurabelle as his partner. He could smell her when she came into his mind and this made obstacles to easy living seem minor. When he thought of her, more and more his mother and Carlow loomed large. He tried to analyse these feelings as he lay on his bed in Elizabethville, but as yet they were both separate in his mind and refused to come together.

Before he left for Leopoldville Tim decided to contact Jack, but it wasn't just a matter of knocking on his door. As his patrol looped the perimeter of the Union Minière compound, he saw an opportunity to contact a UN unit, positioned on the fringe of the town square. He dismounted from his jeep and approached the Ford armoured car, whose turret sported a First World War 303 Vickers machine gun pointing menacingly in his direction. Despite its antique look, this Irish military vehicle and its crew had already proved their worth in active service. As he was obviously not belligerent, a blue-berried NCO climbed out to answer his questions.

"How's it going?"

The informal, Irish-style approach surprised the soldier and he responded in a similar vein.

"Not bad." The Cavalry Sergeant made sure that the Vickers machine gun had the stranger covered.

They had a few words about the weather and Tim explained that he was friendly with Lieutenant Jack Muldoon.

"Could you tell him that I would like to talk and will be in the 'Caruso' bar downtown this afternoon at five?" As the old Ford pulled off, Tim thought that he smelt burning oil from the exhaust.

Jack got the message and on the dot of five, leaving his escort in the jeep, he entered the downtown watering hole. He was anxious to talk about the important information received before the shoot-out in the Baluba Camp, and was also curious about the reason for this rendezvous.

"Over here!" Tim Cope was sitting at the bar with a Simba drinking glass at his elbow. There were a few other customers at the bar, mostly white and probably, Jack thought, Tshombe mercenaries. This particular bar was known as a haunt of Mike Hoare's professional soldiers.

"Hello there."

Tim stood up, pushed back his bar chair and shook Jack warmly by the hand.

"All's well. Will you have a drink?"

"A beer; Simba please - it's hotter than hell out there."

Tim signalled the barman.

"We're due some storms and that will ease the heat a bit. I wanted to have a word with you about the Baluba issue, the shoot-out and the athletics. As you know Tshombe's crowd employs us, with Mike Hoare in charge. We don't make any policy decisions - ours not to reason why and all that shit. In fact, we're sitting on the fence at the moment and at the first sign of Tshombe giving in, we're off, and with our money we hope."

Jack sipped his beer from the tall gold-rimmed Simba glass. He could see that Tim was making big lifestyle decisions, so he just looked and listened and basked in the gentle air current from the ceiling fan whirring pleasantly over their heads.

"As you probably know, the locals here hate the Balubas from the east, and would do anything to get their own back for perceived wrongs when the Belgians were here and employed them. That's only inter-tribal stuff and normal in this neck of the wood, but the Katangan state is different. They're looking at the time when they will have a state separate from the Republic of Congo and Mobutu's crowd, and a group like your Baluba friends sitting astride Katanga and Kivu provinces would not be appreciated. It all depends on the talks in Leopoldville. If Tshombe makes no progress and manages to make it back here and set up a war structure, then the Balubas and the UN better watch out! We're expecting about 200 well-armed ex pats from Belgium this week."

Jack wasn't sure where all this was leading, and in particular he didn't want to be 'piggy in the middle' if Tim sought unofficial support.

"Will you get into trouble if it becomes known that you've passed on this information?"

This was more of a statement than a question in Jack's mind.

"When I came here I thought it was a bit of a lark, but it's become serious and I'm not prepared to continue. If I could be of help to the UN I'd be prepared to keep you informed - until I can get my major payment and scarper that is. The killing just to win the athletics meeting, and the shoot-out with the Balubas at the train, has pushed me over the edge. I'm off as soon as I get the chance."

Anyone with a background in Irish school history would of course prick up his ears at the word 'informed'. Jack felt a rush of blood to his face despite the Simba and the fan.

"I understand your position, Tim, and I will help in any way I can. You must understand, however, that I am but a small cog in a large wheel. I will talk to my people if you have definite information, okay?"

The two Irishmen parted. Jack couldn't see how the meeting and the request could be serviced in the immediate term. He'd gotten into enough trouble over the athletics meeting and the Baluba Camp involvement. 'Anyway,' he mused, as he headed back to the Battalion, 'I don't have to take any action until and if Tim comes back.'

J ack was busy organising his role as support for the move by the Irish UN Battalion to the airport. On the morning of the move he established a section of men in the airport building. He also saw the need to guarantee security of his personal items. He identified a house in Avenue du Tullipiers as home base for the period of the unit's absence in Leopoldville; a place to keep his personal items of clothing and extra uniforms. His last look around the bedroom gave him cause for contentment. His unworn lightweight suit hung in the wardrobe, as did the rest of his army and civilian gear.

Dressed in a shorts and shirt tunic for the trip to the airport, he had a nervous feeling about leaving all that he possessed in the locked but unguarded room. He had bought a cache of malachite stones, carved locally and sold as the makings of ladies' jewellery, rings, and pendants. He spoke to the Indian unit within whose area the house was situated and was assured that all would be secure.

Jack and Corporal Callaghan headed to the airport, saw off the Battalion for the Tshombe deliberations in Leopoldville, and returned to Elizabethville. Having seen off the support company in the Farm Headquarters, Jack and Mickey Callaghan drove the jeep to the house in A Company lines.

"My God, I don't believe it!"

Lieutenant Muldoon entered the house by the front door and realised that what he wore, shorts and shirt, were now his only available apparel. The empty box was testament to the loss of not alone spare ammunition for his revolver, but also any malachite he had bought. In the pith of his moment of loss lay the realisation that he had not followed his instinct. He knew that the arrangement with the UN Indians had been much too loose. A bit like 'will you keep an eye on the old pad until I come back', rather than a detailed military brief with the commander of the unit.

What to do? He was tempted to get into the jeep and drive around like a headless chicken on the off chance that he would see something or somebody suspicious. Just about then, his African orderly arrived. Jack tried to act cool and calculating, but to his own ears his voice sounded a bit frantic.

"Were you here, Patrice, did you see anyone around?"

Patrice's reaction was typical. When the boss man asks questions you answer whether it makes sense or not. In this case there had to be an explanation, and he was seized with the inclination to move some way or another. 'The Lieutenant would expect enthusiasm, results were another question.'

They inspected the room and could see that the window protection, strong wire clipped in place by screws, had been pried open. Not a big space, but enough to allow entry by a medium-sized, reasonably wiry individual - a description of nearly all the African males in the area.

"I know where we look, Sir," said Patrice. "I see men drinking in bar, strange men. I nearly sure."

Jack had wondered if Patrice himself hadn't a hand in the robbery, or even the Indians from whom he had sought protection - he was grasping at straws. Here he was in downtown Africa, bereft of accoutrement except for the clothing in which he stood. He thought that perhaps the smug satisfaction he had felt as he studied his Aladdin's cave before going to the airport was probably responsible for his demise. This sort of irrational thought consumed him, and before he had time to rationalise his actions he, Patrice, and Corporal Callaghan and his Gustaf were on their way to the bar in question. It wasn't a bar in the real sense of the word - more a *sheeben* on the fringes of the now reduced Baluba Camp. As the jeep pulled up Patrice alighted. Two men stood up as he approached; they shook hands and spoke for a while. They looked in the direction of the jeep and without any fuss made their way over and climbed aboard.

"These are the ones." Patrice looked pleased

"How do you know - is there any sign of the stuff?" Jack was thrashing around in search of possibilities.

"I'm sure, but we'll only find out for certain if we bring them to the police."

Jack had a brainwave. "Let's bring them to the Tunisian Commander. This is in his area."

As they made their way to the Tunisian camp nearby, Jack had an opportunity to study the two men. Medium-sized and slim, they wore white shirts, long grey pants, and flip-flops. They appeared so compliant, almost as if they welcomed the experience of being in custody. How come they allowed themselves to be arrested? It wasn't as if one Gustaf would constitute a threat to their lives - not at that distance and from the back of the jeep. What had Patrice said to them? Jack regretted being so impulsive and wished he could reverse reels and start again.

'*Votre Commandant, s'il vous plaît.*'

The sentry at the gate waved them through and lifted the phone in his sentry box. When they arrived at the front of the house, the door had opened and the rotund Colonel of the Tunisian UN Unit approached, uttering words of welcome. The Commander was obviously eating, and wiped his mouth a few times before dumping the napkin on the hall table. Another reason why Jack had decided to approach the Tunisian was because he and the Commander had met at a UN party the week previously. They shook hands and Jack explained his dilemma and the circumstances that had led to the taking of the two Congolese.

Commander Bourguiba listened and approached one of the two men, who had been brought from the jeep into the hallway. They spoke in French for a few minutes, quietly at first and then animatedly. Bourguiba was a small, stocky man. Although about six inches shorter than the Congolese, when he hit him with his fist, the taller man was driven back at least six feet, bounced off the wall and then slumped to a sitting position.

That was the end of the interview, and a shocked Jack was informed that these were probably the guilty ones and that they should be brought to the local police. This wasn't the outcome he had sought, but there was no getting off the train of events at this stage. Obviously he was being dumped on the local police while Bourguiba resumed his evening meal in sumptuous Belgian surroundings.

Back in the jeep, Corporal Callaghan and prisoners in place, Jack headed off. Patrice was engaged in an animated conversation with the prisoners in Swahili; they even laughed! The trip into Elizabethville was increasingly spectacular. Two Tunisian military police jeeps joined them, with two armed policemen ensconced in each and sirens shrieking.

Jack, in tunic and shorts, felt like a bit player in a film, but by now was wishing even more so that he could reverse the clock. They sped through the town and pulled up suddenly, sending red dust into the air from skidding tyres. The Tunisian Military Police corporal paid compliments to Jack and sped away, leaving him and his prisoners to introduce themselves to the Gendarmarie.

Jack tried to approach the issue in a positive manner. He entered the police station and looked around. The place was crowded, women mostly. They sat on the seats around the wall while children played in the street outside and one or two gathered at their mother's knees.

The centrepiece was a uniformed policeman sitting on a bentwood chair, tapping on a Remington typewriter. In front of the table stood a Congolese man looking a bit worse for the wear. When Jack entered, the interrogation stopped and the policeman stood and looked expectantly in his direction. Jack greeted the official in French and introduced Patrice, who deftly explained the circumstances of their visit. As the reason for their attendance at the police station became evident, the policeman assumed a much more serious demeanour. He buttoned his tunic, straightened his cap, and chased a few *manamucks* from their seats to make room for the white officer. Almost without looking, he swung around and struck the man he had been questioning, and sent him staggering to the back of the room, where he landed in a heap on the bicycle he was supposed to have stolen.

Patrice then presented the insider information in French, which was to be the business language in this police investigation.

The policeman assumed a dignified demeanour behind his typewriter, and with a flourish affixed a new page of paper, only then addressing Jack. The two Congolese accused of stealing the officer's goods were directed to join the unfortunate bicycle thief in the back of the dayroom. The light streamed in through a lone window and illuminated further the multicoloured garments of some of the attendant women. The children with them had stopped playing and had fixed their big brown eyes on the strange white man and his bodyguard. The usual smell of body odours permeated. Not a disagreeable smell - the locals washed all right - but soap or deodorant was not usually available.

"Vote nomme monsieur, s'il vous plaît."

Jack decided to deal with the questions in French, and use Patrice only if communication broke down or there was some doubt. In this way he thought he'd be sure of what exact information was being passed between Patrice and the police officer, some of which he figured might be doctored by his houseman's vivid imagination. He also still, and increasingly perhaps, wondered what was Patrice's role in the robbery.

"Lieutenant Jack Muldoon."

With staring eyes and protruding tongue held firmly between his front teeth, the policeman, using the index finger of each hand with determined intensity, tapped in Jack's name and unit and dramatically pushed the typewriter lever fully over to the start position of a new line. The address of the scene of the crime and the time of the incident were then entered into the report, as were details of the circumstances of the robbery and of the apprehension of the two Congolese.

"*Cher Lieutenant . . . Je comprends que tous vos viens et effets etaient dans votre chambre mais a la suite de votre visite a l'aérogare il n'en reste rien.*"

Everyone in the room listened intently as the story unfolded.

"Yes," said Jack, "that's how it happened. I'm not sure about the guilt or otherwise of the two suspects. I only have the word of my orderly Patrice about their involvement."

The policeman didn't pay much attention to the circumstances of the robbery; he had a routine to complete. This was an important day for him and when the case was brought to court in the next week or so, he was going to ensure that all the details required in Form 221 were provided. There wasn't any column requiring information on the likely involvement or otherwise of suspects. Information on the items taken were however central to his list. And so it began...

"*Tout d'abord, un liste de vos biens personelles, s'il vous plaît, mon Lieutenant?*"

Jack couldn't see what an itemised list of personal items would contribute greatly to the charge, but the procedure seemed set in stone, so he had no option but to play along. At least the level of French necessary wasn't too challenging.

"*Alors?*"

"*Une nouveaux Costume.*"

"*Et le prix?*"

He knew the price of the lightweight suit, remembering well the down payment in Siberries and what he owed, to be paid on his return to Dublin. It took a bit of mental arithmetic, and knowledge of the conversion rate, to be ready to answer questions on each item of his civilian and army clothes. He had been involved in some black market exchange in Leopoldville - one dollar equalled 400 Congolese francs, so he used this as a basis for his assessment of the worth of his missing items.

"Deux mille quarante francs."

He wasn't ready for the reaction; from the policeman, yes, perhaps - but it was then he realised he had a much wider audience. The women turned to one another and discussed in animated Swahili the item and its price. Even the unfortunate prisoners at the back of the cell had a word about the exorbitant price of lightweight suits in Dublin. It was doubtful that they'd ever get a chance to visit Siberries, even if they were released!

"Autre chose?"

Although unsure of the prices, he thought shirts and ties might be a logical sequel.

"Chemise troi, a 800 franc, et crevatte, deux a 450 franc."

While these prices were being typed in laboriously, the conversation continued among the *manamucks*, being led now by a large lady seated close to Jack. The price of the tie seemed to be called into question.

Wishing he were somewhere else - anywhere! He next decided to focus on shoes and socks. The shoes were expensive enough and if there was to be any restitution they should be included. Not that he expected any restitution from this exercise, but he knew that the UN had a system in place to cover losses from its members on duty and a copy of these estimates might prove useful.

Losing concentration for a moment, he presented his next item and got the French for shoes and socks mixed up.

"Les chaussettes, 800 francs."

The policeman started tapping, but the rest of the audience couldn't contain themselves. Eight hundred francs for socks! They laughed and stared wide-eyed at one another, while the large lady did a ritual dance on the floor of the dayroom.

Patrice identified the problem to Jack and the policeman, but the damage was done and each item from then on received close scrutiny and analysis in comparison to the local price.

It was a weary Lieutenant Muldoon that eventually concluded his listing of missing items and estimated prices, signed the triple copy document, and took one copy for his information. The prisoners were locked away and the date of the trial was attached to Jack's copy of Form 221. As he, Patrice, and Corporal Callaghan left the station, having shook hands with the policeman, the interrogation of the bicycle thief continued, following a careful replacement of the form whose completion had been interrupted.

The jeep reversed into the street; Jack saw the smiling face of the large Congolese woman framed in the window and couldn't resist smiling back. The trial was to take place in three weeks' time, but he couldn't see how sufficient evidence could be collected, unless the police worked their way back from the statements of the two prisoners and Patrice. That was possible, perhaps!

The Battalion having left, Jack's role revolved around linking with the remaining company in Leopold Farm. He was detailed as orderly officer on one or two occasions, but mostly his duties involved keeping in touch with the unit in Leopoldville. He had responsibility for arranging return transport from the airport on completion of the Tshombe negotiations with the Kasavubu government.

Tim had arranged another meeting downtown and Jack relaxed as he sauntered down Avenue du Leopold. A beautiful boulevard, wide, with rows of stately Aloe trees down the centre for nearly half a mile, planned perhaps to match the European equivalent in Brussels; no Manikin Pee or Grand Place, but unique in its African heritage. The many sellers of carved ornaments and ivory tusks lined the pavement. These *mingie* sellers were a mixture of Arab and Congolese and most spoke at least four languages, English, French, Swahili, and sometimes tribal languages such as Lingala and Kinyamulerge.

With the morning sun beating on the sole uniform shirt he now possessed, Jack strode down the pavement towards the bar/restaurant in which the meeting was to take place.

'It couldn't be, or could it?'

Just in front of him walked a young African. Not unusual that, but what shortened Jack's breath was the suit he was wearing.

'It's very like it - the same colour - everything!'

He kept walking behind what he figured might be his Siberries suit.

The man was shorter.

He looked at the legs. 'He could have had it shortened - the jacket is slightly big for him.'

Jack was being led by the nose again; he had put the robbery behind him and another session like the police station episode should have been avoided like the plague. Nevertheless, he followed the suit wearer. Yes, there was a man-like swing to the suit wearer's stride, shoulders behaving in the John Wayne mode, although this human version of manhood was considerably shorter in stature. Jack wondered why this black man was so on top of his form - could it be the suit? The more he reckoned the more he became convinced that this was his lightweight Siberries suit going walkabout in downtown Elizabethville.

"Bonjour, ça va?"

His quarry stopped and began a conversation with another suited man. They looked like businessmen and suddenly Jack felt less sure of his opinion about the suit and the man. The second African made no issue of the fact that his friend was wearing Jack's suit, or that the suit was new. In his mind's eye Jack could hear the old routine.

'*Jambo*! That's a fine suit. Is it new?'

'Yes I recently bought it, do you like it?'

'Yes, but are the sleeves not a bit long? However just pull up the sleeves and hold your chin down on the cloth and it'll be okay.'

As the two men shook hands and parted, Jack's quarry didn't look like the classic man in the joke, misshapen in an effort to make the suit look well fitting. Instead he strode freely on his way down Avenue du Leopold. Jack turned back to his rendezvous point, passed as he had followed his suit, and felt relieved. He realised that he had missed another chance to do what was his wont: follow an opportunity that contained an open-ended element of risk. A bit like following an unmarked trail in the snow down an obviously difficult route, which might finish at a cliff face. A fine trait with experience perhaps, but otherwise fraught with danger.

Tim and a pretty young woman were seated in the restaurant eating what looked like breakfast. They shook hands and Jack was introduced. As he pulled in a chair a waiter scurried to his side with the makings of a breakfast setting.

"This is Fleurabelle."

Fleurabelle disengaged from her bacon and eggs. Wiping her mouth, she tossed back her hair, gave Jack a smile and offered her hand.

Jack shook hands and noted how beautiful she was, and how her complete focus was concentrated on him for the moments of introduction. He wilted a bit under her deep inspection of his eyes, but she disengaged just as quickly and gave Tim her full attention as he took charge of the meeting.

"You'll have breakfast." Jack nodded as the waiter poured tea into his cup and spread a napkin on his lap. "Fleurabelle is from Rhodesia. She works in Ndola and is here on a visit."

"Tim has told me about you; you are both from Ireland," said Fleurabelle.

"Yes, we are from adjoining counties in Ireland and although we never met, we both served in the same military establishment," said Jack.

She didn't take her eyes from Jack for about two seconds, although she addressed Tim in a firm voice. Too firm, Jack thought.

"I didn't know that you'd served in the Irish Army, Tim. That makes three!"

"Well, I don't consider Katanga to be a country or an official army yet." Tim made the statement in an effort to take control of the conversation.

He appeared embarrassed but concentrated on the arrival of Jack's breakfast. The service was French Belgian in style and with croissants and coffee was a step up from the mess fare either here or at home. Biting into the warm buttered croissant and pursing to sip the coffee, he allowed his eyes to view the apparent close relationship between the pair. As he got to know Fleurabelle he could see why Tim would be attracted to her. They resumed their original conversation about plans to visit Europe, as soon as Tim was free to travel. Their proposed itinerary included France, Germany, Austria, England, and Ireland.

"Is this tour a prelude to something or just a pleasure trip?"

"Well, Fleurabelle is a photographer, has a photography business, and as we travel she can increase her portfolio," said an enthusiastic Tim.

"Our business in Rhodesia involves trading photographs of wildlife with magazines and tour agencies. We send packaged portfolios all around the world. I'm keen to get into the American market; I believe that's where the money is. We also brief filmmakers interested in making films based on an African environment." Fleurabelle was almost breathless with excitement as she opened her bill of fare to Jack.

Jack pricked his ears at the reference to filmmaking and wondered if she couldn't be introduced to the Rank people. He mentioned also his meeting with Leni Riefenstahl, which naturally interested Fleurabelle greatly. Her focus on Jack as he spoke was total and when the waiter arrived with extras, he realised that he was hogging her company.

"The white mercenaries had nothing to do with the terrible shoot-out at the railway, Jack. The Gendarmarie set that up." Tim put his hand on Fleurabelle's arm as he changed the subject of conversation.

"However, I presume that some of Tshombe's advisers would not be sorry that the Balubas were attacked?" Jack held his forkful of eggs at the ready as part of a gesture of inquisition.

Tim met the challenge full on. "I suppose so, but we are made up of non integrated factions, the white mercenaries even more so. Anyway, I'm just waiting my chance. We're supposed to be paid up to date shortly and when that happens this bird's going to fly." He looked at Fleurabelle with unbridled affection in an effort to solicit support.

"There are DC-3s flying around the Congo like taxis. Lumumba, you remember, was flown here in one. Believe it or not, but the pilot, B.T. O'Kane, is from Ireland. I was in touch with him and I hope that Fleurabelle and I can make it to Kano one of these days." Fleurabelle seemed miles away since the mention of filmmaking and Leni Riefenstahl.

Jack made arrangements to stay in touch with the pair. Fleurabelle was keen on getting more information on 'Riefenstahl Productions' in Munich, and perhaps link with Rank in London. She obviously had a keen business brain and was ambitious to advance her career. Jack wondered where, in the long term, Tim fitted in. He wasn't sure he saw the reason for this meeting other than to give the beautiful Fleurabelle on outing.

On his way back to the Farm he didn't see his suit doing the rounds, although he looked!

The Irish troops in Leopoldville were involved in guard duties only, and being away from base, missed opportunities to recreate. It was easy to release the soldiers into Leopoldville, but the likelihood was that suchlike could lead to trouble in the fleshpots downtown. Jack was instructed therefore to take UN transport to Leopoldville and structure some physical and recreational training.

O n duty and sitting in the Orderly Officer's office the week before leaving for Leopoldville, Jack chatted to the Orderly Sergeant, Jock Kiely. Many of his unit had been in the Congo at least once and their experiences were worth hearing. Sgt Kiely was no exception. He had served during a particularly serious period and it was while stationed in the area of Niemba, where seven Irish soldiers were killed in an ambush, that he nearly met his own 'Waterloo'.

"We were stationed in Albertville in Kivu province and C-Company was sent to Niemba. It's a small town, village really, and our lads were billeted in accommodation on high ground close by. We kept in touch with them by radio mostly, but every so often, mail and provisions were brought to the outpost by train. Anyway, one day me and Spud Murphy were detailed to escort the train on its two-hour journey to deliver mail."

"What rank was he?"

Jack wondered about the dangers inherent in moving outside the area controlled directly by the main army unit.

"Spud was a private and I was a corporal then."

"How far was the train journey - just two of you?"

"Yea, me and Spud were to escort the train, two hours there and the same back, he with a bolt action rifle, Lee Enfield and 400 rounds, and me with a Gustaf submachine gun."

"Big deal!" Jack was amazed at the lightness of the guard unit, whereas Jock seemed happy enough with the arrangements.

"Yes, but for the first time in my army career I got an order with no 'ifs or buts'. The Battalion Operations Officer told me that on no account was I to allow the train to stop, or anyone to get on the train between stations. If anyone attempted to mount the train, I was to fire ball ammunition. To tell the truth though, although delighted with a definite operational order, I was shitting myself! Things were a bit edgy at that time and it was known that the natives, the Baluba mainly, were acting up because the Belgians had come back for a while, to support those Belgians who had been left when the pull-out happened."

"So off you went?"

"Yes, we mounted the engine with the driver and set off. This was a normal delivery of mail to Niemba, but as I told you, it was expected that there might be trouble along the way. There was another white man on the train, a guy in the railway uniform called Van Lierde - a railway guard with a braid cap - you know the type."

"So you had someone to talk to, who knew the scene."

"No bloody way! He only spoke French, and Swahili of course, and Spud and me hadn't a word of either. He did his thing at the various stations, flags and all that, and we kept an eye on who got on and off and made sure that there was no stop between stations."

"So, things were okay?" Jack knew there was a story, but wondered if Jock would drown in detail - as was his wont!

"Yes, when we got to the last station before Niemba, Lumande, I saw the railway official arguing with another guy on the platform. They were having a real slugging match in French about something or other. Just before he signalled the driver to carry on, he looked at me, pointed down the line, made a face and muttered 'Baluba'!"

"What did he mean?"

"I wasn't sure," said Jock, "but I gathered that there was trouble involving the Baluba. Obviously this sort of thing was happening and everyone was a bit nervous."

"Were you briefed about what was going on at local level?" Jack tried to push the story along.

"Was I hell! I was told nothing except what I've told you already - shoot if anyone tried to board the train, and I was ready to do that. Anyway, just about twenty minutes out of Lumande, we were crossing a large open kind of scrubby countryside, when I saw a crowd of blacks crossing the line about a mile ahead of the train. There were about a hundred of them and they were waving weapons, pangas, bows and arrows and shooting rifles in the air. As we got closer, we could see that they were very excited and the closer they got the more worried I was. You can imagine all those nut heads waving and shouting, and they weren't a welcoming committee! It wasn't just Spud and me, everyone on board went white, well the whites went whiter and the blacks looked the same colour but their eyes got big as saucers. Especially the women; they gathered the kids around them like a mother hen with chicks."

"Van Lierde looked as scared as the rest. I reckon he had known that something might happen, but I suppose he could do nothing about it because we were in charge and getting the mail to Niemba was a must. He did try to talk to me, but I couldn't make any sense out of what he was saying; so much for the French in the Glasgow primary school."

Jock had been brought up in the Gorbels as a shoemaker's son, and when he got the chance he absconded and joined the Irish Army where, believe it or not and against his wishes, they employed him as shoemaker!

Anyway, panic all around and what to do? Jock noted that the driver had taken his pens out of his shirt and transferred them to his arse pocket. At the same time the Congolese driver eased the throttle lever up and slowed the train. At this stage the 'warriors' were about two hundred yards away and on both sides of the track. Jock's innate Gorbels skills took over; he understood the meaning of the transfer of valuables and the easing of the throttle.

What Jock didn't know however and maybe Van Lierde did, was that an Irish patrol from Niemba had been ambushed at a river crossing on the river Luweyeye about nine miles from Niemba, beyond the villages of Kamanda and Tundula. There were five fatalities on the Irish side, including an officer platoon commander. Many Balubas had also been killed and the guys heading to cut off the train were in no mood to parley.

As they got closer, the unfortunate passengers could see that many faces had been smeared with the blood of brave victims, a practice which was known to give them protection in future battles.

"Keep going, you bastard!"

Sgt Jock Kiely shoved his loaded and cocked Gustaf into the neck of the driver and pushed the throttle lever down with the other hand. The slowing train leaped forward and surprised the Balubas, some of whom just had time to jump clear of the track. Arrows rained on the carriages and some shots rang out. Spud fired his well-oiled bolt-action Lee Enfield in the ten rounds rapid-fire mode, protecting the left flank of the train where most of the attackers were. Jock, having delivered his message to the terrified driver, fired a few bursts on the other flank and kept a few from attempting to scramble aboard despite the increased pace of the train.

When they got to Niemba to deliver the mail and supplies, transport was waiting at the station. On reaching the Company HQ on the hill beside the school, Jock and Spud Murphy had a cup of tea and a wad and prepared to return to Albertville. He was told that the Company Commander had gone out to relieve a patrol which had been reported as being under attack. The journey back was uneventful and the Belgian Railway Guard had relaxed and was prepared to converse in broken English.

"I wish to thank you, Irishman, for your courage and for saving my life."

"Ah, it was nothing - sure I was only doing my job."

"Doing your job Corporal, you're a bloody hero," said an amazed Jack Muldoon. "You should get a medal! Were you debriefed?" Sgt Kiely moved on and left the story hanging.

Jack muddled his way through the rest of the week and organised his visit to Leopoldville. The day he left Elizabethville, the DC-3 soared into a calm, clear sky and headed towards the airfield at Kamina. The plane was a UN-chartered aircraft, but as was normal practice, about twenty Congolese men women and children availed of the free spaces en route to Leopoldville. They must have been moving for good, because they carried what looked like their worldly possessions in a variety of packages, basins and boxes.

One very pregnant member of the group was seated beside Jack. They didn't speak and she covered her face with the sari-type shawl she wore. The plane ducked and dived through the clouds and on occasions followed the line of jungle terrain, as it suddenly fell away into a depression or river gorge. Whether this aerial exercise was necessary or not was unclear. There was a chance that fuel was being saved, or the pilot might just be having some fun.

The changes in elevation were stomach-churning and about five minutes before landing at Kamina, Jack's Congolese companion got sick. It wasn't a violent rejection of the contents of the stomach. This was a silent secretion of fluid and foodstuffs down the front under the shawl, and held there by the women as if it had never happened. The smells in the plane were high as it was, but this added a further dimension. When the plane landed for fuelling the only person to disembark was one of the crew; everyone else stayed put. Okay under normal circumstances, but at midday in African temperatures and with some delay in having the fuel truck attend, it got very hot and uncomfortable. Jack tried to ignore the steaming woman beside him, and isolated his feelings - chin in chest and arms folded. And then an announcement over the tannoy:

"This is a request for all Congolese on board to disembark at once. *Messeurs et Mesdames de Congo, vous êtes priés de quittes l'avion tout de suite, s'il vous plaît.*" Instructions from the cockpit were specific.

It appeared that a contingent of Tunisian troops was required to support operations in Leopoldville and needed the seats at present occupied by the Congolese. Jack was amazed by the easy, calm way the object of this announcement was achieved. The Congolese collected the gear they had stored under seats and in the racks, and quietly made their way down the aisle and out of the plane. Even the children were calm and in about ten minutes they were all ensconced on the tarmac. That wasn't remarkable, but the metamorphosis that ensued was.

In about ten minutes the women and children were behaving as if they had lived on this patch of Kamina tarmac all their lives. The men ranged and collected sticks from around and about, and in advance of the plane revving up and taking off, fires were lit and the children were playing happily in the sun. Jack's companion, pregnant and with sick in her lap, crept out of the plane, with just eye contact, but no word passed between them. He followed her path to join the rest, but failed to see any sign of the contents of her lap being ditched.

'Some woman that! I wonder what future lies ahead for her and her child?'

288

C C This is a bit of a kip, Sir". The driver of the transport that collected him at Leopoldville Airport had been spoiled by the climate and accommodation in Elizabethville, and looked forward to his return there.

"You're not happy?"

It appeared that the billets were not of the same standard as the deserted villas in Elizabethville. Here the climate beside the mighty Congo river, and the angry mosquitoes, made life difficult for everyone

Jack met his comrades again and was able to relay, with some embellishments, the robbery episode. Anyway, they didn't take much notice as the big issue in Leopoldville, apart from the Tshombe government thing, was the rate of exchange between dollars and Congolese francs.

Many rich Congolese were caught with liquidity problems when the Belgians left. Up to then the currency was stable and making money meant getting rich in dollars or Congolese francs. Now, however, the bottom had fallen out of the market and Congolese francs were worth much less. The very rich people, in paper money that is, wanted out, and were ready to convert their truckloads of francs for dollars or sterling and didn't worry about the losses. Four hundred francs for one dollar was a possibility in downtown Leopoldville from agents working for the moneyed businessmen.

"Are you in Jack? We're going downtown tomorrow. We have about a thousand dollars to change." Harry Jenkins was happy that Jack was back with the team and wanted to include him in this group activity.

There was no point, one would think, in changing dollars for worthless francs, but there was another aspect to the operation that made the exercise worthwhile. The American PX was a support part of the UN operation and in its shops a variety of goods were available at nearly half price in the local currency. The range of goods was broad-based, drink of all sorts, watches and cameras. In North Africa even cars were available and their shipment arranged. In the Congo a bottle of best brandy could be bought for the equivalent of five Irish pounds - 100 Congolese francs - but having done the downtown deal, the cost of the brandy worked out at about 15 francs. Imagine what that meant in terms of cameras, cigarettes and jewellery!

"Okay, let's get organised. There are four of us and we'll be confronting one money dealer. These guys are clever. If we don't watch every move, we'll be taken to the cleaners." Harry took charge as he had the greatest monetary input.

"How could that be? After all it's a simple matter to exchange so much for so much." Jack Muldoon had changed money before without difficulty.

"That's what you think. Listen, they may not have school education, but they're like quicksilver. Last week Mick collected a few dollars and headed down full of confidence - he came back down about 20 per cent!" Harry wanted this operation to be super efficient.

"How did that happen?"

"One reason: he blinked, he took his eye off the ball. It's a bit like the three-card trick man." Harry knew that mention of the Irish version of taking suckers to the cleaners would strike a chord with the team.

"Yea, but they generally have others in support that divert attention away from the fraud." Jack found it hard to let go of the argument.

"In this case, that's exactly what happened and poor Mick got his 'cumupins'. But not today - okay, figure it out. There are four places in the jeep, two in front and two in the back. The driver can glance in the rear view mirror, but mostly he just drives and doesn't stop until I say, 'Okay, we're in the clear'. Your job, Jack, is to see the trader into the car and agree the price exchange. He sits in the back between you and Joe, and there he sits until the deal is done. Now, I'll kneel in the front facing backwards and do the deal. Every word and move will be monitored by you two in the back."

"Are we not using a sledgehammer to crack a nut?" Joe Costello was getting a bit fed-up with all the security tomfoolery - as he saw it.

"Don't you believe it. If we don't work as a team we're in the manure business," said Harry.

Lieut Harry Jenkins prepared everything, down to putting the dollars into bundles of twenty wrapped in rubber bands.

Sgt Higgins was the chosen driver. He was orderly room sergeant in A Company, worked closely with Jack in organising sport, and was as cute as a shit-house rat. They pulled out of the transit camp, Camp Martini, full of hope and with not a little trepidation. As they patrolled the main avenue, there were many money exchange people hanging about. They were different than the ornament, leather bag, and tusks salesmen. These were local Congolese in suits, with notebooks and pens as marks of their trade. They had eyes everywhere and as soon as the car slowed, they smiled their way into the vehicle.

"Keep going for a while, until we see one of them who is on his own and appears okay." Harry again!

They drove up and down about twice, and in that time the traders on the street had identified them as dealers.

"Okay, this time let's ask for rates but no decision as yet."

They stopped about five times on the next run and were offered rates from 400 to 450. One spoke only French, so he was ignored. They discussed the options and eventually decided on a younger man and a 435 offer. The rate was good, but in retrospect it might have been better to have a rate in round figures, like 400 or 450. The 35 introduced an element of honours leaving cert maths.

"Try and push him up to 440 Sir," Sgt Higgins couldn't concentrate on the driving role.

Jack tried, but the young Congolese showed the steel behind his smile and wouldn't budge on the rate. Organising another pickup seemed like too much trouble, so they agreed to the offer.

"Ta se giotta ladranach ach leanamid ar aigh."

They had agreed to speak Irish to ensure secrecy. The Congolese figured that they must be Swedes and prepared for a hard deal.

"How much have you to exchange?"

"Five hundred sixty-five dollars."

Jean Pierre's eyes lit up and he prepared mentally for the deal. The group facing him was well prepared, but his motivation came from the fact that he had only a 20 per cent cut, and had to pay a percentage to the friend of the boss man who got him the job. 'Mr Big' was a member of the government who, it was believed, was getting rid of mountains of Congolese money for hard currency.

Jean Pierre had been brought up in the assembly of huts beside the city dump. He had attended a missionary primary school, but living from recycling dumped material was a family business and he was required to play his part, particularly since his father had died. Dumped material had dropped in value since the Belgians left and this money job was a godsend. Some of his friends had jobs in the Gendarmarie. He would like such a job, but working outside the law was almost as lucrative.

"Jean Pierre." He found that introducing himself was a way of gaining the confidence of the white money dealers.

"Well, Jean Pierre, we have an agreement, but we would like to complete the transaction without any confusion." Harry liked the price and felt in control.

"Yes, we would like to make sure that the correct amount of money changes hands - understand?" Jack realised that his intervention displayed an anxiety and was a weak contribution.

Jean Pierre smiled his most becoming smile and focused his attention on the man kneeling in the front seat. He seemed to be the leader of the group. The 565 dollars at 435 he easily translated to be 245775 Congolese francs.

None of them had a calculator so the Congolese was first to announce the amount. Jack and his group used a pen and paper and kept driving as they came to the same conclusion.

"*Sin an cuid is eascaigh. Comead suil ar mo dhuine as seo amach*". Another unnecessary contribution from Higgins, who was beginning to feel like James Bond.

Everyone nodded and intensified their concentration on the piles of money that were being produced and packaged by the money trader. They knew that this was three-card trick time. Who was to hand over first was not a decision they made. Jean Pierre flicked and licked his fingers at speed and handed over the 245775 francs and awaited his bundle of dollars.

"Okay, Jean Pierre, do you mind if we count it before we complete the transaction?"

The six eyes counted and calculated and eventually all agreed that the dollars could be handed over. They all shook hands with Jean Pierre, and dropped him at the same stand of Bottlebrush trees on Boulevard du Leopold II.

Off they went, happy in the knowledge that they could fire the success flare over the operation.

"Give me the last bundle of fives." Harry was dotting the 'i's.

"What bundle?"

It was like a frost falling on an early spring evening. Images that had flowered suddenly suffered a shock and died. It wasn't a disaster, like a girl suffered when she backed into a bacon slicer, but a level of guilt had been inserted and the profit was reduced. They didn't have to relay the loss to the others waiting for their financial return, but they knew that they had been bested and their profit reduced by Jean Pierre the uneducated. So much for the honours leaving certificate and the Military College Infantry course! They had learned about divide and conquer but the application of the principle was another issue.

Jean Pierre, on the other hand, wasn't elated or surprised. This was his daily job and besting the opposition was a '*sine qua non*'. His chicks ate well that evening and he went with pride to the local hostelry to meet and drink with his friend. They had a happy time.

L ife in Leopoldville for Jack and his friends was more of the same. Camp Martini, as the transit camp was called, had progressed; replaced windows and improved sanitation had helped make life easier for officers and men of the Irish Battalion. Nevertheless, the move back to the higher altitudes and Mediterranean climate of Katanga was anticipated. The talks between Tshombe and the Congolese government weren't going well and care had to be taken that he didn't go the way of the left-wing Lumumba. The pressure at higher levels to achieve was manifest surely, but for the lower ranks escape from Leopoldville was a priority. Jack had arranged basketball and swimming in the Leopoldville University facilities and he looked forward to the move to Elizabethville to take part in the UN Soccer Championships.

Meetings were held in the UN offices downtown and the competition draws were to take place in the UN Sports Officers office. Most of the units were in Katanga and its environs, and all the matches, except those involving the Leopoldville based Swedish Unit, would take place in Elizabethville. Certainly if Tshombe didn't come to an agreement, and accept that Katanga was but a province in the new Republic of Congo, then the strength of the UN forces would be centred in the Elizabethville area.

Jack had been detailed by the CO to represent the Battalion and relay relevant information. The listing of applications to take part was completed as follows: The Rajputana Rifles, The Madras Rifles, The Tunisian Battalion, The Irish Battalion, The Pakistanian Battalion, The Malayan Signals Unit, The Swedish Unit, and the Gurkhas; eight teams in all. The competition took the form of a league and finally the top three would play a championship, a draw deciding who played whom. This was an international competition and would draw attention from all the UN unit personnel of course, but also from the Congolese who were very interested in football, but, as yet, had not achieved international status. Certainly all the children in the Irish areas of influence were football crazy. Battalion football coaches were sure the Congolese would make good at international level in the future.

"We're going back." Tim Cullinane, the Battalion Intelligence Officer, brought back the news from the meeting downtown. He slipped his way down the form seat and had his steaming dinner placed in front of him. The officers' mess was in a marquee erected on the patch of ground beside the sleeping accommodation. The Irish food was the same as that served in the Curragh or any other mess. No adjustment was made for country or climate, although the giant cold room in Camp Martini made cooking meat a possibility.

"He obviously has his orders and giving in now is not an option."

The officer with the news about the Tshombe negotiations relished the exposure he was getting. His focus was on the knife and fork manipulation of the spuds and meat, but he allowed his eyes to raise and accept questions.

"Will this lot let him go back?" another question from his brother officers.

He might have thought the question stupid, but he liked the opportunity to play with words, even though he was stating the obvious.

"Well, the Irish and the Gurkhas have control of the hotel and he'll be brought to the airport by helicopter. I expect that he's on his way as we speak."

Next morning as the Battalion did its morning Canadian 5BX exercises, word filtered around that the move back was planned. Jack spoke to the team trainer Quartermaster O'Mahoney.

"I have the team members picked out. Although I'm Eastern Command, I have to admit that the strength of the group is going to be from the south. Gavin is a cert for the goal and of course Larkin as our rough and tumble centre forward." O'Mahoney spoke with confidence.

This was the beginning of team planning and Jack and O'Mahoney had to co-operate closely, Jack to ensure that the team members were released for training each morning and for the matches, and the QM to train and manage the team.

Back in Avenue du Tullipiers life in A Company settled down to a kind of 'Waiting for Godot'. Following the debacle of the Government movement from the Baluba camp, careful group departures by train of about 200 each trip took place.

Presumably there was a degree of watchful supervision of Tshombe and his minions, but this role was at intelligence level and didn't secret down to the Company. Stephen McCoy and his outfit were kept busy mostly feeding and training the men. The level of discipline was measured by neat and efficient turnouts for parade, well-organised patrols, and reduced levels of charges against the men for transgressions against 'good order and military discipline'. Numbers going sick was also seen as a pulse measurement of discipline, as well as of health. On this latter issue the Sgt Major was the main control agent and through him the Company sergeants. Each day a designated Orderly Officer of lieutenant or captain rank took responsibility for Battalion duties, working with the Battalion Adjutant.

Commandant McCoy absorbed the focus of attention from the weekly Commanding Officer's meeting like a litmus paper. As with the previous emphasis on sexual activity and condoms, his obvious excitement at the application of some perceived need from higher-ups was there on this occasion also. He bounced into the 11.00 hrs coffee meeting in Company Headquarters.

"Hi, Benni old flick."

"I'm not either," muttered Brendan in response to McCoy's light-hearted greeting.

Stephen ignored McGonnigle's attitude, and went on to enthuse about the outcome of his last meeting.

"Just like I said in Portobello about Baden-Powell's principles, the CO is worried about morale and sees the solution in leadership - our leadership, that is. I won't go into it now, but I want everyone present at the Company meeting tomorrow morning."

"I have to attend a football meeting downtown, Sir."

"This supersedes all other duties. I want everyone here without fail. Is that understood?" Stephen eyeballed Jack to indicate the seriousness of his instruction.

He softened sufficiently, however, to pass on information about a party being held in Madras Rifles HQ, to which all officers were invited.

"How do we accept the invitation, Sir?"

Mick Keane and Jack were immediately interested.

"Give your names to the Adjutant before 12.00 hrs on Saturday. However, if you're orderly officer or on any other duties you can't go."

"He'd hate to think we're enjoying ourselves, the little shit." Mick Keane had a deep-seated feeling of resentment about all things McCoy, or for that matter about anyone in charge and giving orders.

The following morning broke bright and clear as usual. The Sgt Major was seen setting up the tables for the Company meeting two hours later. The return from Leopoldville and its friendly mosquitoes was reflected in a number of ways, but particularly because of the climate. Harry Jenkins announced the existence of frost on the grass one early morning. Jack went out to have a look and yes there it was - real frost!

"No wonder the Belgians wanted to stay here."

And so, when the day had sufficiently warmed, the A Company officer warriors took their seats around the blanket-covered six-by-four table. Some, who had not attended many company meetings, were there, Enda Ryle and Mick O'Donovan in particular.

Mick was appointed savings officer, and his function was to collect money from those who wanted his services. There were some who either didn't trust themselves to save, or who worried about having money in wallets under the mattress. Mick was useful of course when black-market deals were being done downtown, or as a conduit to the PX, which was under Swedish supervision. Jack worried about how 'the savings officer' regulated his business. He started in a businesslike manner, took notes in a book and gave a receipt. Gradually however, the system, if there really was one, broke down and was replaced with a flourished dumping of the money in 'the bag' and advice to the donor to 'keep a note' of the amounts. Why people trusted or continued to use him was a mystery. Supposedly it showed the level of trust and camaraderie that existed in the forces.

Anyway, there they were, the seven officers of A Company, ready to be briefed yet again on issues of loyalty, trustworthiness, helpfulness, friendliness, obedience, cheerfulness, thrift, bravery, purity and God's glory in mind. The last two qualities had had an innings and were probably now on the back boiler! Because of the availability of cheap booze, combined with natural inclination, the officers drank a bit, some more than others. This could be an issue for McCoy to address.

On this particular morning there was a range of 'afters' evident. Mick had a hangover, but probably wouldn't notice any difference from normal living. Jack Fortune, Eastern Command, (Emergency) Machine Gun Officer, was a hard man and lived life to the full, either on or off duty. He never showed the after-effects of drink and could sit through a meeting asleep, but with eyes open like a golden eagle. On this particular morning, outdoors in the sun in Avenue du Tullipiers, he was feeling no pain and absorbed meeting content through his machine gun officer antenna.

"Gentlemen, I bear tidings of great joy." McCoy again!

"Oh shit, it's going to be one of those!" Brendan McGonnigle rose to the bait.

"The Commanding Officer has received a high commendation from General Gandhi, UN Officer Commanding the Congo Operation, for our contribution to the safe return of President Tshombe to Elizabethville. It is a somewhat double-edged achievement, in that the secession of Katanga is still on the cards, and we are at the cutting edge."

"Cutting edge, what the fuck is he talking about? I know what I'd like to cut."

"Steady, Brendan, keep a cool head." Jack Fortune was a keen supporter of Brendan McGonnigle. They had both served in the Emergency, although similar in age and attitude to younger jumped-up Military College types.

Commandant McCoy gradually got to what he considered to be the crux of the meeting. He kept eye engagement as he sipped from his glass of water. Jack Fortune's eyes didn't release that he was asleep. McCoy wet his lips, did his imitation of a duck throwing water over his head, and uttered the immortal words.

"Gentlemen, the party's over."

"Was there a party and I wasn't invited?" Captain Fortune's half closed eyes opened dramatically.

Fortune had awoken and understood that he had missed out on a 'hale and hearty'. The laughter was uninhibited, but the Commandant, to put it mildly, wasn't amused.

"I expect more from my senior officers," he snapped, unaware that he had just given birth to a catchphrase with legs.

Unabashed, McCoy went on to explain the concern at Battalion level of the amount of drink taken by officers, both commissioned and non-commissioned.

"I agree with this concern fully and I mean to ensure that we take cognisance of the implications for us all. There's no point in coming down on the men; we've got to lead by example. I make a call for loyalty in this regard. Gentlemen, the party 'is' over and from now on I expect a changed approach to lifestyle and the demon drink."

"Demon my arse! I need a shot of something strong to settle my nerves. I think I'll kill him for the *craic*."

Brendan smiled acquiescingly in McCoy's direction and received nodding approval from the man of the moment, while those on his side of the table coughed into their hankies or hands, whichever was appropriate. The Company Commander went on to relay other items from the meeting, but it was the Madras Rifles' invitation to the party that attracted most attention. Best uniforms were to be worn for the occasion, blue scarves, blue beret, and medals where appropriate.

"Will there be drink, Sir?"

"In the light of the tenure of my address this morning, Captain Fortune, I reserve the right to pass on that." McCoy recognised a loaded question.

The chat, as the officers made their way to lunch, was mostly about the coming Madras Rifles' party. There had been a few parties hosted by various contingents before and the general opinion was that the Indians knew best how to organise a *soiree*. They travelled in the tradition of the Raj, a mixture of British regard for the officer class and Indian opulence at the upper levels. They hadn't brought their ceremonial elephants on UN duty, but Battalion silver, furniture, and mess uniforms were seen as part of the unit's need as much as arms and ammunition.

McCoy felt he had delivered the Battalion message well. As he sat down that evening in his room to write his daily letter home, he couldn't resist letting Patricia know of his role in limiting the drinking patterns of the unit. He knew she would agree with any effort to reduce the enjoyment level of the officers known to her.

'They're supposed to be working out there, not living it up,' she thought. She looked forward to telling Mrs McGonnigle about her Stephen's efforts to slow the social life of the officers. This would apply especially to her Brendan, whom she, Eileen, knew to be devoted to his daily tipple. Brendan in fact never imbibed before the sun sank below the 'yardarm' and then only as part of the social scene, via golf or the dogs.

Eileen McGonnigle didn't write much, but she enjoyed getting on to Brendan about the 'the party's over' episode. She really didn't give a damn, but she resented being on the receiving end from Patricia McCoy. They had attended the same convent school together, and Patricia behaved as though she were still head girl. Even on the hockey pitch she remembered that Patricia Googlebanks, as she was then, couldn't resist bossing the rest of the team around.

"She was team captain, but a useless player,' she remembered, "and was responsible for our losing against Loreto, Rathfarnham, in the final that year."

It was St Patrick's Day when the letter arrived. Brendan liked getting a letter, no matter from whom. The news about the meeting with Mrs McCoy and the 'party's over' quip was the last paragraph and it left him gasping for breath.

"I don't believe it, how could he have - I'll kill the fucker."

As he left his reading position on the scratcher, he became entangled in the mosquito net, which brought his temper over boiling point, if it wasn't there already.

Meanwhile, up in the Farm the officers were slipping in and out of the mess, having a drink, reading the paper, or chatting. Jack had met a few Swedish officers that morning, and invited them to the officer's mess, and was engaged telling them stories about Fionn MacCumhail, Cu Chullain, and other ancient Irish historical characters. He was waxing eloquently about the Tain and Cu Chullain's part in keeping the brown bull from Queen Maeve, when it happened. The door burst open and an enraged Captain McGonnigle rushed in, and without pause expertly lifted Commandant McCoy from behind the Irish Times. He stuck him to the wall at the far end of the room with one hand, the other in a clenched mode and withdrawn to the killing position. McCoy was small but stocky, and yet with the strength of a madman Brendan had no difficulty in affixing him to the wall, with his feet dangling about three feet from the ground.

"If you send stories home to your wife about anything to do with me you're a dead man!"

McCoy's mouth opened and closed, but no words formed. The impasse lasted about thirty seconds, after which time he was lowered to his feet and Brendan left as quickly as he had entered.

"It's a St Patrick's Day tradition, that little misunderstandings can be aired without recrimination."

"It's a good idea. We don't have anything like this in Sweden," said a white-faced Swedish officer.

By this stage, a shaken McCoy was again reading a trembling upside-down, two weeks old Irish Times. There may have been some further outcome on the issue, but nobody in the Company knew of any consequences.

"I'm fed up photographing elephants. I'd love to be taking pictures of canals in Amsterdam."

This was a typical outburst from Fleurabelle in recent times. Her business was going well and had been added to by the arrival of the UN in the Congo and contact with a range of Europeans. She wondered about the possibilities of using the film contacts known to Jack, Tim's friend from Elizabethville. In essence, she wanted to get out of Africa for reasons of lifestyle and opportunities to experience different cultures.

"My blood has been more places than I have," she said, in reference to her Indian and Dutch parental background.

Tim Cope, her lover of the moment, had a much simpler approach to life and he considered her blood a splendid mix. True, he loved adventure, but Fleurabelle had changed his attitude to life, and his trips to Ndola had become much more frequent. The idea of taking his winnings and doing a runner was now a top priority. Their two streams of desire, his and Fleurabelle's, had joined and created a torrent - and not just sexual. Between acts of passion, they talked of getting back to civilization. He had a business degree, and linked to her experience of photography and the photo lease business, they figured they could make a living and be together. Still, in the back of Fleurabelle's mind was the American dream. Tim Cope's vision was of a quiet retreat somewhere in Ireland, maybe even Carlow; a far remove from his intent when he started his odyssey five years previously - but now he had a flower to plant!

Tshombe had come back from Leopoldville with an increased passion for Katangan independence. Some of his white advisers had glanced over the abyss, and didn't much like what they saw. They figured that the Congolese government people they had met were on major ego trips, and that included visits to Geneva setting up private bank accounts. Already the Belgian establishments of civilized society, schools and hospitals, were suffering due to a breakdown of systems of administration. No inspectors of schools, no reliable police, increasing army pressure, all added up to chaos in spots and a promise of future mayhem. At least that was their opinion, which reinforced the view that Katanga as a separate state was the best way forward.

This news from Leopoldville convinced the mercenaries that to stay in Katanga meant getting involved in a battle for survival, with little chance of winning. The mercenary policy down the ages - get in, get it, and get out, determined that the time had come to scarper. Tim, with one eye on Fleurabelle and the other on the cash he was owed, was in the start position waiting for the gun - not for battle but to start running.

"I have in mind buying a bit of property in Rhodesia, just over the border. Could I get an advance on my salary, and add it to what I'm already owed?"

Two Belgian women managed the office dealing with the administration of mercenaries and other aspects of Tshombe's government. As well as running the office they were accountable to the Director of Union Minière. Tim Cope tried his most submissive approach to the senior lady in the office. Marie Helene's husband had returned to Belgium, but as they weren't really getting on that well, she had stayed. She loved the climate and the life in Katanga and hated the thought of returning to the boring lowlands of western Belgium. She did, however, miss her teenage children and saw some of their characteristics in this young man.

"An advance would be difficult, but we could pay you up to date I suppose. How much do you need for this purchase, Tim?"

"It's a piece of farmland close to Ndola. I'm told that there could be pockets of gold in one of the deserted mines in the valley. It has a nice house, however, and I could set up shop there."

He guessed that the word house would awaken the mother instinct in her and that she would be more supportive. Marie Helene was indeed excited by the approach of the young man and compared his attitude to the worn-out husband she had recently released. She paid him his dues and managed to get clearance for a small advance. A few days later Tim called again to the office and collected his money.

"Don't forget to invite me down for a visit to your new home," teased Marie Helene.

Tim felt bad about the subterfuge, but realised that everyone cheats a little. His next move involved arranging transport for Fleurabelle and himself north and out of Africa. First stop might be where Fleurabelle had contacts, in the south of France near Bordeaux. The French had a similar business and they executed deals involving photographic shots of jungle life, vineyards, and chateaux scenes.

Flying around central Africa, however, wasn't like taking a bus in a European city or town. It was a four-hour journey by DC-3 to Leopoldville - all in the same country - and it was Tim's plan to avoid Leopoldville if at all possible. Mobutu was searching all flights for subversives, and Tim, a deserter from the Foreign Legion and an erstwhile fighter for Tshombe, would fit that description.

B.T. O'Kane, a DC-3 pilot, flew Tshombe around the Congo and, at another stage, had taken Lumumba from place to place when he was trying to set up a government. B.T. flew into Leopoldville only under UN protection, but knew and flew many other routes out of the Congo. He often touched down in Rhodesia and was known to Fleurabelle. In fact, any red-blooded white male in that area of Northern Rhodesia was suspect if he didn't know and seek to take this flower of Africa out to dinner.

B.T. was born in County Kildare. He studied in Newbridge College as a boarder, and from the beginning wanted to be a pilot. After completing the Leaving Certificate at Secondary school level, he was sent to Surrey to train as a pilot. Although Aer Lingus had started in the thirties and was recruiting its pilots from wartime survivors, and from those trained in the Irish Army Air Training Centre at Baldonnell, B.T. and his family felt that he was more suited to the civilian training regime in England. The course there was three times as expensive however, but his father was convinced of the value of the civilian training course and could afford to indulge his favourite son.

The ex-RAF pilots brought a devil-may-care attitude when they joined civilian airlines after the war, and social life between flights reflected this in many ways. Drink of course, yes, but chasing women and not getting caught was another excitement. B.T. joined Aer Lingus when he had completed his training and settled easily into this environment. He quickly made a name for himself, firstly by safely crash landing a Dakota in Wales. Bad weather and engine failure generally add up to fatalities in some form or another, but in his case all were safely landed. Gradually, however, demon drink took its toll and, although supported by his colleagues, they sometimes had to kit him out when he arrived for duty, without uniform and more than a bit under the weather. It may have been his efforts to loop the loop with a Constellation in Shannon which brought about his dismissal!

There were flying jobs in England, however, and B.T. continued working. He was tall and handsome and could talk his way around most situations, so getting another flying job wasn't a problem. He slowed a bit, however, and was captured by the widow of a test pilot for the purposes of marriage. They eventually split up and B.T. invested in a small transport company, which worked mostly in central and east Africa. The DC-3s they used were the overused residue of wartime and were mostly held together by pieces of string. At least that's the impression they gave, as more and more they were being worked on in some hanger or other. Flying over the vast spaces of central Africa during the seasonal tropical storms or at night was a flying feat in itself, but if the planes were 'iffy' it added to the challenge. B.T. never complained and became famous as one of the flying troubadours of the time.

He loved flying, and got a buzz from the moment when the hostess reported "two locks and four pins on board". Advice that had to be reported to the captain before the DC-3 aircraft was allowed taxi out on the runway.

"Hello, Fleurabelle. Your favourite man is in town for another ration of your charm."

Fleurabelle took the call on her office phone. "B.T., you're a mystery man. I thought you were to get in touch with me soon again?"

The last meeting they had was about a year previously and during their overly conjugal relationship, he had promised to take her off to 'the promised land'. Where that was she didn't know, but he spoke of the charms of the orient, where some friends of his had established a flying company and wanted him in. She knew B.T. however and wasn't holding her breath. She was therefore easily attracted to the younger Tim Cope and his simplicity.

B.T. sat in the foyer of 'The Mammoth', a four-star hotel in Ndola. Fleurabelle was on her way, but he knew she would be late and he relaxed in the knowledge that he had a treat in store. 'This was the beauty of these out of the way places,' he thought. 'Nuggets of precious metal lie in waiting for the next pleasure seeker from out of town. It would be nice to finish life with Fleurabelle.' He had no real reason to believe that she would go with him - but their last meeting had promised so much. He sat back in the extravagant armchair and studied his brandy and ginger ale - Courvoisier and Schweppes. He took out a Carroll's Afton Major cigarette and tap-packed the tobacco into the paper on his silver cigarette case. He lit it with the attached lighter, which took up about one-third of the case's content but added to its cool appearance. Before putting it back into the inside pocket of his linen jacket, he studied the inscription. 'To B.T. O'Kane - From his pilot comrades - Aer Lingus, December 1958'. He thought kindly of his life before Africa, but he had moved on. He kept in touch with Irish culture mostly through books. James Joyce's 'Portrait of the Artist as a Young Man', lay dog-eared and faded on the dash of the DC-3, regularly read by him during the many delays in the African taxi flying business.

Eventually she arrived. She looked the same – sensational - but he sensed an inherent reserve that sent his alarm bells ringing. At this stage of his life he was reduced in confidence somewhat, but he wasn't admitting any slippage and approached the well-practiced man-woman thing with gathered stature.

"Hello Fleurabelle, you look beautiful, as usual."

"B.T. you old charmer."

"Not so much of the old, please."

They embraced warmly, despite the cool verbal exchange. In fairness, she did look stunning in her loose-fitting, simple, girly dress. She had been out on a photo session, and was happy with a range of shots of a tribal wedding which she expected to be much in demand. Her satisfaction with the outcome of the photo shoot was reflected in her personality of the day. Although happy, she had a feeling of independence, which reduced her need for a strong man of B.T.'s quality.

"You look your usual debonair self, B.T., what have you been up to?"

He did look well, bronzed and sporting a recent haircut, which allowed the speckled grey on the temples to add maturity to the devilment in the O'Kane perfect brown eyes. He flicked an errant strand of hair from his brow - the only sign that she had touched a nerve. 'She was so maddeningly young, beautiful, and composed,' he thought.

"Oh the usual, here and there, this and that." He responded flippantly to her question.

"Thanks for the information. I did hear that a group of businessmen from Kinshasa are leaving here for Mombassa?" She steered away from personal chitchat.

"Okay, let's talk business before we get down to the main event of the evening." He recognised the shot across his bows and thought to 'go about' and try again. He looked her straight in the eyes and was surprised to see her blush; he thought they had developed a no-nonsense relationship.

"It's no secret in Ndola. They're staying here in the hotel and were in a talkative mood last night at dinner. It seems that they have sold millions of Congolese francs for sterling and dollars and are opting out. My job is to fly them to Mombassa via Kasama in the north and on to Djibouti on the Gulf. After that they're on their own. It'll take about a week, the round trip, and there'll be plenty of chances for photographs at Kasama and Djibouti. We could call to Dar es Salaam and visit the Ruaha area on the way back. I need to collect some gear for the plane there and have it fitted. It should take about a week, and that would give you plenty of time to get to the wildlife park for some shots and back."

All of the places he had mentioned were ideal photo opportunities, and he knew it.

"Normally I would jump at the offer, B.T., but things have changed a bit since last we met. You remember I told you on the phone about meeting an Irishman from Katanga? Well, there have been developments since then." She identified the import of her changed social status.

"I don't believe it! These mercenaries are the flotsam and jetsam of the world. You can't be serious?"

He knew that she was, and guessed he'd missed the boat again - there was more!

"I was hoping, B.T., that you could get us out of Rhodesia en route to France." She moved closer to him and he felt the full heat of her sexual persuasiveness. This wasn't what he wanted, and he could hardly believe that his chances to sip honey from this flower had been eliminated by some on-the-run Paddy! He wasn't prepared to give up, however, and if a promise to bring them both in the aircraft was a move which could be used to diminish the possibility of total severance, then so be it. Again it was 'the here, the now' that controlled his thinking.

"Okay, as long as you don't mind travelling with a bunch of moneylenders. I'm booked in for the night, so I suppose it's dinner as usual?" B.T. threw out a lifeline.

"Tim is coming down later, so we can have dinner together?" She pouted as she delivered a *coup de grace.*

"I don't think that would work, Fleurabelle, you carry on and I'll see you both in the bar later."

And so they separated. He learned more about his clients for the trip to Djibouti. They weren't 'Mr. Big' in the money laundering operation, but were the next in line and were meeting some Arabs to complete a deal for their leader, who in turn was building a money cache in Switzerland for President Mobutu, described by many as the epitome of the philosophy of *les politique du ventre.*

"I've been told by friends of Antoine Gizenga of the government, that they know that Mobutu is salting it away, but they're all terrified of him. He's ex-army and has the generals in his pocket." Mr Claymore of the Ndola Chamber of Commerce had his finger on the pulse.

"Are we safe flying over the Congo with this crowd?" asked B.T.

"I suppose so, but if there is anything fishy about the deal and it hasn't been cleared by Mobutu, he could be very annoyed and our overall operation could be in danger."

They both had an investment in this trip, so they decided to do a bit of checking on their clients. The trip was planned for three weeks' time, which gave them enough space to investigate the pedigree of the passengers.

"Pass the ball - you don't own it!"

Training for the league was underway. Every morning at 11.00 hrs the team met for training on the ANC pitch close to Leopold Farm. Jack used his allocated jeep to collect drinks from the cookhouse and visit the training pitch. He did some fitness training with the team, but the coach was Quartermaster O'Mahoney, an experienced and qualified FAI coach. He ruled the training session with a rod of iron. The first match was to take place in two weeks and O'Mahoney considered their chances as good, provided they got their act together.

"These Indians are no pushover, Sir. I've seen them playing matches up in their camps, and I'm impressed. They're fit, but they also know the game."

"The draw is taking place tomorrow morning. I'll collect you at your lines at 10.00 hrs, okay?" Jack and the coach quartermaster were in close contact.

Off they sped down Avenue du Tullipiers into Avenue Picpus and into Place des Martyre. The town was moving quietly and there was a policeman controlling the traffic. He stopped everyone to allow the UN vehicle access from Avenue Leopoldville to the Hotel Majestic. Jack noticed a few well-fed mercenaries strutting their stuff with over-painted half African ladies in European clothes. They were in Tshombe's support group, but were a law unto themselves. Ex-Legionnaires mostly, they were much more belligerent than Tim Cope - Jack considered that Tim was getting out just in time.

"Bang!" A shot rang out and somebody who had looked at the mercenaries, or maybe said something, suddenly became a corpse on the sidewalk.

"Welcome to downtown free Katanga!"

They pulled into the hotel car park at pace.

The officer and the NCO left the jeep, and quickly made their way to the meeting of the UN Recreation Committee.

"Ah Jack, great to see you again - have you a team?"

Major Kapoor was his usual debonair relaxed self and smilingly looked up from his section of the paper-strewn table. Jack was about to answer, when Quartermaster O'Mahoney butted in, but in a respectful manner.

"We have a few players, Sir, but I wouldn't call them a team. Not like yours anyway. I believe that the Madras are army champions?"

"This is Quartermaster O'Mahoney, Major. He's our trainer."

Jack was afraid that the QM may have crossed the level of circumspection required in the Indian Army, but he need not have worried.

"Hello Quartermaster, I don't know where you get your information. We don't expect to do very well, I'm sure we won't make the final."

"I'm sorry, Sir, but we were told by the Raj Rifles that you were the favourites."

Jack changed the subject in case the quartermaster's protective attitude to his team caused any problems; he knew that his coach was sensitive and secretive about their prospects. The forthcoming Indian party sounded like a good diversion.

"We're delighted to get the invitation to your party."

"Yes, it should be a good do. Our Commanding Officer is looking forward to meeting our UN colleagues in a social setting." Jack thought he saw amusement in the brown eyes of his older colleague at the obvious change of subject.

They sat down at the top table as the Egyptian Colonel in charge of recreation made a hurried entrance. His assistants had bundles of numbered discs, laid face down on a table, and a pack of cards with the names of the teams printed on one side ready to draw for the League.

"Welcome, everyone. Firstly, we will designate numbers according to the alphabetical listing."

"Jeez, this is as serious as the World Cup!" O'Mahoney was impressed.

"I suppose they have to be sure that there's no hanky panky." Jack didn't know why he responded at all to O'Mahoney's remarks. When he did so, he nearly always finished down an argumentative tunnel of the Quartermaster's making.

"What about the refs. They're the hanky panky merchants." Jack killed the conversation and focused on the proceedings.

The Gurkhas were allocated the first slot, the Rajputana Rifles and the Madras Rifles two and three, Ireland number four, Malaya number five, Pakistan six, Sweden seven, and Tunisia eight.

"Very neat, eight teams, an even draw. Who'd you like to meet first?"

"Anyone bar the two Indian teams, Sir. They're the hotshots in this league and I wouldn't mind if they drew one another to start."

Even at this early stage O'Mahoney had done his homework. He looked in control - an open notebook on his knee, unlike Lieutenant Muldoon who was taking in the social setting rather than being businesslike.

All the numbered discs were placed in an army sock, the team names having been placed face up on a separate table.

"I have asked Colonel Botticelli, of the UN Italian medical contingent, to draw the numbers from the sock. The pairs drawn in sequence will play their first match against one another. From then on the winner of one and two will play the winner of two and three, and so on until each team has played every other team. Colonel Botticelli and I will supervise and we will address any complaints or difficulties on receipt of the case in writing. The top three teams will play off in championship form, having drawn for the first game.

"In the league, points will be allocated; three for a win, two for draws and zero for a loss. The referees will submit the results to us in writing on the same day as the competition in question, and our decision will be final in any dispute. Each contingent will submit the name of a referee, who will be interviewed and briefed by us. In the case of the non-acceptance of the submitted name, a substitute will be vetted, until a full complement of referees is selected. Any questions?"

"All right, the draw will now take place."

The Colonel placed his hand in the upheld sock as the delegates and the meeting secretary, an Egyptian NCO on the Sport's Officer staff, poised with pen and paper to record the matching of teams.

"Number 6, will play - second disc - Number 1 - the Gurkhas versus Pakistan."

"That should be fun." O'Mahoney seriously took notes.

And so the teams were matched. Ireland drew Tunisia for their first match, which was designated a home match for the Irish, to be played on the ANC sports field and refereed by the Malayan referee.

The Madras Rifles didn't draw the Raj for their first match and Jack and Kapoor expressed satisfaction. They talked football as they sipped their Simbas in the hotel bar, but the shooting on the street outside was also raised as a topic of conversation.

"Those mercenaries are a right crowd of 'head the balls'."

"What do you mean?" questioned Kapoor, thinking that Jack was still talking football.

"Oh, I mean they're a dangerous lot."

"That's for sure and they were that long before they came to central Africa. The Legion doesn't ask any questions, and in most cases there are serious questions to be asked. Murderers, rapists, bank robbers, they are a mixture of the worst in your society. By deserting the Legion they have committed the worst crime of all, in the minds of the Legion officials that is. There's a romantic notion about them which attracts some simple young fellas, but in the main they are rats of the lowest order."

Jack had rarely seen Kapoor in such a tense mood, or voice his opinion so strongly. He tried to absorb the tension by making the conversation point more historical.

"There's an element of that in all armies, I reckon. In the courts in Ireland it was, and to some degree still is, the custom by judges to ask the question before sentence: will you agree to go to England or join the army? The Black and Tans, who carried out a reign of terror among civilian populations during the Irish war of independence, were of the same ilk, having been released from prison in England. At least that's the commonly-held view."

"You don't have to tell an Indian about atrocities by the Imperial forces, Jack old fellow!"

They parted, wishing one another well in the first series of matches. As Jack and Sergeant O'Mahoney drove back to the Irish camp, they planned the training sessions and general team strategy for the league, particularly the first match against the Tunisians.

"I have met a few of them," said O'Mahoney. "Some of their team have played in the North African League and their expectations are high."

"What are our chances?"

"We've the best team ever to travel out of Ireland with the Army. I've been involved before with other units, but this is the best and luckily we're stationed in a fairly stable spot. The other leagues were fucked up big time by localised trouble. We won't know for sure however, until we meet the Tunisians."

Jack was aware that other Irish units were getting ready back home, and would benefit from information on recreation and training programmes. Sgt Higgins, the orderly room Sergeant in A Company, had experience of such reports and was Jack's obvious mark in getting such a reporting service

"A weekly sports bulletin, sir - a great idea. I know the lads would love to hear about the matches an' all. An issue every Wednesday!"

The training went ahead and at last the great day arrived. The ANC pitch was marked and the sports office issued the UN-inscribed flags to each participating contingent. Getting the poles into the rock-hard ground was a task in itself, but by 10.00 hrs on the morning of their first match, the pitch was marked, the flags in position and the nets hung.

"What about the penalty spots?" A private on the pitch preparation detail spoke up.

"Oh shit! Hi, Corporal McGann, the spots."

"I only have two bloody hands." Corporal McGann was a known willing worker and as a result attracted work details.

"I always knew there was something wrong with you."

When the level of hassle is high, so is the morale. Everyone was looking forward to this initial encounter and particularly with the Tunisians. There had been a bit of friction between the Tunisians and the Irish for a number of reasons. One evening a young Irish private had bolted into the Orderly Officer's room from the dark. He was frightened out of his wits and the cause of his trouble was in the bushes outside. It seemed that some Tunisian considered young fresh-faced Irish, fair game.

It caused no end of amusement to locals, when on occasions a Tunisian soldier would saunter of an evening down the street holding hands with one of the Congolese ladies. The Congolese never walked beside their women or held their hands, although both sexes behaved not unlike Europeans inside their own compounds, but not in public. The women seemed delighted at this change of status and smiled over their shoulders at the laughing onlookers, as they walked hand in hand with their Tunisian boyfriends.

That was amusing to the Irish, but chasing young fellas was a different story and caused trouble. Luckily the two units didn't meet socially and serious trouble was avoided, but the match was a perceived opportunity 'to kick the shite' out of the Tunisians.

O'Mahoney, in full UN uniform, sat in the centre of the team. The seventeen members, all kitted out, sat around awaiting final instructions. The coach looked at a sheet of paper and coolly described how they would complete their task. He didn't get excited and even on the occasion of their first match he oozed calm confidence.

"I'll be making replacements and they could happen at any time. Just because you're replaced doesn't mean that you've been playing badly, although if you are in crap form you'll be given a rest. I'll be able to see the big picture and so will do what has to be done."

"What did he say about pictures?"

"Nuttin, just you'll be pulled if you play crap."

"Gavin, you're in goal, it's your job to keep the defenders in position and particularly for corners and free kicks. Paddy Murphy, you're captain. Firstly, make sure that the defence is solid. I expect you to feed the wingers and be up for corners. I want you and Larkin to put the fear of God, our God not their Mohammed, into these fuckers when the ball comes anywhere near the square. Got it?"

The morning was hot and getting hotter. The ANC ground was really a drill square surrounded by billets, now unused. Because of a lack of drilling on the dusty bowl for over a year, snippets of grass had emerged creating the image of a field but only in spots. Mostly the game was to be played on packed red dust, particularly around the goals. The markings and flags had created the right image and when four truckloads of Tunisians pulled in to the area, excitement mounted. The spectators from both camps filtered on to opposite sides of the pitch, while the already fully kitted Tunisian team and their management members were shown to their space in front of one of the Armee National de Congo billets.

The situation had all the ingredients of a fully blown international and, as well as the Irish and Tunisian supporters, many Congolese locals also attended. As was the custom with Indian and Tunisian units, all the spectator soldiers were on parade and fully armed. They chatted excitedly, with rifles across their shoulders or carrying submachine guns. The Irish troops on the other hand were unarmed unless on parade or patrol, and were dressed in lightweight uniforms, blue scarves, and blue berets.

The referee blew a shrill whistle, signalled to his linesmen and supervised the exchange of flags between captains. Paddy Murphy handed over his flag and shook hands. He chose heads, which came up, and he selected to play into the sun for the first half, as per his instructions from the coach. The game kicked off and the Irish secured possession and made their way up field.

"Cross it."

The winger swung his right leg but only kicked fresh air. The Tunisian left back had taken the ball without permission and was streaking up the sideline. Murphy came in at speed, missed the ball but instead sent the winger into the crowd. The ball meanwhile had centred and the Tunisian forward Mustafi, ex-player with the Tunis Meridians, had an open track to the Irish goal. Everyone expected him to pass, including goalie Gavin who was tracking a right-winger, onside and running into an open space. In that frozen moment the ball eagerly found the top left corner of the Irish net, impelled by the right foot of Mustafi. The whistle blew: Goal!

The Irish were stunned and silent but the Tunisians screamed, ran onto the pitch, danced in celebration with the team, who showed their jubilation in traditional North African manner.

"Steady lads, it's only a goal, not the end of the world." O'Mahoney steadied the ship and said it as it was.

"The ball is what matters here. Tackle for the ball and make sure you get it. I know you have to watch developments, Gavin, but remember that it's the ball in the net that scores goals. Okay Larkin, show them how Cork Hibs do it."

The Malayan ref wasn't pleased with the invasion of the pitch, and told the Tunisian coach in so many words. When things had calmed down he started the game again. The Irish then ran riot, but not by invading the pitch. Down to the other side of the park, across, and Larkin blasted into the net. In the next five minutes the Irish scored four more goals; fifteen minutes gone and the score was five-one for the Irish!

There was silence at first, but then the referee came in for some criticism and the shouting grew louder and louder. A rip of automatic gunfire rang out! The Irish players stopped and looked in the direction of the shots, but the referee took immediate action. It was probable that the shots were fired into the air as part of an Arabic release of tension, but he was taking no chances. The Malayan jeep arrived on the pitch and immediately the ref and his sideline officials climbed on board.

"What's he saying?"

"He's awarded the match to us and disqualified the Tunisians!"

The ref wasn't taking any chances and in jig time he was up and away. The Irish team followed suit, spectators in tow, leaving a very disgruntled Tunisian team mingling with spectators on the pitch. Despite the unusual ending, the Irish had won a match in the UN soccer league.

Meanwhile in A Company, Brendan McGonnigle, since recovering from his encounter with McCoy over the party episode, was speaking words of wisdom again.

"Speaking of parties, lads, isn't the Madras knees-up taking place this week? I was thinking of sending home for the girlfriend." He wasn't of course, but the idea of attending such a lavish party without women seemed a bit strange.

"The golf match beforehand should be a bit of *craic*."

"Golf! Is there golf?" Jack was immediately interested.

The golf course in Elizabethville was a major social and recreation centre for the Belgians before they left for home. Luckily, the staff from Union Minière and those few who had stayed behind kept the course administered and maintained to a certain degree. The eighteen beautiful holes and well-established clubhouse were an instant attraction to the officers of the UN units arriving for peacekeeping duties. An army of Congolese women carried out maintenance, but a void had been left by the departure of the Baluba Katanga. Quite a few of them were the regular staff, green keepers etc, and were impossible to replace at short notice.

Jack played there regularly, particularly on Sunday mornings.

"We're supposed to submit lists of four balls before tomorrow and they must be a mix of at least two units," said Brendan.

Jack and Mick Keane got together and arranged two others from the Madras Rifles. One was Major Kapoor and as yet they didn't know the name of the other.

"Just write down AN Other, Kapoor will let them know," said Mick, anxious to keep things moving.

Apart from running their business, mining, rubber, and ivory, the Belgians' lives centred on recreational activity and the social life that went with it. When the Irish first came to Leopoldville, there were a myriad of well-supported recreational opportunities. For the troops this was a first opportunity to play in giant outdoor swimming pools, and they indulged themselves. The new togs from the Dundalk businessman stood out from the army issue. Jumping off the high board presented soldiers in a rather exposed position and was christened by some wag as the 'genital leap'. A Company and their fancy togs were spared this indignity, although in fairness the soldiers couldn't have cared less.

There were adjacent recreation areas that were visited by the Battalion members during their stay in Leopoldville. Clusters of circular huts, dotted around a mountainous-forested area, set between groups of lakes and serviced by bars and restaurants, provided potential for aquatic sports. The Irish had been warned of the dangers of attack by a variety of candiru fish from the rivers and lakes, who's penchant was to find an orifice anywhere on the human body, attach themselves to the entrails and feed off your blood. Only surgery could remove it. Local kids were frequently seen playing in pools beside the Congo river, but the Irish soldiers appeared terrified of the fish that went up your bum - swimming in natural pools was not a problem that the medical services had to worry about.

For the first time in their lives the Congolese were allowed into pools being used by whites, but were still very self-conscious and tended to gather in restrained groups. There were still two ball boys on the tennis courts' duty. Although not availed of at first, officers soon followed the custom and a quick return of the balls made playing in temperatures of thirty-plus pleasurable and possible. The Indian officers usually brought their own orderlies with them to act as ball boys.

There was still a big game hunting tradition in the area and 'Park National de Upemba' was famous as an elephant reserve. It was accessible by road from Katanga, and Reggie Morrison had planned a trip there to spot elephants. Despite his terrible back trouble on the way out, Reggie had survived and was making a significant contribution to the Battalions efforts as signals officer. By now his back had recovered, though he still kept a board under his mattress. He had recruited a few interested individuals to hunt elephants; not to shoot them, but to photograph the huge beasts - although there was large-scale poaching in this region and tusks were available at the markets every day. There was still a large export business of ivory to China from supplies of tusks from the many animal reserves in the Congo. Reggie awaited word about a hunt from the local reserve manager.

occer events progressed and by the time of the golf match, two Indian units and Ireland had won one and drawn two matches. The Tunisian incident wasn't mentioned at managerial level, and Tunisia won one of their next matches without firing a shot!

aving arranged the golf representation, the officers got their uniforms dickied up for the party with the Madras Rifles. They knew the night would be a social snippet from the British Raj, crossed with a flavour of the Rajah Indian Prince of Madras. Some of them had been to a party by the Gurkha Battalion and had an idea of how the reception would go. Before the Gurkha Battalion meal, a young goat had its throat cut on the steps of the mess as an offering to the gods. This event was a display of expertise with the Sukri ceremonial sword, as much it was part of a religious ceremony. Jack realised that the UN had brought two very different civilizations together.

Patrice, Jack's and Harry Jenkins's orderly, was delighted with the job of washing and ironing. Ironing in particular was his strength, and his skill with the small native iron was in the higher category. Remarkably so, because the iron was a simple hollow implement into which lighted charcoal was placed as a heat source. Swinging the iron from side to side created a draft that brought the charcoal to a white heat. A damp cloth and the deftness of a concert pianist produced both slacks and uniform with creases fit to slice bread!

The golf competition was to take place in the morning and early afternoon, thus leaving plenty of time to prepare for the reception. The participants were met at the clubhouse by the Sgt Major of the Madras Rifles and a few soldiers, who supervised parking and directed players to the morning food and drink reception in a corner of the lounge adjacent to the competition secretary.

"Lieutenants Muldoon and Keane. We are matched with Major Kapoor and Lieut AN other." Jack presented to the soldier secretaries.

"I'm sorry, Sir, what was the second name?"

"We don't know the name as yet, Major Kapoor has made the arrangement."

"Oh I see Sir, A-n-other." The Sergeant, dressed in immaculate uniform and turban, smiled in recognition of the form of pseudo-name. "Yes, here you are. You tee off at 10.15 hrs, Sirs. Your caddies will take your clubs now, with your permission, Sir."

As if by magic, two soldiers raced forward and took the rather tatty golf bags from Jack and Mick. Shortly afterwards, when they moved outside to look around, one of the caddies came forward: black hair parted at the side, shining black eyes, green sweater, and well creased wide-bottomed slacks.

"Sir, we are cleaning your clubs," he lilted. "You needed new balls so we got them from the competition Quartermaster. Is Dunlop 65 all right for you?"

Jack and Mick were surprised, and having made their arrangements with the caddies and the first tee secretary, they decided to get fully into the spirit of the event, Indian style, and joined Major Kapoor and Captain Ramalingam in the reception area for drinks. Having a tipple before teeing off seemed to be the thing to do, so Jack and Mick asked the Indian barman for iced gins and tonics.

"Cheers!" They lifted their glasses to their playing partners. "May the smoke of poverty never go up your flue."

"What is that you are saying, Jack?" Kapoor smiled in Jack's direction.

"Oh it's just on old Irish saying meaning good luck."

"I'll take your word for it, Jack, but I think you are putting an Irish spell on us."

"I believe you're magic with your putter anyhow, Major."

The banter was good as they prepared to tee off. The official drive-in was the responsibility of the General in charge of United Nations Operations. He and his blond wife were presented with a token of the Madras Rifles' role in setting up this competition. She smiled over an enormous bunch of lilies presented by the Colonel Officer Commanding the Madras Rifles. Being the only woman present she was the centre of attention. The worshiping Indian General, it was said, imported her clothes from Paris.

The General and his party drove off and as was the case any time the General played, a platoon of soldiers, fully armed, patrolled the route of the course, hole by hole. Jack noted the strong, well-executed drive of the General down the first fairway and felt the gremlins beginning to unhinge his nerve at the prospect of driving off the first tee.

"I had a fresh air on the 1st in the Curragh last time I played there," said Mick Keane. Jack was reassured by this remark from his partner and had already split the 440 yards to the 1st green into planned shots.

'That's what a skill is,' he thought, 'when you can eliminate the discrepancy between intention and performance, it's a skill! It's all in the mind.'

Caddies in tow, Mick and Jack answered the call of the secretary to the tee and prepared to drive. It was their honour it seemed, because they were the invited - Kapoor and Ramalingam shook hands and wished them well.

"This is a terrible ordeal. What if I miss the ball on the first tee with all this crowd watching?"

"Remember Mick, you're an athlete and a good one. It'll be a piece of cake for you."

Mick was off first and he mounted the steps to the tee. He took the driver from his caddie and teed up. A broad shoulder, a reasonable stance - but the hurley grip was a giveaway. He clipped a few daisies, or whatever they have in Africa for daisies, and moved in for the kill. He addressed the ball, squared his jaw, and looked into the distance.

"For the honour of the little village, Mick."

Mick started his back swing and began to rotate his shoulders as he carried the driver back a full 180 degrees. At the top of the back swing he flexed his wrists. This was a brave position indeed, and most beginners would have lost the plot by this time, but not Mick. In the blink of an eye he was through the ball and brazenly showing his studs. The ball had been launched by contact with the ivory face at maximum speed.

An expected outcome by most, there was polite applause. Jack was tempted to whoop and holler, but saw that such a reaction to this near-miracle would be very out of place.

"Well done, partner."

Jack took his position on the tee as the secretary announced his name. The flags fluttered and the old clubhouse looked her best; white painted balcony, red tiled roof, and surrounded by smiling Indian faces over a mishmash of rows of cross-legged white slacks. His attention was reduced by the chattering of colourful parakeets fluttering from branch to branch in the trees nearby.

Jack struggled to remain focused as he addressed the white pill, thinking - carry back the left arm on the inside and up. He kept a beady eye on the ball and away it went.

"Nice ball, Jack."

Kapoor, white slacks, blue open necked shirt and what looked to Jack to be a cricket pullover with a battalion motif, sauntered on to the tee. He sported a Ronald Coleman moustache, which emphasised the whiteness of his perfect white teeth as he smiled confidently in the direction of his friends on the steps of the pavilion. His caddy had teed the ball so, without any preliminary swing, he confidently and quickly launched a mighty drive down the fairway. His skills as an Indian international hockey player had transferred easily and he deserved the applause.

His partner Ramalingam was a different kettle of fish and, displaying a definite lack of concentration, he splayed the ball somewhat. At least it finished in the light rough, and not in the jungle. Well not really a jungle, as in tropical regions, more a heavily wooded area with some dense undergrowth containing a number of indigenous animals. Snakes in particular were a problem and could present a deadly risk to golfers looking for lost balls, and that's where the role of the Indian soldiers came in useful. Before they were level with where they had seen Ramalingam's ball disappear, a soldier was standing to attention beside it.

Captain Ramalingam stepped carefully to where his spotter was indicating.

"It's playable Major; and please keep an eye open for the ball as it hits the fairway." The final request by Ramalingam was spoken more in hope than as a definite instruction. He knew before he swung that his chances of getting anywhere near the fairway were slight. He shaped up, but involuntarily closed his eyes as he swung at the ball, which surprisingly he hit, but it bounced off a tree and rebounded deeper into darkest Africa. A few monkeys chattered, upset by the intrusion and they no doubt easily spotted the resting place of the ball.

"I see it, Sir!" His spotter, his village's star cricket fielder, was on the ball before the dust settled, or the monkeys had investigated. Ramalingam spat out a list of Hindu expletives, brushed bits of twigs and dirt from his once immaculate shirt, and gingerly made his way to the new site.

"Are you still playing?" Kapoor was somewhat embarrassed by the display of ineptitude by his brother officer.

"I'll just have one more effort."

Jack and Mick were more than a little interested in the rumble in the jungle, as Jack indelicately called it.

Ramalingam addressed the ball again and let fly. Miracle of miracles, this time Lord Krishna smiled. Wending an impossible route through the trees the Dunlop 65 landed on the fairway.

"Well played, old chap." Kapoor was amazed to see the ball again.

Based on previous experience, his opinion of his partner's golf was poor or less. He had previous reservations about selecting Ramalingam as his playing partner, but considered him to be the best of a bad lot.

"Careful there, Sir."

Striding excitedly through the undergrowth, Captain Ramalingam forgot the possibility of snakes, and trod on a young green Mamba who in fairness was trying to avoid the approaching feet. She only showed aggression when the Indian officer trod on her tail. She bit the juicy brown ankle and fled, taking to the trees when the tail pressure ceased.

"The Captain has been bitten, Sir."

A high level of excitement prevailed, but immediate action in army terms was instituted. The jeep arrived and the unfortunate officer was carted off for treatment, which had to take place within ten minutes of the bite. Poor Ramalingam didn't notice that his ball had miraculously found the fairway, not that he was in a position to continue. The incident caused some delay to the progress of the golf match, but in less than half an hour the game recommenced. Another three four balls had been called through by the Sergeant Major, efficiently acting as competition chief steward.

"Maybe it's just as well," remarked a serious Kapoor, "his game wasn't up to scratch anyway. We'll continue as a three ball."

Jack and Mick considered the remark a bit harsh. "But then, they have a different culture in a land of 100 million people."

"Feck that for a lark," said Mick, "everyone deserves a chance - lily of the field, bird dropping from the sky and all that."

"The Christian Brothers did a good job on you." Jack was surprised at Mick's application of principals from the Gospels.

The rest of the play to the 1st hole was a bit of an anticlimax after the snake incident. The players straightened up considerably and 'conservative' was the name of the game. The soldiers were unfazed and, ignoring local risks, followed one of Mick's balls into the undergrowth from where he had a miracle shot to six inches from the hole.

"Well played, Mick, Vinnie Baston would be proud of you."

Reference to the famous Waterford hurler and army golfer was meant as part of Jack's continuing motivation for Mick.

Pitching on to the elevated green meant that about fifteen *manamucks*, with implements not unlike sheep shears and used as fringe clippers, had to move to one side. They were a swathe of yellow and blue chatter, a plethora of children, big bums, and mile-wide smiles. Jack had had his fill of the observational skills of these African ladies and was happy that his approach lipped the hole and left him with a three-inch putt. He merited a chatter of approval, while poor Kapoor, who ran over into a massive bunker, achieved titters and keen attention. His three attempts to blast out were greeted by whoops of derision and peals of laughter.

"Would you like a drink, Sir?"

The Company Sergeant Major, resplendent in full ceremonial dress, was in charge of a jeep fitted out like a bar. Silver trays were used to carry a round of gin and tonics to the three officers. There were four of these refreshment units on the course, servicing the players at each tee.

"This is the life to which I wish to become accustomed," muttered Jack.

"It was probably the norm in the Curragh before our lot took over."

Kapoor contributed to the discussion about social practices.

"We have a lot of customs, part British Raj and part Indian Royal practice, that still exist. We realize, however, that as we're dragged into the modern world, UN and all that…."

He left the rest unsaid, but Kapoor and the rest of the UN Indian contingent realised that Empire practices in their army would probably suffer diminishment. What they observed as practice among the Irish, or in particular the Swedes, put their own officer support practices from the men under close comparative scrutiny.

On they played, and after about the eighth gin they felt no pain. They finished the eighteen holes to the applause of the earlier starters and non-players, still seated at sets of tables in front of the clubhouse. Kapoor scored 30 points, Jack 32, and Mick 21. They signed the cards and handed them to the competition secretary, before joining the increasingly jolly crowd.

The competition finished before the sun reached its zenith, allowing the officers' time to return to their units and spend three hours at siesta. The results of the golf competition were to be announced at the party in Madras Headquarters that night.

"Patrice, we need the uniforms at seven tonight. *Oui à ce moment précis.*"

Patrice smiled at his officer's attempts to communicate in French and just to keep the pot boiling, he answered in Swahili.

"Sikukusupia kufanya vibaya bwana."

Jack and Mick Keane were too spent by the heat, golf efforts, and gin and tonic to engage in an international conversation, and quickly pulled the mosquito nets into position. In no time flat they were sending snores through the net without disturbing the newts on the ceiling, who also had slipped into slumber, albeit with one fly eye open.

As he ironed, sending clouds of steam skyward, Patrice attempted to put his greatly changed environment out of his mind. True, he was performing the same functions for his UN masters, but the security of working for a permanent family had gone when the Belgians upped and left without warning. They had recruited him and his wife from the east of the province, so he was more or less their property. Having cut his links with his Baluba village in Kivu, he was stranded in west Katanga with his wife and six children. The children had been attending the local primary school and were members of the Boy Scouts and Girl Guides. Little black Belgians so to speak, and they spoke perfect French-the four eldest that is. Now the white teachers, bar one or two, had left, and the voluntary supporters in the scouts had dwindled away, undermining the fundamentals necessary to education Belgian style. Some religious schools were still there, but they could only give a limited service.

Patrice and his family lived in a small hut at the bottom of the garden and depended on the money he accrued from working for the UN. What with the Tshombe problem and the possibility of all-out war, he and many like him were in danger of having to relocate outside Katanga.

"Sir, sir, *Jambo*, time to wake up."

And so the time for the mess party with the Madras Rifles drew close. The uniforms were donned at about 19.00 hrs and transport arrived shortly afterwards. Jack, Mick Keane and Harry Jenkins shared the same jeep and off they went, light of heart and bushy of tail, to attend the reception in the headquarters of the Madras Rifles.

"It'll be all Indian; fancy uniforms and curried food - no birds." Jack was trying to create a picture in his mind of how the party would pan out.

"And drink, don't forget the jar."

The flowering jacaranda wafted extra perfume into the night air as they sped down Avenue du Tullipiers and on to their venue. The Madras Rifles had their headquarters just outside the city in a large, vacated residence.

The gates at the entrance were controlled by a number of magnificent looking senior non-commissioned officers in regimental dress.

"Yes Sir, you're very welcome. Please proceed to the mess." They had checked the list and given them the go-ahead. There was also a military guard on duty at the entrance and the sentry presented arms and saluted as they sped past. Tulip trees lined the approach to the big house, which was about three-quarters of a mile from the gate, but that wasn't all. Every twenty yards or so, a sand-filled brass shell cartridge impregnated with oil was set alight to mark progress. Beside each shell stood a soldier, whose function it was to light the sand again should the motion of the transport extinguish them.

"Get a load of that. I hope our folks at home realise the terror we have to endure in this steaming jungle hell." Harry was trying to imprint the scene on his mind.

The Indian Commanding Officer and his Adjutant met them at the floodlit mess entrance. Waiters in uniform floated by, carrying drink filled glasses on large silver trays. Jack felt good as he selected a drink from an Indian soldier, who appeared delighted that he should be chosen to act as a facilitator to Jack's first drink of the night.

"That was some entrance, Jack. It was like being part of a fairytale - the swish of the car fanning the tunnel of trees and killing the lights one by one, only to have them lit again as we passed. If the Arabian Nights hadn't been written, I'd be tempted to put pen to paper," said Harry.

"The only things I've seen you write, Harry, were charge sheets and they're a long way from Hans Christian Anderson," said Mick.

"Steady, Micheal *a stor*, it wasn't Hans Christian Anderson, it was based on the Thousand and One Nights and translated from Arabic into French by Antoine Galland in 1700."

It wasn't often Harry got a chance to score artistic points, but when he did he milked the occasion.

"I'll take your word for it. You're a bit of an Aladdin, mystery man, yourself. Where do you get this waffle ammunition?" muttered a chastened Mick.

"If I told you, you'd be as wise as I am!" The brother officers were nearly always scoring points from one another as part of a social exercise.

In about an hour everyone had arrived, including the UN Indian General and his wife. More speeches of welcome and the level of conversation increased. The Madras Rifles pipe band had made a dramatic entrance and it took a power of expression to be understood above their contribution. Most of the music they played was Scottish. Tunes like 'Up the Leg of your Drawers' and the 'Irish at Bannockburn' went down a treat with the Gaels present.

The early drinks were having their effect, but just in time the food arrived. And what food! Tray after tray of dishes created by Indian gourmet gods arrived on large silver salvers, supported by a multitude of waiters carrying plates and napkins to everyone, so that the process of eating the curries and eastern delights was carried out with ease. Sets of small tables and chairs were clustered around the fairy-tale garden. While they ate, the regimental brass band played a selection of music - marches, waltzes, popular numbers, and classical pieces.

"This is like heaven."

"Well, we deserve it," said Jack.

"McCoy doesn't think so."

They ate their fill and drank in tandem. The wine was the best and when at last the repast finished, they sat with distended stomachs, sipping on the brandy of their choice.

"Bring on the dancing girls."

Unfortunately, there wasn't such a show, although some very inebriated captains of the Rajputana Rifles engaged in a form of Indian dance while balancing a beer on their heads. Rather British mess-type stuff and no doubt a bit of fun, but lacking in gravitas. Things livened up when a self appointed master of ceremonies took over and facilitated individual song contributions.

A song about 'The Battle of Fontenot' by a Corporal from Clare got a standing ovation. The Officer Commanding had brought him along to perform his well-proven party piece.

"As the French regiments ran down the slope, one regiment was ahead of the others. It yelled its ferocious battle cry: *Remember Limerick, Remember Limerick!* The words echoed grimly in the ears of the English and Dutch. The Wild Geese of Ireland had many scores to settle, not least when they had to be rallied by Lord Clare after a first broadside by the English. The Irish achieved their ambition that day but at a terrible cost."

Having painted a verbal setting, he began to sing and displayed an excellent Irish tenor voice, which like a stellar light, pierced its message into everyone's consciousness.

Fontenoy, 1745. After the battle:

"Mary Mother, shield us! Say what men are ye,
Sweeping past so swiftly on this morning sea?
Without sails or rowlocks merrily we glide
Home to Corca Bascinn on the brimming tide.

Jesus save you, gentry! Why are ye so white
Sitting all so straight and still in this misty Light?
Nothing ails us, brother; Joyous souls are we
Sailing home together, on the morning sea.
Cousins, friends and kinsfolk, children of the land,
Here we come together, a merry, rousing band;
Sailing home together from the last great fight,
Home to Clare from Fontenoy, in the morning light.
Men of Corca Bascinn, men of Clare's Brigade,
Harken, stony hills of Clare, hear the charge we made;
See us come together, singing from the fight,
Home to Corca Bascinn, in the morning light."

The Irish shook the stars when the final phrase of the song rang out, and the Indians joined in as confreres against the idea of centuries of oppression.

A relationship between Madras, Rajputan and Ireland was forged that night, and as they made their way home the Irish were joyous to a fault, but threw down a gauntlet to their new friends from India.

"We look forward to our next meeting on the soccer field. May the best man win."

The Battalion Sports Bulletin was a great success and although no match equalled the bizarre nature of the one against the Tunisians, many notable encounters took place until the results of the League were published. The Madras Rifles and the Irish were first and second, the Raj and the Gurkhas filling third and fourth places. Thus, the Madras Rifles were to play the Rajputana Rifles, and the Irish the Gurkhas, with the winners and losers playing for first and third place.

"So, if we beat the Gurkhas and the Madras win against the Raj, the final will be between us and the Madras Rifles."

"That's a big if. Remember the Gurkhas beat us early on."

And so the football achieved its social aim. There was intense excitement in each camp and even if Tshombe had decided to go to war, it's probable that it would have been put on the back boiler until the championships were over! The Battalion HQ identified that something important was taking place involving the Irish. The Commanding Officer felt that it was necessary to put some of his big guns into the preparation of the teams.

"Didn't Stephen McCoy play for the Eastern Command?"

The Adjutant responded.

"He did indeed, Sir. Do you want me to put him in charge of the operation?"

"Well, we need to keep and support the Sports Officer and Quartermaster O'Mahoney, the coach. But I suppose a senior officer in charge would look better."

"Look better?"

"Yes sir, if we win, reports will be going back to GHQ in Parkgate St., in which case it would be important to have a senior officer involved."

McCoy could have blundered in where angels fear to tread, but his 'footie' background made him realise that the present winning combination deserved support.

"Jack, the CO has asked me to lend a hand to the soccer team. I want you and O'Mahoney to continue as is and I'll generate extra support, transport, grub, drinks, whatever's needed."

It was a bit of a shock. Up to then Jack or O'Mahoney hadn't to answer to anybody and they already had all the Quartermasters on their side, if they needed any provisions. However little extras began to become a part of the support for the team. Mid-morning break included fruit and sandwiches, and transport to and from the training became more easily available. Gradually McCoy managed to winkle his way into the psyche of the already close-knit team and management.

"What about the Gurkhas game? Have we a chance, O'Mahoney?"

"Sir, you'd better not be heard talking like that - Murphy and the team have no ifs or buts in their mind. We have this match won before we take to the field."

That's the way it turned out, but it wasn't easy. The Gurkhas were leading 2-nil until well into the second half, but three goals later, thanks to outside right Barney Hogan, Corporal Denis Larkin, and the team Captain, the Irish were leading five-two; a bit like the Tunisian match, but without the warfare. This finish was amicable and all contestants shook hands and wished the other well in their next encounter.

The matches by this stage were well publicised and well attended, not alone by the UN contingents but also by increasing numbers of Congolese locals. They loved football, although hurling was a favourite attraction - it was considered training for warfare and a cause of great amazement.

When the dust had settled, Ireland and the Madras Rifles were in the final, and everyone, men, NCOs, and officers, were looking forward to a great competition. McCoy the Company Commander was in his element.

"It's just like an international final. I hope they realise at home what a good job we're doing out here."

"It keeps the men happy," said a rather disinterested Chaplin.

"That's not how the other contingents view it, I can tell you."

It was Commandant McCoy's first sharp word to the Chaplin.

B.T. managed to survive without his allocation of love from Fleurabelle. His money-laundering passengers were secure, but he had greater capacity in the old Dakota and had immediate expenses: fuel and servicing, and the spare part had to be paid for in Dar es Salaam immediately it was installed. Because of the fluid situation in the Congo the main hotel foyer in Ndola was a meeting point for all sorts.

'A bit like Casablanca during the war,' thought B.T., 'I could play Rick if I owned this place. The Belgians fecked everything up by doing a runner.'

This was the common opinion among the whites, and hard currency, not property, was the desirable acquisition. An Arab man and a woman were sitting in the foyer. B.T. sat nearby sipping a gin and tonic. The man had identified an advertisement in the bar that stimulated a conversation between him and his female companion.

"Are you free? So are we!" The ad stated.

They were having difficulty relating the first sentence with the second.

"It doesn't make sense."

"I agree with you, husband."

'So they are husband and wife,' thought B.T., from an observation post behind a hotel palm. She appeared in control of their luggage and, more important from a business point of view, tapped consistently on a small portable Remington. Her headscarf accentuated the pallor of her features and of her attractive brown eyes. B.T. normally kept to himself but smelt that they might be potential passengers.

"Have you ever heard of poetic license?" he offered.

She 'copped on' at once and spoke to her husband in a quiet tone, explaining the essence of the concept and how it related to the advertisement. It took a bit of rationalising on his part, due perhaps to his male resistance to change - plus the fact that it was he who identified the phrases which he considered illogical, and obviously he wasn't prepared to retreat without some effort at face-saving. B.T. recognised this dilemma and suggested that his mechanistic approach was perfectly acceptable, but left the option of artistic license open.

Whether the Arab understood the concept or not, B.T. ploughed on, in search of more information about their presence and plans.

"Where are you from?"

"I'm an Arab." His answer was punched out as a final definition of his and his wife's derivation.

B.T. somehow was sucked into a conversation to nowhere.

"I'm a Celt but I come from Ireland."

The Arab's eyes hardened even more and following a pause aimed at chilling the atmosphere, he responded.

"We Arabs belong to the hard world of the present and not just part of the Celtic twilight."

B.T. felt insulted but decided that he hadn't the verbiage or the energy to defend his ancient culture. Anyway, he decided that business came first and two more passengers were a priority. The wife had already indicated that they were intent on getting back to the Gulf as soon as possible and he offered her two places to Djibouti.

"What do you sell?" B.T. still couldn't leave well enough alone. "Camels?"

The Arab's green eyes dilated snake-like and ranges of emotions were displayed in a relay of facial expressions. Finally, when he realised that he held a trump card he allowed good humour to prevail.

"No not camels, but racehorses: Arab stallions. We have secured an order from some rich owners in Cape Town. My client has extensive training farms in St Helena, close to the bay."

He realised that he had allowed this infidel goad him into revealing more about his business than he wished made known and he hated him for that. He got some consolation when his wife refused to shake hands.

"We don't shake hands," particularly not with an infidel, he could have added..

"Hello, Fleurabelle. How are things? I'm working on our trip north."

The hotel phone was no way to run a business; B.T. should have had an office somewhere, but he mostly lived in the air, his heartbeat at one with the throbbing of the engines of his beloved Douglas.

"Tim and me are looking forward to that. He rang me this morning wondering if you could take twenty men from Leopoldville to Elizabethville."

"That would mean bringing them back on the round trip via Djibouti and Dar es Salaam. That's one hell of a trip, would it not be better to get the spare part in Dar es Salaam first, then Djibouti and collect them on the way back."

She knew Tim Cope would prefer to get out of the Congo as soon as possible and also knew that the men from Leopoldville were probably more mercenaries heading to Katanga, who might be one-time colleagues of Tim's from the Legion and might question his departure from Elizabethville.

"You should be in this business, Fleurabelle, I'm only a poor pilot."

"You're more than that, B.T., and I'll miss you when you leave."

"It's you that's leaving, darling!"

His face didn't reflect the flippancy of his remark.

"Being with you B.T., would be like living with a migratory bird."

And so, engagement, disengage, attack, circular parry, attack, hit off target, but like fencing, it was but a game. For Fleurabelle at least, but poor B.T. had a serious intent and particularly as he saw the target slip away.

"I could throw that Carlow shit Cope out at twelve thousand feet!"

Fleurabelle liked B.T. and was slightly uneasy playing games of this nature. America always loomed large at the back of her mind however and although she didn't admit it, or as yet realise it, Tim, her friends in Bordeaux and Jack's friends in the film world were all but stepping stones towards her main objective. Tim's talk of returning to a small farm in Tullow was to her but love talk between the sheets.

B.T. made a few calls from his room. His central manager in Brussels had six other passengers for the trip north. These were Rhodesian business people that he knew, regular clients of the company.

"Nearly there," he muttered, as he threw himself on the bed. He suddenly felt tired.

"B.T., B.T.!" Fleurabelle was at the door. As he opened up she fell into his arms weeping like a schoolgirl.

"Oh B.T., I have terrible news. Tim's been captured on the border by a group of Banyamulenga tribesmen. He's alive, but they want a ransom. The police are downstairs, but they're only carrying the message and say they can't cross the border. What can we do?"

She seemed to forget that it wasn't B.T. and herself as before. He retreated under the pressure of her lithe young body and slowly flopped on to the bed. She was his mirror movement and as if by way of physical conversation and lubricated by her tears, she kissed him, kicking her shoes to the ground, letting her knees envelop his body and her hips melt into his like a bee searching for honey from an open flower. He responded. He wrapped his arms around her waist, slipped her frock over her round bottom and as he slid his hands under her panties she groaned, lifted her hips and kicked the silk to the ground.

"Will you help me, will you help me?" she whispered. B.T. joined her lips to his again and nodded. The answer was received with a frenzied cry of thanks as she opened her femininity totally to him and they made love.

"Locks and pins on board, B.T."

She stashed the flap pins and the locks in the cabin and wrapped her arms around his neck from behind as the Dakota took off. They were heading for a jungle clearing close to the border on the Congo side and known to B.T. as an emergency stop. His information had it that locals would know the whereabouts of Tim and the other captives.

"There it is."

The clearing was visible, split by the only road in the area capable of taking transport. He checked the wind and circled once before landing on the bumpy grass runway. He didn't switch off until he recognised some of the faces that came running out to meet him. They spoke only in Kinyamulenge and stayed around as unpaid keepers of the runway. B.T. enquired about the whereabouts of white men captives in the area. It all seemed a bit unlikely and yet straight away they pointed excitedly north and indicated that bad men had captives for sale. B.T.'s ears pricked because in this part of the world the term 'bad man' usually meant Arab raiders.

"Bad men, how many." Fleurabelle hung on every word and when they spoke of a camp about two miles away, she swept B.T. along in a flood of enthusiasm.

"Oh yes, let's go, B.T. It must be them."

Without realising it, B.T. was out of the plane and on his way into the bush. One of the tribesmen went with them and directed B.T. towards where he thought the camp was. They walked for hours and almost without warning they were in a group of huts and surrounded by about twenty well-armed Arabs, some on camels, which surprised him. Camels didn't normally survive the onslaughts of the tsetse fly and encephalitis south of the Sahara. They had tied together a long line of Congolese, looped around the neck from man to man. It seemed that they were expected, because without much conversation he and Fleurabelle were ushered to one of the huts in response to their questions about white men.

The hut was dark and smelly and when their eyes became accustomed to the light, they saw little of interest. Certainly no white men; there was, however, a canvas bag in the corner. The leader, dressed in traditional Arab gear and black headdress, handed his long-barrelled Arab rifle to one of his group, grabbed the bag and pulled it to the centre of the room. He looked at B.T., indicated that they had a white man nearby and began to talk money. B.T. absorbed Fleurabelle's distraught condition and saw that it was not a time to haggle and quickly passed over a roll of Congolese money, which was taken by the Arab leader without comment. The Arabs stepped back from the centre of the floor in unison and without further instructions a local tribesman, dressed only in a loincloth, came in, grabbed the bag and emptied its contents on the floor. Out rolled three human heads, grinning hideously, and one was Tim Cope from Carlow.

Fleurabelle's screams pierced the silence and B.T. awoke in a lather of sweat. His afternoon nap had trapped his mind in this bizarre sequence. He stared at the ceiling and wondered how much of the dream had been wishful thinking on his part.

Tim Cope and Jack Muldoon had been in contact in Elizabethville following their get-together in the hotel with Fleurabelle.

"Is there a real chance she could become involved in film-making in Elstree?"

Tim was anxious to keep ahead of the posse, as far as Fleurabelle's aspirations were concerned.

"Well, I'm still in contact with the Rank people and Jane is keen that we get back together again." Jack felt a sense of warmth and anticipation when Jane Thornly's name was mentioned.

Tim however, only wanted his steps into the future to be arm in arm with the love of his life. "B.T. is leaving soon, next week I think, so whether arrangements are made or not, we're off to warmer climes. Well, hardly warmer, but different from this shithole."

Jack could see a change of venue for him also, but with a strong sporting addendum. "Our big trick, just before we leave Mother Africa, is to play the inter-contingent final against the Madras Rifles. Not long after, we're bound for Hibernia, love, laughter, and Guinness."

"This is an international contest," he continued, " and winning will place us, the Irish, at the top of the pile. I was talking to Gustav Shorlshrom from the Swedish Battalion and he mentioned that the final was being covered in their national newspapers."

The Company members were impressed, but nevertheless 'going home' seemed to take precedence of attention. *Mingie* boxes were being prepared, and the savings officer, Michael O'Donovan, was under pressure to come up with submitted savings. That should have been a simple matter, but Michael, mostly due to terrible paper accounts, was unable to identify individual amounts, and when the early comers were satisfied financially, he had to resort to bartering through the PX shop.

Just how he did this was never understood. Jack managed to meet the permanently mobile Mick, and was glad to settle for a cine camera and a film projector. They were new, and approximated to the amount due, but how exactly the savings officer survived is still a mystery. For the last month of the stay, any glance down a roadway in the Battalion area might include a fleeting glimpse of the savings officer flitting like an urban fox from point to point. The indulgence of Mick's brother officers had to be seen to be believed. Mick had a great ability to make his officer clients feel concerned for 'his' welfare, rather than demanding their savings.

This was but a minor issue however when seen in the context of the Battalion football team and the final against the Madras Rifles. Training was intense in the last week and team members were excused all other duties. Normally, team or no team, everyone was expected to play their part as soldiers on guard, cooks in the cookhouse or whatever. Jack's experience in the Army School of Physical Culture was at variance somewhat with this philosophy. There everyone lived the good life, sun and exercise, in the mode of '*homo ludens*', as an example perhaps of how life should be lived.

The great day came closer. The match was to be played in the centre of town, on the pitch surrounded by the athletic track, and both finalists sharing training session facilities.

"Just because youse meet these guys regularly is no reason to like them. This is a competition and I want raw hate to be the order of the day."

The coach was worried that familiarity was beginning to build between both sets of players, and tried to inject a suitable level of aggression.

"These Indians are trying to lure you lot into a false sense of security - remember they are the enemy and our job is to demolish the fuckers!"

"Don't you think that's going a bit far, QM? After all it's only a game."

"Game my arse Sir, this is war!"

Jack could see that there wasn't much point in trying to inject a play code at this stage. The Tunisians had probably set the tone when they lowered their knicks and wiggled their organs at the Irish, early on in the competition.

Both contingents' pipe bands led a full muster parade to the pitch on the day of the game. The players were delivered to their dressing rooms in preparation for kit distribution and team talk.

"Okay, men, this is it."

O'Mahoney was thin-lipped and spoke of their challenge in very clear tones.

"Every man has a task, be it in attack or defence. Not alone that, but you must all integrate, so that all the links create a team that cannot be beaten."

"Let me emphasise one thing. Defensive players can't win this game. Unless you, Larkin, and the other forwards do their stuff and score goals, we're in the manure business - understood?"

They all understood of course and with wins against the Tunisians, the Gurkhas, and the Raj, by more than two goals each, they were fairly confidant and said so.

"That may be so, but remember, the shower you're playing in two days' time have the same record."

Jack met Major Kapoor on the day before the match. He was, as was Jack, downtown getting an issue of kit from the sports office.

"Don't feel obliged to let us win because you had such a good time at the party."

Jack looked into his eyes and saw the humour bubbling in the blackness.

"We are gentlemanly above all, old sport! We know, however, that you would expect a real challenge to your men as a mark of respect to the Madras Rifles," said Jack seriously.

Given the short time they had been in the Congo they had developed a friendship, despite the difference in rank. Kapoor's action during the athletics meeting in support of the black man Jessie Jesus appeared exceptional, but was probably normal line of duty in the context of Africa.

"Don't expect any quarter Kapoor; our crowd are all fired up. Nothing personal mind you."

Kapoor's enigmatic smile spoke volumes.

On the morning of the match McCoy was jumping all over the place.

"This is it, lads. I want 100 per cent support from McCoy's Colts."

"Who the fuck let him have anything to do with the team. For Jayses sake, Jack, keep him away."

"The CO appointed him team Captain."

"Don't mind him, he wouldn't know his arse from his elbow."

"Well he has, in fairness, contributed to the effort: food, transport, and all that kind of stuff."

"That may be so, but for Christ's sake don't let him near Murphy or any of the team."

Brendan McGonnigle's opinion of McCoy had deteriorated even further since the 'party's over' episode - if that were possible. Brendan was an excellent soldier, but slow promotion and having to deal with nincompoops from above and below strained his ability to survive in this man's army.

He was past the romance of Jack and his age group, and regular comparisons by his wife of the salary level of her brother the businessman put pressure on his will to survive. The relatively upper crust mess dinners, attended by officers and their wives, were not enough to quiet her tongue on the minuscule nature of the salary cheque. Like most officers, he lived on the extras from uniform allowances and occasional back money from a raise. Living in the Curragh was easier, because civilian comparisons were few, but in Cathal Brugha they lived cheek to jowl with the civilian professions. His Congo trip was strongly money orientated, although he was always the consummate soldier.

Stephen bounced into the Company offices, newly shaved and looking trim on six months of UN rations.

"I will lead our Company on parade, although when we get there my team functions will supersede."

"Will the Chaplain bless them before the match?" asked Mick Keane.

"That's a very good idea," answered McCoy.

A titter ran round the office.

"That's what I mean by keeping him away from O'Mahoney and the team," whispered Brendan.

The morning of the match dawned bright and clear. The night before they had suffered from the fury of a tropical storm. They had seen storms before, but Africa was different. The gods had a field day - well night really - splitting the night sky with fierce stabs of crackling light, followed by a concert of thunderous laughter, which rolled and rolled across the forest canopy. The annual rainfall can total upwards of 80 inches in some places and the area sustains the second largest rain forest in the world after the Amazon basin. The tropical climate has produced the Congo River system which dominates the region. Patrice arrived head first in to the bedroom.

"Washee, washee."

He set about collecting every item of clothing with the intent of filling the machine. He was never happier than when washing was in full flow, and suds growing from the twin tub at a rate of knots.

"If he touches my uniform I'll kill 'im."

"Well you'd better get out there quick. Your slacks are next to hit the suds."

"Jesus!"

Harry Jenkins was due up in the Farm to take over as Orderly Officer.

His white arse was a blur as he scrambled into the washroom to save his uniform - and just in time.

"Nothing like a good laugh in the morning," said Mick Keane, the other officer occupant of the bedroom. "We'll miss this scramble every morning to save a morsel of clothes!"

After siesta the battalion parades began to form. The football coach and his team drove off to the arena in a small convoy. O'Mahoney spoke to each individual player, emphasising the importance of the day in terms of their own motivation. The coach had read somewhere that everyone is motivated individually, like 'you'll have no problem pulling the birds', or 'you'll be able to drop this at your next promotion board meeting', or 'it'll be in the papers at home - think what your oul' fella will think or your ma or whatever'. Some were only motivated by money, so he pushed the idea of getting a place in the local semi-pro team and from there into the big time in the English League. The fact that he knew a club spotter at home didn't go unmentioned! Finally, just before taking to the pitch, he couldn't resist giving them the Caitlin Ni hUallachain line - for Ireland and all that. Most of the older players were cynics, but nevertheless the patriotic pitch hit a chord.

"That sort of stuff would take an Irishman out of the grave," quipped Denis Larkin, as the team rang out the stud's concerto over the concrete apron beside the dressing room, and carried the heady whiff of embrocation down the corridor between the gathered Irish, Indians, and others.

This was the final, and all the Katangese, regardless of commitment, turned up for the match. The UN Commanding Officer had a special role, both as an ex-Rifles man himself and as the General Officer Commanding UN Forces in Katanga. He and the contingent commanding officers sat and talked the social stuff as the two teams ran on to the field, tossed for sides and exchanged flags. The Madras Rifles won the toss and chose to play into the setting sun for the first half. The wind wasn't of any significance, unlike the tornado that had roared through the night before.

"Best of luck." Murphy, the Irish captain, exchanged flags with the captain of the Madras Rifles, Sergeant Singh, and they both joined their teams as the Irish prepared to kick off. The pea rattled in the ref's whistle and they were off!

O'Mahoney called for the ball and got it. A long pass down the wing, centred to Larkin in the square. You could describe the goal as a header from Larkin, but in truth Larkin took man, ball, and all into the net.

There was too much goalmouth confusion to state what exactly happened. The ball was in the net, however, and as the Umpire's flag stayed down, there was only one decision.

"GOAL!" A goal in the first three minutes; Denis Larkin could see the headlines in the next issue of the 'Cork Echo'. At halftime the one-goal lead had its effect - sweating, but confident and happy, the Irish players sat in a circle and drank a special secret mixture, prepared by the coach.

"Would you like a cup of tea, Sir?" The Madras Sgt Major had been sent, private soldier in tow, to offer tea to the officer in charge of the Irish. Jack accepted of course and graciously thanked the soldier. Looking back at the Indian team group he recognised and waved to Major Kapoor.

"They're a nice lot; tea just as I like it, hot, strong, and sweet."

He glanced at O'Mahoney. "They're still the enemy, though."

The match ended in a draw; the final to be replayed two days later.

In Rhodesia, events were progressing. Tim Cope was ensconced in the Pavilion Hotel and despite the best efforts of B.T. in his dreams, ready for the trip north and then what? The contacts with Elstree Studies through Jane and Jack had been made, and the possibility of finding work for Fleurabelle in photography was a runner, or so it seemed.

Later that year, though, she and Tim were to stay with her friend in Bordeaux. Marie Paul was the leading light in the Gironde Region of Gymnastique Volontaire, a Sport for All organization comprising two million members. They were state-funded, and Marie Paul had arranged with headquarters in Paris that Fleurabelle might establish a CODEPT 33 Bordeaux documentation centre, to record in pictures the activities of the 200 or so regional sections in France for Gymnastique Volontaire's 50th anniversary.

Fleurabelle had been in touch with Gymnastic Volontaire regularly over the past few years *apropos* this venture. They had the blessing of Mr Seurin, President of GV, and in the past year she had sent him photographs of activity in the South African region, as a sample of her level of expertise.

She had grown in the photographic sense over the years and particularly in Africa. Her father had bought her first camera, a Nikon with telephoto lens, essential for wildlife pictures. It was a manual focus, a Nikon 400mm lens with f/5.6 telephoto lens and she could make it talk. She was well known around the national parks, complete with camera bag, canvas knapsack, and her sturdy but light Manfrotto tripod. She carried a few other lenses: wide angle 28mm for scenery shots, standard 50mm for general shots, and a 200mm telephoto lens - not quite as long as the 400mm, but useful for shots where she could get a bit closer. The Metz manual flashgun, part of the kit, she rarely used.

Marie Paul had arranged an idyllic house for Tim and Fleurabelle in one of the vineyards. These little houses were used as accommodation for the grape pickers in October and were available for odd bookings between times. The view from their particular house was breathtaking, overlooking as it did the beautiful wine valley leading up to Chateau Margaux - the vineyard of the favourite wine of Hemingway. Close to the village of Issan, they would have access to the little town of Margaux, with opportunities to attend the many concerts and fetes in the chateau in this premier area of the vine in France. Marie Paul had already booked a medieval quartet recital in Chateau d'Angludet. Tim was somewhat bemused by this development; his love for classical music had yet to be discovered.

B.T. wasn't full, but had an economic load. His flight plan was as he had first arranged and now included collecting the group from Leopoldville en route to Katanga. His latest clients, miners from prospective gold mines in Rhodesia, were bound for Dar es Salaam on leave. They were genuine enough but he still was suspicious of the money dealer's reason for travel, but he needed the numbers.

All was ready; he had distributed flight details to his passengers. Take-off was arranged for 15.00 hrs. His crew were already ensconced in the hotel and he had indicated a briefing that evening after dinner.

"Hello everybody; this is our final briefing before take off at 15.00 hrs tomorrow." He wore a blue uniform, white shirt, and college tie.

His co-pilot Dov Aldubi, a Jew, had fought for the establishment of Israel as a State during and since the end of the Second World War. That was okay, but unfortunately for him peace returned to some degree and he became bored. He trained as a pilot in Europe, and finished up with B.T. as a contract worker, flying around the African continent. Some of their contracts were dubious, but the pay was good and the work routine was varied. Although the actual flights were conducted with military precision and became known as a reliable transport system, no questions were asked of passengers as long as the money was paid.

"Dov, our flight plan is as arranged. First stop, Dar es Salaam for repairs, then Mombassa, Mogadishu, and Djibouti, where most will disembark. Kisangani next stop, that's a long hop, and then on to Leopoldville to collect a group travelling to Elizabethville. Any questions?"

"Should we expect any trouble? The money businessmen smell a bit."

"It's illegal to smuggle currency out of the Congo and Kasavubu or Mobutu doesn't like a money traffic to Switzerland unless he's doing it. I'm not sure which side our group is on."

"Then we should expect trouble?" Dov's experience in setting up the Israeli State had made him sensitive to human movement problems.

"Once we're in the air we're okay, although the government in Leopoldville has a few Belgian fighter jets, which are mostly used to embellish national festivals. He has used them on one occasion, to ground transport planes flying over the Congo, but once we reach Bujumbura on the border we should be in the clear."

The rest of the meeting was spent discussing cargo and passengers.

Money traders - twenty-four; six gold miners; two Arabs; Tim and Fleurabelle; and the collection of twenty men of unknown occupation on the way back. There was also a hold containment of goods unknown, being transported by the gold miners going on leave.

"Ask no questions and you'll be told no lies," said B.T. to himself, although he had noted that the price of transporting the cargo wasn't an issue for the miners. He had trebled the price on instinct and it was accepted without question.

"Goal." It was the final and the Madras Rifles had scored - and in the first five minutes. The respective commanding officers touched base in recognition of first blood.

Jack was totally committed to victory for the Irish Battalion for a number of reasons. Firstly, for the men and the work they had put into the preparation, including the contretemps with the Tunisians. There was also the question of national pride. Here in Africa, Ireland had arrived, not as wild geese thrown on the world, like flotsam and jetsam fighting for foreign kings, but as a part of the aspirations of their fathers, who had fought so that Ireland could be part of the League of Nations or United Nations, as it now was.

The essence of the Irish in Africa wasn't only a measurement of the contribution of senior rank, or any rank for that matter. The man on the ground, and his story, deserved to be recognised. Just as in all wars or military expeditions, strategies, reversals, and victories are writ large, while the story of the small cogs in the machine are sometimes not given recognition.

This match, however, offered the Irish soldiers a chance to, as they saw it, make history, and they grasped the opportunity with twenty-two hands. Their coach had seen an opportunity to create a masterpiece and, as well as bringing the team together in far-off Africa, had worked on each individual to ensure that the mixture was potent. Just like a perfect food dish, O'Mahoney had mixed a heady mix of sweet and sour, rough-hewn and smooth, to create a team worthy of national representation.

Larkin, the centre forward, had some slick skills, but mostly he delved into his background of boxing, athletics, and Gaelic football to provide the breath-taking penetration that marked his presence on the field. His main motivation was based on Leeside and his family there. He had scored both goals in the first match and was rearing to go.

"Feck this for a lark, let's get at 'em."

"Steady, Corporal, a cool head brings home the bacon."

They didn't blame anyone for the goal, and certainly not Gavin.

"Let's get moving."

And move they did. The Irish supporters gave it 'lackery' and, in keeping with the rising tempo, the players stepped up the pace. Gavin the goalie venomously landed the 'kick out' at Paddy Murphy's feet who, despite the efforts of the Madras team captain, turned on the red dust and sent the ball running down to the corner flag. Hennessy was on to it, turned inside his marker and, eye on the ball, swung his right foot through in the direction of the square. Everything went into slow motion for Larkin - his leap coincided with the leather about four feet up. A mirror image of his goal in the first match, ball, Larkin, and at least two Madras riflemen, including their goalie, finished in the back of the net. The Malayan referee indicated goal straight away. He figured that the backs had added to Larkin's momentum and crashed into their own goalie. Anyway it was a goal and the Irish supporters, including the Gurkhas, applauded wildly. Larkin had received a belt in the mouth for his troubles, however, and as well as good Cork blood, he spat out half a tooth.

Another cross in the second half was sweetly met by Larkin again.

"Janey, boy, the goalie never saw it!"

Two-one and the Irish were the winners. Trucks were driven on the field, tables and chairs unloaded and the presentation ceremony took place. It was a colourful scene indeed. Gurkhas, Rajputan and Madras Riflemen, local Congolese, Chinese Malayans, Swedes and Tunisians mixed with Irish from all ranks and parts of Ireland to celebrate the winning of a real international competition on African soil. Most excited of all were the shoeless and half-naked African children, who simulated traps, turns, dives, tackles and shots for goal with pieces of paper or imaginary balls: the beginning of a Republic of Congo international football team?

The General in charge of the UN presence in the Congo presented the prizes. "Today belongs to the Irish and the Madras Rifles, and particularly to the Irish Battalion team. I know in football terms what this day means because, as an Indian officer, I am aware of the strength of the Madras Rifles' football prowess. They are Indian army champions and so today was truly an international final. Congratulations again - your coach, Quarter Master O'Mahoney, is the hero of the hour."

The identification of the quietly efficient quartermaster coach caused a bit of a stir, and Commandant McCoy and a few other senior officers stepped back to allow O'Mahoney take a front seat. He and Larkin, complete with a cap in Cork colours, were pushed forward, the cup was presented, and the Irish celebrated with their beaten opponents. There was a planned visit to the Simba Beer factory the following day for the Irish winners, but this occasion was an opportunity for the Indians and the Irish to mingle and celebrate.

"Where we sported and played, neath the green leafy shade, On the banks of my own lovely Lee." Larkin's blood-spattered mouth and gap, where there should have been a tooth, didn't spoil his efforts at leading the chorus.

"She wheeled her wheelbarrow, through streets broad and narrow, crying cockles and mussels. Alive Alive o"

A strong Cork rendition of 'de Banks' was followed by the Dublin national anthem. Some of the Congolese children, who spent a considerable amount of time in Irish cookhouses, were able to join in with the correct accent to boot!

"Well done, Jack. Make sure that the report gets home."

"Yes sir, it's ready for publication. The lads are anxious that their folk at home get the message." Jack and Commandant McCoy felt good!

R eggie Morrison stayed in touch with the guys looking after the hounds in the Curragh, and letters from the Irish Beagling Association were regularly received in the Battalion orderly room.

"Maxi is giving them plenty of exercise and training the pups. We'll have a hellofa pack come winter. By the way, Jack, would you like to come elephant hunting?"

Jack was surprised by the request. Hunting was illegal except as part of a cull in the many designated parks. But he knew that many states, from the Congo to the Sahara, were postcolonial, not politically stable and regulations about elephants weren't applied.

"Where's the hunt taking place?"

"We won't be killing anything. I only want to see them in the wild. We're getting a lift by plane to Kamina, and then on to the Upemba National Park." Reggie was back to full form.

These were the last days of the Battalion in the Congo, and this was another final effort to experience as much as possible, especially by those not likely to travel abroad again. The trip went ahead, but the nearest they came to Loxodonta Africana was a huge pile of still-warm elephant dung! This was a cause of great excitement for the guide, but Jack and Reggie were underwhelmed - to put it mildly.

"**B**ewitched, bollixed and bewildered am I.
Lost my heart, but what of it,
She is cold I agree."

The celebrations in the Simba factory were in full swing and O'Mahoney gave vent to his lifelong party-piece. He was questioned about his poetic license adjustment, vis-à-vis 'bothered' and 'bollixed' but he couldn't credit that 'bothered' was the correct version. "If the coach sings it that way, then that's the kosher version," was the team members' attitude.

The Simba factory produced a fine beer, available all over that part of Africa. The team members were presented with glasses rimmed with gold and with a gold inscription of 'Simba'. The top management was still Belgian and were no doubt very interested in how the Tshombe and Katanga succession issue would unfold. The Manager, Mr Van Dessel, explained his position to Jack.

"My brother is a musician. He left Belgium before the war and got a post as resident musician in a church in Ireland. My father established this business and we have been in charge ever since. I don't trust the new government and would only stay here if Katanga got some degree of autonomy. We have links with the beer industry in Bruges, but don't intend moving there, if we have any choice. We see here as our home and our children do as well. Most of our friends in the rest of the Congo have left, and quite a few of those who lived in Katanga. If we manage to survive here, I expect that there will be a trickle back to Africa. Life in our colony is at a much higher level than at home.

Unfortunately, we are not very well treated when we go back to Belgium - they see us as hicks, rough and ready. This has happened to many, like the Algerian French. Les Pied Noir, black feet, they call them, are poorly thought of, and have difficulty in integrating when they return to France."

As the Irish poured out of the cool reception room in the brewery, they were attacked by the three o'clock heat but felt no pain. They shook hands again, for the umpteenth time.

'This is the life,' thought Jack. 'Best uniform, blue beret and scarf, and full of cool beer. What more could a man want?'

The team members were experiencing the best days of their lives. The sense of comradeship they felt didn't need to be expressed. The Army cosseted them womb-like, food, friendship, career status, all accounted for, plus they had climbed to the pinnacle of success.

Larkin, the consummate goal scorer, summed it up.

"It doesn't get any better than this, lads!"

T he officers of the Battalion had mixed feelings about going home. The savings officer would have liked more time to get his bag in order. He had satisfied, somewhat, his clients, but the killing he'd planned hadn't worked out. Stephen McCoy basked in the victory of 'his' team and looked forward to telling his wife Patricia about his adventures. He indicated in his last letter that she should arrange a coming-home party and invite the wives of 'his' officers. A plaque entitled 'McCoy's Colts' at the entrance would be just right, he suggested. But for the benign influence of the wives, Brendan McGonnigle and Jack Fortune would probably kill him with the ceremonial 'kukri' they had stashed in their *mingie* bags. The 'party's over' still rankled!

Mick Keane was planning to co-operate with Captain Murt O'Brien, the friend of the Balubas in the Elizabethville 'camp', and return with international aid. Five or six trucks filled with essential provisions could begin a system of aid to African countries. He reckoned that a start by them to the Congo would set the trend. He hadn't trashed out the details with Murt, but he figured that the setting up of a food aid project was possible and necessary. He'd been in touch with some business civvies at home who had vaguely promised suitable transport for the aid programme.

Reggie Morrison looked forward to leading his beloved beagle hounds with a firm blast of the hunting horn. "Gone away!"

"Sir, there's a call for you in the orderly room."

"Hello, Jack, Louis here. Did you get the news about the crash in London?"

Jack's heart sank. He knew that Louis could only be ringing about his only serious contact in London.

"What crash?" He wanted to enquire about Jane Thornly, but hoped that there was some other reason for Louis's call.

"A British Airways plane taking off from Heathrow. Belly flopped right beside the main road - went on fire - everyone killed - terrible. I saw on the list yesterday that Jane was one of the passengers - she was killed in the fire - terrible."

Jack stumbled away from the phone. His mouth was dry and he felt shocked and bewildered.

"Maybe it's a mistake." He knew that she was making a film in Paris, the destination of the plane. He sat in an armchair in the mess and somehow his senses were heightened beyond belief. Sight and sound, smell and touch became super active; the smell of the leather in the chair nearly choked him.

"She was so alive and organized."

Jack had enjoyed the way she controlled her career life, and how simply she had included him in her plans.

"We were to ski in Lech this winter."

They had many plans; some involved the possibility of his being in her next film, but now? Last in the pile of considerations was the link with Fleurabelle and Tim. He sank into a despair of sorts and the quartermaster coach's song kept coming back and back into his consciousness.

'I'm wild again, beguiled again, a whimpering simpering
Child again.
Bewitched, bothered and bewildered am I.
Lost my heart but what of it, she is cold I agree.'

He thought of her, cold in death, and shivered in the leather chair in the gathering evening gloom.

Time went by, as it's wont to do. However, Jack and the rest of the Battalion were caught up in a hectic level of preparation to transport their goods and chattels to the airport and thence to Dublin. Instead of the original Globemasters, Sabena was transporting them in jet airliners and apart from the comfort and the food possibilities on board, the plusses in this mode of transport ensured a non-stopover via Brussels; they would be in Dublin on the same day.

"I'll miss the 'ould' Globemasters!"

Jack looked at Reggie Morrison, and accepted the ironic remark in the manner in which it was probably intended. If it weren't for his American ski friend and pilot, Harley D. Wright, Reggie would probably have been returned to Ireland with the turnover unit. He was a happy man now, a few bob in the bank and an elephant hunt under his belt. Neither of them would tell the whole truth - about the warm elephant shit as the only evidence of the fact that the Neolithic creatures were actually out there.

"An adult elephant is about as tall as it's long. They are called pachyderms, which means thick-skinned. The bull I faced up to was about eleven-and-a-half feet tall and weighed about 14,000 pounds. His tusks must have been eight feet long and he was moving around looking in our direction and waving his giant ears. I could see oil secreting from the temporal gland just between his eye and ear and I knew that he was in musk condition and likely to be very dangerous. As you know, the leader of the herd is usually a female, and this guy was a male rogue, separate from the herd and angry. If I had my hounds I'm sure I could have handled him…"

Jack overheard Reggie talking to one of the other officers as a rehearsal for his home account of the hunt in Africa!

One last Battalion parade, into the trucks and they were off. The unit quarters and stores were being supervised by a holding company, who would also collect the incoming unit and brief them on the available facilities. These changeovers were becoming less and less fraught, as personnel with previous experience in the Congo, or at least abroad, formed replacement units. The next unit was very likely to be involved in Tshombe's final effort to set Katanga up as an independent state. Apart from keeping the peace in general terms and supervising the movement of the Baluba Katanga, Jack's battalion had it easy. The move to Leopoldville during the negotiations between Tshombe and the government in Leopoldville was well handled, and probably resulted in preserving peace for that period of time. Without the UN it is unlikely that Mobutu would have allowed Tshombe, self-styled president of Katanga, to behave like a president in Leopoldville for two weeks and then leave.

Cheers from the troops, lined up on the runway, greeted the arrival of the three Sabena aircraft. There was a delay while the planes were refuelled and the cabins cleaned. The new arrivals were greeted with a guard of honour, which was ceremonially inspected by the incoming battalion's commanding officer. Friends greeted friends before the arrivals mounted their transport and headed in the direction of Elizabethville. How pale and anxious the new arrivals looked, compared to the bronzed veterans returning home.

A pipe band struck up. Although they were expecting a goodbye parade from the Indians, the band was a pleasant surprise. Around the airport buildings they strode in their turbans and ceremonial uniforms. Yes, the Madras Rifles had arrived to see off their sports combatants!

Kapoor drove his jeep out on the tarmac and greeted the Irish. A present had been prepared for him by the battalion. He was presented with a solid copper 'Katanga Cross', a once-used form of currency, set on a mahogany base with the words 'Major Kapoor, the Human Bangalore Torpedo', on the base.

Kapoor and Jack talked quietly about events past.

"I wonder how our friend Jessie Jesus is surviving as President of his tribe in the east?"

"It's a pity he can't keep throwing. He had one fast arm."

"Keep an eye on the next Olympics - he might turn up."

As his plane banked and headed north, Tim saw Kapoor and the pipe band reduced to specks and he felt sad.

"Goodbye, Madame Mosquito." He wasn't sad to see the end of her!

Fleurabelle had heard about the death of Jack's contact in the film world, which meant in turn that her chances of getting a photography contract with the film studio was reduced. She still had her own connections in Europe, and the chance to sell still more of her extensive portfolio, but she knew that wide and all as her range of product was, it was still only African and mostly wildlife. Jack had spoken to her about the Riefenstahl work in Sudan. Leni's wonderful coffee-table book containing photographs of the Nubian Sudanese in their villages had just arrived by post. Jack had enthused about this wonderful artiste and Fleurabelle had ordered the book straight away. She studied the male form in Riefenstahl's book and realised that she needed other influences and a broadening of her portfolio.

Tim Cope's plans for Fleurabelle were different. He had visions of returning home with this gorgeous creature and walking her down Main Street, Carlow. He knew his mother would love her and all the criticism of him, as an adventurer without roots, would be dispelled. This surely was a fertile place to plant his roots! In truth he was at the stage of hormonal romantic attachment where rational thought wasn't possible. It was clear to him, however, that he had to take her out of the range of influence of B.T. as soon as possible. The flight to Dar es Salaam seemed straightforward enough, and from there to Bordeaux before returning to Ireland.

The death of Jane Thornly had reduced the risk of Fleurabelle getting sucked into the film world. He was sorry for Jack and all that, but the crash certainly made Tim's plan a lot easier. Fleurabelle said yes to everything when they were in bed, which caused him to believe that he was in total control.

B.T. taxied out on the runway from the dilapidated hanger. He tested the systems and watched the starboard flap to see if it was working okay, including the flap position indicator. That had been one of his problems on the last flight. The chief engineer cast a black and white smile in his direction. "*Masouri*", all okay. B.T. gave a thumbs-up and went through the rest of the check in accordance with the check card. He tapped the directional gyro, which sometimes stuck. It was okay. A glance at the overhead electrical panel - two position switches - clicking in this area toggles the switch between on and off.

"Locks and pins, Captain."

Fleurabelle was acting airhostess, not passenger duties, just an odd service for B.T.

"Thanks honey. Why don't you take this job up seriously?"

"You're a fake, B.T. You had your chance to make me permanent."

She joked with him between trips to her seat in the back of the plane with Tim.

"A full load, thirty four passengers and all's well." He whispered to himself as he taxied out on the runway facing nor' west. Dov was stretched with an African bug of some sort, so he had no co-pilot as far as Elizabethville, where he would pick up a pilot cum navigator for the round trip. Although he could manage alone, the DC-3 manual prescribed two as the lowest crew level, and he didn't want to risk being delayed or aborted at any of his touchdowns by flight officials.

Tim noted the direction at take-off and was expecting a change towards the east and Dar es Salaam, but it didn't happen. He could see the road below; straight through the jungle to Elizabethville and B.T. was following its path like an arrow from a bow.

"Shit! Fleurabelle, why are we flying towards Elizabethville? I thought that getting out of the Congo airspace was a priority. Ask B.T. what's going on."

"Please!" The lady wasn't for taking orders. The blood had risen from her neck and reddened her cheeks at Tim's commanding tone.

"Fleurabelle, this is important. I'm on the run from Tshombe-land, you know that."

She reacted better to his pleading tone and wriggled her way up the passageway to the cockpit.

"We have to pick up a co-pilot there, but we won't be disembarking." She brought back the information he sought.

She thought to herself that Tim's world was getting smaller. The Congo, French possessions anywhere in the world, and mainland France were off limits to some degree.

"If he keeps on like this, Carlow will be his only refuge."

Tim knew that he would be missed by this time, and if he was spotted on board by anyone in Elizabethville, it was curtain time.

"Why didn't he get his co-pilot to come to Ndola by road?" Tim asked.

Fleurabelle raised her shoulders and pursed her beautiful lips, more as a reaction than a response.

The DC-3 droned on until the tall chimneys of the copper mines came into view. The radio crackled into life and B.T. responded. Having received permission to land, he banked over the airport, turned into the wind, and lined up for the runway. The cirrus clouds in the sky were evidence to the fact that the wind was gusting and a storm was brewing. He skewed slightly on the approach as he floated in for touchdown. The well-worn Michelin aviation tires screeched as they grabbed the runway. Flaps down fully, brakes on, release and on again, until about three-quarters down the runway he swung around and taxied back to the parking lot at the building.

Tim had his face glued to the window. A truck carrying one passenger sped out towards the plane, which still had its engines running. He watched as Fleurabelle opened the door and the passenger in the truck clambered on to the roof of the cabin of the open backed truck and climbed aboard. No bother with steps - get out, get in and get going! He was reassured by the simple efficiency of the operation.

"Close the feckin' door." He wanted the operation to finish and the Douglas to get to hell away. Seconds felt like hours as Fleurabelle helped the co-pilot aboard and she and he went into the captain's cabin.

And then it happened! A convoy of Gendarmarie jeeps screeched out across the tarmac and encircled the plane. At the same time the steps were pulled into position at the open door and the props stopped rotating - the engines were switched off!! A group of Gendarmarie, one a white mercenary, boarded. They were armed to the teeth, submachine guns and grenades attached to their web belts.

Tim's mind was in turmoil. This could be it; they were coming to take him back. In a few seats to his front, however, the moneylenders seemed just as agitated and one of them ran to the back of the cabin and into the toilet. It all happened quickly. The armed police acted on the French-language instructions of the mercenary, and bundled the group of Congolese out the door and into the truck, while one burly Gendarmarie kicked the toilet door open and dragged the protesting man towards the plane door. He didn't even give him a chance to pull his trousers up! They knew exactly who they were looking for; the white man had a list which he checked as his captives were unloaded.

To say that Tim was agitated would be an understatement. He was slightly relieved that the moneylenders were the target group, but until that door was closed and they had become airborne again he was in serious danger!

'Where the fuck are B.T. and Fleurabelle? After all, he is the captain and in charge. Did he have word that this was going to happen - he must have.' These thoughts and others ran through his mind as he buried his face in the dog-eared Sabena in-flight magazine, which B.T. regularly managed to illegally secure from passing Sabena traffic. The page, inches from his face, gave advice on how to make Christmas pudding!

"*Bitte, Mein Herr.*"

Tim's heart sank even lower as he looked up and saw the white mercenary. He recognised him as one of Tshombe's crowd, a German and an ex-Legionnaire.

"Mr. Tshombe wants a word with you." The mercenary grinned in realisation of a successful intervention.

Tim saw that any protest or attempt at escape was useless - not with this geezer and his armed friends. There was still no sign of B.T. and Fleurabelle. As he grabbed his hand luggage and made his way out of the plane he shouted towards the cabin, but there was no response; a Gendarmarie and probably one inside guarded it. The heat hit him and he began to perspire.

As they stuffed him into the already-packed truck, he was aided by a stream of Swahili invective from the Congolese. They didn't often have a chance to give a white man a going-over. Events were moving fast now and even before they had reached the buildings, the plane started up and begun to move. He thought he could see Fleurabelle's face at the window of the cockpit looking in his direction. As the plane sped up the runway, he broke his rule about turning before departure and looked one more time!

The jeeps sped out of the airport and were waved on by the Gurkha guard at the entrance. Tim tried to attract the guard's attention from the back of the jeep, but a swift jab of a rifle butt in the chest reduced his words to an unintelligible mutter. Away they sped towards Elizabethville and on towards Tshombe's headquarters near Union Minière.

"I'm in deep trouble," he muttered and yet his thoughts were with Fleurabelle. 'She must be distraught, poor love.' He could see her in his mind's eye bewailing his absence. Somehow, the thought of B.T. giving her reassurance was no consolation.

At last they reached the Tshombe headquarters and he suddenly realised how isolated he was. He wasn't the responsibility of any national Embassy; the French wanted him, but only to be returned to the Legion for punishment - he thought he might be a deserter from the Irish army also, and now even a renegade army like Tshombe's had claims on his life.

'*Jesus.*' He suddenly realised that he had deserted during a state of war - or at least the threat of immediate conflict. The sham court martial story told by Corporal Denis Larkin and relayed to him by Jack Muldoon filtered into his mind; would that he could inject humour into this situation.

His exact position was quickly established, when some of his erstwhile colleagues called to his cell and offered advice for the court martial.

"Court martial! Will there be a court martial?" The mention by an English mercenary of court martial gave Tim a real shock.

"What do you expect; you're a deserter."

"But this isn't a real army."

"Try telling that to Tshombe. I wouldn't use that approach if I were you. Have you a defence council?" His military colleague was trying to be helpful.

"I haven't been charged yet."

Tim was still in denial. He couldn't believe that the last hour had happened and struggled to take in his new surroundings and the threatening behaviour of everyone. He had so often been on the other side and hoped that by blinking the shutters of his eyes he would reverse the situation. Alas! To no effect.

"You're not in an established country, Tim. They will see this as an opportunity to dissuade any others who might have your idea in mind. I think you should prepare for the worst - have you written any letters?"

Tim hadn't of course written any letters; it had all happened so quickly. Shortly after the visit of the English-speaking mercenaries, a guard, wearing creased camouflaged denim battledress, swaggered into his cell and read a notice in French outlining the crime and the form of the court. He was not to be given the privilege of a real court martial, if privilege it was.

"Because of the wartime situation, you should be shot immediately, but instead a short trench court will establish your crime and award the punishment."

He asked a question or two, where the French of the guard wasn't clear. In particular he asked why no mention was made of the possibility that he might be innocent. The punishment, was, it appeared, a '*sine qua non*'.

The streets of Carlow rushed into his mind. He could see his mother collecting her grocery provisions from O'Sheas, wearing the fur-trimmed coat she had bought in Dublin when 'himself' and she were up on their annual visit to the Horse Show; that was her time to spend the turkey money. All these thoughts were against a background of the beauty of Fleurabelle and how she must be missing him. He realised that it was indeed a time for writing letters, but not just yet. After all, there was a trial and despite the predictions of his visitors, all was not yet lost.

"They would hardly go that far. I've given a good service so far and I'm but a mercenary. Whatever about our man in charge, Mike Hoare being upset and even giving vent to some spleen, Tshombe has only rented this military service from him."

He was uncomfortable in the dank, hot cell, and while his rationalisations gave him some consolation, it was not sufficient to give complete clearance. He still had the hope that the nightmare would end, and he'd be free again to move and make decisions on life and living.

"I can't sit here like a gobshite and do nothing. There must be some solution."

He dredged his child mind in search of a story where the hero escaped.

It wasn't easy to think; apart from the activities of the giant mosquitoes that kept his defence mechanisms ticking over, his mind was a blank. He searched the cell for a sign of weakness, but found nothing. The bars of the cell at head height were set in holes in the stone and sealed with lead and to what depth he didn't know. He scraped a bit with his nail at first and then tried a biro pen, but the effect was infinitesimal and then the top of the pen broke.

"Shit and double shit."

The effort to shift the bars, although ineffectual, gave him some satisfaction and more than that, his failure galvanised him into further action.

"Guard, *s'il vous plaît*."

The timber hatch rattled open, revealing an unshaven, one-eyed Gendarmarie guard. It took him a few seconds to chew and swallow whatever he was eating.

"*Oui*." The unguarded garlic laden belch said still more about his lack of interest in the welfare of the prisoner.

Thinking on his feet now, Tim tried to get behind the gruesome grin and present his problem.

"*Bonjour, monsieur. C'est possible pour moi de visiter aux toilettes s'il vous plaît?*"

The jailer obviously wasn't used to being addressed as monsieur and so instead of barking some order or other in rhythm with the slapping closed of the hatch, he engaged Tim in Belgian-type conversation.

"*Vous avez un seau la.*"

Tim tried to explain that the bucket wasn't usable for him because of an injury he had sustained on being captured: he couldn't squat without a seat. The guard thought that was funny, and as he laughed his eye alighted on Tim's gold wristwatch; it was handsome indeed. Tim saw the lizard-like eye movement of the guard, and slowly removed the watch while awaiting a response to his request to visit an outside jacks. The guard followed the watch and without taking his eye from the black and white face of the timepiece, drew the bolt, opened the door and stood with one hand outstretched, the other holding his carbine, steadily pointed at Tim's stomach.

Words weren't necessary. Tim passed over the watch and the guard stepped to one side, indicating with a nod of his head where the toilet was, and covered his movement to its door with his submachine gun. The smell was indication enough and Tim entered another foul example of accommodation in this hellhole.

This was it; he looked around. No window, no way out, except down the open shithole in the corner. Not totally impossible, depending on one's girth that is. He even went so far as to scrape the shit from around the hole and tried. The billion or so flies and mosquitoes screamed blue murder; it must have been their lunchtime. No go; he couldn't squeeze down for many reasons, but mostly because of the fact that the hole narrowed at one point, even though past the crux it looked like access was possible. Access, but to where?

A noise at the door; he jumped to his feet and wiped his trousers with his hand.

"Vous avez fini?"

"Oui."

He had given it a shot but realised that to focus on the mock trial was now his best bet. When he arrived back at the cell a mercenary soldier was waiting for him. He spoke English - an ex-British army man.

"You're in trouble, old sport. Tshombe has a thing about Katanga being a corporate state and he sees you as an opportunity to have a Dreyfus-type trial and an execution. My God, but you smell!"

He explained also that Mike Hoare knew about the court martial of one of his members, but Tshombe, it seemed, was using this case to bring the mercenaries to heel, and that included their leader, in case an all out conflict with the UN arose. Hoare had been detailed to visit Kivu for some defence purpose; his influence as far as Tim was concerned was not in question.

Shortly after that visit, he was informed of the court martial and the charge. Charged with desertion during active service, the penalty as outlined in the document left him in no doubt but that he could be executed by firing squad. He sat in the cell and mostly slumbered, albeit uncomfortably. He was dreaming that help was on its way, when he heard the unmistakable sound of the *bodhran*, the famous Irish percussion instrument. Diddly dum, diddly dum, diddly dum, dum, dum. He thought he was dreaming, but then he realised that the distinctly Irish sound was being played right outside his cell window. He stood on the bed and looked out. There, immediately below his window, stood a ragbag group of three to eight-year-old Congolese children. Two of them had a *bodhran* and were giving it lackery, while some others were keeping time with sets of bones. One chubby chap was doing his best to be heard over the racket. The song he was attempting to sing was 'The Boys of Wexford' and the words were a mixture of west of Ireland English, French, and Swahili. When they saw Tim, they increased the tempo of their presentation and added movement as an art form.

'How did they know I was here?'

They had heard their parents talking about the Irish man who was going to be executed and they had decided to play for him.

"We want you to be happy, *bwana*."

They had been taught to play the *bodhran* by an Irish battalion and were left the instruments when the unit repatriated. The sound outside the cell had not gone unnoticed by his jailers and as the 'orchestra' scattered Tim shouted after them.

"You have made me very happy!"

'Dear Mother, I'm sad to have to write to you with such bad news. We may never meet again and if so, I want you to know that I love you. I apologise for the pain I have caused since I left home...'

His first letter started thus and went on to try and explain why he had arrived in his present position. The letter to Fleurabelle was in much the same vein.

'My Dearest Fleurabelle, I love you more than I can say. This journey to Ireland was to have been the beginning of our lives together, but now all is lost, dearest one...'

He passed the letters over to the English-speaking mercenary who had visited his cell and was assured that they would be posted. On the second day of his incarceration, he was paraded for trial in the same filthy clothes and without a body washing opportunity. He presented a pathetic picture in the adapted courtroom.

"Although we are in conflict with the UN, which we do not accept represents the voice of the world, we are an emerging small nation and must harness whatever resources are available. The mercenary army recruited by General Mike Hoare is an example of such a resource."

"What has this to do with the case before us this morning?"

Tim had a defence council, a young Belgian employed by Union Minière, but with legal training in Belgium.

"I don't know whether this is a military or a civilian trial. If it's military then the laws of the Army in question will prevail, but if not then we are dealing with a State without a legal system. Even if I was another Emile

Zola, and I'm not, your chances are poor to nil."

Tim swallowed and blinked at his only hope of surviving. He was keenly aware of the pathetic picture he presented, shitty slacks and all.

"I don't want my trial to be a blip in the historic evolution of Katanga. I just want to be set free. I've served my time well for six months and need to move on."

"You may feel that, Tim, but this court appears to be set up to establish that Katanga is a State. Nothing does that better than an execution, French-revolution style."

Tim's heart sank. Looking around the court he could see that the set-up reflected this opinion. A Tshombe-type black judge, six black Gendarmarie jury, a white mercenary prosecutor - he had often seen him in Tshombe's company - constituted the trial team.

"We are at a seminal stage of our evolution as a State."

The prosecutor directed the eyes of the room towards the full-size Katanga flag with a dramatic wave of his hand.

"Anything that militates against this noble cause must be eliminated, stamped out, spurned, rebuffed, and repulsed. A guilty of desertion verdict, and nothing else, will set the tone for our new State."

He went on to describe the importance of the recruited mercenary army and of its discipline code.

"Without a keen regard for discipline we can't depend on the army and therefore cannot plan or survive. Anyone who deserted the front line during the Great War 1914 - 1918, was shot at dawn. Following the example of the British Empire, I seek the same treatment for this prisoner."

Tim stood up and attempted to speak, but wasn't allowed continue. The thin veneer of civilization cracked in the 'court'; he received a blow from a baton to the back of his head. When he recovered the 'hearing' had continued and his representative was on his feet.

"As a professional soldier this young man has already contributed to the establishment of Katanga. He was paid for his services and was unaware that his contract involved staying for any period of time. He fought bravely at our first encounter with the UN and we decorated him for his contribution at the battle for the Tunnel, which was an important event in our evolution as a national army."

He continued in this vein for a while, but it was clear that the court had their minds made up. Apart from a general lack of interest in what he was saying, an occasional outburst from the jury made it clear that this wasn't a court of justice.

"La justice pours Katanga mais la mort pour ce traître."

More in keeping with the cry from the French rabble at the open courts in Place Nation, than a civilised version of the passing of justice. Since he received the baton stroke Tim couldn't follow proceedings clearly and only partly realised that his goose was cooked.

"Guilty, take him away and shoot him."

"What did they say?"

"You're to be shot this afternoon."

He felt sick as he was hustled out of the court, back to his cell. Time passed quickly and in what seemed like seconds he was led on to the square, placed in front of a whitewashed wall and had a piece of paper placed on his left chest. He only began to come to as his eyes were covered with a scarf, and the firing squad shuffled out of the guardroom, loaded their rifles, and awaited orders. While the scarf was being placed in position, he had one last chance to look beyond the walls, to where the African sky stretched to the skyline decorated with pieces of cotton wool like clouds.

The sounding of a bugle call and a roll of drums enhanced the charade of a national execution procedure.

"Have you any last request, a cigarette perhaps?"

Tim knew what was happening and asked only that his letters be sent to his mother and his faithful lover, Fleurabelle. His very last thoughts were, however, of his mother and how kind she had been to him when his penis had picked up an infection. He was only thirteen, and she provided a cure to a nasty rash which had developed over about a week and about which he was too embarrassed to seek help. She had been so tender and caring…

As the fire party lifted their rifles and aimed, he wondered if he would hear the shots before he died. And what then?

"Aim, fire!"

'A thousand pigeons fluttered excitedly into the air in St Mark's Square!'

The Sabena jet sped onward over the Sahara at 33,000 feet. At this height the cumulus clouds shone and left a series of dark spots on the Sahara below. A beautiful view and enhanced doubly as the blue Mediterranean came into view.

"There, look, the Alps. Up now to Brussels and then left to Ireland."

"If we took a shortcut and avoided Brussels, I'd be in O'Mearas of Ringsend in an hour."

Two young privates discussed the flight.

Jack returned the friendly nod of McCoy, as A Company Commander beamed his way down the aisle, stopping occasionally to chat with soldiers, NCOs, and officers. He was a happy man and his bonhomie overflowed particularly to the officer corps in A Company.

"We've done a good job, Brendan, and we deserve whatever kudos comes our way."

"What fucking kudos?"

"A now, Bene don't be like that."

He skipped on quickly, thinking that a phalanx of empty mini brandy bottles might expose the dark side of his second in command.

The plane landed in Brussels, refuelled and headed off to Collinstown Airport. The reception area was wild with mothers, wives and children, to which the fathers and sons gravitated quickly. There was no customs delay; they had decided not to inspect the *mingie* boxes. This was usual practise at this stage, although Jack heard that later contingents had to go through the usual custom inspection. Most of what was brought home was innocent stuff and not worthy of inspection. Carved African figures, ivory tusks, malachite jewellery. Bush paintings were popular and some of the paintings by local African 'artists' were of Irish landscapes.

The homesick soldiers commissioned copy paintings of cards sent from home. The Lakes of Killarney painted by Harry Mena in Katanga was a favourite with everyone and his Irish lakes' paintings and African lake scenes were similar, except for the type of boat displayed. One scene contained a black African, standing in a dugout at one corner of a lake in Connemara. Anyway, Harry churned out these masterpieces, which no doubt now have pride of place in the front room beside the Pope and Jack Kennedy.

Not all was such, however. The PX system and the rate of exchange of hard currency ensured that many items of real value were brought home. In particular, cameras, film equipment and watches were popular, although the spurt of use of the photo equipment was short lived, which is in the nature of things. The many 8mm films stashed up in the attic - rarely seen, and expensive photo and film equipment barely used - are evidence that fools and their money are easily parted. Maybe not fools, but there was a euphoria which needed to be expressed, and that happened in a variety of ways.

Some half-white babies might now be important social leaders in the

Congo and wondering about their differing DNA. The friends made and the influence of the many human contacts, posits the view that the overspill, social system on social system, is as necessary for human survival as the movement of the Celts or Norsemen through Europe, or the influence of the Ottoman in the middle ages. The UN in Africa, or before that, the colonisation of the continent by European powers and their proselytising religious, might eventually be seen as a necessary part of positive evolution.

In the Curragh Camp life went on as usual. Jack was in charge of a Standard Physical Training course which catered for unit physical training needs. Twenty-five NCOs and five commissioned officers would spend twenty weeks being trained in fundamental fitness training and sports specialisations, and then apply their skills in their respective units. Jack was fully involved, but with a heavy heart.

Apart from her loving significance, Jane Thornly was a friend; friendship forged on the ski slopes and in his toe-tip experience in the film industry. Her death, when he was in the Congo, was a shock, but the reality, the void was emphasised starkly on the Curragh plains.

'When a lovely flame dies smoke gets in your eyes.'

The words of the song on the radio seemed appropriate. His plans for skiing again in St Anton were on hold until Louis rang the mess.

"Jack, I'm going in February. I have to - why I don't know, but I am."

And so the plans were made in a 'life must go on' mode. The few Congo bob made planning easier for Jack. There was still a limit of money that could be taken outside of the State, but that had increased to 200 pounds, officially that was. He took a little more, stashed away in the ski boots. Getting off for four weeks was a bit easier now that the ice was broken.

"Are you doing a bit today, Sir?"

The lads in the Army School of Physical Culture were never far from involvement in some physical activity.

"A run across the plains this afternoon?"

With three weeks to go before St Anton, fitness was a factor. Away they went, out by the back of the magazine to Corrigan's Cut, up to the Stand House and back. A few throws, or a run, or a weights session were normal practise among the staff as part of their personal recreation and fitness regime. After work hours, 16.30 under normal circumstances, reminiscences of service in the Congo trapped discussions. Training had a new focus; for the first time the world of the 'emergency' was pushed into the background. The Lee Enfield rifle and the classic Vickers machine gun became part of folklore, just as the threat to show the watermarks of the Blackwater on the lower legs wasn't considered a 'break' anymore.

Jack hadn't heard about or from Tim Cope, and expected that he and Fleurabelle were in Bordeaux with Marie Paul, developing Fleurabelle's photo portfolio. He realised that he had promised to see if Fleurabelle could meet Leni Riefenstahl.

He had received a letter from Riefenstahl Productions, Munich, seeking support in a programme to identify the location of her Olympics films. Riefenstahl Productions was now in a position to reissue the original film without the Nazi influences or close-ups of Hitler and other Nazi leaders. Leni had questioned him before about this, but was planning an early visit to American film centres as soon as the investigations into her possible war crimes were completed. She expected to be declared innocent by this Allied commission and had been told so by some of her contacts on the commission.

Riefenstahl Productions figured that a readjusted and edited version of the Olympics film might go down well in the United States. They had of course misgivings about how the Jewish film fraternity would treat her efforts to create a career there or in Europe.

Come February, Jack, complete with Kneissl Combis, new ski slacks, and Trinity Street blazer, hit the road again, starting on the bus from the Water Tower. He and Louis were intent on moving on despite personal setbacks. What else could they do? A few days as *Pistenhelfer* were sure to push the past into the past - at least that's what Jack figured.

He searched in the Bahnhof the first evening and sure enough his contact of his last ski trip was there and ready to sign him on as *Pistenhelfer*. Things had progressed however, and the administration detail now included a photograph and the issue of an identity card. Some of his friends of last time were there still, adding to his sense of security.

"Hi Jack, hope you have another bomb."

Australians, New Zealanders, South Africans, Americans; some of them had spent the summer in the Med sailing or travelling around Europe and were up for what the snow could throw at them.

"The snow's fantastic; wait 'til you see the Valluga! Wow!"

In no time it was as if he had never left St Anton, and yet he was a different person and his world had changed. The boy in Jack had received a layer of adult change, and as he strode through the village he realised that the previous St Anton experience had set in train a series of events, some tragic and most carrying heavy responsibilities. He didn't realise it, but post Congo the boy had become a man. He looked forward to checking out his local friends, and in particular how Heidi and Peter the tailor had developed their relationship. As he walked back to his hotel that first evening, he did a detour via the Hotel Post for old time's sake.

"Hello, Herr Muldoon, it's good to see you again." In four weeks you do get remembered. "Frau Riefenstahl is here again this year - have you met her?"

Jack told Louis about Leni. This time he was staying with Louis in the Trittkopf - the Congo money had made it possible to upgrade his accommodation.

Louis was up to speed. "She has an apartment on the next floor. You'll see her tomorrow at breakfast if you call back after work."

It was cold next morning, and the glow in the east was a forecast of good ski weather. He crunched his way down from the Trittkopf and across by the Vallugabahn to the Gampen lift. He said goodbye to the sad black suited figure of Louis, as he headed down by the Bahnhof to the main street and the church. He could see the shadowy figures of other *Pistenhelfer* workers as they arrived from a number of directions.

"*Grüss Gott* Jack! William, it's Romeo!"

His romantic name didn't mean that he would have to tread any less, and this time he was viewed as an experienced worker and expected to lead. The hut before the start wasn't any less smelly, but Jack soaked in the atmosphere and contributed to the male-oriented conversation. Out and away, shovel in hand, push right, push left, and sit forward over the tips heading for the first area of need on the slopes. They spent about two hours digging out hard ice bumps, or moguls as the Americans called them, waited for the sun and off again.

"A golden dawn - it's great to be alive!"

When they had finished, Jack headed back to the Trittkopf to meet Louis. As he stacked his skis outside and pushed open the double doors, he heard a voice.

"Jack, good to see you." It was Harley D. Wright, the American pilot. They'd made an arrangement in Africa, not really expecting to meet again, but here they were! They'd a lot of catching up to do; Jack instinctively ran his hands over his eyebrows - no more bomb play, Horse's Neck or no Horse's Neck!

After breakfast he headed up to Leni Riefenstahl's suite of rooms and knocked on the door. She must have seen him arriving because the door was flung open at once and he was welcomed in.

"*Willkommen* Jack. May I introduce you to my assistant Fleurabelle?"

Fleurabelle glanced a smile in his direction. Dressed in polo neck sweater and slacks, she carried the compulsory light meter around her neck. She held a set of negatives up to the window for inspection and looked a clone of Leni Riefenstahl the film editor - Jack thought her smile faded somewhat quickly.

B.T. O'Kane was hovering in the background, but there was no sign of Tim Cope from Carlow.

The End

Ski terms

Arlberg method – From simple snowplough through stem christie to parallel turn; begun in St Anton by Hannes Schneider-'father of modern skiing'.

Arlberg Kandahar ski race – First international ski race- held on Gampen /Kapal in St Anton from 1928.

Attenhoffers – Swiss timber skis.

Ski Binding – Method of attaching skis to boots-with release in case of accident or fall. Kandahar and Marker-two types in the 1950's.

Safety Strap – Geared to keep the ski under control when released by the binding.

Pistenhelfer – A worker whose job it is, in cooperation with others, to step and thread down the slope and prepare the run for skiers.

Tips up! – An admonition on arriving at a chair lift terminal as a caution to beginners.

A rescue sledge – A sledge equipped with four dismountable handles used to bring accident cases down the mountain. Sometimes irrevently referred to as the blood wagon.

Coloured Pole marker – To indicate the standard of run-black being the highest and most difficult.

Edged to a halt – Taking the downward pressure on the inside edge of the skis to slow down or halt.

Bumps – Nowadays known as moguls.

Sitting back – A mistake usually employed by beginners afraid to ski with weight forward-in the fall-line.

Slalom – A ski race through gates placed sometimes in close proximity and on difficult terrain.

Ski pants – Slacks designed to fit neatly, with elastic band under the foot inside the boot and zipped pockets.

Toboggan – A small two person or one person sledge with a canvas seat and steel edged runners.

Weighting and unweighting – A weight emphasis by the skier, which presents an opportunity during the unweighting to change the direction of the skis and then use the new direction to progress.

Short swings – Not a term used in the Arlberg technique, but parallel turns employed even then to display a smooth series of turns. In the 50's in St Anton it was expected that the skis would be parallel and the knees not together, but one pressed into the back of the other on each turn. This technique was discontinued when Arnold Frank's films were studied in detail and later racing film studied.

Kneissel Combi – An Austrian Ski-very popular in St Anton in the 50's

Deep snow skiing – A very different mode of skiing, not usually within the compass of beginners.

Avalanches travel from their origin high up on the mountain and follow the natural contours of the mountain using available gulley's as would water in a stream bed.

Army Terms

(These terms are meant only as a guide to a civilian understanding of army life).

Ranks – Officers, NCO's and Men.

Men are the soldiers in the Army. They are trained as recruits and progress within their Corps-Infantry,Cavalry,Artillary or other specialisations, to serve within a Unit, be it Section(ABOUT 12 MEN) , platoon,(FOUR SECTIONS) Company (Four Platoons) or Battalion(four Companies).

Non Commissioned Officers are the next rank above private. Corporals, Sergeants, Quartermasters, Company Sergeants and Sergeant Majors are non commissioned officers.

The commissioned officers grade starts at 2nd Lieutenants and progresses to Lieutenants, Captains, Commendants, Lieutanent Colonels and Colonels.

All commissioned officers are entitled to be saluted by NCO's and Private soldiers and to be called Sir. Senior Officers - from Commandants upwards are entitled to be saluted by all ranks below their rank and to be called Sir.

2IC -2nd in Command.

Commander in Chief – Usually a General who is in overall command.

Military Police – They are comprised of NCO'S and Officers and are the military equivalent of civilian police.

Adjutant – The chief officer administrator in a Batallion.Works directly to the Commanding Officer.

Trigger Finger – The finger used to press the weapon's trigger.

Ambush – A surprise attack from a concealed position.

Drill – A method used in army training to promote immediate action to legitimate orders and used also for weapons practice.

Bulls Wool – A term used to describe the First World War type of wool uniforms worn by Irish troops on the early United Nations contracts in The Congo.

Glossary

Lee Enfield rifles – The bolt action rifles on issue to some Irish troops.
Bren Gun- a .303 light Machine Gun.
Scrambled Egg – The gold braid on a Colonels cap is often described as scrambled egg.
Mortar – An uncalibrated weapon, which fires mortar bombs using a high trajectory for effect.
Grenade – A hand launched explosive.
Gustav Machine Gun – A 9mm personal machine gun.
Bangalore Torpedo – A pipe stuffed with explosives and used to clear a way through ground obstacles such as barbed wire.
Mercenary soldiers – The term applies to non nationals working for money and not part of the National Army.